FEAR THE NIGHT...

FEAR THE DARKNESS INSIDE YOURSELF.

WHAT EVIL GROWS BENEATH THE CITY OF ANGELS?

Thousands of years before cars and cities and civilizations, it was worshipped—a dark god nourished on primal fear and blood.

For millennia it slept, while humankind trembled, healed, and eventually forgot.

But it sleeps no longer. Strengthened by rest and awakened by hate, it spreads like a fiery plague across an unsuspecting nation—seeking out the darkest souls to devour.

The world will soon learn what nightmare means. Rousing the dead evil within the worst of humanity, it will turn the streets bloodred, as day becomes night and the sky bleeds black in its wake.

Heroes will rise to fight for a future. But they will be forced to confront the epic horror as cold as the moon . . . and as unstoppable as the dawn.

BLACK DAWN

BLACK DAWN

D.A. STERN

HarperTorch
An Imprint of HarperCollins*Publishers*

To everyone at 10 E. 53,
for whom this book was a horror
long before it was a novel

———

This is a work of fiction. Names, characters, places, and incidents are products of the author's imagination or are used fictitiously and are not to be construed as real. Any resemblance to actual events, locales, organizations, or persons, living or dead, is entirely coincidental.

HARPERTORCH
An Imprint of HarperCollins*Publishers*
10 East 53rd Street
New York, New York 10022-5299

Copyright © 2001 by HarperCollins Publishers
ISBN: 0-380-81486-2

First HarperTorch paperback printing: October 2001

HarperCollins®, HarperTorch™, and ◆ ™ are trademarks of HarperCollins Publishers Inc.

Printed in the United States of America

Visit HarperTorch on the World Wide Web at www.harpercollins.com

10 9 8 7 6 5 4 3 2 1

God has weighed the world in the balance,
By measure he has measured the hours,
And by number he has numbered the times,
He will not disturb nor stir them,
Until the said measure be fulfilled.

.   2 Esdras 4:36–37

Note: The Book of Esdras is part of the Apocrypha, and not considered canonical Scripture.

Prologue

Thursday 9:43 P.M., PST

COMPTON, CALIFORNIA

The trash barrel on the corner was squeaking. Pearl Coleman leaned over the edge and looked in.

The squeaking was coming from a little baby mouse, stuck to a glue trap. Writhing and squirming frantically, patches of bare skin gleaming in the light from the street lamp above, its wide frightened eyes looked up at Pearl. She felt like she could read the terrified creature's mind.

Help me. Please help me.

"Poor thing," Pearl said.

Garbage filled the barrel to the halfway mark. The glue trap rested on the top of the heap. Pearl bent over the edge to reach the trap, and grimaced—the fingers of her left hand refused to open. Her arthritis was getting worse every day now. She supposed that was what happened when you got old. And Pearl was old now; sixty-three years old last month, her birthday coming the day after she was widowed.

Pearl picked the glue trap up gingerly in two hands, careful not to touch any of the sticky top side, and put it down on the sidewalk.

The little mouse began squeaking even more frantically. Pearl wondered why for a moment. Then she decided it was being out in the open again, out of the trash barrel, and seeing freedom—the open sky, the sidewalk, the boulevard behind her—so seemingly close at hand.

But that freedom was an illusion. The glue in the trap was too strong. Really, there was only one way out for the mouse.

An empty beer bottle lay next to the curb; Pearl bent over and picked it up. She knelt down next to the mouse.

"Poor thing," she said again. The mouse squeaked in reply. It looked up at her hopefully.

Pearl raised the bottle, and slammed it down. There was a crunching sound, a noise like a piece of hard candy snapping in between teeth, and a single loud squeak. The mouse stopped wiggling.

Pearl lifted the bottle. To her surprise, the mouse's head was untouched. She thought she could see the outlines of a smile on its face.

Pearl stroked the top of its head with one gnarled finger.

"No more pain now, is there?" she said softly.

It was just like the dark-haired woman had said to Pearl in the dream. To be released from the trials and tribulations of this world, to be free of all the suffering and sadness—why, it was a blessing.

Throwing the bottle and the trap back in the garbage, Pearl stood and faced the building in front of her.

The Mount Zion Baptist Congregational Church, at 1251 South Central Avenue, in the heart of Compton. The ghetto to some. To Pearl Coleman, home for the last forty years of her life.

This part of her home was sorely in need of repair right now. The church looked like a wreck, paint peeling, foundation cracked, garden overgrown. A wreck, and Gordon gone not much more than a month. It looked, in fact, much the same as it had thirty years ago, the first time Pearl had seen it, just after Gordon had been named pastor.

She remembered that day, how Gordon had stood next to

her, his arm around her shoulders, sensing her disappointment.

"What's that they said about Rome?" he asked.

She had smiled then and chucked him on the arm.

It wasn't long before a new coat of paint went up, and they started making themselves a congregation. Gordon went up and down the nearby streets, introducing himself, getting people to come once to the church, then come back a second time, then to bring their friends. He'd met the neighbors, organized block parties, and even started a summer camp so the kids could get out into the country once in a while. He kept the gang-bangers, if not out, at least at bay. Mostly because he treated them with respect, the same way he treated everyone.

In between her work at the library, Pearl balanced the books, ran the bake sales, and organized the choir. Every Sunday morning there was services, every Wednesday night there was a meeting, and there was something to do every other day of the week as well, for both of them.

And when all was said and done, what had it been for? The last few years, everything had fallen apart. The roof started leaking, the soup kitchen shut down, attendance at Sunday worship fell by half. A few weeks ago Gordon had even admitted for the first time that he was looking forward to retirement. Too late to have the kids they'd talked about so long ago, Pearl thought, but at least they'd have each other.

Or so she thought.

Pearl walked to the front door, and pushed it open. It swung wide—unlocked, just like the dark-haired woman had promised—and Pearl stepped inside.

The chapel was a single large room, with pews lining both sides of a central aisle. At the front of the church was a raised stage; behind the stage, looming high above the floor, was a large wooden cross. A banner underneath the cross read JESUS IS LORD.

The banner was burning.

The fire gave a faint, eerie glow that transformed the inside of the church, tinting everything—the walls, the pews, the glinting steel of the microphone stands stacked to the left of the stage—in tones of orange and red.

Shadows flickered and danced around her as Pearl walked forward. She took a seat in the front pew, and set her bag down next to her. Graffiti etched into the wood covered the back of the pew in front of her, and she remembered a time when those pews were brand-new. George Carter, a woodworker who used to have a shop over on Alondra, had built every single one of them, doing the work on his own time. Pearl still recalled the look of pride on the man's face when he and Gordon had finished unloading and positioning them in the freshly-painted church.

Everywhere she looked, memories.

Pearl closed her eyes and saw Gordon at the pulpit, pounding a closed fist into the palm of his hand, exhorting the congregation. She saw him standing with the choir, his body swaying, his voice raised loud and clear in song. And she saw him at the breakfast table, slumped forward with his hand reaching for hers in the moment of his dying.

They were having pancakes. Gordon was passing the syrup when he suddenly dropped the bottle and looked at her, his face ashen.

"Oh Lord," he'd said, grabbing his chest. "Please, no."

It sounded as if Gordon was begging for more time.

But the Lord had none for him.

Why should he care about taking Gordon Coleman two days before retirement, a week before he and Pearl were to leave for Hawaii?

Why should he care about leaving Pearl to clean up, to pull Gordon's face from his plate, wipe off the butter and syrup, and get on with her life?

He didn't care. Gordon's God was a harsh master. He'd

killed Moses in sight of the promised land, had his own son tortured on the cross, and let his followers be eaten by lions and burned alive in ovens. To her way of thinking, Gordon's God demanded much in the way of sacrifice and returned little.

But there were others.

Most of them had long since faded from memory, the people who'd worshipped them swept away in the tides of history, the Gods reduced to footnotes in the story of the Almighty Creator.

But still . . .

They were out there. Waiting.

All you had to do was get their attention.

Pearl reached into the bag next to her, and pulled out the knife she'd brought. It was an old steak knife, one of a set of five she and Gordon had gotten as a wedding present. Stainless steel blade, inlaid wood handles. This was the last of the set left; the others had all disappeared over the years.

Holding the knife firmly in her right hand, she drew the blade across the palm of her left.

Blood pooled up in the cut.

Blood, the dark-haired woman had told her, would speak louder than any words.

Pearl turned her palm over, and a drop hit the concrete floor. Then another, and another. The ground beneath her feet shivered—once, twice, like a car engine turning over.

Like something trying to wake up.

Pearl put the knife down, and reached into her bag again.

She pulled out an old, thick book, the cover pulling away from the binding, the pages yellow, the corners brown and crumbling. A worn metal bookmark held her place; she flipped the book open, and began to read.

The book was not in English. Not long ago, the symbols on the page, the words they formed, would have been incomprehensible to her. Not now.

Now they spilled off her tongue as if she'd been born speaking them. They echoed in the empty church and gathered strength.

Come, Pearl chanted. Come, she beseeched.

The hour is at hand.

The banner flared and disappeared into a cloud of ash. The cross above it began to burn. Tongues of flame reached like fingers toward the exposed wooden beams of the building above and the wooden bench at the back of the altar as well.

The cross toppled to the ground and cracked into countless smaller pieces. A cloud of ash flew up in the air. Pearl tasted smoke, thick and acrid in her mouth, and gripped the metal bookmark tightly in her hand.

Blood from her cut oozed up around its edges.

The floor buckled: boards splintered and bowed upward, as if something was trying to push its way into the church from below. She felt a presence now, something pulsing with barely contained power; it washed over her like a wave and in its wake, she felt something else.

Hatred.

The hatred of something trapped for ages and ages, something that was awake now, and straining to be free.

Awake, and burning up with anger.

The fire drew closer.

Pearl felt the skin on her arm beginning to blister, and gritted her teeth, and tried not to scream.

She pictured the dead mouse, and the smile on its face.

The pain would end, she told herself. Soon enough, it would all be over. For her, at least.

The rest of the world would have to wait a little bit longer.

BOOK I

CONVOCATION

Friday 1:15 A.M., EST

NEPTUNE BEACH, FLORIDA

Peter Williams stepped around the side of the Quickie Mart just as Tarek reached for the front door.

"Tee," Peter called quietly. "Over here."

Tarek stopped dead in his tracks. He turned to his right and squinted into the darkness.

"Who's that?"

Peter took another step forward, letting the light from inside the convenience store fall on his face.

"Holy Jesus." Tarek's face registered astonishment for a second. Then he smiled—a fake, insincere smile. "Officer Williams. Long time no see. What—"

"Not officer," Peter said. "Not anymore."

"Right." Tarek nodded. "I heard."

"I'll bet you did," Peter said. He studied Tarek. The man looked exactly the same as he had the last time Peter saw him. Tarek Aziz—"Tee" was his street name—was six feet and a hundred seventy pounds of solid muscle. Tan, good-looking, when he wasn't supplying marijuana and coke to the street-corner dealers out here on Justina Avenue he was playing gigolo to the rich widows down in Ponte Vedra Beach.

"You keeping busy, Tee?" Peter asked. "What you been up to?"

"Not much." Aziz shrugged. "Getting by. You know."

"Uh-huh." Peter did know. Back when he'd been a cop, Tarek had been one of his main snitches. Aziz gave Peter information, Peter gave him money and helped him stay out of jail.

"I want to talk to you, Tee," Peter said.

"So talk."

"Not here," Peter said. "Walk with me."

Aziz followed Peter around the side of the Quickie Mart. A sputtering fluorescent bulb above a steel delivery door lit up the sidewalk.

"I need some help, Tee. I'm looking for a guy." Peter reached into the pocket of his coat and pulled out a piece of paper—an artist's sketch. He handed it to Tarek. "This guy. You know him?"

Aziz held the sketch up to the light and studied it.

"Why you want this guy?"

"That's my business."

Light dawned in Tarek's eyes. "This is the guy. The guy who shot Kelly?"

Peter nodded. No use denying it. "That's right. Kelly and the girl." Peter—at five-eight a good half a head shorter than Aziz—looked up at the taller man and caught his eye. "This is a bad man, Tee. I want him."

Aziz shook his head. "I cannot help you. I have never seen him." He tried to hand the sketch back to Peter.

"Do me a favor," Peter said. "Keep it. Show it around."

Tarek hesitated.

"Please, Tee," Peter said. It burned him to have to do this, to ask a small-timer like Aziz for help, but where else was he going to go? The police? Fat chance of getting help from them.

Tarek sighed. "I don't know. The people I work for. . . ."

Peter gritted his teeth. When Tarek was snitching for him, and Peter said jump, Tarek not only asked how high he didn't even dare land until Peter told him it was okay. And now this?

But he held his temper. He needed Tarek's help. Tee knew a lot of people up and down the Florida coast. Over the last six months of looking, Peter had pretty much exhausted his sources around here. He needed to widen the search.

"You do this for me," Peter continued, "and I won't forget it."

Aziz was silent a moment.

"A lot of people," he said finally, "not me, of course, but a lot of people—they're happy you don't be a cop anymore. They don't like you."

"Uh-huh." Peter could understand that: he'd made this part of Jacksonville a pretty uncomfortable place for the criminal element to hang around in. With Tarek's help, of course. But he didn't point that out right now.

"Don't say it's for me, then. Say it's for you. Say you want to know who the guy is."

"Why?"

Peter shrugged. "That's up to you. You come up with a story that works."

"No. That's not what I mean." Tarek shook his head. "Why should I help you?"

Peter stopped himself—just barely—from exploding.

"Because I'm asking, that's why."

"That's not enough, I'm sorry."

Peter gritted his teeth. "What are you looking for—money?"

Tarek smiled. "That would be a start."

"If you find the guy, there'll be money."

"But still you want me to work? For nothing?" He shook his head, and held out the sketch again. "I can't do that."

"You mean you won't do that."

Tarek shrugged. "That's right. I won't do that."

Peter glared at him. Tarek's back was to the store parking

lot. Over the man's shoulder, he saw the car Aziz had driven up in. A light blue minivan. Hard to tell from where he stood, but it looked like the van had out-of-state plates.

"What you got in that car of yours, Tee? A little something for the dealers around here?"

Tarek sneered. "It's none of your business what I got."

"Really?"

"Yes, really."

"Suppose I make it my business?"

"You can't do anything now," Aziz said. "You're not a cop."

Peter smiled and shook his head. "You got that all wrong, my friend. Now that I'm not a cop, I can do whatever I want."

Tarek flinched, and stepped backward.

He tripped over a row of milk crates behind him on the sidewalk. He fell hard to the ground. The sketch floated up in the air and landed on the sidewalk next to him.

Right at that instant, a patrol car cruised by on the avenue. It made a quick, screeching turn into the Quickie Mart lot, and two cops hustled out. Peter recognized them both right away. Hibbard and Shannon.

They made right for the side of the building.

"What's going on here?"

Tarek climbed to his feet, fuming. "This man is harassing me."

"Williams." Hibbard's glare burned. He had been tight with Kelly. "What are you doing here?" His eyes went to the sketch on the ground, and he sneered. "Still trying to peddle that line of bullshit, huh? Looking for your mystery man?"

Peter glared right back. "I'm looking for the guy who shot Kelly, Hibbard. Same as you ought to be doing."

"Yeah?" Hibbard snorted. "I'm looking at the guy who shot Kelly, as far as I'm concerned. So—"

Peter growled and took a step forward.

Hibbard's hand went to his nightstick. "Try it, Williams. Please. I'm begging you."

Hibbard was well over six feet tall but starting to go to pot:

Peter, who carried exactly the same hundred and sixty pounds of solid muscle he'd had since high school on his five-eight frame, would have loved the chance to kick the big man's ass. It would almost be worth a few nights in jail. Almost.

"Hey Shannon," Peter said, "I can see your partner's too busy harassing me to worry about doing his job, but you might want to check out Tee's car there." He nodded to the minivan. "Ten to one he's got something he shouldn't in there."

Tarek glared at him. "Ridiculous."

Shannon turned and gave Tarek a quizzical eye.

Peter bent down and picked up the sketch.

"Have fun, gents," he said, and started walking.

Back at his apartment, he pulled out a beer from the refrigerator and cracked it open. He crossed over to the kitchen table and sat down.

Peter lived in a one-room concrete box a block and a half from the ocean. He'd lived there for almost ten years, but still had trouble thinking of it as home. Especially now.

Right now there were blank spaces where the couch, the TV, and the stereo had been. They'd all been repossessed or sold. The phone had been shut off last week, and yesterday he'd gone down to the street to get his car and it wasn't there. Repo man. He'd known it was coming.

Peter was down to his last few hundred dollars. His pension was supposed to get freed up soon, and he'd get a paycheck next week from Leo, but the funny thing was, he didn't even care about the money.

He'd missed Lee Crane's farewell party last month, and a chance to interview with the P.I. firm Sharkey had set up in St. Augustine, and he didn't care about those things either. Janet had called him twice last week to take her to the movies, and he'd been so rude the second time he was sure she'd never call again.

He didn't give a good goddamn about any of it.

The only thing he cared about was finding the guy in the sketch.

He unfolded the copy of the drawing he'd tried to give Tarek and pressed it flat against the kitchen table.

The man in it stared back at him.

The man was somewhere in his fifties; he had a thick, gray-black mustache and skin badly pitted and scarred, as if he'd been burned in a fire a long, long time ago. The sketch was as close to lifelike as a drawing could be; Peter had paid for it out of his own pocket, after deciding that the one the police artist had done was crap.

Neither had gotten him a single solid lead.

He got a lot of crank calls because of that sketch. That, and the $1,000 Leo had put up as a reward.

Jesus, Peter realized suddenly. That all happened six months ago, almost to the day. And he remembered it like it was yesterday. Only he didn't remember it.

That was the problem.

Six months ago, Peter had been a cop on the Jacksonville police force. The night of June 19 he and his partner, Jack Kelly, were out on patrol, just like they'd been every night that week.

They were parked on South Mayport with the lights off, talking about the Jaguars. Peter had his window down. It was a humid summer evening, with a warm, salty breeze coming off the water. Noise from the bars a few blocks away on Beach Boulevard filled the damp air.

"Listen," Kelly had said. "They oughta trade that guy while they can still get something for him."

Kelly was talking about Mark Brunell, who he was convinced was the only reason the team hadn't gotten to the Super Bowl yet. Peter thought he was wrong: Brunell was the only reason they'd gotten into the playoffs in the first place.

Peter took a bite of his own burger before answering.

"Come on, Jack, they had a guard playing tackle. They had a center playing guard. They had a guy who came out of retirement trying to remember signals. They—"

A woman screamed.

Peter and Kelly looked at each other.

"You heard that?"

"I heard that."

Kelly, who was driving, hit the gas.

Peter hit the siren and picked up the radio.

The scream had come from somewhere ahead of them.

As they shot down Mayport, Peter glanced to his right, where an alley ran perpendicular to them. He saw two shapes struggling in the darkness.

"There!" he shouted.

Kelly hit the brakes and slammed the car into reverse. He backed up and shone the headlights down the alley.

The two shapes stopped struggling. One of them lay on the ground—a woman. Peter saw her bare legs crumpled beneath her.

The other was a man, his features shadowed by darkness. In his hand he held a knife.

"That's a dead-end alley," Kelly said, stepping out of the car.

Peter got out as well.

"Police!" Kelly shouted, drawing his gun and walking forward. "Police officer! Step back from the girl!"

The man raised his hands above his head, but he was still holding the knife.

"Drop it, chief," Peter said. "Drop it or I'll drop you right where you stand."

Kelly moved in and knelt down next to the girl's body. "Goddamn," he said.

The man still held the knife.

"Five seconds!" Peter yelled. "Then I shoot!"

The man dropped the knife and looked at Peter.

"It's not a knife," he said. "See for yourself."

Peter bent down and reached for it. The man was right, it wasn't a knife, it was—

"Like what you see?" the man had asked.

And that was the last thing Peter remembered of the alley.

When he woke up he was lying in a hospital bed with a gunshot wound to the shoulder. Jack Kelly was dead. So was the girl.

The man from the alley was nowhere to be found.

The police artist did a sketch right then and there, with the doctors screaming to get him out of the room, to let Peter rest. When the sketch was done it went out all across the state, but with zero results.

Peter had imagined all sorts of scenarios that first evening in the hospital as he tried to figure out what had happened. The guy must have had an accomplice who shot Kelly. The accomplice must have been hidden. That made the most sense, but for some reason he was blacking out the memory. Maybe when the facts came back from ballistics, Peter thought, maybe if they could find a witness, maybe they could piece it all together.

But the next morning all his carefully crafted scenarios fell apart.

The lieutenant walked into his hospital room with a grin on his face.

"What's up, Lieutenant?"

"Pete, I'm not going to give you any bullshit about this."

"What?"

"The bullet that killed Kelly came from your gun."

Peter was about to say "You're kidding," but when he looked at the lieutenant's face, he realized that the man was dead serious.

"My bullet?"

He tried to think.

"The guy must have gotten the gun away from me somehow."

"The only fingerprints on it are yours."

The two men stared at each other for a moment. "This is bullshit, Lieutenant," Peter said finally. "I don't know who's trying to—"

The lieutenant shook his head. "I don't know what to tell you, Pete." He stood up. "Call for a lawyer. And get the union rep." He nodded toward the doorway, and Peter saw two stone-faced men in suits staring at him.

He knew who they were without even asking.

Internal Affairs.

Peter called the rep. He got the lawyer. But it didn't make it any easier to sit through the interview or to listen to the scenarios Internal Affairs had come up with. Maybe you had a thing for Kelly's wife and wanted to get him out of the way? No. Well, maybe the two of you were fighting about something else. Ever use drugs, Peter? Ever smuggle drugs? What about Kelly? What was he into? And so on and so on. Ridiculous charges, all of which Peter denied vehemently.

It was all a bunch of horseshit. He kept thinking it would blow over.

But the day before Kelly's funeral, the lieutenant suggested that it might be better if he not attend.

It didn't take a rocket scientist to figure out why.

"Somebody talked," the lieutenant said. "The word is out that your bullet killed Kelly."

Peter tried phoning Diane, Kelly's wife. She wouldn't take his call. Visits from his buddies on the force dropped off too. After a while the only guy who would talk was Leo Beauchamp.

Leo and him had been best friends since they were kids. They'd joined the force together, right out of high school, only Leo had quit being a cop five years ago and started a construction company; done pretty well for himself. He told Peter to relax, let things work themselves out. Wait.

Peter wasn't good at waiting, though. He checked out of the hospital a week earlier than the doctors would have liked and went to the station house. Ignoring the dirty looks from his former colleagues, he went through every book of mug shots dating back ten years, looking for the guy. He had his own artist's sketch done. He went over to the FBI building and got access to the National Crime Information Center database.

But he couldn't find the killer anywhere.

It became an obsession with him: he stopped seeing his friends, he stopped calling his family. He spent every night at the station house, going through old crime reports, looking for something, anything even remotely resembling a clue.

Two months after the shooting, the lieutenant called him into the office.

"Good news, Pete. Looks like Internal Affairs is going to put the shooting down as an accident."

"Uh-huh." Peter didn't smile.

"That doesn't make you happy?"

"Only one thing's gonna make me happy, Lieutenant. You know what that is."

The lieutenant shook his head. "You gotta face facts, Pete. This guy may never turn up."

"I'll find him."

The lieutenant shrugged. "Maybe. Maybe not. In the meantime, you gotta get back to work."

"Oh yeah?" Peter snorted. "Some critical filing has to get done?" He'd been on administrative duty while the shooting was being investigated, but he'd let what little paperwork that job required slide too while he searched for clues.

"Yeah. That's right. But don't worry, I'll get you back on the street soon enough. Just as soon as IAB comes back with their finding."

"I gotta keep looking," Peter said.

The lieutenant shook his head. "No. What you've got to do is lighten up, Pete. My gut tells me this is going to be one of those cases where we're gonna have to get lucky."

"Is that what you're telling Kelly's widow?"

The lieutenant's face darkened. "Don't. Don't start with that."

"Then don't tell me to stop looking, Lieutenant. Or have you forgotten what this guy did?"

"What you say he did."

Only the fact that there was a big desk between the two of them stopped Peter from punching the lieutenant right in the face then.

"Fuck you," he said, and slammed his badge down on the desk.

Both of them stared at it a moment.

"You don't want to do that, Pete," the lieutenant said. He slid the badge back across the desk.

"I'm not going to stop, Lieutenant," Peter said. "You can't make me stop."

The lieutenant sighed.

Peter left the badge lying on his desk.

That was back in August, and Peter was no closer to finding a clue now than he had been then. Farther away, probably, because the trail had grown even colder in the intervening months.

And still, the only thing Peter had to go on was his memories of that night.

Two months back, when he let slip the fact that he was running low on money, Leo offered him a job working on one of his construction crews. It was hard work, and physically exhausting, but Peter found it suited him just fine. It took his mind off the search for awhile at least, and some nights, when he'd worked really hard, he was so tired he had no trouble sleeping at all.

Not tonight, though.

Tonight, the scenes from the alley just kept playing in his head, over and over.

Like what you see?

He glanced over at the clock on the wall. It was late. He

had work tomorrow. He should be getting to bed. Letting it rest, just like the lieutenant had said.

He took a long, slow swig off his beer, and stared down at the sketch on the table.

Let it rest? Like hell.

He could rest when he was dead.

ASHEVILLE, NORTH CAROLINA

Betty toweled herself dry and climbed into bed.

Pulling the covers up to her neck, she turned the television on to Craig Kilborn. Harold had once said he was funny, and Betty wanted to see for herself. Not surprisingly, she thought differently. But to be fair to Kilborn, she had a hard time paying attention to the television.

Her eyes kept returning to the knife on her bedside table.

It was a big knife—the biggest one they had. The sharpest too, as she'd just recently bought it to slice bagels. She hadn't needed it before. She used to get their bagels from Dunkin' Donuts on the interstate. They had that automatic slicing machine. You dropped the bagel in the top, it made kind of a buzzing noise, and then wham! the bagel popped out the bottom, sliced neatly in half.

Betty used to get up every day a little before six A.M. and go to Dunkin' Donuts for fresh bagels, two of them: blueberry for her, plain for Harold. Get there at six, you got 'em hot, just as they were coming out of the oven.

Just the way Harold liked them.

Truthfully, Betty didn't mind waking up then: she was always a morning person, and after a week or so of this ritual, she discovered a bonus to getting up that early. She became part of the regular early morning crew at Dunkin' Donuts. There was Janis, who worked behind the counter, and Mike, who made the doughnuts. She learned their names pretty quickly, as well as some of the other customers—like John, who worked for the logging company in Somerville, and Nick, a big, tall guy who was the nighttime security guard at the Coca-Cola plant just outside of town.

Usually, when she walked in, the four of them were all spread out around the horseshoe-shaped self-service counter near the front of the store, telling stories about their kids, their jobs, their spouses. Betty would order her two bagels and a glazed doughnut and go sit by herself at one of the booths in the back. Taking care not to get any crumbs on her dress (it wouldn't do to have Harold find out she was sneaking a doughnut before breakfast), she'd eat her doughnut, listening to details of everybody else's lives. She never offered any of her own, and nobody ever talked to her directly, but even so, after just a few days she felt as if everyone had accepted her as one of them: the proverbial regular. One of these mornings, she kept telling herself, I might even start talking to them.

Instead, one of those mornings, while she was listening to Janis talk about her cheapskate husband, Harold walked in.

Her first thought was that the clock on the wall must be wrong: it said six-ten, but that couldn't be right, because Harold never got out of bed this early. He was a night person.

But he was there.

She met his gaze. He had the same look on his face he'd had that night when he picked up the phone in their last apartment, in Philadelphia, where they'd lived before moving to North Carolina, and found Lou, her coworker from the magazine, on the other end. The same look he wore just before he hit her.

He was staring at the doughnut in her hand, and she'd dropped it like it was on fire, but not soon enough. Harold smiled and started toward her.

She jumped up from the booth, dropping the bag of bagels.

Harold reached her side and grabbed her arm so hard she knew she was going to have black and blue marks the next day. She winced reflexively.

A shadow fell across them and she looked up to see Nick, arms folded, staring down at them.

Harold was a big man—close to six feet tall and a solid 200 pounds. But Nick dwarfed him.

"What's the problem?" Nick asked.

Harold glared at the bigger man. "There's no problem."

"Doesn't look that way to me. Looks like you're hurting her."

Harold put on a smile. "Well," he said, "I'm a little upset. A family emergency." Then he turned to her. "Honey, it's your mom."

"Oh," Betty said reflexively. Harold hadn't called her honey in years. Her mom had been dead even longer. "We'd better go."

"That's right." Harold nodded. "We'd better go."

Nick didn't move. "You all right?" he asked her.

She lowered her head and nodded. "I'm all right," she whispered. She felt tears come to her eyes and forced them back.

Nick stepped out of the way—reluctantly, it seemed to her—and let them pass.

Harold led her away from the counter and toward the door.

As they pushed through it, she turned and offered a half smile to everyone. Then she followed Harold meekly out to the parking lot.

She hadn't been back to the Dunkin' Donuts since.

They drove back home that morning in their separate cars, but when she walked into the house, Harold was waiting for her.

That was all she cared to remember about that.

She hadn't left home for a month afterward. When she did, it was only to go shopping: Harold had made a list of the things for her to buy, and he now double-checked them against her receipts. One of those things was bagels: a dozen, frozen. He'd also decided they needed a new knife to cut them with.

The knife.

Betty reached over and took it off the night table.

Its serrated edge was still sticky with blood.

She set it down and glanced at the clock on Harold's side of the bed: it flashed 1:22 in big red numbers.

She was hungry. She couldn't stomach the idea of cooking right now, but maybe there was a diner open by the highway. Or maybe . . . the Dunkin' Donuts. It was too early in the morning for the regulars she knew, but she could always just grab a cup of coffee and wait for everyone: Mike, Janis, John, Nick.

Oh wait. Not Nick.

Nick wouldn't be at Dunkin' Donuts anymore.

One night, a few weeks after he'd caught her there, Harold had come into the bedroom smiling and thrown a copy of the local paper down on the bed next to her.

"Hey, your fat friend made the news," he said. Then he turned and walked out of the room.

She picked up the paper, and there, above the fold, was the headline SECURITY GUARD KILLED IN BOTCHED ROBBERY.

It was a picture of Nick. Nick Cheetham was his name. The article went on to say that the night before, Nick had apparently surprised someone trying to break into the bottling plant. Someone with a gun. Someone who shot and killed him. What the robber was hoping to find in a bottling plant, the article didn't mention. But Betty knew. She knew the intruder had found exactly what he wanted. Nick.

She learned a few things she hadn't known about Nick from that article. That he was married, for instance, and left behind a wife and two daughters, ages four and six.

She felt even worse about Nick than she had about Lou, who was a bachelor. At least when Lou mysteriously disappeared (though to her, of course, there was no mystery about it), he didn't leave a family.

She used to think Harold was jealous—that he couldn't stand other guys looking at her. And at one time she even thought it might have been partly her fault. She was a good-looking woman—or at least, she had been: Lou used to tell her she looked like Susan Sarandon, only without the dark circles under her eyes—and she liked to wear clothes that showed off her figure.

But after Lou was killed, she knew the real problem.

She had married a monster.

That's how she thought of her life with Harold: like she was acting out the plot of one of those old 1950s B films; *I Was a Fugitive from a Chain Gang, I Was a Teenage Werewolf, I Married a Monster.*

The monster looked like an ordinary man. He masqueraded as a programming consultant, wrote a regular tech column for *OnLine* magazine, did work for a half-dozen local businesses, and looked good in a suit. He'd seemed like a regular guy when they were courting: he liked taking her shopping on South Street and eating Jim's cheese steaks; he'd wooed and won her over stromboli at Doc Watson's. Somehow, he'd even gotten them into half a dozen soldout Hooters shows when they were dating. And of course, he'd given her the most romantic evening of her life, proposing to her in Rittenhouse Square on New Year's Eve, walking out on his own party to be with her when the clock struck midnight.

The monster's true nature came out slowly: he started by begging her not to work late, to be home by five-thirty so they could eat dinner together. He'd slapped her one night after an argument and then apologized vociferously, swearing to never do it again. He'd somehow arranged his own schedule so she kept missing her regular Thursday night drink dates with her friends (God, she couldn't even remember half their names now) . . . until finally she'd given up her job, her friends, her family, and the only thing left was Harold.

Their relationship descended into the truly horrific only after that phone call from Lou, who'd called her at home about a week after she'd left her job. Harold must have been listening in on the extension in his office, and he must not have liked what he heard.

He'd woken her in the middle of the night a few days later and said he thought she might want to go for a drive with her friend from work.

"He's in the back, honey," he'd told her.

And when he took her out to the car, there was Lou, propped up in the backseat, duct-taped in place, eyes wide and unseeing.

She'd started to scream, and Harold hit her, really hit her, for the first time.

Later that night, after they'd gotten rid of the body, Betty realized there was only one way she would ever get rid of Harold.

She looked at the knife again.

Slipping out of bed, she put on a dress and walked out of the bedroom.

The television was still on in the living room. Two TV dinners, her Weight Watchers lemon chicken, his Hungry Man salisbury steak, both untouched, sat on the coffee table. The paper was stacked neatly beside them, just like Harold liked it, so he could eat and read and watch TV at the same time.

Harold himself lay on the floor exactly where she'd left him, his feet still in the kitchen and the rest of his body in the living room. He was staring up at the ceiling, eyes open wide, looking like he had asked God a question and was awaiting the answer.

Actually, he'd been in the middle of asking her a question when she cut him with the knife. He was rolling up his sleeves and advancing on her as he talked.

"*Did it occur to you that I had it set aside because I wanted to save it?*"

Harold always talked so calmly, even when he was really angry, but he always managed to make her feel like he was shouting, like she was really stupid.

He was yelling at her about some magazine he'd wanted to save, which he swore she'd thrown out. He already had the belt in his hand. He was either going to hit her with it or use it to bind her arms before he took her into the bedroom. She didn't know which would be worse.

She'd felt this explosion coming all week: his coffee was always just a little too cold or too dark, the office a little too messy or too neat, his food too spicy or too bland. She didn't know what it was. But something was in the air, building like a storm.

She backed up as he advanced.

Feeling the kitchen counter behind her, she grabbed the knife.

"*You know how important those articles are to my work,*" he said.

"Just leave me alone," she said, pulling the knife out from behind her back.

"Well well well," he said, stopping.

"You just leave me alone," she repeated.

He shook his head. "Now you are definitely going to have to be punished for this. The question," he began, "is how—"

In mid-sentence he swung the belt.

Betty stabbed at him with the knife.

After that, things had gotten messy.

Things still were messy: there was a pool of blood around the back of his head, gone a dull brown against the gray carpet, and it occurred to her how difficult that stain was going to be to get out. She might have to send it to the carpet cleaners. That would be expensive, and expensive wasn't good. Harold didn't like expensive.

But that's when it really hit her: it didn't matter what Harold liked anymore.

The monster was dead.

Except, in the movies, the monster always came back to life. Which she wouldn't put past Harold—not for a second.

She looked down at him again, expecting to see his eyes open: to see that familiar, terrifying smile cross his lips, or to see him climb to his feet.

But Harold was still lying there, dead.

Betty turned around and walked back into the bedroom. From the closet, she grabbed the biggest suitcase she could find and packed it full of clothes.

She walked back out into the living room, set the suitcase down, and reached into Harold's pocket. He always carried a lot of money, and she wasn't surprised to find a roll thick with twenties in there, held together by the gold money clip he always used. That would be a start.

Shoving the clip into her purse, she grabbed her suitcase, took one more look at Harold, then headed for the door.

AUSTIN, TEXAS

Steve Crescent rolled over in bed and looked at his wife. Alison was snoring gently. They'd gone out for Mexican in the old town. They'd drunk three pitchers of sangria. She'd had most of it: Steve made sure of that. He didn't want her waking up until morning. By which time, of course, he'd be long gone.

He pulled down the sheet and slid out from under the covers. He slipped on his jeans. The note he'd written was crumpled in his front pocket. Steve unfolded it and laid it down flat on Alison's vanity, in front of a picture of all three of them from vacation last summer. Kerry in the middle, burnt brown by the sun, he and Alison on either side, all of them smiling at the camera, arms wrapped tightly around each other. The loving family.

Steve looked from the picture to the note. It read:

Alison:

> *I'm taking Kerry to a place where she can get help. If I'm wrong for doing this, God forgive me.*
> *If I'm right, I hope you will.*
> *I love you.*

Steve

There. Simple and straightforward.

Unlike what he was doing.

He looked back at the bed. Alison hadn't moved.

Steve felt suddenly guilty. Was he being a shit, or saving a life?

No way to be sure. At least he was doing something.

He padded barefoot down the carpeted hall to Kerry's bedroom. He stood in the doorway a moment, letting his eyes get accustomed to the darkness.

Kerry lay in bed, twisting and turning, moaning softly.

She was having another nightmare.

Dr. Chandra, the first psychologist they'd sent her to, told Steve and Alison that Kerry had a lot of unresolved anger.

"How do we resolve it?" Steve had asked.

"Encourage her to express her feelings more openly," Dr. Chandra had suggested. "That may help."

The next day at school, Kerry got into a fistfight at lunch. She chipped an older girl's tooth. She got a two-day suspension.

"How did the fight start?" Steve asked.

"The cow tried to cut in line," Kerry sneered. "I expressed my feelings to her. Isn't that what I'm supposed to do?"

Steve almost slapped her. That wasn't the first time

Kerry's behavior made him long for the days of corporal punishment, when "spare the rod, spoil the child" was the rule, not the exception.

Back in those days, Steve wouldn't have to spend his hard-earned money to send Kerry to a psychologist. He wouldn't have to argue with Alison about whether their daughter was going through a phase, or doing drugs, or drinking. Whether she needed more space, more supervision, or new friends.

Back then, he would have just taken Kerry over his knee and given her a good paddling.

That's what his dad had done with him, and Steve thought he'd turned out all right. Steve Crescent was forty-one years old, a tenured professor of history at the University of Texas at Austin. He had a beautiful wife, a nice house just outside of the city, and a daughter who he loved more than anything in the world.

A daughter who, over the last six months, had somehow slipped away from him, turned into a stranger who never spoke to him anymore, filled with anger whose source he couldn't even begin to guess at. Steve simply couldn't stand by and watch it anymore.

He leaned over the bed and touched her shoulder.

"Kerry," he whispered. "Kerry."

She moaned louder. He shook her again.

She sat bolt upright, her eyes wide open.

She looked scared to death.

"Good God, honey." Steve sat down on the bed. "Are you all right?"

For a second, it seemed as if she was about to cry. Steve reached out his hand.

She twisted away.

When she looked back, the fear in her eyes was gone, replaced by a dull stare.

"I'm fine," she said. "Is it time?"

"Yes," he nodded. "Was that a nightmare?"

"No."

"Kerry . . ."

"Dad, I'm fine. Just leave me alone, all right? I need to wake up."

He held up his hands in surrender. "All right, all right. Just keep your voice down."

She nodded. Then she reached under her bed and slid out the suitcase there.

"Two weeks' worth of stuff?"

"Yes," she said exasperatedly. "Two weeks' worth of stuff."

"Good," Steve nodded. It was the first time she'd done what he'd asked in months. That's because she thought she was getting a trip to San Francisco out of it. A trip to Uncle Doug's place, so that she and her mom could have a little space between them, after what had happened today.

But Kerry was wrong.

She wasn't going to San Francisco. She was going to Tucson, Arizona, to the Jessup Institute. Steve had found the Institute on the Internet. He'd called up the director one day and spoken to her for close to an hour. They sent out an information packet. Alison had taken a quick look through it and pronounced the whole thing a terrible idea.

"It sounds like one of those boot camps they send juvenile delinquents to," she said. "It's no place for a young girl."

I've got news for you honey, Steve felt like saying. Our daughter is a juvenile delinquent. But he'd held his tongue. He'd acceded to Alison's wishes—then. Not now. Not after today.

Not after Kerry had hit her mother.

He'd come home from the university to find Alison sitting at the kitchen table, halfway through a bottle of wine, holding an icepack to the side of her face.

Kerry wouldn't even come out of her room to talk about what had happened.

This wasn't the first fight the two of them had. There had been a lot of them lately—even before the school year started, it seemed to him. This was the worst.

And Steve swore it was going to be the last.

He'd called Jessup Institute from the guest room, so Alison couldn't hear what he was doing. He'd talked to the director, given them a credit card number, and a hefty deposit.

Sometime late tomorrow, or the day after, he was giving them Kerry.

She climbed out of bed. Underneath her nightgown, she was wearing jeans and a T-shirt. Also like he asked. He smiled. They were off to a good start.

Steve led Kerry out to the van. She collapsed on the bench seat in back. Then he went into the house and got his overnight bag and the cooler he'd packed. The cooler was full of Mountain Dew, bottled water, and Oreos. Caffeine and sugar; the drugs of his choice for this evening.

Steve was planning to drive all night.

When he climbed into the driver's seat, Kerry stirred and opened her eyes.

"Go back to sleep," he said. "I'll wake you for breakfast."

She shook her head. "I'm awake."

She looked exhausted. But Steve didn't feel like arguing. She could stay up all night if she wanted.

He was sure Jessup Institute would get her back on a regular schedule.

He turned back around and reached for the ignition key.

Alison was standing at the driver's side window, staring at him.

"Steve? What are you doing?" She looked utterly, totally at sea. Dumbstruck.

He hit the automatic door locks and started the van.

"No!" Alison screamed. She grabbed the door handle, yanked at it hard. "Don't take her! Don't take my baby!"

Steve started backing out the driveway.

Alison ran alongside the van, slamming on the window with her fists.

"Stop it! Steve!"

He saw a light go on in the Druckers' house next door.

Christ, what a nightmare.

He backed over the driveway hedges, going too fast, and bumped over the curb. The van landed on the pavement with a thump.

Alison ran out into the street in front of them, waving her arms and running straight at the van.

"Dad! Watch out!" Kerry screamed.

Steve hit the gas hard. The van, still in reverse, shot backward. The tires squealed. A few hundred yards down the road Steve stopped and did a 360.

As they pulled away, he saw Alison in the rearview mirror, still running after them.

Kerry leaned forward anxiously. "She's all right, Dad, isn't she? Mom's all right? You didn't hit her, did you?"

"No, I didn't hit her. She's fine. Jesus Christ," he said, running a hand through his hair, his heart pounding. This changed everything. Alison would be on the phone to the cops the second she got back to the house. He couldn't use the highway. He couldn't take any of the main roads. Could he even do this anymore? Would Alison know where he was bringing Kerry?

He heard a muffled sob from the back seat. He turned around. "Kerry?"

She was crying.

"It's okay, honey. It'll be all right."

"No!" she screamed. "It is not all right! Nothing is all right!"

Steve sat there with his mouth hanging open for a good five seconds, trying to think of something comforting to say. Finally, he gave up.

Nice job, professor, he thought, hunched over the steering

wheel. Good thing you decided to take matters into your own hands before your whole family fell apart.

He sighed heavily.

In the back seat behind him, Kerry kept on crying.

NEW YORK CITY

Danny Garber always followed his instincts.

People used to ask him when to buy, what to buy, when to move from tech to biotech, when to diversify, the time to bet big on chips, and how to move into foreign currency. He hardly ever answered, though, since he liked to cultivate an air of mystique. He liked people to think he knew more than he did, and a helluva lot more than they did.

Danny didn't have many close friends, but there were a couple of people he hung out with—Andrew, and Amy, a few of the suit-and tie types from PaineWebber—and sometimes, when they asked why he'd made the moves he did, why he'd sold the day before and not the day after as they had, and managed to save himself and his clients a few hundred thousand bucks, sometimes, if he'd had enough to drink, he would look them in the eye and give them the God's honest truth.

"Instinct, baby," he told them, trying to sound as much like Frank Sinatra as he could. "It's all instinct."

For the last couple of years, Danny had ridden those instincts to a multi-million dollar fortune.

Now he was down to $2,400 in his bank account, and sixty dollars in his pocket, which he was about to blow on another lap dance from the same stripper he'd been buying lap dances from all night.

"Come on, man," someone said.

Danny looked up and saw his cousin Ezekiel standing over him. Zeke looked uncomfortable, as he had all night, ever since he found out it was twenty-five dollars admission and ten dollars a beer. Danny had paid the cover for him, and when they'd walked into the club and the girls had come up to Danny—pressing themselves against him, asking him to buy them drinks, asking if he wanted a dance, a limo ride, a trip to the champagne room—Zeke found himself an inconspicuous spot at the bar and shrunk down as small as he could get.

Zeke was the look-don't-touch type. The kind strip bars hated. All the bouncers—big, thick slabs of beefcake stuffed into tuxedos—had gone over to Zeke at least once to try and intimidate him into spending money. They only stopped when Danny pulled one of them over and explained the situation to them. That his cousin was a drip, but that he, Danny, was there to spend money. He flashed the five hundred bucks he'd walked in with, and the bouncers went away smiling, leaving Zeke alone.

And Danny went off to have his fun. This was certainly his last shot at it—God knew there weren't any girls like this back in Lansing, Michigan. Which was where he was headed after tonight, with his cousin as chauffeur. Back to Lansing, to work in his dad's furniture store.

The thought made him almost sick.

"Come on, Danny," Zeke said again. "We should go if you want to get any traveling in tonight. It's two in the morning."

"Don't worry," Danny snorted. "I'm not gonna turn into a pumpkin." He waved at the stripper he'd been conducting his business with. She caught his eye and smiled.

But as she walked toward him from the left, another girl stepped in front of her, blocking Danny's view.

"How about a dance?" she said.

Danny looked up at her and swallowed hard.

Maybe he was drunk—hell, no *maybe* about it, he must have had eight beers since he'd walked in the club—but he couldn't recall ever having seen a girl as beautiful as this one in any strip club or nightclub or party he'd ever been to. She was tall and thin in all the right spots and curvy in all the others, with straight dark hair and a perfect, perfect face.

Danny smiled widely. "Yeah," he said. "I'd like a dance very much."

The girl took his hand.

"What's your name?" she asked, leading him to a table in the back of the club.

"Danny."

"Well, Danny, you can call me Claire."

He slipped her two twenties. She slipped them into her G-string. Then she danced.

It might have been the fact that he knew this was absolutely his last taste of what this kind of life was like, because soon he'd be in Lansing, living in his parents' basement and working in his father's store. Or maybe it was just that it was almost two in the morning. But as far as he was concerned, even when you threw all those things into the mix, it was still the best goddamn lap dance he'd ever had in his life.

And the funny thing was, as beautiful as Claire's body was, he found himself watching her eyes for most of the dance.

He knew he was no Don Juan; hell, he was nothing more than a stockier version of Woody Allen without the sense of humor—which was what his first and only college girlfriend had yelled at him when they were breaking up—but looking at Claire, he had the sense she could see past all that, to the real Danny within, to the Danny Garber that had been worth a million bucks a few short months ago, and could very well be worth that much again, someday soon.

He found himself fantasizing about going out on a date with her. A part of him knew she did this for every customer, but that was his brain, and that part wasn't working too well right now. What was working were his more primal instincts, and those were telling him: Why not? He was always reading, in celebrity profiles, how the actresses and models wished that regular guys weren't so intimidated by them. Maybe Claire was the same way. Maybe she went home at night to an empty apartment and wished that one of the guys she'd seen that night—one of the intelligent-looking guys—was there with her, to maybe share a little wine, watch a movie, and then—

She stopped dancing.

"What's the matter?" he asked.

"Nothing." She smiled. "You want another dance?"

"Yeah, sure as hell do." Danny reached into his pocket and pulled out his last twenty. He held it out.

"It's forty," she said.

He turned around without hesitation. "Zeke! Hey, Zeke!"

His cousin came running quickly. "What? Are you ready to go?"

"Give me twenty bucks."

"Twenty bucks?" Zeke frowned. "What for?"

"Never mind. Just give it to me."

Zeke looked from Danny to Claire, then shook his head. "No. No way." His eyes widened. "Wait a minute. You spent all your money already?"

Danny didn't bother to answer.

"Five hundred dollars?" Zeke shook his head in disbelief, and Danny knew this story was getting back to his parents—that he'd spent five hundred dollars that night on booze and lap dances, so you can guess what he did with that couple million he used to have.

Fine, Danny thought. Just fine. Fuck the dance. He would talk to Claire for a minute, and then they would go. Or they wouldn't.

But when he turned around, she was gone.

Ten minutes later they left. Half an hour after that they were through the Lincoln Tunnel and in New Jersey. Danny made Zeke stop at a diner then, since he needed coffee to clear his head. They ordered, got their food, then started arguing. Zeke wanted to find a place to stop for the night, but Danny said that if he was so concerned about money, they should get a little farther out of the city first.

Two cops entered the diner as they were eating and walked through the restaurant, looking at every customer. When they'd made a complete circuit, they stopped at the cash register. One of them talked to the guy behind it, who shook his head a couple times, and then they left.

After they finished eating, they got up to pay. Danny asked what the cops had wanted.

The guy behind the cash register shook his head. "They were lookin' for someone."

"Yeah, I got that," Danny said. "What's up?"

The guy hesitated.

"Come on," Danny urged. "It's gonna be on the news in fifteen minutes anyway."

The guy leaned forward and lowered his voice.

"Somebody got killed in the motel back there," he said, jerking his head in the direction Zeke and Danny had come from. "They're looking for who did it."

Zeke's eyes went wide. "Killed?"

"Killed," the guy nodded, "in a nasty way."

Zeke swallowed, and Danny could tell he was going to have another story to tell about the big bad city when he got to Lansing.

"What'd the guy look like?" he asked.

"Not a guy. A woman, if you can believe it. What's this world comin' to?"

Danny paid, they got back in the car and onto Route 80, headed west.

Zeke put on a tape: Creed. Danny frowned. He hated that shit. Bunch of rock 'n' rollers singing about God. That wasn't rock 'n' roll. Rock 'n' roll was sex and drugs and parties, and that got him thinking about Claire again.

It was an alcohol-inspired delusion he'd been having back in the club, taking her on a date. As if. Now his thoughts were even more sexual. He kept thinking about her long legs, and how good they would feel wrapped around his body. God. He wondered how much money that would cost.

He looked up, and there was someone standing on the shoulder of the highway, far enough back from the road that she was almost hidden.

Danny squinted into the darkness as the car moved past. He could just barely make out what she was wearing, some kind of fur coat, white spotted with black.

Or maybe the spots were—

His eyes locked with hers for a second.

He blinked, realizing that the woman was Claire.

"Holy shit. Stop the car!" he yelled.

"What is it?"

"Pull over, Zeke. It's her!"

"Huh?"

Danny grabbed the wheel.

"Are you crazy?" Zeke yelled. "What are you doing?"

"Stop the car!"

Zeke pulled the car to a screeching stop. "What's going on?"

"Back there. That was Claire."

"Back where?"

"Right there, on the side of the road. A couple hundred feet back. It was Claire, from the club. The dancer."

Zeke snorted. "Danny. You need more coffee, man. You—" Then he started like he'd seen a ghost.

Danny turned, and Claire was standing next to his window.

He rolled it down eagerly.

"Claire." Danny smiled.

She looked at him blankly.

"I'm Danny, from the club. Remember?"

"Sure," she said. "Of course I remember."

"This is my cousin Zeke."

"Hi, Zeke," she said, staring at Danny.

She was wearing a black leather jacket and jeans. A real rock 'n' roll outfit, Danny thought.

But a minute ago she'd been wearing a fur coat.

Impossible.

And now that he thought about it, she couldn't be here now, because when they left the club she was still working, and she would be working until closing time, which was still an hour or so away. So how . . .

He shook his head again. Impossible. This couldn't be Claire.

On the other hand . . . how could it not be?

Danny looked into her eyes then, and for a split second thought he heard a little voice in his head say *Run*. Tell Zeke to hit the gas to get as far away from this girl as the two of them possibly could. Because he was right the first time, it was a fur coat, and he knew what those stains on it were and—

"Aren't you going to invite me in?" Claire asked.

Danny blinked.

He looked at the swell of her breasts under her jacket, at the way her legs seemed to be poured into her jeans, and suddenly that little, rational voice in his head shut up. His instincts took over.

"Sure," he said, unlocking the back door.

She hopped in.

"Where are you going?" he asked.

"West," she said.

Danny laughed off Zeke's surprised look and said, "Isn't that something. So are we."

MANHATTAN, KANSAS

It was the wind that always got you. The wind that made Midwest winters such an ordeal. Came rushing through the prairie, building up speed all the while, and when it hit town, it was howling like a banshee, blowing strong enough to draw tears from your eyes and freeze them to your face.

Bert Lyons wondered what those pioneer families had thought the first time they felt that wind: for some reason, he kept picturing the actor Slim Pickens, sitting on the buckboard of a stagecoach, urging his horses back home, back east, away from the howling wind, which (in Bert's mind) was chasing after them like the twister that took Dorothy.

"Giddyap! Giddyap, you horses! Go!" he imagined Slim saying, shaking the reins like there was no tomorrow, looking over his shoulder the whole time. "Faster, faster!"

Of course, it hadn't been like that, really. It couldn't have been.

The pioneers who came west to the wide-open prairies, who built the towns, and the railroads, who went toe-to-toe with the Indians and exterminated them and the buffalo, why, they were made of stronger stuff than old Slim. Yes sir, what kept them fighting on, through good times and bad, let them suck it up and do whatever was necessary to survive, was a simple thing when you got right down to it.

They believed, the pioneers did. They had faith.

All those corny old sayings were true: faith could build bridges, move mountains, change lives. And here he was: living proof. A man with faith could do just about anything.

Six months ago, Bert Lyons had none of that faith. Six months ago, what he had, more often than not, was a glass of beer in one hand and another waiting for him on the bar. The Aggie Lounge—the Aggie Lou, to all its regulars—opened at six in the morning, and there were times he was there, waiting for those doors to swing wide. Six in the morning, and drinking beer.

Beer was all he ever drank. Since seventh grade, when he and Johnny Graham broke into a refrigerator at a construction site one night and made off with a six-pack. They ran like bats out of hell, laughing the whole way home, even though no one was chasing them. When they got to

Johnny's, they snuck into the doghouse with Johnny's old German shepherd, Ranger, and opened each can, one at a time, passing it back and forth between the two of them. It was the worst thing Bert had ever tasted, except that Johnny kept drinking it, so Bert did too (later on, Bert found out Johnny also hated the taste, and he would've stopped a few sips in if it wasn't for Bert). By the time they opened the third can, it wasn't so bad. By the fourth, they were giggling hysterically.

About a month later—if you went by the Program's standards, which Bert was intimately familiar with—he was officially an alcoholic.

Took him close to fifty years to break the cycle.

Fifty years where he spent more time drinking with Johnny and his friends than with the two women who'd been foolish enough to marry him, fifty years of letting people down, of not following through on opportunities, of not even recognizing opportunities, of losing jobs, friends, family until finally he was living all by himself in a little apartment in Aggieville, two rooms and a hot plate for a kitchen.

Aggieville was that part of Manhattan where all the University of Kansas students came to get drunk: three blocks packed with bars, bad food, and loud music. Some nights Bert would just sit up in his apartment, a Budweiser in one hand, and enjoy the show. Frat boys stumbling to their cars, co-eds giggling and puking all over the street.

One night he'd gone out for a drink, and somehow ended up bringing one of those girls—he couldn't even remember her name now—up to his apartment. Him past fifty, and her not even out of her teens yet. They couldn't look at each other in the morning; he couldn't look at himself in the mirror for a couple days afterward. He'd stopped drinking . . . for the whole of that afternoon.

Looking back now, it amazed him that for virtually the whole time he was an alcoholic, he managed to hold onto a job of one kind or another. Most of it was security work, because of his size. Bert had been a football player in high school, and if he'd gone to college, he could have been one there, probably. Even now, at six three and two fifty (with just a little bit of a beer gut), he had the look of an ex-athlete. The look of a man you could count on.

He'd fooled a lot of people with that look.

The fooling had stopped one night last June. He'd been working as a night watchman at one of the university buildings. Just before work, he'd stopped in at the Aggie Lou for a drink with Johnny. One drink turned into two, two turned into three and before you knew it, he was fifteen minutes late to work, and less alert than he should have been.

Making his rounds, he'd walked right into an open elevator shaft. He'd fallen two stories—twenty-five feet—straight down the shaft onto concrete. And walked away without a scratch.

It was like a miracle.

"Like God himself was saving you for something, Bert," Johnny said the next night when Bert walked into the Lou and sat down at the bar next to him.

Bert had laughed that off, of course.

"What would God want with me, anyway?" Bert asked. He'd raised his hand then, to get Mickey's attention, intending to order a beer.

But the words wouldn't come out of his mouth.

"Bert?" Johnny looked at him strangely. "You all right?"

Bert shook his head, and continued to stare straight ahead, at his reflection in the mirror.

Bert always carried around this image of himself as a younger man—when he saw people looking at him, he imagined they saw the Bert Lyons he was in his early thirties. The Bert Lyons he'd been in the pictures from his second wedding: with a full head of thick, black hair, a flat stomach, tall, muscled, with a sparkle in his eye. That was one of those times in his life when he'd stopped drinking—well, stopped drinking heavily for a few months, anyway—and lost a little weight. He and Sharon had made a great-looking couple: all the pictures proved it.

The Bert Lyons looking back at him from the mirror behind the bar bore no resemblance to that man.

This Bert Lyons was fifty pounds heavier: puffy and pale. There was a roll of fat underneath his chin. There were dark circles under his bloodshot eyes. His clothes were wrinkled. His nose was red.

He looked exactly like what he was—a drunk.

"Sweet Jesus," he said, turning away from the sight. His stomach was rolling.

And then he looked at Johnny.

His friend wore a Chiefs baseball cap, a long-sleeved T-shirt a size too small for him, stained and stretched tight across his belly, and a pair of jeans. He saw those things, same as everyone else at the bar could.

But he also saw something else.

Johnny was dying.

There was something black and horrible growing inside of him: something twisting its way around and through and into the very fiber of his being. It was going to kill him, and soon. Bert could see it.

Only *see* was the wrong word. It wasn't as if Johnny's body had suddenly become transparent to him. It was more like somebody—something?—was whispering in his ear, telling him what to look for. You see that, and that? Well, you know what those things mean for your friend, don't you?

Don't you?

"Bert?" Johnny repeated. "What's the matter?"

He pushed back from the bar without saying another word, and strode out of the Lou. Climbed into his car, and headed for Denver and his sister Connie's place. She, her husband Don, and their two kids were just about the only family Bert had left in the world. It took him half a day to get

there, and the whole time he spent convincing himself that
nothing strange had happened, that Johnny Graham was
fine, that he just needed a little break from work to get back
to his old self. There was a little bar right around the corner
from his sister's, he'd walk in, have a beer, and everything
would be fine.

Funny thing, though, the first place he walked into was a
church. A cathedral, actually. St. John's-In-The-Wilderness, a
magnificent structure six blocks from Connie's. He walked
in, knelt down in one of the pews, and started to talk. Sometimes out loud, sometimes to himself. He talked about all the
mistakes he'd made in his life, about all the things he'd done
and hadn't done, the lies he'd told, the people he'd hurt, how
he was sorry to have wasted the gift of life he'd been given,
and how he wished it wasn't too late for him to maybe make
up just a little bit for the error of his ways.

When he finished, he felt clean for the first time in years.
Like he was ready to make a new start in life.

Bert stayed in Denver for three months. He never got to
that bar he'd been thinking about, but he sure did go back to
church. He became a regular—"a real god-fearing man" in
his sister's words. He hadn't though, not really.

The God he was talking to, he didn't fear. None of that "I
am the Lord your God, you shall have none before me" talk
mattered to him. He didn't even really listen to what the
priest was saying, the sermons, the prayers, the songs. He just
stood when the other people stood, sat when they sat, sang
when they sang. What brought Bert back to the church time
and time again was the fact that it was a place built to communicate with God. A holy place, where he could talk to the
presence he felt growing in his life. The presence that had
shown him what was happening to Johnny Graham, what
very well could have happened to him. Sometimes he even
felt like that presence was talking back.

Last night, sitting in that church, kneeling down in the
pew that he'd come to think of as his, he had the sense it was

time for him to go back to Manhattan. Right then—immediately, if not sooner. So he had. Grabbed his things out of the spare bedroom at his sister's, packed his car, and drove right back down I-40 into the center of town. Parked across the street from the Aggie Lou, and walked right in.

"Holy mother of God." Mickey Hendrickson, behind the bar, was the first to see him.

"Hey, Mickey." Bert slid into one of the stools at the bar: there was a basketball game on the TV at the far end.

"If it isn't the prodigal son himself." Mickey smiled and reached a hand out. Bert shook it. "Bert, it's good to see you."

"It's good to see you," Bert said.

"I heard you gave it up," Mickey said. "The booze."

Bert nodded. "Six months ago tonight."

"Good for you, Bert. Good for you." He smiled. "So where are you livin' now?"

"I've been staying with my sister in Denver. Now . . ." He shrugged. "I may be here for a little while." Bert looked around. "So where's Johnny?"

Mickey's face fell. "Oh, jeez, Bert. You ain't heard?"

Bert shook his head.

"He got sick, Johnny. Real bad."

"Ah." Bert nodded, remembering what he'd seen that night six months ago. "He's dying, isn't he?"

"Jeez, Bert." Mickey leaned across the bar, and lowered his voice. "He's dead."

Bert felt like he'd been punched in the chest.

"Oh," he said, slumping back in his chair.

I should've warned him. I should've called.

"It was a couple weeks back. We tried to find you for the funeral, but . . ."

Bert nodded.

"His mom was askin' for you," Mickey said.

"I'll stop by, then. Pay my respects."

Mickey nodded. "She'd appreciate that, I know."

Bert gathered himself, and stood. "I'll see you around, Mick."

The front door flew open, and two women walked in. The shorter of the two—a curvy, fiftyish redhead—literally stopped in her tracks when she saw Bert.

"Oh, my Lord!"

The woman—Donna Stanley—practically flew into his arms.

"I knew you'd come back," she said, squeezing him in a bear hug.

"Easy, you'll break my back, girl." He smiled.

"Well." She let go and stood back from him. "You look good, Bert."

"So do you," he said. But then, Donna always did. They had a thing going once, right after his marriage to Sharon broke up. It fell apart, and for the life of him, he couldn't remember why.

"Let me buy you a beer."

"Whoa," Bert said. "I'm not drinking anymore, Donna."

"Say that again, Bert."

"I gave it up."

She smiled—hesitantly at first, and then a little more genuinely. "Good for you, Bert."

"But I'll take a ginger ale, if you want to buy me something."

She did—and if he wasn't drinking, well, enough other people were that by the time midnight had come and gone, the nighttime scene at the Aggie Lou turned into a celebration of Bert's return. Old faces came by the bar and raised a glass to him on a regular basis, and at one point, Donna started everyone singing "For He's a Jolly Good Fellow."

"You are some of the worst singers I've ever heard." Bert lifted his own glass of ginger ale, and smiled. "But here's to you."

Later, all the celebrating started to wear thin. Started to feel wrong, too, without Johnny there.

Bert hated goodbyes; he snuck out without making any, and started walking. School was out of session; the streets were deserted.

He wondered what he was doing back here. He had more of a life in Denver now. Guided by voices, he thought. Is that any way to live your life?

A sudden gust of wind almost knocked him off his feet.

Bert righted himself, and smiled.

All right, he thought to himself. I get the message. I should stay right here.

There was a Holiday Inn sign lit up just down the street, beckoning him.

He went to see about a room.

Friday 4:45 A.M., PST

COMPTON, CALIFORNIA

Someone was shaking his shoulder.

"Church! Get up. Now!"

Church opened his eyes. "Wha? Whassup?"

Carl Royce, dressed in his firefighter's uniform, was leaning over him. His face was streaked black with soot and he was sweating hard.

Behind Carl the sky was colored red, and Church heard sirens wailing. People shouting and running in all directions.

Church rubbed his eyes and slowly got to his feet. He smelled smoke, and his head hurt something awful.

"There's a fire," Carl said. "It's big and getting bigger by the second. You've got to get out of here."

Church nodded and rolled his neck from side to side. He'd passed out in the alley between the nail salon and the restaurant after polishing off half a bottle of Old Granddad, and now he was stiff. He smelled bad too. He wondered if Mrs. Lee at the nail salon would let him get a shower at her place.

"Church? You all right? You understand me?" Carl asked, looking into Church's eyes. "You have to go."

Church nodded. "Whatever you say, Carl."

Carl was always looking after him. He worked down at the fire station on Walnut, and stopped by every night after he finished work. Sometimes he brought Church a little money. Sometimes they even went to the dollar theater together, to see a movie.

"Head up Central," Carl told him, "away from the highway, okay? Toward the theater, right?"

Church nodded, and pointed north.

"That's right," Carl said. "Now go. I'll see you later."

Church watched Carl walk back toward a blue car parked at the curb, with a siren flashing on top of it. Three other men were standing there waiting for him. One of them was a policeman, the kind with the high boots and the sunglasses. Church shuddered: he'd gotten into an argument with a policeman in a uniform like that once, and it turned into a very bad fight.

Church didn't like fighting. Luckily, he was so big that not too many people wanted to mess with him—but that highway patrolman sure did. He made Church and Cliff Jackson, who was driving, get out of the car. Then he put handcuffs on Cliff and shoved him around a little. Then he tried to do the same with Church. Except Church's wrists were too big around to put the cuffs on. That made the policeman angry, and he hit Church. He hit him a lot.

There was only so much of that Church was going to take, so it turned into a fight, and then a few more cops showed up, and it turned into a big fight. The cops beat Church up pretty badly, sent him to the hospital, then to prison.

"Downey's sending another engine," one of the men said to Carl.

"All right," Carl said. He walked over to the car and studied a map spread out on the hood. "Okay—tell them to get off at Acacia and hook up with the Lynwood companies."

The first man nodded and began talking into a walkie-talkie.

Carl turned to the policeman with the boots. "How many men you got coming?"

Church looked back down Central. One whole side of the street was burning. On the other, people were standing behind a line of yellow tape. Fire engines and ambulances and police cars were parked in the center of the big wide avenue, lights flashing. There were a lot of cops milling around, talking to each other. They kept turning around and glancing at the fire at their backs, as if they expected it to sneak up from behind and burn them.

The man holding the walkie-talkie walked up to Carl and shouted something in his ear.

Carl shook his head. "Christ, give me that." He took the radio and started shouting into it.

". . . AFF will stop a gasoline fire . . . What do you mean it didn't work? . . . Uh-huh, uh-huh, I hear you, I'm just saying you can't have used enough." Carl rubbed his eyes and listened to the voice on the radio for a moment, nodding. "Then move a block and do it again."

Church looked over to the highway patrolman and noticed the cop was glaring at him. He smiled at the man, trying to be friendly.

"What are you, a fucking retard? Get the hell out of here," the cop said.

"Okay," Church said, bowing his head and walking off, heading in the direction Carl had told him to go. A block down the road he turned and glanced back at Carl, who was still shouting directions into the walkie-talkie.

Church kept walking. Helicopters passed him in the sky above, and three fire engines in a row came roaring down Central toward the fire, with three police cars right behind them.

Church looked across Central and saw a boy—nine, maybe ten years old—standing on top of the cement wall in front of McDonald's. There was something awfully familiar about him, and a second later Church had it. It was Eldon Patterson. Eldon lived with Church's sister, because the boy's mom was dead and his father . . .

Church frowned. No one knew what happened to Eldon's father.

Eldon saw him and turned away.

Church crossed the street. "Eldon!" he yelled. "Eldon! What are you doing up there?"

The boy turned back to him and gave him a sullen look.

"Watching the fire," he said. The wall he was standing on ran between the McDonald's drive-through lane and the little shopping center next to it. It was not much more than three feet high, and Church stepped up carefully and stood beside Eldon.

Compton was flat, so if you got even a little bit of a vantage point you could see pretty far. Standing on the wall, Church could see down to the highway—Route 91, which ran east-west out to the ocean.

It looked like all of Compton was burning.

The fire was so close that Church could actually feel the heat. It was like when you opened up the hood of your car to change the oil on a hot summer day. It might be 100 degrees out. You could be sweating like a greased pig. But the second you got your head near the engine you realized how much hotter things could get.

Fighting heat like that had to be hard work, Church

thought; no wonder why Carl looked so exhausted. On all sides of the fire he could see flashing lights.

A low rider pulled into the drive-through lane behind them, bass thumping. Church heard the drive-through speaker say, "Welcome to McDonald's," and then the sound of another voice ordering. The music was lowered, then: "Yo, Eldon—what's up?"

Church turned and saw the passenger window of the low rider rolled down. A young guy—maybe early twenties, with fancy-looking clothes, dark sunglasses, and a big shiny earring in one ear—was looking up at him and Eldon. He had a big E tattooed across his shoulder.

That "E" was a gang tattoo. "E" for Eighteenth Street. They were one of the biggest gangs in the city. Even in Compton, where the Crips and the Bloods used to own pretty much all the turf, Eighteenth Street was moving in strong.

Church watched all this going on and frowned. He didn't like the looks of the guy in the car, and didn't think Eldon should be hanging around with him.

The guy stared up at Church. "What's your problem?" he snapped.

"I ain't got no problem."

"You lookin' at me like you got a problem," the guy said.

"No," Church said, bowing his head. "I ain't got no problem."

Eldon waved a hand in front of Church. "Ah, don't mind him," he said. "He's always got that stupid look on his face."

The guy laughed. "You hungry?"

Eldon nodded. "Sure. You buyin'?"

"Of course. What do you want?"

"Quarter pounder meal. Chocolate shake."

"Hey, what about you, Tiny?" the man in the car said, turning to Church. "You want something?"

"Tiny." Eldon laughed. "Hey, that's a good one. Tiny."

Church didn't think so. And he didn't like it that Eldon was laughing at him. Not at all.

He opened his mouth to say something about it.

At that moment everything went dark.

The streetlights, the car headlights, the McDonald's lights, everything, just like that.

Eldon hopped down off the wall.

"Damn, I was hungry too."

The guy at the McDonald's got out of his car and walked to the front of it. He opened the hood and clicked on a flashlight. It didn't work.

He kicked the car a couple of times. "Shit!"

"That's a weird kind of blackout," Eldon said. "A blackout ain't supposed to work on cars, you know?"

Church nodded. He looked all up and down the street. The power was out as far as he could see.

Everybody was coming out of their houses now: men, women, children, old folks.

A policeman came running toward them. "You all better clear out of here. That fire's headed this way."

"We're all right here," Church said. "My friend Carl is fighting that fire."

The policeman shook his head. "Nobody's fightin' this fire."

"But Carl—"

"Listen, pal. The power's out, so the water pumps aren't working, get it? That means the hydrants got no pressure. No pressure, no water. Understand?"

Church nodded.

Eldon's eyes went wide. "Shit, man. Compton's gonna burn!"

"Compton?" The cop shook his head and turned. The fire lit up the sky behind him. It looked to Church like the whole city was burning. "We'll be lucky if it's just Compton. The size of this fire, if we can't get the power back on . . ." The cop shook his head again. "This'll keep on burning until it hits the big city. It'll set all of L.A. on fire."

SAN DIEGO FREEWAY, LOS ANGELES

"No one talked to me all night, Carol," Abby said. "You saw that, right?"

Carol kept her eyes on the road, her thumbs twiddling on the steering wheel.

"Look, I am not imagining things," Abby said. "My name is mud in this town, and you know why."

They passed the exit for Sawtelle. Two miles to the 10, and then east to Santa Monica. Abby couldn't wait to get home.

"Okay," Carol said finally. "Tell me why you think no one at the party talked to you."

"Because they're afraid that Bobby will blackball them too," Abby said. "They know he's got it in for me."

"Abby." Carol shook her head. "You're imagining things."

"You think I'm paranoid? You don't think he cares anymore."

"No, I didn't say that." Carol chose her words carefully. "Look, Bobby is a busy man. He's producing two TV shows. He's got a movie wrapping. He's casting a pilot for Paramount—"

"Which pilot?" This was news to Abby.

Carol hesitated.

"It's not *Calamity*, is it?" Abby begged. "Tell me it's not *Calamity*."

Carol nodded. "It's *Calamity*."

"*Shit!*" Abby slammed her hand on the dashboard. "That was supposed to be my show! He wrote that for me!"

Carol nodded sympathetically. "I know. I didn't want to tell you, but . . ."

Abby shook her head. *Calamity*. She was there the night that show was born. Hell, she even helped come up with the concept. A female time traveler who was drawn to pivotal events in human history—would Bobby have come up with that without her? No. That was the answer, and he'd told her as much. She was the science fiction fan, not him.

Damn, she should have fought for that show.

The thing was, at the time she hadn't wanted to fight. For anything. That was a year ago, and she'd been a star, the female lead on *Island Patrol*, a top five syndicated show. She was the number-one downloaded swimsuit model on the Internet, a regular guest on the *Tonight Show*, a regular face on the cover of the supermarket tabloids. She'd even been talking to Paramount (and Dreamworks on the side) about doing a multipicture deal and—the icing on the cake—she was Bobby Stevens's girlfriend. Not just his girlfriend, hell, the two of them practically lived together. He was even buying her clothes and jewels on Rodeo Drive, and had her try on rings at Tiffany's and Cartier.

"Just in case," he had said with a smile. And she knew that meant he was going to propose any day, and she was going to be Mrs. Bobby Stevens, the wife of the man who was generally known as the creative genius behind all the best network dramas of the last twenty years—*Chicago One, Angels of Mercy, Hard Time*, to name a few.

The papers loved doing stories on the two of them. Beauty and the Beast, that was the usual headline, the subtext being that she didn't have a brain but looked good in a bathing suit. Heck, that was all right with her, being a television actress was just a start to her career. After that, she wanted to be in a profession where people took her seriously.

That was why, when *Island Patrol* went on hiatus, she went in to talk to the producers about wearing a few more clothes in front of the camera for the next season. And yes, maybe Carol was right, maybe that had cost her a few jobs, but she wasn't looking for those roles anymore, the ones that called for her to be half-naked for every line she had. And no, she wasn't worried when the first day of shooting the new season of *Island Patrol* rolled around and she reported for work to find her character was now a deputy force commander (translation: bathing suits *out*, polo shirts in) who spent most of each episode behind a desk, with fewer and fewer lines as the season wore on. She wanted to cut back her hours on the show anyway, so that when the juicier roles came along, she could take them. And it was all right that those juicier roles were slow in coming. Abby was willing to be patient. She started taking classes again. She bought a computer and started working on a screenplay of her own.

She had her friends. She had Bobby—when he wasn't busy. Everything was fine.

And then she stopped by the set of *Angels* for a surprise visit and caught Bobby on the couch in his office with one of the nurses from the show. They split up. They got back together.

She caught Bobby again, read him the riot act, and they split up again, this time for good. Her idea.

"Nobody walks out on Bobby Stevens!" he yelled at her while she was leaving.

She didn't bother to reply. Not to the flowers he sent, not to any of the friends or flunkies that came around groveling on his behalf.

And then one day Bobby stopped calling. Coincidentally, that was around the time Abby's job offers suddenly dried up. She even had job offers taken back. Fine, she thought. But then friends—or at least people who she thought were friends—stopped being friendly, and second-tier producers who'd been kissing her ass suddenly stopped returning her calls.

Worst of all was the day she pulled up to the Paramount gate for her one-day-a-week spot on *Island Patrol* and found out she was fired. Not to be admitted onto the lot. Persona non grata. She knew Bobby was at the bottom of it. And now this. *Calamity*.

"All right," Abby said, "tell me, who has the part?"

"No one yet," Carol said, "I've been trying to contact him. I want to pitch Jane."

"Jane Carteret?"

"That's right," Carol said. "But he's not even returning *my* calls. Which only goes to show you—he's not trying to black-ball you. He doesn't have time. He's swamped."

Abby shook her head. "Carol, Bobby doesn't need to call around. Everybody knows how he feels. That's why I'm not getting any auditions."

"Okay," Carol sighed. "Can we stop talking about this?"

"Sure," Abby snapped, "why don't we talk about why I'm not on the *E!* special?"

E! was doing a special on *Island Patrol*. A tenth-anniversary special/sweepstakes, which involved the network booking some of the show's cast members and then drawing the names of a hundred lucky viewers to accompany them.

Carol shook her head. "They didn't invite everyone on the show."

"No. Just the stars."

"You're not one of the stars anymore, Abby. And that's by your own choice."

"Oh, right. So you don't think it has anything to do with the fact that Charlie Frankel is producing the special? And that Charlie and Bobby are best buddies. Come on, Carol."

Carol didn't say anything for a moment.

"Stop obsessing," she finally said. "It's not healthy."

Abby sighed heavily. Maybe Carol was right. Maybe she was obsessing. Maybe the best thing she could do would be to just lie low for awhile, stay out of the public eye. Spend some time working on her screenplay; spend some more time with her computer, which had become a little hobby of hers as well, getting under the hood, finding out what made that machine tick.

Hell, maybe she should give up acting altogether, become a computer programmer.

The thought made her smile.

"What's so funny?" Carol asked, shifting into the exit lane.

Abby opened her mouth to answer. The dashboard lights went out. The steering wheel locked.

Carol screamed, and the car drifted to the right and smashed into the guardrail.

Abby was wearing her seat belt. She jerked forward, then slammed back into her seat.

All around her, she heard metal crashing on metal, the sound of a million fender benders happening at once.

Then silence.

"Jesus," Abby said.

Carol was gripping the wheel, breathing heavily, eyes wide.

"I couldn't turn the wheel. Ohmygod. I couldn't turn the wheel."

Abby put a hand on her shoulder. "It's all right. We're okay."

She looked out the windshield in front of them. The 405 was an eight-lane highway—four lanes in each direction. Every single car was stopped. Every single headlight was out.

The streetlights were out too.

In the car next to them a woman was hunched over the steering wheel, sobbing hysterically. A young man was sitting next to her, trying to comfort her. Noises came from all around: the sounds of people crying and cursing. Car doors slammed. Abby opened her door and stepped out onto the highway.

There was a full moon floating high above her. She spun slowly around. Behind her, to the south, there was a faint orange glow in the sky. A fire?

"Abby, look." Carol came and stood next to her. She pointed to their right. East.

Abby looked.

The entire city of Los Angeles was dark

LOS ANGELES AIR FORCE BASE

Private First Class Jimmy Maartens was sitting in the Command & Control center of Los Angeles Air Force Base, listening to the fire department dispatch truck after truck to County 41 to assist the Incident Commander in fighting the blaze.

County 41. Where was that? Jimmy looked it up in the book and snorted. Compton? Jesus, why go to so much trouble? Let it burn.

Jimmy was surrounded by computer monitors that gave him automatic updates on what was happening throughout the Los Angeles area. They were tied in to fire, police, and all emergency systems. In the event of an emergency, the Air Force base was supposed to serve as the command center for all Los Angeles air-based traffic. But that was for a real emergency, like a power failure at LAX or a bunch of Iraqis landing at Worldport. Not a fire that, as far as he was concerned, was only helping urban renewal.

Jimmy looked up at the television monitor in the corner of the room, which was always tuned to CNN. So far they had nothing on the blaze. He didn't care, though, because what he was watching was a lot more interesting. CNN *Entertainment Watch*, and they were showing a scene from Lil' Kim's newest video.

"My lord," Jimmy whistled. Damn, when he got out of the army and started making some serious money, he wanted a girl like that around, 24/7. He could see it now. Him and Kim, in a Bel Air mansion, with a swimming pool and a flat-screen color TV in every room. They'd have parties where people ate fancy food off silver trays and drank expensive liquor and danced until dawn, and he wanted the guys to come up to him afterward and say great party, man, great party, and he wanted the girls to look at him like, gee Jimmy, I wish you were my boyfriend instead of the loser I have.

In fact, the more he thought about it, he wanted a Jimmy Maartens party to be like a rap video, with lots of barely dressed, booty-shaking half-naked girls dancing with basketball stars, actors, musicians, and him sitting on a red leather chair in the middle of his living room like a king's throne. With Lil' Kim sitting next to him.

"Get back to work in there," someone shouted.

Jimmy turned and saw Tina Chou standing up in her cubicle, staring at him.

"I *am* working," he said. "I'm monitoring the fire."

She snorted. "Yeah. I see what you're monitoring."

Jimmy blushed. Then he got mad. Chou was always giving him grief. Every chance she got, she was on his case.

When he started working in Command & Control, they used to be friends. She showed him the ropes, warned him not to screw around with Martinez, because Sergeant Martinez had no sense of humor, and she even took him out drinking a couple times. But then she'd tried to fix him up on a date with a loser friend of hers who Jimmy had ditched about half an hour into dinner, and ever since then, Tina had been cold to him. She kept riding him about being a little overweight, about his acne, about his work habits. Jimmy hated it when they got stuck working the same shift.

"Did you do the logs yet?" she called out.

"No, I didn't do the logs yet."

"Then why don't you shut that off and get to work?"

"Why don't you kiss my ass?"

"In your dreams," she said.

He shot her the finger.

Then the lights went out and the room was plunged into darkness.

Command & Control was two stories below ground level, an electronically shielded, sealed environment. No windows, no natural light, no natural air. It was pitch-black and dead quiet.

"Jimmy?" Tina's voice cut through the still air like a foghorn.

"I'm on it," he said.

His knees touched the main console in front of him, and he bent forward and opened the cabinet door.

"Here we go," he said, feeling the rubber grip of a flashlight in his hand. He flicked on the switch. Nothing happened.

"Shit." He flicked the switch again. Still no light. "What the fuck is wrong with this?" Could the batteries be dead? That didn't make sense; they checked the light regularly. And speaking of lights . . . Where was that emergency generator? C&C had its own dedicated power supply that was supposed to kick in automatically.

This was a damn weird blackout.

"Easy, Private."

Jimmy almost jumped out of his skin.

Sergeant Martinez was standing right behind him, holding a candle. Jimmy hadn't even heard him approach. That was the way Martinez was, always sneaking up on you. That's how Jimmy had gotten in so much trouble last month, when he'd been on a personal call during a C&C shift. Martinez had come on him without making a sound, and next thing he knew, he was on the guy's shit list—permanently, it seemed.

After that incident, somebody told him Martinez used to be in Special Forces, which he could totally believe. Not only did the guy sneak around like a shark, but Jimmy had caught a glimpse of him in the shower after a pickup basketball game, and he was built like a motherfucking tank.

"My flashlight's dead too," Martinez said. "And the phones are out—I was talking to an officer down at Pendleton when the line just went dead." Camp Pendleton was the big marine base just about an hour south of L.A.

"How is that possible?" Jimmy asked. He looked around the room. All the status monitors—L.A. Emergency Services, Satcomm, Reuters—were dark. So were the computers.

Jimmy slid across the floor and picked up the phone at his desk. He tried one line, then another. He shook his head and made eye contact with Martinez.

"Nothing," he said.

"Shit." The sergeant rubbed his forehead. "I was afraid of that."

Jimmy looked up at Martinez. The guy—for the first time that Jimmy could ever recall—looked nervous.

Then he got it.

The computers weren't working. The phone lines were down. The batteries were dead.

"Christ," he whispered. "EMP."

Jesus. His mom, and his older brother—both of them lived right over in Venice. If there'd been a nuke . . .

"EMP?" Tina was standing behind Martinez now, looking worried too. "A nuclear explosion? But wouldn't we have had a warning of some kind? There was nothing on the system." Her look hardened. "Was there, Jimmy?"

"All right. Let's go up top and try the satellite phone. Chou . . ." Martinez turned and waved at Tina. "You get in here and start checking these systems. Top to bottom. Find out why the emergency generator hasn't kicked in, okay?"

"With no power for diagnostics? That's not—"

Martinez handed her a candle. "Do what you can, okay?"

Chou nodded. "Yes, sir."

Martinez lit another candle. Jimmy grabbed the gray suitcase that contained the satellite phone and followed him up the darkened stairwell.

They emerged outside in a large courtyard where most of the base's night shift personnel—both civilians and military— were huddled together, talking in hushed voices.

The base was located just off the 405 highway near the El Segundo exit. The military kept a pretty low profile at normal times. But these weren't normal times.

"Sergeant Martinez!" A tall blond man in uniform broke from one of the huddled groups and headed toward them.

"Lieutenant Rogers," Martinez said, saluting.

"At ease, Sergeant. We were just about to send a man down to you."

Rogers was the deputy base commander: in Jimmy's opinion, another hardass who liked nothing better than yanking your chain. The kind of guy who got pissed when your shirt was untucked.

"Nothing worth seeing down there, sir. Power's out, emergency backup hasn't kicked in, no battery power, nothing."

"Same here," Rogers said. "Satellite phone?"

"Gonna try it now. Maartens?"

"Aye, sir." Jimmy set the suitcase down on the ground and flipped it open. Inside was a Mitsubishi A900 cell phone. With the aid of the little satellite dish in the suitcase, the A900 could broadcast a signal directly to a geosynchronous communications satellite orbiting above them. It gave them a hot line directly to other bases nationwide.

When it had power.

"This is dead too," Jimmy said. He tried the spare battery. "Nothing."

"Damn," Martinez said. "That's not supposed to happen. It's supposed to be hardened against an EMP. So is the whole command center."

"He'll figure it out," Rogers said. "First thing first."

He separated himself from the group and whistled sharply.

"All right, everyone, can I have your attention, please." The lieutenant waited a moment till the talking around him stopped. "You can all see the situation we're in for yourselves. Power is out, communications are down, and to answer the question before you ask, we don't know why." Rogers took a deep breath. "We can hazard a few intelligent guesses, however, which is why I am ordering the base to Condition Charlie, effective immediately."

There was some muttering at that, mostly from the people in uniform. Going to Charlie meant they'd have to stay on duty until additional personnel arrived. And just about everyone had families nearby. No doubt they all wanted to go check on them, make sure they were all right and hadn't been harmed by the . . . whatever it was that had knocked out all the power.

"We'll be sending runners to Vandenberg to bring back additional security forces. In the meantime, all available personnel will see me for a schedule of guard duty assignments. Beyond securing the base, our priority for the next few hours is to restore power and reestablish communications. Those operations will run out of Command and Control, under the direction of Sergeant Martinez. Any civilian personnel who can assist, please see him.

"All enlisted personnel will alternate guard duty shifts. Guards will be issued weapons from the armory and must wear them at all times while on duty." Rogers paused. "This is serious business, people. In the absence of hard information, we are assuming that Los Angeles—and quite possibly other areas of the country—have been targeted by hostile forces. We are going to do whatever is necessary to safeguard our assets and the integrity of our command post. I hope that's clear to everyone.

"Dismissed."

For a second no one moved.

The civilians, Jimmy saw, all looked a little green: the army guys, by and large, didn't look much better, with the exception of those who had been in combat duty before. Like Martinez, specifically, who Rogers now pulled aside again and started talking to very animatedly. No doubt the lieutenant was making a whole bunch of half-assed suggestions which Martinez, in turn, would see carried out to the letter.

Jimmy, no doubt, would do the carrying out part.

Grumbling to himself, he started packing away the cell phone.

INTERSTATE 40, EAST OF NASHVILLE

Once or twice in the early days, those first few years when the marriage was starting to go bad—the way she'd heard other marriages sometimes went bad, the way friendships and business partnerships and just about every other kind of relationship you could think of went bad—Betty wanted Harold to come to counseling with her. She even mentioned the D word to him.

"Divorce?" He shook his head. "Oh no, honey. You and me, we're joined at the hip. One flesh, one destiny. For now and all time, till death do us part."

She kept hearing those words now, and the funny thing was, even with the road disappearing behind her at seventy miles an hour, with the image of Harold lying there on the floor as she scurried out the back door, the idea—the thought that Harold wasn't dead, that he somehow was going to get up, put on a turtleneck to cover up that horrible gash in his neck and come after her—the idea just wouldn't let go.

She knew it was ridiculous. His skin had been cold, his eyes vacant: he'd lost way too much blood. But still . . . it was Harold. He'd surprised her before and she didn't firmly, one hundred percent believe he couldn't do it again.

She kept having visions.

Vision number one: she'd stop at a restaurant and the hostess would smile and guide her to a table for two, and Harold would be sitting there, waiting for her.

Vision number two: she'd pull off the road—into a service plaza, or a rest stop, or maybe just onto the shoulder off the blacktop to grab a few winks of sleep. She saw herself leaning the seat back, snuggling up underneath her coat, closing her eyes . . .

And then someone was tapping at her window.

She'd roll it down, and a police officer would be there, shining a flashlight into the car.

"Mrs. Garson?" he'd say, and before she could stop herself, she would nod and then he would nod back as if he'd known all along and say: "We've found your husband."

She'd try to explain about what had happened, how she didn't mean to hurt him, how he'd come after her, and she was only defending herself, and then—

Harold would appear at the policeman's side, looking the same as he always had, smiling his big, perfect, shiny white-teeth smile.

"Thank you so much for getting us back together, officer," he was saying, and then he was opening the driver's side door, and she couldn't stop herself from sliding over to make room for him, from shrinking back down into the little ball of nobody that she'd been the last ten years.

And so Betty didn't stop to rest.

She could go for days without food.

She could go for almost as long without sleep.

The one thing she couldn't go without, though, was gas. The car was three-quarters full when she started. About half an hour shy of Nashville, driving on I-40, the fuel warning light started flashing.

Betty took the next exit. There was a Texaco station at the bottom of the ramp: not a big one, only two pumps and a run-down-looking minimart, but the lights were on, which was good enough for her.

She filled up, then headed into the minimart to pay. A little bell tinkled as she pushed the door open. Two men were in the store: an older man behind the register and a young cop leaning across the counter. They were both listening to the radio.

The cop turned and fixed his gaze on Betty. "Morning."

She nodded back to him. "Morning."

She felt his eyes raking over her, studying her.

And she told herself: he knows. He knows who you are and what you've done.

Suddenly the fantasies she'd had earlier about Harold showing up to reclaim her seemed ridiculous. Now, the image that came to her mind was of a policeman kneeling down on their living room floor, pulling a sheet over Harold's body, then turning to another cop and saying: "Put out an APB on her."

Forcing herself to remain calm, she walked up to the register and pulled out her wallet.

"I was on pump number two."

There was a tray of shrink-wrapped muffins next to the register. She grabbed two and set them down on the counter.

"And these."

"That's $22.10 all together, ma'am," the older man said.

She handed him twenty-five.

"Where you comin' from, ma'am?" the policeman asked.

"Oh, uh—Asheville," she answered. Now that was brilliant, she said, mentally kicking herself. Why don't you just come out and give him your name? Why don't you just tell him that you're the woman they're looking for, that you're the one who killed her husband?

"That's a nice town," the cop volunteered. "Went to the arts festival there once. Bought a painting."

The old man put the muffins in a bag and put her change down on the counter.

"You want my advice," the policeman said, "give old Cal back his muffins and head on down to Flynn's for a real breakfast. You look like you could use one."

"Flynn's?" she repeated numbly.

"It's a little coffee shop about ten minutes down the road that way." He pointed down the road in the opposite direction from the highway on-ramp. "Opens in a half hour or so."

"Oh, no, really," she said. "I've got to get back on the road."

"Uh-huh," he said. "Well, you take it easy now. Make sure you find a motel if you get tired."

"Oh, I will, officer, I will. I'm planning on stopping real soon."

She rushed out as fast as she could.

Back on the highway, she kicked herself again for talking to the cop and telling him where she was from. Why couldn't she have had a simple lie ready? Her plan—you couldn't really call it a plan, she supposed, since it had only come to her after she'd gotten out of North Carolina and realized she had no clue where she was going or what she was doing—had been to get to Nashville, ditch the car, and take a bus down to Memphis. She didn't know anybody there, nobody knew her, and she could dye her hair and disappear.

"Stupid," she said out loud. "Stupid, stupid, stupid."

Keeping her left hand on the wheel, she reached into the paper bag with her right and pulled out one of the muffins. She ripped the plastic off with her teeth and ate it in three bites.

A real breakfast would have been nice, but there was no way she could stop now. That cop had fixed her in his mind, she knew it. She'd have to get out of the state completely. Memphis wouldn't do now.

She had to keep going west.

SR 34, EAST OF DALLAS

It was a perfect summer day.

Kerry spread her towel on the beach and lay down.

Behind her, she heard her mother and father talking, laughing. From the water in front of her she heard a splash and then giggling; children playing in the lake. Mudge Pond, it was called, though why they called it a pond was beyond her. It was the biggest body of water she'd ever seen in her life. So big you couldn't even see the far shore from where she lay now, so big that there were whole towns that made a living off the summer vacationers that came to rent the cabins along the lakeshore.

Summer vacationers like them. Kerry and her mom and dad. They'd been coming to Upper Salisbury, one of the two towns next to the lake—every Fourth of July weekend since Kerry was three years old. She knew the town as well as Austin—better, in some ways, because it was so much smaller.

The downtown was two blocks long, with a police station on one end and a library on the other. Kerry had never been inside either one. In between was a five-and-dime, an ice cream parlor, and an antiques store. That was where she'd bought the bracelet. A plain metal band—not her usual style, but something about it had spoken to her. She spun it on her arm now, and lay back on her bed.

She closed her eyes.

It was a perfect day.

But it wasn't going to last.

It never did.

The lake around her grew still and the warmth of the sun vanished. And stretched out in the backseat of the van, Kerry stirred and moaned and tried to wake up. Her dream, the dream that she'd been having every night for the last six months, was about to get very, very bad.

A cool breeze blew in off the water, and Kerry opened her eyes.

It was night. The beach seemed deserted.

She stretched and rose to her feet.

Now, in her dream, she was someone else. Someone wearing heavy black boots, jeans, and a dark sweater. Someone whose skin was the color of strong coffee.

Someone who crouched low on the beach and began walking silently forward.

On the sand ahead she saw two teenagers lying on a blanket and making out, oblivious to the world around them. A transistor radio lay next to them, and Kerry could hear, very quietly, one of those old Beatles songs her dad was always insisting on playing for her.

She saw a coffee-colored hand reach into the pocket of her jeans and pull something out. It was a switchblade, and as the knife flicked open, she saw that the edge of the blade was crusted with blood.

The girl on the blanket looked up. She had a ridiculous bouffant hairstyle, the kind that had been popular twenty years ago. The girl screamed.

Suddenly, impossibly fast, the knife flashed.

Kerry saw blood and smiled. The dreams had given her quite a taste for it.

In the van, she sat up with a start.

"Kerry?" Her dad was twisted around in the driver's seat and looking at her with concern. "Are you all right? Did you have a nightmare?"

"Yes," she said weakly. "It was a nightmare."

"You want to come up front?" he asked. "You can put on a CD."

"Okay," she said. "Give me a minute."

Her dad turned back around and watched the road.

Kerry reached down and found her purse. She snapped it open and found the bag of little black pills she'd bought from one of the seniors at her school. She'd stolen twenty dollars out of her mother's purse to pay for them.

"Amphetamines," the boy had said, handing her a handful. "They'll keep you up all night."

Which is just what she needed, Kerry thought, swallowing two.

She should've taken them before the drive, but she really needed sleep, a long ten hours, twelve hours, without the dreams. Blissful, restful, peaceful sleep.

Sometimes it seemed she would never have it again.

———————————

Friday 6:05 A.M., PST

COMPTON, CALIFORNIA

Eldon and the guy with the E on his arm were both pushing down on one end of a crowbar, trying to use force to open the steel gate in front of Jeremy's High Fashion for Men and Women.

Church was keeping lookout. He didn't like keeping lookout. He knew it was wrong. He knew it was something Carl wouldn't like him to do. But when he told Eldon no, Eldon had cursed at him and called him a big dumbass. So Church had changed his mind and said yes. Eldon said there was nothing to worry about anyway, since the cops were so busy doing crowd control for the fire they had no time for anything else.

Still, Church didn't like it.

Off to his right, Church saw that the sky was just starting to get gray. The sun would be coming up soon. Behind him, the fire was so big you couldn't even see the other side of it nymore.

Big, and getting bigger all the time. It made Church nervous.

"Hey, Eldon!"

The boy looked up and made a face. "What?"

Church crossed the street. "I think the fire's getting closer," he said.

"Of course it's getting closer," the other guy said.

"Well, I'm just keepin' a lookout, like you told me to."

The guy rolled his eyes. "Look out for *people*, all right? Not the fire. We can tell—"

"Hey!"

The voice came from behind him. Church turned around.

The cop with the boots, the one who'd been arguing with Carl before, was running up the street toward them, a nightstick in hand.

"Shit." Eldon and the other guy both dropped the crowbar and ran.

Church started to follow them.

"Hold it!" the cop yelled. "Hold it right there!"

Church stopped.

"You're Royce's friend, aren't you?" the cop asked.

"Carl?" Church said. "Yeah, I know Carl."

The cop walked closer, the fire behind framing him in red and orange. Shadows flickered across his face. He tapped the nightstick in his hand. "What were you doing with that crowbar? Trying to help yourself to a few extra-large-size outfits?"

"Oh no," Church said, walking backward. "I wasn't—"

Church tripped over the curb and landed hard on his butt.

The cop stood over him. "You weren't what?"

The wind shifted then, or it seemed that way to Church, and he really smelled the fire, for the first time since he'd been right up next to it. Burning wood, burning rubber, all sorts of nasty smells . . .

And something else too.

First he thought it was just a blast of air, a little taste of how hot the fire really was, a hot wind against his face. But then it was like that breeze went inside him and found something there that had been hidden a long, long time. A feeling that belonged not to Church, but to the man he'd been before those cops had all ganged up on him and hurt him. Billy Ray Patterson, that was his name, and he got angry at himself now for lettin' the folks call him anything else. And he got angry at the people who made fun of him and tried to make him feel stupid.

Like this cop here. Like this cop who reminded him of the other cops, the ones who needed five-to-one odds to whip his ass and then had kicked him when he was down. Billy Ray owed them plenty, he owed everyone plenty, and the way he felt right now, he had plenty to go around and he was only too happy to share it, starting now. Right here and now, with this cop in the motorcycle boots, who had an expression on his face that said the cop felt about him just the way he felt about the cop.

The cop swung the nightstick at his head.

Billy Ray caught it in one hand and yanked hard, pulling the cop toward him. Billy Ray slammed a knee into his chest and down he went on the ground.

Then Billy Ray had the nightstick.

"Motherfucker," he said, and he started to swing it right at the cop's head, which was going to pop like a nice ripe canteloupe. "You're Royce's friend, aren't you?" the cop had asked, and that was wrong. Billy Ray was nobody's friend, Billy Ray was—

Church held the nightstick in the air. He looked at it, then let it drop to the ground.

What was he doing?

He felt the warm breeze, whatever it was, blow by him and on down the avenue, like a rolling wave.

The cop was doubled over on the ground, wheezing for breath.

"I'm sorry, mister." Church bent down and offered him a hand.

"Fuck you," the cop snarled and got to his feet, holding the side of his chest and grimacing. "I think you broke one of my ribs, you retard."

Church held out a hand. "I said I'm sorry."

"And I said fuck you." The cop drew his gun, pointing it right at Church.

Something slammed into the cop's head then and knocked him to the ground.

Church looked up, and there was Carl, standing before him and holding a shovel high above his head, both hands clasped tight around the handle. He looked like a crazy person. Blood was spattered all down the front of his uniform and all over his face.

"That fucker," he said. "That motherfucker. That was for you, Church! That was for you!"

Carl laughed like a madman, then turned and ran down the street, the shovel held high over his head.

On the ground, the cop was twitching, his eyes still open, staring straight ahead. The whole top of his head was gone. There was blood and bone and other stuff, and Church thought for a moment he might be sick.

Someone screamed.

Down the block, where Carl had gone, Church saw three firefighters with shovels raised above their heads, slamming them over and over into something on the ground.

Glass smashed. At the minimall across the street, someone had pushed a car through the window of the liquor store, and Church watched people shoving their way inside.

He heard gunshots from farther down the street, then closer, then all around him, coming from every direction.

Right across the street, a woman ran out of the house, screaming. Someone fired out the front door, and Church saw the flashes from the gun as the woman fell to the ground and lay still.

Church looked around wildly. Where was Eldon?

"Eldon!" he shouted. "Where are you?"

There was no answer.

Church ran off, shouting the boy's name.

LOS ANGELES AIR FORCE BASE

The sky was turning gray. Tina and Jimmy—on orders from
Martinez, with no power in sight and nothing for them to do
but sit and twiddle their thumbs—made their way to the
base's main entrance. Two men, M-16s slung over their
shoulders, were leaning up against the fence.

"Tell me some good news, Tina," the first man said. "Like
you got the generator working and coffee is on."

"Sorry, Ian. No coffee yet. But we did come to relieve you
guys for a while. This is Jimmy Maartens."

"Ian Currie. This is Jason Evans." Currie's partner was a
tall black soldier Jimmy had seen around base but never
talked to.

"So what's goin' on down there?" Ian asked. "You guys figure out what the hell happened?"

"EMP, right?" Evans said.

"Nobody knows for sure. What's going on up here?" Tina
asked.

"Runners been coming back all morning," Currie said. "As
far as we can tell, power's out all over the city. There's a big
fire over there." He pointed almost due east. "You can see the
smoke."

"Jesus," Jimmy said. "There was a big fire in Compton last
night. It was on all the monitors. They must have had half
the fire trucks in the county there." He thought of something
else. "When the power went, the pumps would have gone."

"Yeah," Currie said. "That thing's still burning."

"Eyes front," Evans said. He pointed down the street.
"Here they come again."

The base fronted El Segundo, a major commercial avenue four lanes wide. At six-thirty in the morning those lanes were normally jammed with traffic, cars crawling by on their way to the beach or the mall or the interstate. Not now. Now the road was full of stationary cars, many of them abandoned by their owners.

Heading toward them, just on the other side of an underpass, was a group of about two dozen people.

"Who are these clowns?" Tina asked, squinting into the darkness.

"Clowns is right." Currie shook his head and took his rifle off his shoulder. "Some kind of gang, I think."

As the group drew closer, Jimmy could make out individual faces: Latinos with shaved heads and soul patches, blacks with dreads and sideburns, a short, stout white kid with biceps the size of grapefruits. A whip-thin Hispanic boy at the center of the group stepped forward, holding his hands at his sides. The inside of his right forearm was tattooed with a six-inch stylized E.

"Hey, soldier."

Evans stepped forward, so that twelve feet of asphalt and the wire fence were all that separated the two men.

"What do you want?"

"What's the news?"

"No news."

"When's the power coming back on?"

"Don't know."

The boy smiled. "You just full of information, huh?"

"Not at the moment."

The boy turned and said something in Spanish to the others. They all laughed.

It was just light enough now that Jimmy could see that everyone facing them was packing a weapon of some kind. Gun butts protruded from waistbands and pants pockets. A black kid who looked all of twelve years old had a big hunting knife tucked into a scabbard hanging off his belt.

The leader turned back to Evans. "We check back with you in a while, okay?"

"It's a free country," Evans said.

The boy nodded. "That's right."

The two stood rock-still for a moment, staring—no, glaring—at each other. Finally, with a nod at Evans, the leader spun on his heel and led the others back down El Segundo.

"If the power's not back on soon, those guys'll be looting every store in sight," Currie said.

"Those guys were all packing—you saw that, right?" Tina asked.

"Kind of hard to miss," Evans said.

Currie unslung his rifle and handed it to Jimmy. "Which is why you get this." It was an M-16, same as the one Jimmy had trained on, but with a thicker barrel.

"It's the A-2 model," Currie explained. "Sight's a little different."

"Does three rounds in a burst," Evans added, handing his own gun to Tina. "Now, listen," and for the first time Jimmy noticed the sergeant's stripes on his shoulder. "Don't even think of taking this off your shoulder unless the base is in imminent danger, understand? You get into it with civilians like those clowns, we're gonna have a big mess on our hands."

"Yeah, sure," Jimmy said.

"Of course." Tina nodded.

"The other thing is," Evans continued, "we had a few guys come in from Vandenberg last night. More may be on the way. Now I know this is a fucked-up situation, but everybody has to have ID to get in, okay? If you have any problems, any questions, come and find me, or go see Alston at the post in the courtyard. We'll make it a short break. Half an hour."

Currie yawned and put a hand on Tina's shoulder. "Try not to fuck up."

Then they were gone.

"I don't know about this," Jimmy said, hefting the gun Evans had given him. "It's a whole different feel."

Tina shrugged. "Then get used to it." She took the gun off her shoulder and sighted down the barrel. She swung the gun around slowly, sighting on the overpass down the road, on the Burger King past it, on the funeral home across the street, and then . . .

Pointed it right at Jimmy.

"Bang," she said.

"Hey, that's not funny."

She lowered the gun. "You have no sense of humor. You ought to try it out. It's definitely a different feel."

"Don't tell me what to do."

"I'm just saying you should get used to the gun, Jimmy, that's all."

Behind her, Jimmy saw a cloud of black smoke rising from the fire down in Compton, and at that moment he swore he felt the heat from it blow right through him.

And he got angry.

He looked at Tina, and realized he was angry at her. No, not angry. Furious. Telling him what to do.

"Why don't you just shut the fuck up?" he said.

Tina blinked. "What did you say?"

"I said, why don't you just shut the fuck up?"

Suddenly, Tina looked furious too.

"Look, just because you're too much of a chickenshit—"

"Shut up!"

She shook her head. "Make me."

Jimmy glared at her. "Don't think I won't."

"That's exactly what I think." She was holding the gun in front of her with both hands, and suddenly she lunged forward, slamming it into his chest and shoving him backward.

"Come on, butterball," she said. "Make me."

"Fuck you," he said. He raised his own gun chest high and shoved right back at her.

She dodged out of the way, and Jimmy stumbled.

Tina slammed the rifle into his back, and he fell to the ground.

She put a boot on his head.

"You're such a fucking loser," she said. "Somebody ought to put you out of your misery."

Then he felt the barrel of her rifle against his forehead.

"Maybe that somebody oughta be me," she said.

Jimmy heard the bolt slide back. Jesus Christ, he thought, I'm a dead man.

The next thing he heard was the sound of glass shattering. He raised his head.

Something was happening at the Burger King.

"What the hell?" he heard Tina say. The rifle barrel moved away from his head.

He turned and looked up at her.

She was staring at the rifle like she didn't know what it was doing in her hands.

"Holy Christ," she said, the anger gone from her face. "Jimmy, I'm sorry. I didn't mean to—"

Jimmy pushed himself off the ground, and picked up his gun. He wanted to shoot her. God, he wanted to shoot her.

She was looking down the street.

"Trouble," she said.

Jimmy followed her gaze. A thick black cloud of smoke was rising from the Burger King. People were pouring out of the restaurant, running in all directions. One—a massively overweight black woman—ran right past them, holding her hands to her face and screaming. Blood oozed from a cut that ran the length of her cheek.

"Shit," Tina said. She started backing away from the gate. "I'll go get Evans."

"No time," Jimmy said. "Look."

The gang was headed their way again, the same whip-thin kid front and center.

"Hey, soldier," he said, swaggering up to the gate. "What's new?"

"What's new?" Jimmy raised his gun. "What's new is you got ten seconds to get the fuck out of here."

He smiled. "I thought it was a free country."

"You thought wrong."

The boy shook his head.

"You don't want to fuck with us, soldier."

"You don't want to fuck with me," Jimmy said, and he suddenly realized it was true. They didn't want to fuck with him, because he'd start shooting, he really would. He was actually kind of looking forward to it.

"Then start counting, soldier. Let's see what happens when you reach ten."

"I know what's going to happen," Jimmy said. "But like I said, I'll give you ten."

A grin tugged at the edges of the boy's mouth. He didn't believe Jimmy at all.

"One," Jimmy said.

"Jimmy, what's the matter with you?" Tina said quietly into his ear. "Remember what Evans said?"

Jimmy shook his head. "Don't distract me now."

"I'm going to get Evans."

"Shut up," Jimmy barked. "Two."

"Better do like your friend says!" the kid called out. "Put down the gun."

"Jimmy." Tina put a hand on his shoulder. "Come on."

That did it.

He spun and squeezed the trigger. *Rat-a-tat-tat.*

Tina flew backwards, crimson roses exploding on her chest.

His gun was trained back on the gang leader in less than a second.

Jimmy smiled. "Now . . . where was I?"

The thin boy's eyes were wide.

"You fucking crazy, man."

"That's right." Jimmy smiled. "Three. Four."

The leader shook his head. "You know, man, you can't shoot all of us."

Jimmy nodded. "I know. But I can get you for sure, homeboy."

The kid stared. Jimmy's finger tightened on the trigger. Then the gang leader laughed.

"Homeboy," he said. "That's a good one. That's funny."

"Glad you think so."

The boy nodded to the others, and they started backing away from the gate.

"We'll see you later, soldier."

"Uh-huh," said Jimmy. In the distance, he heard the sound of gunfire coming from the opposite side of the base.

And suddenly, from somewhere deep inside came the certainty that the power wasn't coming back on anytime soon, that the cops weren't suddenly going to show up in force, that the cavalry wasn't coming over the hill in the nick of time. That the world had changed in some real basic, fundamental way, and it was going to be a struggle for survival for a while. A real dog-eat-dog world.

The question was, which pack of dogs was he going to run with?

"Hey," Jimmy called, still staring down the sight of his rifle at the gang leader. "What's your name?"

The boy stared at him a moment before answering. "Hector."

"I'm Jimmy." He lowered the rifle, and slung it over his shoulder.

"I want to talk to you."

SAN DIEGO FREEWAY, LOS ANGELES

"Damn, I'm hungry," Carol said.

Abby nodded. So was she. "Let's get out of here and get something to eat."

It was the third time she'd suggested doing that in the last few hours. Then, as now, Carol shook her head.

"I don't want to leave my car. Besides, don't you think we should stay here and find out what's going on?"

"I think we have a better chance of finding out what's going on if we get off the highway," Abby said. It seemed pretty obvious to her, yet few people had left their vehicles. Almost everyone was still sitting right where the blackout had left them, stranded on the 405. People were huddled together in small groups, sitting on the hoods of cars, hanging out by the median. Abby had smelled pot more than once during the night. She heard laughter and the sound of a guitar playing, a few people singing along. She went for a walk, and saw more than one set of car windows steamed up. People passing the time, doing what comes naturally.

It seemed to her that everyone was waiting for something to happen. But she was tired of waiting.

"Come on, Carol, what do you say? Let's lock the car and get out of here. There's got to be a gas station, or a minimart—something—right around here."

"I'm going to wait." Carol shook her head. "The cops will be along soon, I'm sure. They'll tell us what to do."

Abby shook her head. "I don't think they're coming, Carol. At least not for a while."

It was mind-boggling that no one in authority had made an appearance yet with a highway full of stalled cars and passengers.

"Ladies."

Abby groaned softly. She knew that voice. She looked up and saw the Hispanic guy from the car next to theirs leaning over their window. "How's it going?"

"Same as it was going an hour ago," Abby said. "And the hour before that."

The guy had been over to check on "how they were doing" pretty regularly since the power went. He was a little starstruck. He kept calling Abby "Cristina," which was the name of her character on *Island Patrol*.

"Hey, listen," he said, "I was talking to this dude on the other side of the highway. He said that maybe what happened was an EMP. Like an electromagnetic pulse, like after a nuclear explosion. Really screws up everything electronic."

Abby shook her head. That possibility was one of the first things she and Carol had discussed. An EMP would not only knock out the power, it would fry cars, cell phones, pagers, everything that seemed to be on the blink.

But they hadn't seen an explosion. "Not an EMP," Abby said. "There was no bomb."

"Maybe," the Hispanic guy said. "Look."

Behind him, Abby got out of the car to see. He was pointing south, toward the orange glow she'd seen earlier. The fire. It looked a lot bigger.

"What is it?" Carol called out.

"Come see for yourself," Abby said, leaning over the guardrail. Maybe the guy was right, she thought. Maybe there had been a bomb.

She stared into the faint orange haze for a second.

And for a second, she felt as if something was staring back. A chill ran down her spine. Suddenly, Abby wanted to be someplace else—anyplace but the highway. She turned to tell Carol she was leaving.

Carol was looking at her strangely. No, not strangely, Abby realized. Like she was mad about something.

"What?" Abby said.

"Nothing."

"Why are you staring at me like that?"

"I'm just wondering why I keep wasting my time on you."

"What do you mean?"

"You know what I mean. I'm never gonna make a dime off you again. You have managed to make a lifetime enemy out of one of the most powerful guys in Hollywood." Carol shook her head. "I quit. Get yourself another agent."

Abby couldn't believe what she was hearing. "After all the money I made you? You lousy bitch."

"Yeah, I might be a bitch, but you're a talentless, stuck-up little—"

Abby clocked her right in the jaw. Carol went down like a sack of wet sand.

Suddenly, just like that, the anger Abby had felt was gone. She bent down and started to help Carol to her feet.

"God, Carol, I'm so sorry. I don't know what—"

Carol snarled.

She walked over to her car, reached into the backseat and pulled out Abby's bag. Her laptop and a hard copy of the script she'd been working on for the last six months were in it.

Carol took the strap by both hands and flung it over the guardrail.

"No!" Abby screamed, trying to grab it. She watched it smash below, and then whipped around to face Carol. "I can't believe you did that," she whispered.

"You all right, Cristina?" Abby looked up and saw the Hispanic man standing next to Carol's car, pointing at Carol. "This bitch fuckin' with you?"

"Fuck you," Carol said. "Who you callin' a bitch, you fuckin' wetback? How about I get Immigration to check you out, huh? You and the twenty people in your van."

"I got a better idea," he said. He started walking toward them.

He picked up Carol and slung her over his shoulder.

"What are you doing?" Carol screamed. "Put me the fuck down!"

"That's just what I had in mind," he said.

He walked to the guardrail and tossed Carol over the side. Then he turned to Abby and smiled.

"Looks like you need a new agent, Cristina."

Abby backed away and started to run.

NEPTUNE BEACH, FLORIDA

Someone was hammering on his door.

"Pete! Pete, goddamnit are you in there?"

Peter Williams opened his eyes. He looked at the window and saw the sun blazing through. He looked at the clock next to his bed and saw it was eight-thirty. He looked at the empty beer cans next to the clock and groaned.

Shit.

"Pete!" The hammering at his door got more insistent.

Peter sat up in bed, and rubbed his eyes. He threw on a shirt and opened the door.

Leo Beauchamp stood there, glaring at him. Leo glaring was an impressive sight, six feet two inches and 250 pounds of angry black man.

Appearances could be deceiving though, and in this case, they were. Leo was big, but he was a teddy bear. Even as a cop, he'd been hesitant to use his size to any advantage. Part of the reason why he'd left the force.

"You know what time it is?"

Peter rubbed his eyes. "I do now."

"Good." Leo folded his arms. "Would you please get your ass down to Ponte Vedra then?"

Ponte Vedra was Ponte Vedra Beach, where Peter was running a renovation job for Leo on a big mansion. A big fancy mansion, because all the houses in Ponte Vedra Beach were big and fancy. Ponte Vedra was where Leo got most of his work from.

Peter was supposed to have been there an hour ago.

"Hold on," he said. "Just let me get dressed."

Leo's eyes widened as he looked past Peter into the apartment.

"What the hell—where is everything?"

Peter shrugged. "I decided to redecorate. Minimalist look."

Leo frowned. "Yeah. Right. You out of money?"

Peter pulled a crumpled five off the nightstand.

"I'm flush. See?"

"Peter, come on. Are you out of money?"

"Don't worry about it. The union says my pension gets freed up soon—next week, probably. Everything's fine."

"Well, let me give you something to tide you over." Leo reached into his pocket and pulled out a thick wad of cash. He peeled off a few bills. "Five hundred do you?"

Peter shook his head. "I can't take your money. You've given me enough already."

"You saying you ain't gonna have five hundred next week?"

"I'll have it."

"Well, you can pay me back then," Leo said. "Right?" Leo shoved the bills into his hand. "Take it. Get dressed, and I'll see you at the mansion."

He turned to go.

Peter sighed. "Wait."

"What? You need more?"

Peter shook his head.

"No. I need a ride."

"What?"

"My car got repossessed yesterday."

"Oh, man." Leo rolled his eyes. "Just how were you planning on getting to work if I didn't show up?"

"The bus. That's how I got there yesterday."

"The bus?" Leo held up a hand and shook his head. "Never mind, I don't want to know. Just hurry up and get dressed."

Half an hour later they were pulling down the long shaded driveway that led up to the Beaulieu mansion. Peter's crew had been working nonstop on the house since the beginning of November, getting it ready for a big New Year's Eve party that the owner, a tobacco heiress from Richmond, was planning. All the big jobs—moving walls, raising ceilings, laying new floors—were done now, and they were racing the clock to get the finish work completed in time for the big event.

Before leaving last night, Peter had told the crew—who usually started around six-thirty in the morning—to concentrate on painting the entryway above the grand staircase, which was the centerpiece of the house and was also planned as the centerpiece for the party. That's where he and Leo found them when they walked in.

But they weren't painting anything. They were ripping up the stairs.

Leo stopped short. "Jesus Christ."

Peter came up behind him. "What the hell is going on?" he yelled.

Mike Gormley, who was his best man on the crew, stepped forward. "Miss High-and-Mighty herself dropped by first thing this morning. Miss Cornelia."

"Oh, God." Peter groaned. Every time Cornelia Beaulieu dropped by to see how things were going, it turned out they were never doing as good a job as she expected.

"I thought we were going to get away clean," Gormley said. "I took her over every inch of the house, showed her what we'd done since last time, and I could swear she had a smile on her face. Then as she's walking out the door, Burton"—Gormley turned and pointed at Jim Burton, who was one of the biggest guys on the crew—"comes down the staircase, and all you can hear is the wood going squeak squeak squeak."

"Oh, no."

Gormley nodded. "Oh yes. Now she walks up the staircase

a few dozen times, and even though she doesn't hear a single thing, she insists we have to fix them because she's going to have so many guests going up and down the staircase. Rip 'em up and fix 'em, she says. Now."

Peter shook his head. Damn it, he should have been there, and he could tell by the look on Leo's face that he was thinking the same thing.

"You should've waited for me," Peter said.

"I tried to, but she was standing there, screaming about calling in another contractor on the job if I didn't do what she said, and so . . ." He shrugged.

Peter sighed. "It's all right," he said. "We'll make do." He nodded toward the staircase. "So how's it look?"

Gormley shook his head. "Not good. They really nailed some of those treads down tight. We already split one trying to get it up off the riser. Here," he said, leading them over to the partially disassembled staircase. "Take a look."

Gormley handed over one of the treads, which had three big old-fashioned nails sticking out of it.

"Look at the size of those things," Gormley said. "Man, they don't make them like they used to."

Peter turned the board and looked at the nails sticking out. They were big, all right. And old. The kind of nails that didn't have heads and were shaped more like spikes.

Peter frowned. Something about that shape seemed familiar.

"Pete?" Leo said. "What is it?"

"Hold up a second," he said, because something was coming to him.

A memory.

He squeezed his eyes shut, and a second later he had it.

The man in the alley.

The night Jack Kelly was killed.

"Pete?" Gormley said. "You all right?"

Peter didn't answer. He was seeing the man, raising his

hands and stepping away from the girl, just as he had that night. Seeing him smile, and then hearing himself say, "Drop the knife! Drop the knife!"

The man dropped it.

"It's not a knife," he said. "See for yourself."

But Peter couldn't. His memories of that night ended right there. At least they had for the last six months.

Until now.

Now they played on.

In his mind, Peter was back in the alley. Looking down at the ground, seeing that the man was right. The thing lying there wasn't a knife. It was a bigger version of the nails the builders of Beaulieu mansion had used.

It was a spike. An old-fashioned railroad spike.

WALNUT GROVE, MINNESOTA

Thomas slept in his car again, bundled inside a sleeping bag in the back seat. When the sun woke him up, he went outside to piss. Then he came back to the car and made an entry in his journal.

December 17

> *It may, in fact, be a candlestick. Much to my surprise. I thought that reference was just an analogy.*

He paused. There was a package of Saltines on the front seat next to him. He ripped it open with his teeth, and swallowed each cracker in a single bite. Breakfast.

He wrote for another minute. Then he started up the car and drove.

The house stood far off the road, hidden behind a thick curtain of pine and evergreen forest. Yesterday he'd driven past two times before spotting it, and the narrow break in the trees that indicated the driveway. There was a barn at the back of the house. That changed things—the story he'd come up with for one. He sat in the parked car for a moment and thought up a new one. Then he got out and walked up to the front door of the house. He pressed the doorbell and waited.

A sturdy, handsome-looking woman in her mid-forties opened the door. She was wearing an apron and her arms were covered with flour.

"Mrs. Johannsen?" he said.

"Yes?"

"I'm sorry to disturb you at home. My name is Thomas Kelleher." He handed her his card.

"Americana?" She frowned. "What—"

"Antiques," he said. "I'm a collector."

"You want antiques from us?" Now the frown became a smile. "I'm afraid you have the wrong place, Mr. Kelleher."

"What is it honey?" someone called.

A man came to the door. He had a pipe in one hand and a newspaper in the other. The woman's eyes were blue. His were a brilliant, piercing green.

"This man is looking for antiques, Marcus."

The man shook his head. "Well, I'm sorry to disappoint you, but—"

"Not antiques, exactly," Thomas said quickly. "Excuse me for interrupting. This part of the country, we find a lot of valuable old farming tools."

"Farming tools?"

Thomas nodded. "Tractors, hoes, harnesses, wagons . . . threshers, rakes, saddles, churns. Things like that are getting pretty valuable."

"Huh," the man said. "We might have some stuff like that out in the barn. I can't guarantee what kind of shape it's in."

"That's all right," Thomas said. "I just want to take a look."

The wife frowned. She looked suddenly suspicious.

"You don't have to sell to me," Thomas said quickly. "But I can tell if you've got something valuable."

"Hmmm." Johannsen nodded. "Can't see what harm it'd do. Let's go see."

Thomas followed the man along a narrow path that led behind the house.

"Where are you coming from, Mr. Kelleher?"

"Out of Boston originally," he said, the words flying out of his mouth before he could stop them. He'd meant to say Kansas, that fit his story better, but the truth had popped out instead.

"That's an awful long way to be coming for antiques."

He attempted a smile, but it felt forced. "You have to go a long ways to find the good stuff. Traveling's part of the job description."

"I couldn't do it." Johannsen shook his head. "Stay away from home so long. And at your age—if you don't mind my saying so—it must be quite a haul."

"You get used to it."

"But still—isn't there someone else who could handle that part of the business for you? Do you have a partner?"

"I had a daughter," Thomas said suddenly, and stopped dead in his tracks.

The image of Julie filled his mind.

Why had he told Johannsen that? His tongue was loosey-goosey today. His mind was going, as he knew it had been for quite some time.

Johannsen was looking at him funny.

"Mr. Kelleher? Are you all right?"

He realized he'd stopped walking, and shook his head. "Of course I'm all right." This wasn't going the way he'd planned at all. "Lead on."

"My wife is making strudel," he said. "We could go back into the house and relax for a minute."

Thomas looked up. The kitchen was at the back of the Johannsen house and he saw Mrs. Johannsen staring at them through the window.

Sure. They would love for him to go back into the house. As if he didn't know what they would do to him in there.

"There's coffee too," Johannsen said.

"Maybe after," Thomas said. "For now, I'd really like to see what you have."

At the barn, Johannsen reached up and unlatched the big wooden door, and Thomas helped him swing it open.

As Johannsen had said, there wasn't much inside. Shafts of sunlight shone in through a row of windows along the far wall of the barn.

"We gave away most of the tools over the years," Johannsen said. "But if you see anything . . ."

Thomas began searching.

In one stall he found an old saddle and a riding crop. In a corner were some parts that looked like they belonged to an old-style farming machine of some kind. Underneath a hay loft he found a couple of hoes, a shovel, a pickaxe, and a pitchfork. On a long wooden bench next to one of the walls there was an overturned candle holder and a box of matches.

"I don't mean to pry," Johannsen said, "but you said you had a daughter. Did something happen to her?"

"She died." Thomas smiled. "It was a long time ago."

Johannsen nodded. "I'm sorry."

Thomas picked up the pitchfork and held it in his hands. "How old do you think this is?"

"Well, I don't really know." Johannsen took a step forward. "Maybe there's a date on the—"

Thomas swung the fork and stabbed him square in the chest.

The man gasped and grabbed at the wooden shaft. Blood dribbled out of the corner of his mouth, as he stared, unbelieving, at Thomas.

"You bastard," he said.

"My daughter," Thomas screamed. "I think you know exactly what happened to her!"

Johannsen tried to speak but staggered backward. Then, to Thomas's surprise, he clutched the shaft tighter and started to pull it out.

Thomas grabbed the pitchfork again and slammed the man back into the barn wall. Putting all his weight into it, he drove the pitchfork forward till he felt the tines catch wood. When Johannsen's eyes went blank, he let go of the handle and stood back.

He was just starting to turn around when something heavy hit him on the head.

He staggered, finished turning, and saw Mrs. Johannsen holding a shovel.

Blood trickled down the side of his face.

He reached his right hand into his coat pocket and felt the barrel of his gun. She swung the shovel again. He held up his left arm to block it and heard bone crack.

He brought the gun out of his pocket and shot her.

Once.

Twice.

Then he slumped to the floor.

The pain in his arm was incredible. His head was spinning. Closing his eyes, he drifted off into darkness.

NEWCASTLE, OKLAHOMA

Steve had gone north instead of west, in case Alison remembered about the Jessup Institute. Even going north, he'd been careful to avoid a straight-line route, staying on the interstate only as far as Round Rock, after which he'd ducked over to Taylor and onto the back roads.

Some 250 miles later they were across the Red River and into Oklahoma. A little town called Yuba, where he stopped to gas up the car and get coffee. A couple hours after that they picked up the interstate again and were heading west into Oklahoma City. Steve felt he could go another few hours, but just outside Norman he saw a sign for a Motel 6 and decided to stop. Kerry had barely slept through the night and he was worried about her.

He was also worried about Alison. He still couldn't shake the look on her face when they'd pulled out.

Not for the first time that night, Steve wondered if he was doing the right thing. He'd made the decision to take Kerry away so quickly, and now here they were in Oklahoma, and he was more miserable about the situation than ever. Kerry was miserable too. He could tell. She was also exhausted. She'd only gotten a few hours' sleep right after they left Austin, and she'd been wide awake next to him throughout the rest of the trip.

At the manager's office, Steve paid cash for their room, leaving his driver's license as a deposit so they wouldn't run a credit card. Then they parked and went into the motel.

The room had two double beds on either side of a little night table. Looking at those beds, a wave of overwhelming exhaustion hit him. He put their suitcases down and realized he wasn't even going to change. He was just going to stretch out on the bed and collapse.

"Which bed do you want?" he asked.

"Whichever. I'm not going to sleep yet."

Steve shook his head. "Kerry . . . you've got to get some rest."

"I did—remember? In the van?"

"That was only a couple of hours."

"And the couple hours before you woke me up," she said. "Dad, I'm fine."

"We should get on the same schedule, Kerry," he said. "It's going to be a long drive."

"I'll be all right," she said, opening the drawer of the night table and taking out the remote control for the TV. "I'll watch television for a while."

"Kerry—"

"Dad! Stop treating me like a baby!"

He sighed heavily. He was too tired to fight. "All right, Kerry."

He flopped down on the bed nearest the door. Then he remembered he had to make a call.

He picked up the phone on the nightstand and dialed the number for Jessup Institute.

An operator's voice came on. "We're sorry. All circuits are busy at this time. Please try your call again later."

Dial tone.

He hung up the phone. That was odd.

"Dad?"

He looked up. Kerry had been clicking through channel after channel. "All I can get is news."

She'd stopped clicking on an image of a grim-faced woman talking into the camera. Superimposed behind her was a map of California. Los Angeles was shaded red. As the woman kept talking, the shaded area expanded.

". . . the White House will still neither confirm nor deny reports of a nuclear explosion, centered in the metropolitan Los Angeles area. The President, flying back from Pakistan this morning, issued a brief statement to the press expressing his concern and stating that he was planning an immediate meeting with national security advisers. CNN further reports that the communications blackout appears to be spreading in all directions, as both Ventura and San Bernardino . . ."

Steve leaned forward on the edge of the bed, suddenly wide awake.

TOLEDO, OHIO

When Danny got up to go to the bathroom, Zeke went with him.

"What are you doing?" Zeke asked.

"What do you mean what am I doing?" Danny unzipped his pants and stood at the urinal. "I'm taking a piss."

Zeke stood at the urinal next to him, glaring.

"You know what I mean."

"No, Zeke, I don't. Why don't you tell me?"

"You're going to bring that stripper home to your parents' house? What is the matter with you, Danny?"

Danny finished his business and washed his hands. He'd been holding his tongue, trying to come up with a smart answer, but seeing Zeke there, fuming, hands folded across his chest, just itching to get into a big argument with him, he decided he wasn't going to give his cousin the satisfaction.

Besides, he'd realized something important over the last few hours. Actually, two things.

Number one was that he wasn't bringing Claire home, because he wasn't going home.

And number two, the girl riding with them wasn't Claire.

The realization hit him late last night, after Zeke had fallen asleep and the two of them were talking. Actually, he did almost all the talking—all Claire did was give short, enigmatic answers to the questions he asked her.

The first of which came about half an hour after they'd picked her up, when Zeke started yawning and making noises about finding a motel for the night.

"I'm not tired," Danny said. "Not at all." And he wasn't; he was wired. Mostly because every time he turned around in his seat, Claire was sitting in the backseat, smiling at him.

"How about you?" Danny asked her. "How do you feel?"

"Fine," she said, and so she came up front and Zeke went in the backseat to lie down while they drove.

"So you got off work early?" Danny asked.

"Yes," she said. She opened and closed the glove compartment, then did it again, as if she'd never seen such a thing before.

Danny lowered his voice. "That's good, 'cause I'm glad

to see you again. I was thinking about you after I left the club."

"I know," she said.

He laughed. "I'll bet you hear that from a lot of guys."

She shook her head. "You're the first."

Danny glanced at her out of the corner of his eye. Was she putting him on?

No. She looked dead serious.

They drove on in silence. A while later Danny tried to start up the conversation again.

"So you're headed west?"

"Yes."

"Where?"

She smiled. "I'll know it when I get there."

"Maybe you should try Lansing," he said half jokingly. "That's where we're going."

She asked him where Lansing was, but when he told her it was west, then north, she shook her head.

"That's too bad," he said, half kidding. "I was kind of hoping you might want a change of pace for a while."

"No," she said. "Do you?"

He laughed. "What do you mean—me come with you?"

She nodded. "Yes."

They were having this conversation just as the sky was starting to lighten, and as Danny turned to look at her to see if she was serious, he got a good look at her in the light for the very first time.

She wasn't Claire.

For one thing, her hair was a different color, pitch-black, whereas the girl in the club, he remembered now, had streaks of red in hers—which he'd only seen during the lap dance, when she bent over him and draped her hair across his face.

For another, her eyes. They were dark brown, verging on black, just as the girl's in the club had been, but these were somehow more serious. More intense, more probing.

Smarter.

That was the word he was looking for.

But beyond those subtle things, what he really noticed was just the way she held herself, the way she sat in that seat and spoke to him, the way she looked at him, the way she carried herself when they got out of the car to stretch. He had sat in meetings with some of the biggest big shots from the biggest companies, and they had the same air about them. An air of command; the air of someone used to being in charge.

All right then, said the little voice in his head, *she's not Claire.*

Then who was she?

For a second Danny flashed on the cop in the diner and the woman he'd been looking for. He thought about the coat he'd thought he'd seen Claire wearing, just before she got in the car. He thought about the fact that during the eight or so hours they'd been driving, she hadn't had anything to eat or drink. She hadn't had to use the bathroom. Yet she looked as fresh as she had when she'd climbed into the car.

Who is she? the little voice in his head asked.

"So?" Claire had said, her eyes locking on his. "What do you want to do?"

Danny saw she was dead serious, and he knew right then that he was facing one of those life-changing decisions people always talked about. He was either going back home to Lansing to live in his parents' basement or he was going west with Claire to do God knows what.

And when he thought about it like that, there was really no choice at all.

He just had to work out the details.

"Danny?" Zeke said. "Come on, when are you going to tell her?"

Danny looked at his cousin. They were both standing at the bathroom sink now, staring in the mirror. Zeke's clothes were all rumpled. He looked funky and he smelled even worse.

Danny supposed he looked—and smelled—just the same.

He tried as best he could to neaten himself up, and then went back to the table.

Claire was sitting there, waiting for them. There was a muffin on the plate in front of her, untouched.

"I'm ready," she said.

"Then let's get going."

Halfway down the concrete path leading out to the parking lot, Zeke tugged Danny's sleeve and held him back.

"Danny? Aren't you going to talk to her?"

Danny didn't even respond.

But to his surprise, Claire did. She turned to Zeke and stared at him. "You want to get rid of me, is that it?"

Zeke flushed. "No. It's just that we're going north here. And you said you're going west. I'm sure you can pick up another ride, or—"

"Danny, do you want me to go?" she asked.

"No." He shook his head. "We'll take you wherever you want."

"No we won't," Zeke said. "This is ridiculous. Danny, look, I'm taking my car and I'm going to Lansing. You want to go with this girl, fine. Just give me the keys."

"You're not taking the car," Danny said.

"It's *my* car," Zeke snapped. "Give me the keys!"

Danny shook his head.

"Give me the fucking keys!" Zeke yelled, and it was the first time Danny had ever heard his cousin swear.

"No," Danny said, and that was when Zeke pushed him— hard. Danny went flying backward into a parked car. It broke his fall and he came up swinging.

Zeke raised an arm and blocked Danny's punch, then threw one of his own. It hit square in the stomach. Danny gasped and bent over, trying to catch his breath.

Zeke hit him again, and Danny fell to the hard cement. Zeke reached into Danny's jacket pocket and grabbed the keys.

Danny almost let him take them. Then he looked up and saw Claire staring at him.

Danny's right hand fastened on Zeke's wrist.

"Danny, goddamnit let go!"

Danny was on his knees on the ground. Zeke stood over him, half dragging him down the path.

Danny cried out. In a second, he knew, Zeke would rip free of his grasp. His cousin would take the car, and go to Lansing. Then Claire would leave him, and he couldn't let that happen.

The concrete path was bordered by a row of hedges. Stones lay scattered underneath them.

Danny picked up a stone the size of a melon in his left hand and, almost before he knew what he was doing, slammed it into the side of Zeke's head.

There was a soft *thump*, and then Zeke crumpled to the ground and lay still.

Danny stared at the rock in his hand.

"What did I do," he said, shaking his head. He looked up at Claire. "Oh my God, what did I do?"

She smiled. "You got the keys."

Danny got to his feet. He looked down at Zeke and then back up at the rest stop, where people were staring out the window at them. One woman pointed at him, and he could see, although not hear, her scream.

"Shit," he said. "Let's get the hell out of here."

"Wait," Claire said. She put a hand on his arm. It was the first time she'd touched him.

Danny looked into her eyes and felt suddenly, unaccountably, terrified. "Bring the body," she told him.

Danny turned and looked at her.

She was dead serious.

BEVERLY HILLS

Abby was hiding in a big construction Dumpster, underneath a piece of Sheetrock, when she heard voices and a second later, the noise of the Dumpster lid being raised. She clutched the board studded with nails next to her, and thought: If I'm going down, I'm not going without a fight.

Abby had been in the Dumpster for a while. A couple hours at least. She had no way to keep track of the time. She had no idea what time it was now, she had no idea what time it was when she'd climbed in.

She was in one of the public lots north of Wilshire, she knew that much. She remembered getting off the highway, running through Westwood, UCLA, and down Sunset, the riots exploding around her.

When she saw the Dumpster, she climbed in, too tired to run anymore. She'd burrowed under a piece of Sheetrock and thought that she might try and grab a few hours of sleep. Maybe her brain would start working again. Maybe then she'd be able to figure out what the hell was happening, because right then she had absolutely no clue. But she'd been too wired to sleep; all she kept seeing in her head were scenes from the last few hours of madness, her laptop and then Carol flying over the edge of the guardrail, three teenagers holding a woman down and spraypainting her, inside and out, the woman twitching and screaming the whole time and finally lying still on the sidewalk. The East Gate to Bel Air, on fire, the sounds of shouting and things smashing coming from beyond it.

Now it seemed the riots were catching up to her again.

Someone lifted the piece of Sheetrock away. Abby screamed and swung the board—

And stopped.

An LAPD officer was staring down at her.

She thought: Thank God, Thank God, and started to cry. She dropped the board.

He reached a hand down. Abby took it, and climbed out.

"God, thank you," she said.

"You're somebody," the officer said. He snapped his fingers. "Cristina Goodman."

She had to laugh. "No, that's not my name, that's—"

"Sure, that's your name," he said. "Cristina. I've seen you on that show."

"My name is Abby," she said.

"Whatever." The officer smiled. "You like to party, Abby?"

Her mouth dropped open.

"What?"

"I asked if you like to party," the man said. Bright was the name on his badge.

Abby shook her head. This wasn't happening.

"I'll bet you do," he said. "I seen you on that show. You know how to get down." He leered at her. "Don't you?"

"Please," she said. "I just want—"

"Don't be scared, honey." He smiled, and took a step closer. "We're gonna have—"

Abby punched him in the face. The man stumbled backward. She started running.

He tackled her from behind and landed on her.

All the breath went out of her body at once. He rolled her over, and leaned closer.

"We gonna have a good time, Cristina. We gonna have a party."

His breath smelled like the bottom of a garbage can.

She tried to roll, throwing her hips from side to side. He had both her wrists: he pushed down, pulled her wrists together so that he could hold them with one hand, and then with his other reached down and grabbed her dress.

Abby screamed.

"Shhh, Cristina," he said, and his free hand caught around her throat.

Oh God.

She couldn't breathe.

God, please. She pushed up with her arms, punched at his chest, pulled at his shirt, reached out on the sidewalk, and there was something sharp there, and she grabbed it, and struck at the man, once, twice, again, and again, and—

The hand at her throat relaxed.

It started to rain, and in the middle of the rain, Abby heard herself screaming, screaming, and so was he, but his was more of a kind of gurgling noise, and there was water everywhere, it was really coming down now, in buckets, and—

Abby realized the wetness she was feeling wasn't rain at all.

Her stomach churned, and she got to her feet, gagging, saw the man twitching on the sidewalk, blood spurting from his body, and she screamed again, and turned away.

Just then, an alarm began to sound.

The power had come back on.

The alarm was echoed by another, across the street, and then another, and another, until the air was full of shrieking, howling sirens.

Abby—barefoot, her dress torn, her skin sticky with blood—was one of them.

MANHATTAN, KANSAS

Bert had breakfast with Sharon, who he hadn't seen in ten years. He went back to the factory where he used to work. He visited Johnny Graham's grave for over an hour.

He felt like he was marking time, waiting for something to happen.

In the early afternoon, for lack of anything better to do, he headed back to the Aggie Lou. This time, his arrival wasn't an event.

Everybody was watching the television.

He took a seat at the bar and ordered a ginger ale from Mick, who was scooping ice from a bucket into the bins under the bar.

". . . confirming reports that we have now lost contact with Las Vegas as well, this as reports trickle back in to us of the devastation in Los Angeles. For more on the situation there, we now have one of our Los Angeles-based reporters, Patrick Taylor. Patrick, are you there?"

There was a moment of silence. The screen switched to a picture of a distinguished-looking older man, superimposed over a map of Los Angeles. At the far end of the bar, Bert noticed Donna in the middle of an animated discussion with another woman, whose back was to him.

"Patrick, are you there?"

"I'm here, Jane."

"Where are you calling us from?"

"I'm on Sunset Boulevard in Hollywood, Jane. A few blocks north—"

A crackling sound came over the line.

"Patrick, we're losing you."

Silence.

The woman turned back to the camera.

"We apologize for the break in our coverage of the Los Angeles crisis: we'll be back in a moment with more from Patrick Taylor, we hope. In the meantime, as we await an appearance from the President in Washington, D.C., we want to show you—"

"Want a slice, Bert?"

Mick held out a pizza box with a couple slices left in it; Bert shook his head. The picture on the television had switched to a shot of a highway bumper-to-bumper with cars. Even the breakdown lane was packed.

"—Interstate 80, people fleeing the oncoming Blackout Zone by heading north and east. At the same time, in Sacramento, Governor Brown and the state legislature, meeting in emergency session, have invoked an emergency compact between several western states calling national guard troops to service here in California." The woman on screen paused.

"I'm told we now have Patrick Taylor back again in Los Angeles. Patrick, can you give us an idea of the situation?"

And as she spoke, the map disappeared and was replaced by a shot of an older man. Bert recognized him now.

Patrick Taylor. He used to anchor the network news, until they shoved him aside for a more photogenic face. Taylor had a reputation for being the "distinguished elder gentleman" of broadcasting. You never saw him in anything but a suit and tie. He never had a hair out of place.

But that wasn't what Patrick Taylor looked like now. Now he looked as if he'd woken up from a deep, deep sleep and been given five minutes to get dressed. He wore a stained sweatshirt and jeans, with beard stubble on his face and dark circles under his eyes.

He looked terrible.

But compared to the devastation behind him, he was in great shape.

Bert had expected to see Los Angeles as he knew it, if a little worse for wear, like after an earthquake; some damage, but basically the same fancy cars and fancy people.

But the city on television looked like Baghdad after the Gulf War. Dresden, after the fire-bombing. Hiroshima.

"This is Los Angeles," Taylor said, walking down a sidewalk littered with glass. He walked past trash cans smoldering with fires, cars overturned in the street, and bodies—dead human bodies—scattered everywhere. "This is hell."

"Jesus Christ," Mickey said. "What happened? It's like a goddamn slaughterhouse."

The camera fizzed again to black and white. The audio went to static.

The anchorwoman came back and offered a weak smile. "We're going to have to take a break. More from CNN in a moment." The words CRISIS IN LOS ANGELES filled the screen, and then a commercial came on.

"Goddamn." One of the college kids put an empty pitcher on the bar and a five dollar bill next to it. "Shit is fucked up."

"Watch your language," Mickey snapped, moving the pizza box and grabbing the pitcher.

The kid saw the pizza box and his eyes lit up. "Sorry, man . . . you gonna eat that?"

Mickey glared at the kid. "Yes, I'm gonna eat that. I set it aside because I wanted to save it, genius."

Bert heard a gasp behind him and turned.

The woman Donna had been talking with was on her feet, staring at Mickey.

She looked terrified.

Bert got off his stool. "Miss? Are you okay?"

Still staring at Mickey, the woman started backing out of the bar.

"Keep away," she said.

Five feet from the door, she turned around and ran.

Mickey shrugged.

"What's that all about?" Bert asked.

"I don't know," Donna said.

Bert went after her.

He found the woman leaning up against a street lamp, sobbing hysterically.

"Miss?"

"Keep away from me!" she said. "Just keep away!"

"No one's going to hurt you."

She shook her head. "You don't understand," she cried, looking over Bert's shoulder and staring at the bar door. "He's not dead. He's here. He's coming after me."

"Who?" Bert asked. "Who's coming after you?"

"I broke down," the woman said, ignoring him. "Triple A towed me in. They said they would find me when my car was ready."

"I'm sure they will then," Bert said. "But you don't look in any shape to drive right now."

She looked, in fact, ready to fall over from exhaustion.

"When's the last time you slept?" Bert asked.

She shook her head. "I can't sleep. I can't stop. I have to keep going."

"Miss, at least let me get you something to eat. Will you do that?"

She looked up and nodded.

"Good." He held out his hand. "Bert Lyons."

"Betty Garson." She shook her head. "No. Betty Monroe."

She smiled, and Bert suddenly noticed two things.

She was beautiful.

And her clothing was stained all over, with tiny dark spots.

They looked like droplets of blood.

Friday 3:08 P.M., PST

BEVERLY HILLS, CALIFORNIA

There was a parade of Ferraris heading down Wilshire Boulevard, weaving in and out of stalled traffic, occasionally veering up onto the sidewalks. Hector and Jimmy were in the lead car, the other Eighteenth-Streeters were following. Hector had a bottle of tequila in one hand and the steering wheel in the other. He held out the bottle to Jimmy.

"You want some more?"

"No man. I'm cool," Jimmy said. He had a portable DVD player in his lap. He was watching *The Matrix*, freeze-framing on the first fight scene between Neo and Morpheus. Damn. What a kick-ass movie.

They'd been looting all day. A dozen Ferraris from a dealership on Wilshire, all sorts of electronic doodads from the Sharper Image on Rodeo, booze and cigarettes and chocolate and whatever else caught their fancy. It was a nonstop party. Jimmy had never had so much fun in his life. His only regret was not having a bigger car to carry the stuff they'd stolen.

"Hang on," Hector said. He took a sharp left; Jimmy lost his balance and banged into the passenger door.

"Hey!" he yelled. "Take it easy!"

"You ought to wear your seatbelt, man."

"You ought to learn how to fuckin' drive."

"Whoa. Relax." Hector looked over at Jimmy. "Don't spoil the mood."

Jimmy forced a smile. "Yeah. All right. Just slow down a little."

"Sure," Hector said. He turned back to the road, and his eyes widened.

A tractor-trailer was stalled out right in front of them, turned sideways, blocking the entire road.

"Shit!" Hector yelled.

He slammed on the brakes. Tires screeched.

They crashed right into the side of the truck.

Jimmy lurched forward. The DVD player went flying out of his hands and smashed into the windshield with a crunch. He bumped his head on the dashboard.

"Damn." Hector shook his head. "You all right?"

Jimmy picked up the DVD player. The screen was dark.

"Fuck." He looked over at Hector and glared. "Now look what you did."

"Sorry, man. I didn't see that coming."

They both climbed out of the car. A blue Ferrari pulled up next to them. One of the other gang members leaned out the window.

"You all right?"

"Yeah, yeah, fine." Hector waved them on. "How you doing?"

There were two of the gang and two half-naked girls in the Ferrari. Jimmy guessed they were doing all right.

"Hey," he said. "How about a ride?"

"Sorry man," the driver said. "Ain't got no room here."

Hector laughed, and took another hit off the tequila.

"It's all right," he said. "We'll catch up."

They walked awhile down Santa Monica, sharing hits off the tequila.

They found two old men hiding inside a parked car. Hector dragged them out and made them dance in the street, just like in the old westerns, he and Jimmy shooting up the ground until both men collapsed in tears.

Jimmy had never seen anything so funny in his life. He ran across the street to a Rite-Aid, reached into the smashed window and pulled out two bags of holiday candy.

"Merry Christmas, gents! *Feliz Navidad!*" he said, pouring Hershey kisses all over them.

They kept walking.

Farther down the road, they came to a three-story concrete building. Letters above the front door read "Division 7."

"What is that, a police station?" Jimmy asked.

Hector shrugged. "Let's check it out."

They went inside. The first room they came to was a lounge with a pool table and a soda machine. Jimmy shot the machine open, and grabbed a Coke.

Hector was frowning at a sign on the wall. "MTA," he said. "This is like an employee lounge, or something."

Jimmy wandered towards the back of the room, and found a doorway. A staircase led him down two flights.

He pushed the door at the bottom open, and was suddenly outside again, facing a parking lot that had to be two football fields long.

"Holy shit," Hector said, peering over his shoulder. "That's a lot of buses."

Jimmy nodded. Hector was right, there had to be well over a hundred city buses in the lot here.

"We should grab one," he said.

"Huh?" Hector looked confused.

"We should take a bus, man. That way we can carry around all the loot we get. The gang can stay together, too."

"Sounds like a good idea." Hector smiled. "But what the hell do I know? I'm shitfaced."

"It is a good idea," Jimmy said. "Let's see if we can find some keys around here."

"Freeze!"

Jimmy turned around.

A policewoman had emerged from behind a row of buses. She had her gun out and trained on them.

She was young. Young and scared. The gun shook in her hands.

Jimmy stepped out in front of Hector.

"It's all right, officer. Corporal James Maartens, U.S. Army."

She relaxed a little, but didn't lower the gun.

"What's the army want here?"

"Maybe some of those buses," Jimmy said. "Troop transport. If you could show me where to get the keys."

The woman eyed him closely a moment. Then she holstered her weapon. "They're inside," she said. "I'll show you."

"I'll find them," said Jimmy. "Thanks anyway."

He took out his gun and shot her.

"Oh, man," Hector glared at Jimmy. "What'd you do that for? She was cute. We could have had some fun with her."

"In case you didn't notice," Jimmy pointed out, "she had a gun." He stood over her body. Hector was right: she was cute. Probably had been a lot cuter before he shot her.

The name on her shield was Kim.

"Lil' Kim," Jimmy whispered.

"What?" Hector said.

"Nothing." Jimmy kept looking at Kim. She was wearing a short-sleeved uniform shirt. It was soaked through with sweat, and he could see the outlines of her nipples.

"Let me get her gun," Jimmy said, kneeling down, his voice thick and strangely nervous. He reached for her weapon, and his hand brushed up against her skin. It was still warm.

Jimmy suddenly realized he had a hard-on.

"I'm going to go find those keys, okay?" Hector stood at the doorway, by the stairs leading to the main building. He looked back at Jimmy. "You coming?"

"I will be," Jimmy said. He unbuckled Officer Kim's belt. "In a minute."

Saturday 8:10 A.M., EST

JACKSONVILLE, FLORIDA

Peter had trouble sleeping again that night, but now it wasn't because he kept seeing that same scene from the alley. It was because for the first time in a long while, he could see a light at the end of the long, dark tunnel of his life.

It had been a spike—not a knife.

"Now *that's* something we can use," Manny Gleason had

said when Peter called him from the mansion. "A weapon like that is very distinctive. Lots of people get killed with knives, but spikes . . ." Peter could almost see Manny nodding. "That's unusual. It's not much, but it's something. Let me see what I can do."

Manny was FBI, working out of the Federal Building in downtown Jacksonville. Peter had met him during a big drug bust several years back and they'd hit it off immediately.

Manny knew how to work NCIC—the computerized database of the National Crime Information Center—better than anyone on the face of the planet. After the shooting in the alley—after Peter had exhausted every possible police department resource he could think of and come up empty—Manny had gone into the NCIC database and worked his magic. He'd pulled down pictures of almost sixty additional suspects—killers whose modus operandi matched what Peter knew of the man in the alley. None of them had turned out to be the guy, but now, armed with this new information, he hoped at long last that Manny could help him put a name to that face that had been haunting him for the last six months.

When he'd called yesterday, Manny was in the middle of about two dozen other things.

"But you're lucky," Manny had told him. "Tomorrow's Saturday. Meet me at the back entrance of my office around nine. We'll see what we can do."

Peter was there at nine. Leo was with him.

"You bet your ass I'm coming," his friend had told him after Peter used his phone to call Manny. "You had your little revelation today on my time, and I figure that makes me entitled to watch over your ass for a while."

Peter wasn't going to argue with him, especially since it meant he'd have a ride.

Manny showed up forty minutes late with a cup of coffee and an apology.

"No need to apologize," Peter told him. "This is above and beyond, Manny. I appreciate it."

Manny was the kind of guy you knew at a glance was law enforcement. He had a buzz cut, a craggy, weathered face, and a clipped, no-nonsense manner that reminded Pete of Joe Friday from that old TV show *Dragnet*.

"All right," Manny said, holding the door open for them. "Let's see what we can find."

The FBI office in Jacksonville had three NCIC terminals on various floors. Manny took them up to the fourth floor—the one they were least likely to get bumped from—and logged on.

Even though it was Saturday, the system was still busy, and they had to wait a few minutes for the log-on to go through.

"You hear about Los Angeles?" Manny asked, taking a swig of his coffee.

"Who could miss it?" Peter replied. Part of his restless night had included several hours of late night TV watching, mostly CNN, where all they were doing was broadcasting information on the blackouts and the riots. "But it's not just Los Angeles now. It's still spreading. We heard on the radio driving over—it's in Arizona and Nevada too."

"Yeah," Leo added. "Whatever the hell 'it' is."

"They'll figure it out, don't worry," Manny said. He didn't seem too concerned. "I was talking to an agent in Washington. He says the buzz there is it's an electromagnetic pulse weapon. Maybe a terrorist attack."

The terminal behind them beeped.

"All right," Manny said. "Here we go."

He rolled his chair to the terminal and started hitting keys.

Peter had a rough idea how NCIC worked. It was basically a database of all active cases nationwide, information entered by local law enforcement and processed in Atlanta. You could search that database like any other on a computer, using various parameters.

Peter watched as Manny entered the term "spike" and told the system to begin searching.

Thirty seconds later a list of eight cases popped up on the screen. Seven of them, Peter saw at a glance, were active. The inactive one had been marked closed a few years ago.

"Seven suspects." Manny smiled. "I have a good feeling about this. Let's see if we can find this guy."

He hit another key, and a picture flashed on the screen: a man with long hair and an earring who looked like a pro wrestler.

"No," Peter said.

A man who looked like an accountant.

"No."

A man with a shaved head and more tattoos showing than bare flesh.

Peter shook his head and felt deflated. "No again," he whispered,

They went through all four other active cases, with no results.

"All right," Manny said. "Not to worry. Let's try something else."

He entered a new search term: "blunt force objects."

They got a bigger pool to choose from; twenty-one more suspects. But none of them were the guy.

"Lots more," Manny said, punching in the word "spoke."

"Just in case somebody screwed up entering the data."

No one had, though. There were no matches.

They stayed there for another half hour while Manny tried every trick in the book. But all leads came up empty.

"Shit," he said, shaking his head and pushing his chair back from the terminal. "I'm sorry, man. I thought we were going to get it."

"It's all right," Peter said. He tried to look on the bright side. "Listen, it's a good sign, me starting to remember things from that night."

"Yeah. I know, but—" Manny shook his head. "Jeez, when

those first seven came up so quick, I was sure we were going to find him."

"Weren't there eight?" Leo chimed in.

"One was inactive," Peter pointed out.

"Yeah, but . . . shouldn't we still take a look? Maybe the guy got out?"

"Couldn't hurt," Manny said. He turned back to the terminal and hit a few more keys.

A picture flashed on the screen.

A picture of a man with a thick, gray-black mustache, whose skin was badly scarred, as if he'd been burned in a fire.

Peter stared into the man's eyes and felt a chill run down his spine.

"That's him," he whispered. "That's the guy who shot Kelly."

Manny read his name off the screen: "Diego Novarra. Wanted for questioning in the murder of Linda May Burke, apprehended Little Chaparral, Texas." He turned to Peter. "They probably got him stuck in the state penitentiary outside Fort Worth. Let's give them a call and see . . ."

His voice trailed off. "Pete. Look."

He pointed to a line of text at the bottom of the screen.

Suspect shot and killed by Sheriff John Walker, Little Chaparral, Texas 10/01/93.

"Shit," Leo said. "The guy's dead."

"No," Peter said. "No, he's not. I'm telling you, this is the guy."

Manny shook his head. "Pete . . . how can that be?"

"I don't know, but it is. Let's call Little Chaparral."

"That's crazy," Manny said, but he picked up the phone anyway and made the call. When it started ringing, he handed the phone to Peter.

A woman answered.

"Good morning, sheriff's office."

"Good morning," Peter said. "I'm looking for Sheriff John Walker."

There was a pause on the line. "I'm sorry, sir. Cade Curtis is the sheriff here now. Would you like to speak to him?"

"No," Peter said. "I really want to talk to Walker. You don't happen to know how I could get in touch with him, do you?"

"I'm afraid that would be impossible, sir. Sheriff Walker is dead."

"I'm sorry to hear that," he said. "Can I talk to Sheriff Curtis then? This is a very important matter."

"One moment."

Peter waited while the line clicked over.

"Sheriff Curtis here."

"Good morning, Sheriff, my name is Peter Williams. I'm calling you from Jacksonville, Florida, in reference to a murder case we're trying to solve here."

Curtis's voice snapped suddenly to attention. "Go on."

"We've got reason to believe that a man named Diego Novarra—"

"Wait," Curtis said. "I know who that man is, but he's dead."

"Yes, sir, that's the information I have here as well. But an eyewitness places him at the scene of a murder here six months ago. A police officer's murder."

"I think your eyewitness is wrong, son."

"Sheriff, I'm the eyewitness."

There was a pause on the line.

"Let's start over again," Curtis said. "Your name is . . ."

"Peter Williams. The cop who got shot was my partner."

"Well, I'm sorry about that, Officer. But I can tell you for sure that Diego Novarra couldn't have shot anyone six months back. The man who had this job before me—John Walker—saw to that."

"Walker killed him?"

"That's right."

"Were you there?"

"No. No, I wasn't."

"But Novarra is dead? You're certain about that."

"They buried him in a graveyard not a dozen miles away from where I'm sittin'. Least that's what Walker told me when I came on the job, and I got no reason to doubt him. He sure was torn up enough about it."

"How so?"

"Shooting gave him nightmares, he said. He quit halfway through his term. About two months later he had a nasty accident."

"All right," Peter said. "Thank you. Is it all right if I call you later with some more questions?"

"That's fine," Curtis said. "I'll be here."

Peter hung up the phone.

Peter thanked Manny, and he and Leo went back to the car.

"What the hell," Leo said, starting up the car. "It's not a total loss. You could get another sketch done off that picture. Pass that around."

Peter shook his head. "That's the guy, Leo."

"Novarra?"

Peter nodded.

"The guy in the grave?"

"He's not dead."

Leo switched off the ignition and turned to face Peter.

"Pete. It was night. It was dark. You got shot. Isn't it possible you're wrong about this?"

"No, it's not. I know what I saw, Leo. Besides, the spike. This guy Novarra used a spike too."

"Yeah." Leo nodded. "But—"

"I'm going there, Leo."

"To Texas?"

"That's right," Peter said. "I'm going there, and I'm going to talk to whoever put Diego Novarra in his grave and make sure that they ID'd the right guy. Hell, I'll dig up his goddamn grave if I have to. But I'm going."

Leo folded his arms. "And who's gonna handle the Beaulieu mansion?"

"Gormley can do it," Peter said. "You know he can. He should be doing my job anyway."

"Uh-huh," Leo said. "You think so?"

Peter turned and looked his friend in the eye. "I'm going, Leo. Come hell or high water, I'm going."

Leo broke into a big smile.

"What's so damn funny?"

"You're going?"

"That's what I said, isn't it."

"Uh-huh." Leo was still smiling. "I was just wondering how you're going to get there."

Peter's face fell. Then he shrugged. "I'll rent a car."

"You could do that," Leo said. "Or you could borrow this one."

"Really?"

Leo nodded. "Uh-huh. On one condition."

"Which is . . ."

"I go with you."

"You go with me?"

"That's right."

"What about work? What about your jobs?"

Leo smiled again. "Like you said, Gormley can handle it."

OMAHA, NEBRASKA

Thomas was looking at a picture of Jesus.

It was on a Xeroxed piece of paper, the top sheet of a stack on the table in front of him.

In the picture, Jesus was sitting on a heavenly throne, floating in the clouds, holding a Bible open on his lap.

There were seven candlesticks floating in the air around him.

There was a long, gleaming sword next to his face.
There was a caption underneath the picture. It read:
"St. John's vision of Christ and the seven candlesticks."
Thomas opened his journal and made a note.

December 18

   I have the first candlestick.
   God forgive me, I had to kill two people to get it.

Their faces suddenly popped into his head.
He sighed, and laid his pen down.
Minnesota was almost a full day behind him now, but the
memory of what had happened there was still fresh in
Thomas's mind. After he'd shot the woman, he'd dragged
both bodies out into the field behind the house and poured
lighter fluid over them. Then he lit a match and watched
them burn. It was gruesome work, but it had to be done. He
didn't know any other way.
"Hey, mister."
Thomas looked up.
A little girl in a blue and white flowered dress was stand-
ing at the edge of his booth, hands folded behind her back.
"You look sick," she said.
Thomas smiled at the little girl. She was right. He didn't
feel so good. Breakfast had not been a good idea. He wasn't
ready for a meal yet, not after yesterday.
"I'm all right," he said.
"What's all that stuff?" she asked, pointing to the stack of
paper on the table.
"All this stuff?" Thomas said to the girl. "I guess you could
say it's my work."
"You still work? My grandpa doesn't have to work any-
more."
"It isn't that kind of work," Thomas said.
"Do you get paid?"

"No." In spite of himself, he laughed. "I don't get paid."

"So it's like a hobby?"

"Well . . ." He didn't even know how to begin answering that one.

"Are you gonna eat that?" the girl asked, pointing to his hash browns, which sat untouched on the table.

"No," he said. "I'm not. Help yourself."

She plopped up in the booth across from him and did just that.

He watched her eat and smiled.

"You remind me of my daughter," he told her.

"Really?"

"Mm hm. Her name was Julie. What's your name?"

"Sandy."

"You live around here, Sandy?"

"No. We live in Casper—in Wyoming. At least we did. But now my daddy says we have to live somewhere else, on account of the—"

"Sandy!"

Thomas looked up. A big, bearded man in a down parka was staring down at the two of them.

"You come away from there right now!"

The girl darted out of Thomas's booth and disappeared into the other side of the restaurant.

"You didn't have to yell at her like that," Thomas said. "We were just talking."

"She should know better than to talk to strangers." The man glared. "And I'll thank you not to tell me how to raise my daughter."

Thomas's head was starting to hurt.

"I'm sorry," he said. "I don't want to make any trouble."

His backpack was on the seat next to him, and Thomas opened it and slid the stack of articles inside. At least, he tried to. Half of them missed and went flying across the floor. Thomas reached for them, but the man was quicker. He picked up the entire stack and put them back on the table.

The article about Julie's murder rested on top.

The man took one look at it—at the headline, LITTLE GIRL SLAIN, at the picture of Julie, who had been eight years old when it happened—and his face went bright red.

"You sick bastard," he said, grabbing the article and thrusting it into Thomas's face. "What the hell is this? What were you trying to do?"

"Nothing," Thomas said. "Just—please, give me that back now. Don't crumple it."

The article was the only picture of Julie he had left.

"I'm calling the cops," the man said. "I don't know what the hell this is all about, but I'm calling the cops."

Thomas couldn't let him do that. Not with Minnesota just one day and a few hundred miles behind him.

He stood up and ripped the article out of the man's hand.

Then he grabbed the man by the neck, spun him around, and slammed him hard into the table.

The man's eyes rolled back in his head and he fell off the table to the floor.

The little girl had come back and was screaming. People stopped and looked around.

Damn it, Thomas thought. Damn it, damn it, damn it.

He picked up the articles and put them in his backpack.

It was all falling apart, he thought, and there was nothing he could do to stop it.

MANHATTAN, KANSAS

Harold didn't come back that night. Betty was free to talk all night, until the sky was light and Betty could no longer keep her eyes open.

Free to talk about the past: about Nick, and Lou from the office, about the family and friends she'd left behind, and the horror her marriage had become. Free to tell Bert about leaving Asheville in the middle of the night—for reasons she didn't get into—and about running as far and as fast as she could go.

Harold stayed quiet while Bert talked about his two failed marriages, about Johnny Graham, and all the people he'd hurt in his old life, and all the friends he'd made at his new one in Denver.

When the talk ended Harold let Bert walk Betty down the street to the Holiday Inn where he was staying, let him get her a room and put it on his credit card. He even allowed the two of them a chaste kiss good night, or good morning, if you really wanted to get picky about those kinds of things.

He gave her two solid hours of sleep.

Then Harold came back.

Of course it was a dream. Harold was dead. She knew that.

The problem was, being dead didn't seem to make any difference.

She was home, in the kitchen in Asheville, making dinner.

The back door opened.

"Hello, sweetheart," Harold said.

He set his briefcase down on the kitchen table and smiled. "What's cooking?"

His neck was still bleeding—dripping, a vast, gaping wound—his head wobbling on his shoulders, like it might fall off any second.

Betty clapped a hand to her mouth and stepped backward.

"No," she whispered. "You're dead."

"Oh no. Not me," Harold said, blood dribbling out of his mouth. "Old Harold's got a hearty constitution. I take good care of myself too, you know, eat right, get plenty of rest. Don't want to get sick and spend all my hard-earned money on doctors." He frowned, and reached into his pocket. "Say, where is my money, anyway?"

He looked right at her and gave her one of those smiles that let her know she was in trouble.

Deep, deep trouble.

"You wouldn't have any ideas about that, would you?" he asked.

Betty took a step back and almost tripped over the coffee table.

" 'Cause I was thinking about surprising you, you know? Maybe taking you on a little trip to California." He pointed at the television. "I have friends in Los Angeles, you know? I'm sure you'd like them. Give you the clothes off their back. So what do you say?"

He started walking forward.

"We could make it a second honeymoon. A chance for the two of us to start all over. Really get to know each other. Get into each other's heads, you know what I mean?"

Betty ran for the door. He caught her two steps away from it and spun her around.

"You don't want me in your head anymore?" he asked sadly. " 'Cause I don't mind if you look in mine."

His head flopped backward on his shoulders.

Betty screamed.

She flew up out of bed screaming as two hands grabbed her shoulders. She screamed again and looked up. It was Bert.

"Hey, it's all right," he said. "It's all right."

He was standing over her, gently holding her shoulders. Behind him Betty saw the nervous face of a young kid in a Holiday Inn uniform.

"What—"

"You were screaming. The desk clerk"—Bert pointed to the boy—"came by and woke me up."

"I was dreaming," she said, looking up at him. "About Harold. He came back."

"It's all right now," he said, and turned to the clerk. "It's all right. You can leave us alone."

The clerk looked over at Betty. She nodded, and he left the room, closing the door behind him.

"I thought it was over," Betty said.

"It *is* over," Bert said. He sat down on the edge of the bed and took her hand. "Your husband's back in Asheville. He can't hurt you anymore."

"I know that," she said. "But still—"

"Do you think he followed you here?" Bert asked. "Is that it? Because I know some people in the police department, we could circulate a picture—"

Betty laughed aloud. "No no . . ." She smiled, wiping away tears. "He didn't follow me here."

He shook his head. "I don't know, guys like this can do crazy things. You read about it all the time. If Harold's as crazy as you say, he's probably out looking for you now."

"No, he's not."

"You're probably right," Bert said soothingly, "but it wouldn't hurt to be a hundred percent sure, would it?"

She pulled her hand away.

"I am a hundred percent sure."

"You can't be," Bert said. "You left while he was asleep. If he woke up—"

"He didn't wake up."

"But if—"

"He didn't wake up!" Betty screamed, then burst into tears.

"Okay," Bert said. "He didn't wake up."

"I killed him," she sobbed, crying harder now. "He was going to hurt me again. I couldn't—" she gasped. "I couldn't take it anymore, I just couldn't."

"It's all right," Bert said.

She was sitting up in bed and Bert was holding her in his arms: she didn't know when that had happened.

"No." She half sobbed, half spoke the word. "It's not all right, I killed him, and so—and so—" She stopped talking, couldn't breathe to get the words out, but it was all she could think: killed him, call the police, go to jail, her life over, and she'd never even really lived, never got to do anything, go anywhere, love someone.

And all the time Bert was holding her, letting her tears wash up against him and fall right off, a rock, an island of strength.

"I have to call the police," she sniffed. "I have to tell them what I did."

"Call the police?" Bert shook his head. "No. You don't have to do that."

She pulled back from him and wiped her eyes. "But I do. They're going to find Harold. They're going to come looking for me, soon enough."

"No," Bert said. "I don't think so."

"Why?" She sniffled. Bert handed her the box of tissues from the bedside table. "What makes you say that?"

"I think soon enough the police are going to have other things to worry about. A lot more important things."

"I don't understand."

"The blackouts. They're happening in Phoenix now, all over Arizona. They're spreading."

They'd talked about that too last night, what was happening out west. Half out of her mind with exhaustion, more worried about what was going to happen to her than the rest of the country, she hadn't paid too much attention to what Bert had been telling her.

She suddenly realized how serious it was.

"Phoenix." She'd never been much on geography. "How close is that to here?"

"Not very. But it's closer than Los Angeles. A lot closer. And the thing is . . ." His voice trailed off.

"What?"

"The blackouts aren't going to stop. The craziness isn't going to stop. This isn't some kind of military attack, like they said on the news, or a glitch in the energy grid. I think everyone's going to realize that soon enough."

"You sound like you know what's happening."

"I think I do."

"So? What is it? What's causing all this?"

He shook his head, held her at arm's length. "Now I'm the one who's going to sound crazy."

"No. Never." She looked at him. "Tell me."

He got up then and walked over to the window. The curtains were drawn, but bright sunlight peeked through into the room around the top and bottom of the fabric. Betty wondered what the weather was like; she remembered cold and windy from last night, but not much more.

Bert turned and looked at her.

"Betty," he said. "Do you believe in God?"

Saturday 10:18 A.M., PST

JEFFERSON AND 141ST, LOS ANGELES

Church had found Eldon unconscious in front of a big electronics store with a gash across his forehead and his arm. He slung the boy over his shoulders and carried him all the way to the hospital on Hawthorne. Except the scene there was the same as it had been in front of the electronics store; there were people fighting with one another and carrying all sorts of things out of the hospital. Church tried to stop a few of them and ask for help, but no one would listen to him.

Finally, he decided he would have to take care of Eldon

himself. He broke into a 7-Eleven and got ice and aspirin and bottled water for the boy to wash it down with. Except he couldn't wake him up to give him the pills. Church felt like crying for a while, then he decided that wouldn't do any good so he carried Eldon a few blocks deep into what looked like a safe neighborhood. He broke into a house and watched over Eldon while he slept or while he was unconscious; Church didn't know the difference between the two.

When morning came he found Eldon awake and moaning on the couch he'd put him on.

"You all right?" he asked anxiously.

"My head," Eldon said. "It hurts like hell."

"I got some ice," Church said, but when he went into the kitchen he realized he'd forgotten to put it into the freezer the night before, and now what he had was a very wet bag and a very wet bottle of aspirin.

Which is when he decided he'd break into the house next door and see what they had. He looked out the little window to the house across the yard and didn't see anyone moving inside.

"See if they got soda," Eldon said. "I could use some soda."

"I'll get what they have," Church said. He needed food too. He hadn't eaten since the 7-Eleven, and he'd only had potato chips and Honey-Nut Cheerios then. He should have gotten more food, but he'd been scared the cops were going to come along, and he'd also been thinking about what Mrs. Lee always said to him, about how important it was for kids to eat healthy, so he didn't want to feed Eldon all that junk food.

"You stay here," Church said. "I'll be right back."

He opened the door and walked out onto the driveway.

The sun hadn't completely cleared the horizon and it was still gray outside. Over the houses across the street, Church thought he could see smoke. He could still smell fire too. How far off, he couldn't tell, but he decided that after he brought back the food and water, they should get going, not wait for dark and take their chances on the street, because he didn't want to get trapped by that fire again.

He walked across the driveway past a big green jeep, keeping his eyes open.

A policeman on a motorcycle cruised by.

Church quickly knelt down behind the green car. The policeman turned right and left, looking carefully over each house. Church heard the low murmur of the motorcycle engine.

The policeman stopped in the middle of the street, put down the kickstand to his bike, and stepped off. He pulled off his helmet, took a radio off his belt, and spoke into it. Church was too far away to hear anything, but the cop didn't look happy.

Behind Church, the door to the house he'd come from opened.

Eldon stood framed in the doorway. "And see if they got any . . ." His voice trailed off as he saw the cop.

The cop saw him too. "Hey. Hey, kid!"

Eldon froze. So did Church.

The cop broke into a brisk walk and started coming up the driveway. Eldon slammed the door shut.

"Damnit." Church heard the cop swear.

As the cop walked past, Church jumped up and tackled him.

They hit the driveway hard, with Church's hands wrapped around the cop's chest. The buckles on the cop's leather jacket dug into his skin, and the skin on the back of his hands scraped pavement.

The cop reached for his gun.

Church's hand got there first. He pulled at the grip of the pistol, but the holster was still snapped shut. The cop slammed his other arm against Church's throat and started pushing him back. Then he rolled, and suddenly Church was on the bottom. But he kicked up his legs and caught the cop right in the balls with one of his feet. The cop grunted in pain and then Church had the gun. He pointed it up at the cop.

He had a clear shot but couldn't do it.

The cop slammed Church's gun hand down against the driveway and held it there with both of his own.

Church saw the door open, and Eldon look out again.

"Run!" Church yelled. "Run!"

Church knew the cop was going to hurt Eldon the way they'd hurt him, and somehow he found the strength to push the cop over again. He was on top, but the cop had both of his hands on Church's hand that held the gun, and his two hands were stronger than Church's one, so he bent the arm, bent it so Church's hand was pointing the gun at his own head. The cop's finger was reaching for the trigger, and then he had it and Church knew he was going to shoot.

Church's eyes went wide and wet. "Please don't hurt my boy," he pleaded.

He'd said it without thinking, "my boy," yet somehow knew it was true.

"Why the hell would I want to do that?" the cop gasped.

Church had no answer and couldn't think of anything to do but repeat himself.

"Please don't hurt my boy, mister, please don't hurt him."

"Let go of the gun," the cop said. "I'm not going to hurt anyone. I'm trying to help you, for Christ's sake."

Slowly Church let go.

The cop took the gun and got to his feet, rubbing his throat and shaking himself off. "Damn," he yelled. "The whole world, the whole freaking world is crazy!"

Church looked at him.

The cop had a little name tag on his jacket that read CON-NORS.

Connors shrugged his shoulders and holstered his gun. "Listen," he said, "this part of town isn't safe. I'm trying to help you. We have to get you to the base."

Church got to his feet. "The base?"

"Los Angeles Air Force Base," the cop said. "It's not far at all." He looked at the green car in the driveway. "Let's try and get that started."

Eldon stepped out the door then, walking gingerly.

"You all right, son?" the cop called.

Church frowned, then remembered something very important.

The cop shouldn't be calling Eldon "son."

Eldon was his boy.

SANTA MONICA BOULEVARD, LOS ANGELES

Jimmy had a wicked hangover.

It wasn't helping his mood,

He was stretched across a row of seats in one of the buses they'd stolen, wearing sunglasses and drinking a longneck Corona, his second one of the morning.

Hector was driving, heading southwest on Santa Monica Boulevard. Actually, they weren't on the boulevard, they were on the sidewalk, because the boulevard was full of abandoned cars and burning cars and overturned cars. The sidewalk was full of broken glass and garbage and the occasional body, but that wasn't a problem for the humvee, just for Jimmy, whose head hurt every time they bumped over something.

"How many times I gotta tell you to take it easy?" he snapped.

Hector grinned. "Hey, we got to be there on time, man."

They were heading to some sort of gang meeting. Omar the Colombian ran Hector's crew and the rest of the Eighteenth Street gang. Up until two nights ago, he'd run it from prison.

Now he was out, and taking a more hands-on approach.

They were having the meeting at the Division 7 parking

lot. Jimmy's idea about using the buses had gone over big, apparently.

When they pulled into the parking lot it was filled with people—kids, mostly, tough-looking kids, like the ones he'd seen Hector with at the gate by the Air Force base yesterday morning. A bunch of them were spray-painting the buses with the number 18, or a big "E." Both were gang signs, Hector had told him.

They climbed out of the bus.

"Hector!"

The crowd swallowed up Hector, people back-slapping and hugging him. "Wassup? How you doin'?"

A few of the people stared beyond Hector to Jimmy. There wasn't anything welcoming in those stares.

Jimmy had his rifle slung over his shoulder, and two more clips to go with it. But he knew if he got into trouble with these boys, he was going to need more ammo.

He realized then just how out of place he was.

He thought about Martinez, how he was always talking about the importance of having a plan, of setting a goal, breaking it down into small, achievable tasks, and then doing it.

For the first time he knew exactly what Martinez meant. He'd made a lot of moves over the last day or so without stepping back and seeing where they were going to take him.

Now he had the feeling he was about to find out.

Hector waved him over. "Yo, Jimmy! I want you to meet somebody."

Jimmy approached and the crowd parted, and then he was face-to-face with a guy as broad as he was tall, who stared at him like he had daggers in his eyes.

"This is the soldier?"

"Yeah, this is him. This is the guy who got the idea about the buses. Jimmy. Jimmy, this is Omar."

Jimmy held out his hand. "Hey." Omar ignored it.

"What the fuck are you doing?"

Jimmy was confused. "What do you mean?"

"What makes you think you can hang with my boy Hector?"

Omar had taken a few steps closer, and now he and Jimmy were no more than two feet apart.

Jimmy set his jaw. He wasn't going to let this guy intimidate him. "Hey, man—"

Omar slapped him.

"Don't you hey man me."

Jimmy blinked. That hurt.

"Omar, it's cool, it's cool," Hector said. "This guy—"

"Shut up, Hector." Omar didn't turn away from Jimmy for a second. "I decide what's cool around here."

Hector shut up and shrank back.

"So, soldier . . ." Omar folded his arms. "I'm gonna ask it one more time. What you think you doing hanging with my boy?"

A crowd had gathered, forming a rough circle around the two of them.

"You want to run with E Street, you got to pay your dues."

The crowd murmured its assent.

"Dues?" Jimmy said, sweat beading his forehead.

"That's right," Omar said. He pulled off his jacket to reveal a sleeveless T-shirt underneath. The guy was built like Martinez, only bigger. He had tattoos up and down both arms, and muscles that moved like they had minds of their own.

Two other guys Omar's size stepped forward.

"Unless you don't want to be part of what we're doing?" Omar asked.

Jimmy swallowed hard. He had a feeling there was only one answer to that question.

"No, man. I'm down for it. Paying the dues."

Omar smiled. "Good. Hector, you too."

Hector shrugged and took off his coat as well. "Hey, Jimmy," he said. "Everybody got to go through it."

Jimmy cleared his throat. "Through what?"

"Initiation, soldier." Omar smiled. "You probably run an obstacle course before, right? Like in basic training, shit like that?"

"Yeah. So?"

"Well, this is like our version of the obstacle course, I guess."

Jimmy looked around. Everyone in the crowd was smiling.

"Who got a watch?" Omar asked.

A girl stepped forward. "I got it."

"So here's how it works." Omar took a step closer to Jimmy. "We see if you can take it for eighteen seconds, right?"

"Take it?" Jimmy asked. "Take what?"

"Take this."

And before Jimmy knew what hit him, his head was snapping back. Omar had punched him or kicked him, something like that, then he had his hands raised to defend himself, but that was no good, because something slammed into him from behind, and he half turned, and a fist from one of the other guys caught him right on the chin.

Jimmy took a step backward, not quick enough. He was hit again, in the nose, and felt blood begin to flow. Then something hard hit him in the ribs, and then he got clipped again on the jaw, and he saw Omar smiling and his vision blurred.

Fight back, he thought, and lunged and swung and caught nothing but air. He wobbled at the knees, and then two quick punches caught him in the chest. He looked up and saw Hector standing there, and then it was Omar again, punching, and his chest was so sore he couldn't even feel it, and he fell back, and someone pushed him forward, right into another shot to the stomach. The air went out of him. He stumbled to his knees.

"Time!" someone shouted.

He knelt there a moment, his breath coming in spurts, his chest a mass of bruises. It was all he could do to keep from crying.

"How you doin', soldier?"

Omar was leaning over him, smiling.

"Never been better."

"Yeah? That's good. Say, this is a nice gun you got."

He looked up.

Omar was holding his M-16.

"Gimme back my gun," he whispered, already feeling one side of his face swell up.

Omar cocked the rifle and held it over his shoulder, swinging it around till the barrel was pointing right at Jimmy. "Tell me why I should."

"Because I passed your initiation."

"All that means is that I'm not gonna kill you here and now," Omar said. "Now tell me why I should give you back the gun."

Damn, Jimmy thought. He was hurting too much to think about anything but the pain. Martinez was right, you had to think things through, and from now on that's exactly what he was going to do. He shook his head. His own damn fault, Martinez and all those jerks from the base would probably come along and find his body lying out here in this parking lot and laugh themselves silly.

The base. That was it.

Jimmy smiled.

"What's so funny?" Omar asked.

Jimmy got back to his feet. "So you like that gun?"

"Didn't I say that?" Omar snapped.

"Yeah, yeah you did." Jimmy rolled his neck and winced. Damn, those guys had hammered him. "So how about I get you one of your own?" Jimmy did a slow 360 with his eyes, taking in the crowd gathered around him. "How about I get you all one?" For the first time, Jimmy saw something besides contempt in Omar's eyes. "For real?"

"That's right," Jimmy said.

Omar's eyes glinted. "How's that gonna work?"

Jimmy explained.

When he finished talking, Hector stepped forward and high-fived him.

"You see?" Hector turned to Omar. "What I tell you, man? My boy's all right."

Omar handed Jimmy back the rifle. "We'll see about that."

"Don't worry," Jimmy said, slinging the M-16 back over his shoulder. "I'm a man of my word."

And it was true: he was going to get the guns, one for everyone, Omar included. But after that . . .

Jimmy had plans of his own.

Saturday 3:30 P.M., MST

ALBUQUERQUE, NEW MEXICO

When they found another motel room, Kerry pretended to fall asleep. She was getting good at pretending; she'd done it for several hours on the drive across Oklahoma and into New Mexico. The only problem was her hands, which sometimes shook uncontrollably. It was all the pills she was taking. The kid who'd sold them to her had warned her about that side effect, but at the time she hadn't cared to listen.

Now she was afraid her dad would notice, so she clamped her hands between her legs. But after a while like that her hands fell asleep, and that was more uncomfortable for her than trying to hold them still. So eventually she just rolled over and faced away from him.

When the van stopped, she'd started pretending again, fluttering her eyelashes as if she was waking up. When her dad came back with the keys to their room, she'd pretended to do a half-asleep stumble from the back of the van into her bed. When her dad had crashed —which took all of ten minutes— she finally stopped pretending.

She popped another pill and turned on the TV, keeping the volume down.

After clicking through about fifty channels, she finally found something else on besides news. Cartoon Network; a repeat of *Scooby-Doo on Zombie Island*, where, according to the ominous voice-over, the monsters were real.

Kerry had never been a big Scooby fan, but she'd heard all she could stand about the blackouts and the riots. Her dad had kept the radio on during the whole drive last night. Most of the stations were calling it mass hysteria, and it seemed to be something you could catch, like a disease.

It was also spreading, and at some point that night she knew they'd run smack into it.

Kerry wasn't too worried, though.

How much crazier could she feel?

She'd been having nightmares since last summer. Almost a whole year that she'd been afraid to go to sleep. That was when she and her mom had started having their knock-down-drag-'em-outs too, when she'd stopped hanging out with Deb and Suzie and—

No, wait a minute. The fights had started even before that.

The first one, now that she thought about it, had come on the Fourth of July, which had started out as a good day—a swim at the lake, lunch at the Ice Cream Castle, finding the bracelet in that antique store. Things had only gone wrong that night, when she and her mom got into a little spat because she took a hit off the jug of wine when it went around the campfire.

She still remembered how embarrassed she'd felt when her mom had yelled at her. Usually when her parents yelled she just bowed her head and took it. But that night . . .

She'd gotten angry. Really angry. And the next thing she knew, she was yelling back at her mom. Screaming stuff she couldn't even remember now, and things that made her mom angry enough to banish her from the fireworks display.

Boy, she'd known exactly which buttons of Mom's to push that night; her mother's face had just about turned purple.

Kerry had felt terrible afterward.

But the next day she'd done it again. Pushed those exact same buttons. And for the last six months she'd made a habit of it. Almost as if she enjoyed it.

What the hell was wrong with her?

She turned to the TV. Scooby and Shaggy were fighting zombies. Real zombies, dead men rising up out of the ground and walking again. It was actually a bit scary.

Kerry smiled.

A monster movie. Just the thing to take her mind off her troubles . . .

She must have fallen asleep, because the next thing she knew she was back at the lake.

It was a perfect day. An idyllic day.

But it was a different dream.

Now she stood on line at the beach snack bar. Her skin was the color of coffee. The blade was in her pocket.

She stepped up to the window: HOT DOGS 35 cents, SODA 5 cents.

Cheap prices, she thought.

And then, just as she was about to order, she felt a hand tap her shoulder.

"Mr. Topher? John Topher?"

She turned around.

Three grim-looking policemen were staring at her. Two of them had their hands on their guns.

The third had a pair of handcuffs.

"Yes," she said. "That's me."

"You're under arrest, sir. Please come with us."

The cop held out the cuffs.

She pulled out the switchblade.

One of the other cops drew a gun and fired.

Kerry fell backward and heard screams. She looked down and saw a red stain spreading slowly across her chest.

Screaming, Kerry jerked bolt upright in bed. Sweat covered her body. She looked around and saw that the room was empty. The sun shone through the window.

The clock said 4:45 and there was a note next to it.

Kerry—

> *I'm in the pancake house across the street. If you wake up before I get back, come meet me.*

Kerry touched her chest.

John Topher? she thought. Who the hell is that?

Steve Crescent took another swig of coffee.

This is not my life, he thought.

My life is back in Austin. My life is grading papers, a two-inch stack of which are currently on my desk. My life is Ancient Near East Religions next semester. My life is getting up at five-thirty in the morning to work on my book for a couple hours before the day actually starts. My life is coming home to my family at six o'clock every night and eating dinner, helping Kerry with her homework, watching TV with Alison, and on Friday nights heading downtown with her for dinner and some music.

My life is not this nightmare of driving all night and sleeping all day, of hiding out like some criminal in sleazy motels.

My life is not sitting in an IHOP watching a dozen senior citizens eat the early bird special with their eyes glued to the television set and the little clock in the corner of the screen, ticking down the minutes until whatever decimated Los Angeles rolled on eastward.

"Dad."

Steve looked up and saw his daughter.

"Hey, honey," he said. "Have a seat."

Kerry slumped down in the booth opposite him.

Steve sighed as he looked at her. His life was messed up, no doubt about it, but Kerry's was worse.

He could tell with a single glance; whatever good he thought he'd been doing by taking her away, it wasn't working. Kerry looked terrible; to go along with the bruise from her mother, she now had dark circles under both eyes. He knew she wasn't sleeping much; he'd heard her muttering silently to herself in the back of the van for most of the drive, but this was the first time he'd seen her out in the light, and he was surprised at how utterly exhausted she looked.

"You want something?" he asked. "Pancakes? Eggs?"

"Not particularly."

Steve sighed again. Kerry hadn't really been eating on this trip either. They'd been living off fast-food drive-through meals for most of the journey, but he had the feeling she'd been throwing away most of the food she ordered when he turned his back. He'd never considered the possibility that she had an eating disorder before—his daughter always had a healthy appetite—but now he wondered.

"Have a little something," he told her.

Kerry's eyes blazed, and Steve could see she was about to tell him to leave her alone again.

"Excuse me!" someone shouted from behind him. "Excuse me, people!"

The manager was standing in the middle of the restaurant. A police officer stood next to him, hands clasped tightly behind his back.

"Can I have your attention, please?"

Conversation around the restaurant died.

"Officer Jackson here tells me that as of five o'clock this afternoon—that's in about ten minutes—all businesses are being asked to close down, and all people to return to their homes in preparation for the blackout. So I'd like to ask those of you who haven't ordered to please do so immediately so we can get your food cooked for takeout. Those of you who are still eating, we don't want to hurry you, but please do finish as quickly as you can. And those of you who are finished eating, please settle up your bill and leave. Thank you very much. And now, Officer Jackson wants to say a few words."

The police officer cleared his throat.

"Just to repeat what Mr. Holland here told you: we're putting a curfew into effect, statewide, to try and keep people off the streets once the power goes out. So again, when you finish here—"

Mr. Holland tapped the officer on the shoulder and spoke quickly into his ear, pointing to the TV.

"All right, folks," the cop said. "The President is about to go live. I'm sure you all want to see what he has to say, so I'm going to shut up and let you watch. But then, like I said, we'd like everyone to please clear out of the restaurant."

Steve looked up at the television where the words PLEASE STAND BY were flashing.

The manager crossed to the set and turned up the volume.

"Ladies and gentlemen," a deep voice came on, "the President of the United States."

The screen faded from the presidential seal to a shot of the President himself, seated at his desk. He looked down at a piece of paper and started to read from it.

"Good evening. As I'm sure you are all aware, a disaster of unprecedented scope has recently struck the western portion of our country. I've been speaking via satellite with civilian and military commanders in the affected areas, and I want to assure all of you that National Guard troops are on the streets and have begun restoring order."

"That's a load of bull," someone said.

Everyone in the restaurant went "Shhhh."

"Secretary Sheehan, the Joint Chiefs of Staff, and I continue to explore additional measures to improve security in those areas, such as bringing in federal troops to assist the Guard. We will continue to explore these options as events unfold over the next few days. Now . . ."

He shuffled papers on his desk.

"As to what is causing this wave of blackouts, I have spoken with both Energy Secretary Kennedy and General Eisenhardt. Based on these discussions, we have concluded that the power outages across the West Coast are unrelated to the national energy grid. We can therefore not rule out the possibility—indeed, the strong probability—that these blackouts are the first wave of a hostile foreign attack. I am therefore ordering our national forces to their highest state of readiness. All commercial air and rail traffic are suspended, and our interstate highway system will be closed to nonessential traffic. For those of you in the immediate path of these blackout zones, I ask you to remain calm, remain in your homes, and stock up on water, candles, and food."

The President tried to smile but it came across as forced.

"I will continue to update you throughout the next few days as this situation evolves and as, I am sure, we bring this crisis to a close. In the meantime, please stay tuned to your local emergency broadcast system for further updates. Thank you, and God bless America."

The screen switched to a studio set and two men in suits.

"That was the President of the United States. Not much information there, wouldn't you say, John?" one asked.

"Not much is right," Steve replied.

He looked across the table at Kerry, who was still watching the TV. "Kerry, are you sure you don't want something to eat before——"

She shook her head without moving. "No. I'm fine."

Steve sighed and waved for the check.

On the TV, the two men in suits had been joined by a third, an older man, in a green army uniform ablaze with medals and ribbons.

Across the screen flashed the words: GENERAL THOMAS DOOLEY USMC (RETIRED).

". . . I am disappointed by the President's remarks," Dooley was saying. "Disappointed and greatly disturbed. Immediate and forceful action on the part of our government is imperative at this time."

"What would you recommend, General?" one of the men asked.

Dooley smiled, but as he opened his mouth to speak, the screen went black.

Everyone in the restaurant started

"Folks," the police officer said, "that's the satellite dish going. It's about ten miles northwest of here. Everyone needs to start clearing out now."

"Come on," Steve said to Kerry. "Let's get back to the motel."

Steve paid for the check and a few candy bars.

Water, candles, and food, the President had said.

He wondered if it would be enough.

BEVERLY HILLS, LOS ANGELES

Abby heard her next door neighbor's television set blaring away and thought, Shit, I overslept again.

She lived in a bungalow-style apartment in Santa Monica. The next bungalow over—about five feet over—belonged to a guy named Matt Jordan, who was a cameraman for _L.A. at Dawn_, a very early morning news show. Work for Matt started at midnight and ended at nine in the morning. When he got home, he liked to sit back in his living room and turn on his television as loud as it could go. Or at least it seemed that way to Abby.

After she got canned from _Island Patrol_ and stopped having to wake up at six A.M. for makeup call, Abby discovered she could figure out the time by Matt's TV-watching habits. Five days a week his set started blaring at nine-thirty. She liked to be up and out of the house by nine, so whenever she heard Matt's TV, it meant she'd overslept.

Today, she guessed, oversleeping probably had something to do with the crazy nightmare she'd been having. It had seemed so real. Los Angeles getting blacked out and people going crazy and Carol flying over the side of the highway, that cop trying to rape her—God, she thought, what a great idea for a screenplay.

The whole city suddenly gone completely insane. People killing each other for no reason; things burning, things blowing up . . . She flashed on another part of her dream then—the East Gate of Bel Air on fire, what a great image— and that was just one of dozens floating around in her brain, each more vivid than the next.

Opening her eyes, Abby became completely disoriented.

Instead of her bright sunny bedroom and extra-firm king-size bed, she was in complete and total darkness, trapped between what felt like two hard boards. Her feet were bare and she smelled sweat and stink and vomit.

She realized the smell was her.

Dream and reality flipped, and she suddenly remembered everything. The highway, Carol, the Hispanic guy, Officer Bright, and climbing back into her cozy little Dumpster.

She had slept through the night. Now she was up. Hungry and thirsty, scared and confused, but at least her brain was firing on all cylinders again. At least she knew what time it was, thanks to Matt's TV.

Except that wasn't Matt's TV.

". . . National Guard. To anyone within the sound of my voice; the city of Los Angeles is now under martial law. All citizens are required to report to camps being established . . ."

The voice drifted away into the distance.

Abby shoved the Sheetrock off her, opened the lid of the Dumpster, and boosted herself up into the sunlight.

It was morning.

A small convoy—two jeeps sandwiching a green canvas truck and a smaller van—was pulling away down Wilshire Boulevard.

She was out of the Dumpster and on her feet in a flash.

"Wait!" she yelled. "Please wait!"

The power was back on.

There were people.

She was saved.

She ran barefoot down the street, waving her arms, screaming for the convoy to stop.

A soldier in the rear jeep must have heard her. Turning around to see her coming, he tapped the driver on the shoulder. A second later the entire convoy came to a stop.

The soldier hopped off the jeep.

"It's all right," he said, as she got closer. "You're safe now."

She stopped running five feet away from him and broke down crying.

"It's all right," he said. "Come on."

He put an arm around her shoulder and brought her over

to the rear of the truck, flipping up the canvas flap. Behind it a hundred pairs of shell-shocked eyes stared back at her.

The truck was jammed full of people; refugees, Abby thought, and realized a moment later that was exactly the right word. They were refugees—men, women, and children—just like she was, and the look on their faces was the same look she remembered on the faces of Bosnian refugees after the war started there. They were dirty and they smelled and they looked scared.

"See if they got room in the van, Sarge," said a soldier standing in the middle of the crowd. " 'Cause I don't rightly think we could squeeze another body in here."

The soldier who'd brought her over to the truck lowered the flap and then walked Abby toward the front of the convoy.

He stuck his head in the window of the van and spoke to someone. A second later the van door slid open.

Abby found herself looking into a mobile broadcast van. There were two soldiers up front and three men in the cabin, occupying three of five very comfortable-looking cushioned chairs bolted to the van floor. All three men wore CNN ID badges around their necks.

Abby recognized one of them: Patrick Taylor, one of the network's most familiar faces.

When he saw her, Taylor's eyes widened in recognition.

"Cristina?" he said. "Cristina Goodman?"

Abby sighed and climbed into the van.

After introductions, they all got one another's names straight. In addition to Taylor, the other CNN personnel in the van were a cameraman—Billy Atkins—and the producer, Andrew Luka. The three of them, Abby learned, were what was left of CNN's Los Angeles-based staff.

Luka filled her in on the events of the last thirty-six hours in Los Angeles and across the rest of the country. She filled them in on what had happened to her.

Then she asked about the camps.

"They've set up a bunch of them all over the city," Luka

said. "I guess we've seen what? Four, five hundred people come in with the trucks. There must be ten thousand or so at the camp right now."

"Ten thousand?" Out of how many million? Abby shook her head. Where was everyone else?

She was about to ask Luka those questions when the van made a sharp left and Abby saw the Hollywood Hills and the world-famous Hollywood sign, directly through the front windshield.

Only it didn't say Hollywood anymore.

The last D was gone. Now the sign said "Hollywoo."

"Oh yeah. Let's get a shot of that," Luka said, all business.

Atkins tapped the driver's shoulder and the van pulled over to the side of the road.

The rest of the convoy drove past.

"Please, let's make this quick," Taylor said, hopping out of the van. "I've had enough excitement for one day."

"Yeah," said Atkins, who had also hopped out of the van and was now panning around the street with a camera on his shoulder. The camera was on a direct feed to one of the monitors in the van, and Luka watched the monitor as he slipped on a headset.

"Check one, two. Check. You got me, Taylor?"

Taylor's voice came into the van. "I have you," he said.

Abby peered over Luka's shoulder and saw the newscaster holding his microphone, hand raised to one ear. She recognized the buildings behind Taylor. They were on Sunset Boulevard in Hollywood. The strip. The one place in town all her friends who came to L.A. wanted to visit.

When she'd first come to L.A., she spent a lot of late nights here. The hotel bars, the after-hours hangouts, even— once or twice—the rock clubs. One night, in fact, she'd gone to Club Lingerie to see Keanu Reeves's band. Five minutes before the show started, the crowd around her started buzzing, and she turned and saw Jack Nicholson himself walking in the door. She'd almost fainted.

"All right," Luka said. "Billy, pull back the camera, we want to get that sign right over Patrick's shoulder. That's it. Hold it. I'm going to get Atlanta, see if they want to go live."

He punched a button on the console before him and waited.

"Jamie? This is Andy Luka. I can give you a thirty second spot, right now. Live if you want. Okay." Luka punched another button on the console. "We're going to go live in about a minute. Hang tight, guys."

On the monitor, Taylor glanced around nervously. "I'm hanging," he said, "but I'm not enjoying it. I do not want a repeat of—"

"Relax," Luka said. "That was downtown; we knew that was going to be trouble."

"Really?" Taylor frowned. "I wish someone would have told me."

Luka smiled. "Don't worry, we're fine. Hold tight. I'll count you in."

"What happened downtown?" Abby asked.

"We got shot at," Luka said quietly. "We were live right in front of City Hall and suddenly bullets were flying everywhere. Taylor almost lost it." He shook his head. "The old guy's nerves are shot. I'd be surprised if he lasts another day."

A red button flashed on the console in front of them and Luka punched it.

"All right." He punched a second button. "Billy, Patrick, we're live in ten, nine, eight . . ."

On the monitor, Taylor smoothed back his hair and straightened, fixing the camera with his gaze. He suddenly seemed like a different man to her, and Abby realized that he was getting into character.

On the monitor, a city bus turned the corner behind Taylor. She saw that someone had spray-painted a big number eighteen on the side of it.

A bus? Abby thought. They're running bus service? That's ridiculous. Impossible.

"Shit!" Luka screamed. "Atlanta, we are down, kill our spot—Patrick, Billy, let's go go go!"

Luka threw off his headset and ran to the open side of the van. He grabbed Atkins's camera and handed it to Abby, then pulled the cameraman into the van. Taylor came next, and even before he was all the way in, the van spun into reverse and flew down the street.

Taylor hit the floor hard.

"Damn it!" he swore. "That's the last time!"

"What is going on?" Abby asked, totally confused. "Why—"

Bullets tore up the street in front of them.

Abby looked up through the windshield and saw the bus heading straight toward them, half a dozen guns poking out the windows.

"Who are those guys?" she asked—just as the driver slammed on the brakes.

Abby went flying the length of the van and slammed into the back door. She had visions of flying out onto the street, but the door held.

They shot forward, to their right, around a collision in the middle of the street, then wove through a few streets before they slowed down.

"Nice work, Corporal," Luka called to the driver. "I think we lost them."

"Yes, sir," the soldier said.

"For now," Taylor snapped angrily. "This isn't safe anymore, Andrew. It's not safe. And I won't do it."

He folded his arms and glared.

"We'll talk about it when we get back to base," Luka said.

Taylor went to the back of the van and glared daggers at the producer.

The van was turning again, and Abby looked up and saw they were on Melrose Avenue. Her old stomping grounds.

She sat down next to Luka.

"Why were they shooting at us?" she asked. "Who was in that bus?"

"Some gang," Luka said. "We ran into them this morning, too. They must be all over the place."

"So what do we do now? Bring in reinforcements, track them down?"

"No," Luka said. "We've got enough problems. We go back to the base."

"Which is where?" Abby asked. She knew Melrose Avenue pretty well, and she couldn't think of any base.

They passed Gower.

"That's it," Luka said, pointing to his left.

There was a long wall of white concrete running the length of the block. Painted on the wall, in bright blue letters, were the words PARAMOUNT PICTURES CORPORATION.

Abby started to laugh.

ALBUQUERQUE, NEW MEXICO

The clock on the dresser said 5:43, but Kerry thought it couldn't be. The sun was long gone, and the only light in the room came from a candle on the dresser—the last of the six they'd gotten from the front desk.

Her dad was sitting in a chair by the window, staring out at nothing.

Waiting.

Kerry knew it wouldn't be much longer now.

A memory came to her then, of one summer a few years back, going for a long walk around the lake with her grandfather—her mother's father—before he died. When they set out, there wasn't a cloud in the sky. But her grandfather had insisted on bringing umbrellas.

"It's gonna rain hard," he said. "I can tell."

Kerry asked him how.

He tapped his shoulder and said he could feel it, right there. A little ache he carried around with him that got worse whenever a storm was coming. And it was worse now, he said. A lot worse.

Sure enough, he was right. An hour into their walk the sky had grown suddenly dark, and even though they turned around, they got caught in a thunderstorm to end all thunderstorms. The umbrellas didn't keep them from getting wet, since the wind blew so hard.

In school the next year, Kerry had learned there was a scientific reason why her grandfather's pain could predict the weather, at least to an extent. Something to do with air pressure.

Kerry knew there was no such scientific reason to explain what she was feeling now, but the sense was the same—something bad was headed their way, and she knew she was right, just as her grandfather had been.

Her dad was nervous too. Even though he was sitting still in the chair now, for the last few hours he'd been bouncing up and down all over the room. Kerry was glad when he'd been doing that, because it hid her own nervous energy; she was still wired from the pills, so she was doing a good amount of bouncing too.

But it wasn't just nervousness she was feeling now. There was another part to it, which she couldn't quite put words to. It was a little bit like the feeling she'd had when she was dreaming about Mudge Pond, she realized, a feeling of dread, helplessness, and anticipation, of knowing that something terrible was going to happen and there was nothing she could do about it. The feeling she got when she found herself lying on the beach again, knowing that in a few moments she was going to wake up and—

"What?"

Her dad was looking at her, and she realized she'd been talking out loud.

"Nothing, Dad," she said. "Just talking to myself."

Even in the dim candlelight she could see the concern in his eyes.

Maybe she should tell him about the dreams, she thought. But she'd tried that with Mrs. Hungridge, her guidance counselor, who had listened patiently until she got to the part about flicking open the switchblade, at which point the older woman had visibly blanched and suggested that maybe she might want to consider a session or two of aggression therapy. Which was, in fact, what she was already getting from the psychologist her dad had brought in to iron out the problems with her mom.

And a lot of good that had done.

On the other hand . . .

She was falling apart.

"Kerry," her dad said, "are you all right?"

Kerry looked at him and burst into tears.

"Hey . . ." He sat down next to her and put his arm around her shoulders. "Don't worry, honey. Everything's going to be all right."

"I hope so," she cried.

"I know so," he said. "The power's going to come on again in a few hours and then we'll get going."

"It's not just that," Kerry said, wiping away tears. "It's just that—things are so screwed up, Dad. Me and Mom, I mean—I don't know how it all got so out of control."

She wiped her eyes with the edge of her sleeve, and her bracelet banged against her watch.

"We'll fix it," her dad said. "I promise you, we'll fix it."

She shook her head. "How? I don't see how."

Kerry stood up and walked to the window. The only light outside came from the moon, nearly full in the clear night sky above, but it was enough to show her the outlines of the mountains looming above the city.

A shadow passed across the night sky, and Kerry straightened. Whatever they'd been waiting for was here.

The motel stood on the top of a small hill. At the bottom was a minimart where they'd gotten snacks coming into town, and from that direction a woman screamed and glass shattered.

Another scream followed.

"Dad?" Kerry whispered.

"It's all right."

He came to the window and wrapped her in his arms. Kerry leaned on his shoulder.

She looked at the candle burning on the dresser.

Something slammed into her then. It knocked her backward and out of her dad's embrace and threw her to the ground. Her vision swam, and she looked at her arms—they were the color of coffee and there was a bloodstain spreading across her chest.

Something slammed into her again—a heavyweight boxer getting in a good solid shot to the gut—and she skidded back and hit the wall and in her hand was a switchblade, with fresh blood glinting along the edges of it and—

She got hit again, and this time was the hardest of all. She looked up, and there was a dark-haired woman standing over her. And in that instant, Kerry knew exactly what had been happening to her these last few months, and why. And she knew what she had to do next.

Her dad was on the edge of the bed, shaking.

"My God," he said, looking at his hands. "My God, what was that?"

Kerry got up and stood before him. "It was for me," she said.

She picked up the lamp off the night table and slammed it into the side of his head. Slumping backward on the bed, he lay still.

She pulled all the cash out of his pocket.

She took her coat out of the closet.

She thought about taking the car keys, but decided

against it. The power wouldn't be back on for several hours yet and she wanted to get started right away.

HONEYVILLE, INDIANA

Claire hadn't moved a muscle for hours.

She was just sitting on the edge of the motel bed, staring off into space.

Zeke's body was on the bed behind her. He was still bleeding from his head, but that wasn't the worst part.

The worst part was that Zeke was still alive.

Either he hadn't hit him hard enough, Danny thought, or . . .

He didn't know.

He didn't know anything anymore. Yesterday he thought he knew how the world worked, and today he was discovering he knew about as much about that as he did about the stock market, really, when you got right down to it.

Which was nothing.

Nothing, because after a nerve-wracking day and night of driving on the back roads into Indiana, of checking his rearview every few minutes for flashing sirens, of driving until he couldn't keep his eyes open anymore, they'd finally stopped at a dingy-looking motel and he'd paid and then carried Zeke's body up to the room.

His cousin had been dead; he wasn't breathing. Danny was sure of it.

He'd laid Zeke down on the bed and started crying, because he'd really done it now, fucked up in such an unbelievable way, and for what? A chance to score with some lap dancer he'd met two nights ago?

As he sat there holding his cousin's cold hand, Claire had put a hand on Zeke's forehead and closed her eyes for a second. And the next thing Danny knew, his cousin was breathing.

Danny had dropped Zeke's hand like it was on fire and jumped back from the bed.

He started to speak, and realized he didn't have a clue what to say.

Claire hadn't said a word either. She simply sat down in a chair and went into her trance.

Now Danny was scared. He was scared of sticking around to see what Claire was going to do next, and he was scared to leave because a few hours ago he had tiptoed to the door, thinking that maybe he was in way deeper to whatever this was than he wanted to be, and just as he touched that knob he heard her say "Danny?" and he turned and she hadn't moved a muscle.

"Just going to get some air," he said.

And she said, "Don't," and then went back to whatever it was she was doing.

Danny hadn't moved since.

He'd managed to convince himself, though, that his cousin must have been alive before Claire touched him, because otherwise . . .

Otherwise, he really didn't know anything.

He got up from the chair and walked over to Zeke.

His cousin was unconscious but breathing; short, shallow breaths that it hurt Danny to even listen to. Zeke sounded like he was in pain, like he was trying to cry but couldn't. Like he was having a nightmare that he couldn't wake up from.

Danny brushed Zeke's hair back from his eyes, and he felt a hand on his shoulder.

He almost jumped.

When he turned, Claire was standing next to him, holding a knife.

No. Not a knife. What she held was the hilt and six inches of blade of what had once been a far larger weapon. A sword, with stains on it that looked like—

No.

He took a step back, away from Claire.

"Whatever the hell you're going to do, I don't want any part of it," he said, his voice trembling. He was going to walk out the door, take the car and drive someplace far, far away—

"There's no place to run," Claire said.

Danny blinked.

"What?" She must have read his mind, but that was impossible. He could still do it. He could still run—

"There's no place to run," Claire repeated.

Danny's mouth fell open.

Claire turned around and pointed at the television. With a faint popping sound, it went on.

"How—" Danny said, then stopped.

A news show was on, but the sound was down too low to hear. A very serious-looking newscaster was talking, and behind him, in big type, it read:

MASSACRE IN LAS VEGAS

The newscaster disappeared.

Vegas Vic's head filled the screen.

Vegas Vic was the fifty-foot-tall neon cowboy who was one of the city's oldest landmarks. Every time Danny went to Vegas—and back when he was rolling in cash, he'd gone almost once a month—he made a point of stopping by to see old Vegas Vic.

He wouldn't be seeing Vic anymore. No one would.

Vegas Vic's head was lying in the middle of Fremont Street. The head, but not the body.

The body was nowhere in sight.

But there was an arm sticking out from underneath the head. A human arm.

There were also plenty of other bodies lying around the head as well. Fremont Street, in fact, was full of them.

A great deal of Fremont Street was also on fire.

"What the hell . . . what is this, a movie?"

He turned to Claire.

She pointed at the TV again, and it started flipping through channels.

He saw Los Angeles, San Francisco. Las Vegas, again and again and again. All the same images. But it wasn't a movie.

"What's happening?" he asked. "What's going on?"

"You might say a friend of mine is trying to wake up."

"I don't understand."

"You don't have to," she said. "All you have to do is serve."

Danny looked in her eyes.

Of course she wasn't Claire. She wasn't even human. She was like the Devil, or Satan, or—

"Satan?" Claire laughed, long and hard.

It was the first genuine laugh he'd heard from her. "The world is old, Danny," she said. "Older than you dream. And that name is young. It is a name the fools in Rome gave to their own fears: it has no meaning."

First among the many thoughts running through Danny's head was the realization that Claire was reading his mind.

He had to get the hell out of there.

"You're right," she said. "We both do."

Claire raised the blade and brought it down square in the middle of Zeke's chest.

"Oh God," Danny said, stumbling backward.

Zeke seized up and his eyes shot open. He screamed, but no sound came out of his mouth.

Claire pulled the blade back out of his body. Blood glistened on the edge.

She walked past Danny, to the wall behind him. Raising the blade again, she drew a perfect square with his cousin's blood.

"What the hell are you doing?" Danny asked. "What—"

Claire slashed downward with the blade, stripping off the wallpaper, and that was when Danny lost it, really lost it, because behind the wallpaper there wasn't a wall.

Behind the wall was a city of dazzling neon. Danny saw a sign.

THE FLAMINGO.

Behind the wall was Vegas Vic's head, lying in the middle of a burning Fremont Street.

And Danny could smell the fire.

He started to laugh.

"This is not happening. I'm asleep somewhere, dreaming this shit, because this is not happening."

Claire turned to him.

"Are you coming?" she asked.

"Are you out of your fucking mind!" he screamed. *"Coming where?"*

She didn't answer.

She just held out her hand.

Danny swallowed hard.

He looked into her eyes and realized what she was really asking him: Do you want to live?

When he looked at it that way, there really wasn't a choice.

He lowered his head. "I'm coming," he whispered.

Danny took her hand, and together they stepped forward.

BOOK ⅱ

BATTLEFIELD

Sunday 3:22 A.M., CST

ORANGE, TEXAS

Peter and Leo made it all the way to the Texas-Louisiana border that first night, taking turns at the wheel and tilting back the passenger seat to grab some occasional sleep. But just past a WELCOME TO THE LONE STAR STATE sign, the caffeine buzzing around in their systems finally gave out and neither of them could drive another foot.

They pulled off onto the shoulder and passed out.

Peter woke up to the sound of something rapping hard on his window.

He opened his eyes. The sky was still pitch-black. A light was shining through the window and he saw a face peering in at him. A face attached to a U.S. Army uniform.

He rolled down the window.

The soldier leaned in. "Sir, the interstate highway system is closed to civilian traffic."

"Yes, I know that, but—"

"I'm going to ask you to follow me to the next exit and leave the road."

"Wait, wait. We've got a letter—hold on."

Peter reached across Leo, who was lying on his side, fac the passenger window and snoring, and opened the compartment. He grabbed the fax they'd received ye afternoon from the governor of Florida's office—

a friend of a friend of Leo's—describing their journey to
Texas as essential state business, and handed it out the window to the soldier.

They'd had to show it half a dozen times since the high-
ways were first closed yesterday. State troopers, highway pa-
trolmen, National Guardsmen; each time they'd been waved
on without a problem.

The soldier looked at it and frowned.

"Hold on a minute." He stepped away from the window.

It took a moment for Peter's eyes to adjust to the darkness
again after the dazzle of the flashlight beam. The soldier
who'd stopped them stood at a jeep parked twenty feet up
the road. A second soldier stood out in the highway, watching their car with a rifle held straight across his chest.

"What time is it?"

Peter turned and saw Leo rubbing his eyes.

He squinted at his watch. "Three-twenty in the morning.
If we're still on Central time." He leaned out his window, and
called to the second soldier. "Excuse me, is this still Central
time here?"

"Yes, sir. Central time all the way through Texas, except
for the western tip, right next to New Mexico. El Paso, Fort
Bliss." He hesitated a second. "You headed west?"

"Just to Houston. Then we're going north. Why?"

"Well . . ." The soldier took a few steps closer to the car.
Peter could see his name tag now—Jeffers—and his face. He
looked to be all of eighteen years old. "That's where I'm sta-
tioned out of—Fort Bliss. Got a wife and daughter there. I
was gonna ask if you could check up on 'em. They're right
on the base, so I'm sure they're fine, but still . . ."

Peter realized he was worried about The Waves.

That was the name the media had now bestowed on the
⎓dness sweeping across the country. When they began the
⎓ it was just "the strange pattern of blackouts and de-
⎓on that originated in Los Angeles," but that was a

mouthful, and by dinnertime yesterday the verdict was in, and the riots and the killing and the madness sweeping across the country had a new handle.

The Waves.

They were all radio and news stations were talking about, and the later it got, the harder it was to find a station that was covering anything else. Music practically disappeared from the dial; broadcasters at the big football games, college and pro, were relegated to giving updates during coverage of the crisis; and every call-in talk show host changed the subject of their afternoon/evening/late-night program when it became obvious that it was all people wanted to discuss.

Peter and Leo had been switching back and forth between all of them. From the talk shows they got a lot of interesting speculation. From the news shows they got the hard info. There were two "waves," spaced about four hours apart and traveling outward in pretty close to a perfect circle from Los Angeles at roughly twenty miles an hour.

The first wave blew out everything that worked off electricity, AC or DC. It didn't matter whether it plugged into a wall or ran off a battery, when that wave hit, it stopped working. Cell phones, computers, CBs, cars, trucks, trains, speedboats in the middle of Lake Tahoe, planes 30,000 feet up in the air. Everything.

This knowledge hadn't come cheap. When the first wave had hit San Francisco, at least two dozen aircraft were circling the airport, waiting to land. Every one of them had been lost without a single survivor. One of the planes had struck the heart of a shopping center in San Bruno. Deaths from that disaster alone were reported in the thousands. All commercial flights had now been cancelled.

Even places that thought they were prepared to operat on their own were out of luck. Emergency generators w affected too. Hospitals scrambled to keep patients scrambled to keep blood supplies cold, organs fresh, c ing rooms lit. They scrambled but they failed, and no one had yet to calculate the number of lives lost.

But the first wave of blackouts wasn't the biggest problem. The country had dealt with blackouts before.

The problem was the second wave.

That problem, nobody could put a handle on. The media struggled to find one: "the riots," "the violence," "the mass hysteria"—some of them settled for "the madness" and left it at that. Or left it to their experts to try and find a way to explain a thing you couldn't see, couldn't find a way to measure, couldn't find a way to hide from, a thing that could apparently turn a town full of law-abiding citizens into a mob, could turn a bunch of beat cops into cops ready to deliver a beating. It was a thing that could walk right through the locked front door of your house and turn the husband, wife, son and daughter into strangers.

The experts used terms like "psychosis" and "predilection for violence" and others that Peter didn't pay a lick of attention to. None of them sounded to him like they knew what they were talking about.

Far truer to him were the words of those who'd survived the second wave, who'd somehow managed to fight off whatever it was that caused their neighbors to go temporarily insane, and found a way to a phone or a news station or a CB to report the hell they'd been through.

Because whatever kind of magic was making the power go out, nine hours or so later that same magic made it come back on. Everything that had stopped working started up just as suddenly. The lights went on, people were able to start up their cars, heat their houses, and most important in the larger scheme of things, people could use their cell phones. They could reconnect with the outside world.

Reporters who depended on satellite technology were ~ng the first to be heard from. Correspondents from San ~isco and Las Vegas, Salt Lake City and Albuquerque and all points in between, were able to sign back on and talk about what had happened when the second wave hit.

Some people hadn't noticed a thing.

Others had felt a sudden, inexplicable burst of anger at whatever it was that they happened to be looking at, standing next to, thinking about. Anger that passed as quickly as it had come.

Half the country, it seemed, had gone crazy.

"And why are you headed to Little Chaparral?" Jeffers asked.

"We're working on a case," Peter said, leaning across the seat.

"You guys are cops?"

He decided to steer the conversation in another direction before the soldier started asking more questions. "You said your family's in Fort Bliss?"

"That's right." He smiled, glad Peter remembered. "My wife and my daughter. They live right on the base. I'm worried sick about 'em, though. That's why I was hoping you might be going that way. So you could check up on 'em."

"If they're on the base, I'm sure they'll be all right. When are the waves supposed to hit there?"

Jeffers frowned. "They already have."

The news hit Peter like a kick in the gut. They were at one end of Texas and the waves were at the other. All day and night yesterday, he'd been listening to reports of what was happening out West and thinking it was half a world away.

Suddenly, it was right next door.

"I was talking to Jeri—that's my wife—at around seven last night, and the phone just went out. I haven't heard from her since."

Jeffers suddenly straightened up.

The other soldier was back and sticking the fax through Peter's window. "I'll ask you to follow me to the next exit," he said stiffly, turning around.

"Hey!" Peter called out. "Wait! What about the letter? Didn't you read the letter?"

The man didn't even turn around.

"Hold on," Leo said, opening his car door. "I'm sure there's been some kind of mix-up. Why don't you—"

The soldier swiveled and pointed his gun at Leo. "Get back in your car, sir. Right now."

For a moment Peter thought Leo was going to complain, but the soldier didn't look ready to argue.

He looked prepared to shoot.

Leo, thankfully, saw the same thing. He got back in the car and slammed the door.

"What the hell?" he snapped. "You see that?"

Peter started the engine.

"Goddamn army."

They followed the soldier to the exit ramp, which ran for a good half mile. It was supposed to lead to a clear state road that would get them into Houston in no time. But as they came to the end of the ramp, it curved down into a ribbon of headlights that stretched for miles in one direction: east.

Leo's mouth fell open. "Jesus Christ," he said. "What's next?"

But Peter wasn't paying attention. He was looking at a man selling newspapers on the side of the road. The man was holding one up and in the glare of the oncoming headlights, Peter read the headline: EXTRA—MILITARY COUP IN WASHINGTON.

DENVER, COLORADO

Outside the cathedral a light snow had begun to fall.

Bert stood in the shadow of the huge stone building and watched the snowflakes come down, sparkling in the moonlight before they settled to the ground. The moon was the only source of light outside the cathedral. The torches were no longer lit, and the darkness spead from the streets below to the vast city beyond.

The first wave had come to Denver.

Bert and Betty had, too. They'd driven all day and into the night at Betty's insistence that they keep heading west.

Bert stared once again at the paper in his hand. On it was written a simple message:

JOIN CARDINAL HANLEY
TONIGHT PRAY FOR PEACE—
ST. JOHN'S-IN-THE-WILDERNESS CATHEDRAL

Hundreds of Denver residents had taken the cardinal up on his offer. The cathedral had been filling up since midnight, just before the power went out. Even now, at what Bert guessed was after four in the morning, a few stragglers were still pouring in.

The night was calm and still, and prayers could be heard filling the sky.

But the second wave was yet to come.

"Bert?"

Bert turned and saw Betty push open one of the cathedral doors.

"They've started again."

"I'll be right there," Bert said, taking one last look at the snow-covered steps of the cathedral and the street below.

Two hundred police in full riot gear stood there.

His brother-in-law Don was captain of the Denver police force. "Don't worry," Don had said. "We're not going to have any problems at the cathedral. We'll have cops two deep around the building."

Bert didn't doubt the numbers.

He doubted numbers were the solution, though. That's what they'd thought in Salt Lake City and now the city was burning. He'd seen the flames on television, lighting up the sky as the city went up in smoke. They'd had National

Guard troops on every street corner (per the governor's orders), the police and the fire department prepared (again, according to the governor), and it hadn't made a damn bit of difference.

When the power came back on, Salt Lake City looked the same as Los Angeles, Las Vegas, San Francisco, and Portland, Oregon, the same as every other city that had been touched by the blackouts.

Fire, devastation, and death.

People—people in power, specifically—seemed to have a hard time grasping the fact that it didn't seem to matter if you were a cop, a crook, a soldier, or a saint before the second wave hit. You could line up four hundred cops around a building, but after the wave hit, two hundred of them might try to burn it down.

So numbers didn't give Bert a warm feeling.

In fact, the only thing that had given him any peace of mind were the last few hours he'd spent in the cathedral. He felt a sense of safety there, for reasons he knew would sound downright silly if he tried to put them into words. Partly it was the praying, the singing, the sense of strength he drew from the people gathered around him—but more than that, it was the sense that there was somebody—something—in there watching over him.

He followed Betty into the cathedral vestibule.

At the cathedral doors a young girl handed each of them a white tapered candle.

"God be with you," she said.

Bert smiled at her and lit their candles. The wicks flared as they stepped into the cathedral proper.

The massive chamber was bathed in yellow light from the candelabras crowding the altar, from the torches hung on the walls, and most especially, from the candles that virtually every person in the cathedral held.

The place was filled to overflowing. People were jammed

into the pews, standing in the aisles, leaning up against the walls. Many were sleeping. Many more were only half awake, wearing the sort of dazed, disbelieving expressions Bert had only seen on television on the faces of accident victims or train-wreck survivors—on people who somehow still believed that the events around them were part of a horrible dream that would soon go away.

Their seats were toward the front, first behind a stone pillar that partially blocked their view of the altar. Bert's sister Connie slid down the pew to make room, but she didn't look at Bert. She had tried to convince Don to stay in the cathedral earlier and failed. The two of them had fought, and now, Bert suspected, she was regretting how they'd parted, as her eyes were bloodshot and dark.

He sat down next to her.

"Just in time," Connie muttered. "The cardinal is next."

Bert peered around her. "You going to wake the girls?" he asked, referring to Mary and Linda, his nine- and eleven-year-old nieces, asleep on the pew next to Connie.

She shook her head. "Best thing in the world would be if they could sleep through this."

Bert nodded.

At the front of the cathedral the priest who'd been running the service—Father Larsen—stepped up to the pulpit and the choir of praying voices slowly came to a stop. Father Larsen looked at everyone in the cathedral before he spoke.

"It's been a long night already, so I won't bore you with any long-winded introductions, except to say that we are blessed to have this man here with us tonight, and I am doubly blessed to be able to call him my friend." Larsen smiled and stood to the side of the pulpit. "Please welcome Cardinal Hanley."

A man with a red cardinal's cap and flowing white robes rose from a chair near the altar. Cardinal John Patrick Hanley. Cardinal Hanley had been born and raised in nearby Aurora; he'd been priest and bishop in this very diocese before becoming a cardinal ten years ago. This was the man's home; these people were his flock. He was the shepherd, come home to watch over them.

The cardinal was a tall, vigorous-looking man in his early sixties. He strode confidently to the pulpit and clapped Father Larsen on the shoulder as the two men passed.

From beneath the pulpit the cardinal pulled out a Bible and laid it open before him. He took out reading glasses from his robe and put them on.

"I would complain about the light," he said, "but . . ."

The crowd laughed, and Bert joined in. He looked over at Betty and saw that she was smiling too.

The cardinal put his hands on the pulpit. Despite the lack of amplification, his voice was clear and strong.

"May the Lord God bless and keep you."

"Amen," the crowd echoed back.

"Why are we all here tonight?" the cardinal began. "In the midst of all these terrible things that we see happening on our television sets, all these things the experts say are going to happen to us too now—why come to the church? Why not hide ourselves away in our homes, bolt the doors, barricade the windows, seek refuge in our cellars with our loved ones? Why come here at all?"

He paused and looked out over the congregation, as if waiting for an answer.

"Can it be," he began, "that inside our cynical, hardened hearts, we still believe in the possibility of a miracle? That in this horrific moment, when all our fantastic machines and the wonders of our technology have failed us, we are ready to return to the Lord's embrace, to seek his protection?"

He held up the Bible.

"I am here to tell you that protection is here, my friends. Inside these very pages—God's own words, as passed down to the prophets. Immutable, eternal truth. Commandments that must be obeyed, in return for which we are promised the gift of eternal life.

"Revelation," the cardinal said. "Chapter twenty-two, Verse fifteen. 'Blessed are they that do His commandments, that they may have the right to the tree of life, and may enter in through the gates into the city. For without are dogs, and sorcerers, and whoremongers, and murderers and idolaters, and whosoever loveth and maketh a lie.' "

He looked up. "My friends, I am here to say that if we live our lives by the words in this book, we have nothing to fear. Not this night, nor any other.

" 'Put on the whole armor of God,' " he said, raising his voice. " 'That ye may be able to stand against the wiles of the devil. For we wrestle not against flesh and blood, but against principalities, against powers, against the rulers of the darkness of this world.' "

Bert shifted in his seat.

When he was a kid, the priest at their church in Manhattan had talked of the devil constantly. Particularly when the man had dealt with him and Johnny. But Bert had never taken the word—or the concept—seriously. Not then, and not in all the weeks he'd been coming to services here at the cathedral over the last six months.

But now . . .

It struck him suddenly that maybe the cardinal was right. That the reason why numbers and guns and the National Guard and all those rational things didn't matter anymore was that the waves were really about one simple thing. Maybe what was happening in the world outside was nothing less than a war between good and evil.

A war between the higher powers.

Next to him, Betty gasped.

"What's the matter?" he whispered.

"I don't know. I feel . . ." She looked up at him.

Her eyes were round as saucers.

"It's here," Betty whispered. "Oh God, Bert, can't you feel it? It's here."

The Cardinal was still talking.

" 'Stand therefore, having your loins girt about with truth, and having on the breastplate of righteousness, and your feet shod with the preparation of the gospel of peace; above all, taking the shield of faith, wherewith ye shall be able to quench all the fiery darts of the wicked.' "

Fire, Bert thought, looking at the candelabra behind the cardinal.

Fire, he thought, looking at the candle in his own hand. And then a sudden wave rushed through him, and every candle in the cathedral flickered out and went black.

Betty screamed and reached for Bert, searching for his hand in the darkness. She found the sleeve of his coat and clutched it tightly.

A few pews behind them someone else screamed.

"It's all right," she heard the cardinal say.

A hand brushed against hers.

"Easy," Bert said. "It's going to be okay, just—"

The wave rushed through Betty. It wasn't physical, but like a gale-force wind, a speeding car, a million volts of electricity.

She shot backward, away from Bert, and hit the back of the pew—hard. Her vision blurred. And suddenly, instead of the dark inside of the cathedral, she was seeing Nick from the Dunkin' Donuts kneeling on the ground before her, crying.

"Please, mister, don't do it. I got a wife and kids . . ."

Why was Nick calling her mister? *It's me, Nick, it's Betty, what's the matter with you? Why are you crying?*

But none of those words came out of her mouth.

Instead what she heard was:

"I got a wife too, you nosy bastard. Remember?"

It was Harold's voice, coming from her mouth.

But how could that be?

Where was the cathedral? Where was she? It was like she was watching a movie of the past, except it wasn't her past, it was Harold's past, and somehow she was reliving it.

Harold had a gun. Now he was raising it and Nick was crying, begging really, asking him please, please, please. But to her horror, she wasn't listening, and she was just raising the gun and pressing it to his forehead and—

The wave slammed into her again.

She was vaguely aware of the cathedral around her, the hard back of the pew, the stone floor as she slipped off the bench and landed hard.

Now she was holding a bloody baseball bat. Lou was lying on the ground and she was picking him up and dragging him into the trunk of the car and then stuffing a sock down his throat and tying him and—

The wave hit her again, and she was seeing herself, back in the house in Asheville, stumbling backward into the bedroom and falling and screaming—

Everything went black.

The cathedral was madness.

In the haze of moonlight that trickled through the building's great stained-glass windows, Bert saw a mother shouting at her children. He saw two white-robed members of the choir turn on a third. He saw Betty scream and slump to the ground.

In the row in front of him two men stood up. One grabbed the other's shirt collar and cocked a fist.

"Take it back," the first man said, and from the look on the other's face, Bert knew he wouldn't.

No one was taking any steps back, they were running pell-mell on their way down that slippery slope, going from words to fists to worse. It was going to happen here, just as it had in Los Angeles, and Phoenix, and Salt Lake City— just as it was going to happen everywhere else across the country.

The two men in front of him started swinging. They fell to the ground and began to wrestle.

Bert looked at them, and the cardinal's words came rushing back. Men were fighting, but the war here was between good and evil.

Bert stood up and grabbed the collar of the man on top. He spun him around.

"Who are you fighting?" he yelled, angered, frustrated, and scared. "Do you even know who you're fighting?"

The people were like tinder, the wave had just passed through like gasoline, and in a second someone was going to strike a match and set the whole cathedral on fire.

Fire.

Bert reached into his pocket. He pulled out his matches and struck one. He lit his candle.

"Look at me!" he shouted, holding his candle up high. "Look at each other! Look at what you're doing!"

Heads turned his way.

He looked down for a second and saw Connie holding Mary in her arms. On his other side he was aware of Betty stirring.

Bert pulled Connie to her feet and handed her his candle.

He picked up another one off the floor and used hers to light it.

Other candles flickered randomly around the church. Light came back to the cathedral.

At the pulpit, the Cardinal stood. His eyes found Bert's, and he smiled.

"God bless," he said.

Bert smiled back.

And in that instant, he felt the presence again.

Betty, it whispered.

Bert spun around and looked for Betty.

She was in Connie's arms, eyes wide with horror. Sobbing.

He rushed to her side.

Sunday 6:30 A.M., PST

PARAMOUNT STUDIOS, LOS ANGELES

Abby slept on a cot in the middle of Soundstage 8, along with several hundred other people. "Slept" was maybe the wrong word; suffered was more like it, lying there in the pitch-darkness, listening to the snores, the whispered conversations, the children crying, the farts, all those noises echoing back and forth throughout the vast empty space above her. The soundstages—she guessed there were two dozen on the Paramount lot—were huge warehouse-like buildings several stories high, with catwalks and wires and cables running throughout the rafters. They were housed where all the company's TV shows and movies got filmed.

Normally, every soundstage had at least a couple of standing sets in it—*Island Patrol* shot over on Soundstage 23, across the lot, and they had four.

Now, though, she had no doubt that Soundstage 23 looked just like Soundstage 8, a big empty building, and that all the *Island Patrol* sets had been hastily knocked down, just like the ones here had, in order to make way for the refugee population of Los Angeles.

It made her wonder what the rest of Paramount looked like; she'd only caught a brief glimpse of the lot when she came in yesterday with Luka and the CNN team, tents and trailers everywhere, policemen and National Guard troops hurrying from point to point in every direction she turned.

After she'd gotten over laughing at the irony of her coming to Paramount again under these circumstances, she had to admit that the studio made a good choice for a base. The concrete wall she'd glimpsed coming in ringed the entire lot, and the land around the studio was flat enough that from the roof of any of the taller buildings you had a good vantage point on the surrounding area.

For the first time in a long while, she felt safe. Still, she had trouble sleeping, and after a while she realized it wasn't just the noise. She'd lived in New York City for six months, right on St. Mark's Place. Noise, she could deal with.

But the thoughts running around in her head were driving her mad. The images of what had happened the last few days, the blackout, the highway, Wilshire Boulevard, the Hollywood sign, the bus, all those things kept playing over and over in her mind.

None of it made any sense. And craziest of all, she decided, was the look she'd seen on Carol's face, back on the highway. Carol, who'd been a friend for almost ten years, looking at her like she was a total stranger. Looking at her with an expression of complete and utter hatred; like a woman possessed.

"Good morning, everyone." It was a soldier's voice, coming through a megaphone. "It is six o'clock."

Abby groaned. She had barely slept. Opening her eyes, she saw that the overhead lights were on. The soldier with the megaphone was in the middle of the soundstage floor, turning as he spoke.

"We will begin latrine calls with the far row, by the north exit." He pointed at a line of cots. "Five minute latrine calls, now please be considerate of your neighbor's time and be as quick as possible. Latrine calls, then breakfast. Let's go, everybody up."

Abby was wearing the combat fatigues Luka had gotten for her yesterday. While she waited for the latrine, she ran her hands through her hair and straightened up as best she could.

After the latrine, it was time for breakfast. Some Guard troops brought in boxes of stale cornflakes and powdered milk. Abby brought her rations back to her cot and wondered what delights the rest of the day held.

She felt a hand tap her shoulder and looked up.

It was Luka.

"I need you," he said.

Luka pulled her out of the soundstage and led her outside, down a narrow path between tents on the studio grounds, flashing the CNN badge around his neck whenever soldiers stepped forward to block their way.

"There was a coup," Luka said. "The President is under house arrest. General Dooley—you remember, from Libya?—is now in charge. The National Guard has been federalized."

Abby stopped walking and looked up at him.

"You're kidding, right?"

Luka shook his head. "I never kid. I have absolutely no sense of humor. The army's taking over here. They're taking over everywhere. They're having a briefing in—" he glanced at his watch—"fifteen minutes."

Jesus, Abby thought. A coup? Coups didn't happen in America, they happened in places like Haiti and the Congo and Libya. Here in America, the army took orders. At least, they usually did.

But then, here at Paramount Pictures Corporation, usually they made movies, not cornflakes and powdered milk.

"What do you need me for?" Abby asked.

"Taylor took off last night. Him and Atkins. Which leaves me up the creek."

"I'm sorry about that," Abby said, "but—I still don't understand what you need me for."

"I need a reporter for the briefing." Luka looked her right in the eyes. "Can you do it?"

"Me?" Abby laughed. "I'm an actress, remember? Not a reporter."

"Yeah. I know that. But you've been in front of a camera."

"So?"

"So odds are you won't freeze up if you have to ask a question."

"Odds are I won't have the first idea about what question to ask too."

"That's what this is for," Luka said, holding up a little black circular pad with a wire leading off it. "It's an in-ear monitor. I talk to you through this. I feed you questions, I even feed you a follow-up, all your lines." He shrugged. "Just think of it as another acting job."

Abby frowned. "Why can't you do it?"

"I've got to handle the feed back to Atlanta."

Abby thought a moment.

Abby Keller, CNN reporter. She remembered thinking about a career change, but that seemed so long ago now.

"I could try," she said. "But—"

"Great." Luka smiled, not giving her a chance to back out. "Let's walk and I'll explain."

By the time they reached Soundstage 14—where the press conference was going to be held—Abby had the basics down; how the event was going to run, how the two of them were going to communicate, the kind of questions he was going to feed her.

"We've got a bunch of experts lined up back in Atlanta to do commentary," Luka told her. "So the questions I give you are going to play to their strengths."

That made sense, she thought.

"All of us—the four networks and CNN—are going to run off a single camera feed. We're going to stay tight on General Scott the whole time."

"Who's he?"

"General Davis Scott. He was one of Dooley's guys in Libya. Now—apparently—he's going to be Dooley's West

Coast commander-in-chief. In charge of everything out here. Starting with this briefing."

Luka went on to tell her she wouldn't be on camera at all for this press conference, which Abby thought was just as well, given what she looked like. Then he gave her the two things she would need—the wireless mic, which Luka pinned to her lapel, and the in-ear monitor through which he could speak to her. Both of those ran off a single transmitter, which he clipped to her belt. Any problems with the transmitter and she was to tap the side of her head. He'd be at a special broadcast console toward the back of the soundstage.

Just as he finished explaining those things, they crossed a line of orange barrier cones and entered Soundstage 14. There were more soldiers crammed into it than Abby had ever seen in a single place. In the middle of the soundstage a raised platform had been set up, behind which was a huge American flag. There was a podium at the center of the platform, and a soldier stood there now, fiddling with a microphone.

Two rows of folding chairs were set up in front of the platform and half a dozen people milled around them: network reporters and techs, Abby found out when Luka introduced her. He put her in the second row of chairs.

"All right." He smiled, and tapped the side of her head. "I'll be right here. Good luck."

Then he clapped her on the shoulder and strode to the back of the soundstage, behind a row of identical-looking broadcast consoles.

The soldier who'd been testing the microphone stepped up and spoke.

"Ladies and gentlemen, General Davis Scott."

An officer separated himself from the massive group of soldiers and walked up to the podium.

The general struck Abby as Hollywood's version of what a commanding officer should look like. Well over six feet, powerful-looking, with close-cropped gray hair. The kind of man who barked out orders and had men hopping to obey them.

"Good morning, ladies and gentlemen," Scott said into the microphone. "I want to thank you all for coming. You've all heard General Dooley's statement, and let me just reemphasize everything he's said. We have taken this unprecedented step because we feel in the face of this extraordinary situation the normal mechanisms of government grind too slowly for effective action. I can tell you that it's not too much of a stretch to say that the President himself felt somewhat constrained by those mechanisms in the action he could take. Having said that, let me get right to your questions, because I'm sure you've got a lot of them. Yes, ABC?"

General Scott pointed to a woman in the front row.

"Where is the President now?" she asked.

"He's safe. That's all I can tell you at this moment. And I want to stress again—and I've spoken personally to the general on this subject—as soon as this crisis is over, the general will turn control of the government back to the President and surrender himself for any possible prosecution."

"Abby?" Luka's voice came in her ear. "Ask what their immediate plans are for dealing with the crisis."

She shot her hand in the air, but Scott pointed to a man in the row ahead of her.

"General Scott," the man said, "can you tell us what sort of decisions General Dooley has made with regard to the crisis, and when we might expect to see some of those decisions implemented?"

"Our question," Luka said in her ear. "Good enough. Ask if they have any further information on stopping the blackouts."

Abby nodded, trying to listen to both Luka and Scott at the same time.

". . . we advocated treating this as you would a criminal investigation," Scott was saying. "Now we're seeing the re-ults of that investigation starting to bear fruit. Unfortunately, I'm not at liberty to reveal what we've found just yet, but within a relatively short amount of time, I do expect to have more details for you."

"Could you define 'relatively short'?" the man followed up.

"Within the next twenty-four hours," Scott said. "Possibly sooner."

Abby's hand shot up again. Scott pointed elsewhere.

A man with a thick black beard stood. "Yes, General. Greg Reed, *L.A. Times.* Talking about the overall situation here in Los Angeles, we've seen a great increase in the number of troops, Can you tell us when you expect to have order restored throughout the metropolitan Los Angeles area?"

"We're not willing to put an exact time frame on it, but sometime in the next few days, I would think. An important part of our strategy, as you know, is to move the civilian population into the base camps we've established so we can more effectively deal with the hostile forces in the area."

"You mean the gangs?"

"That's right," Scott said. He pointed to another reporter then, who followed up on Reed's line of questioning about the gangs. As did the next reporter, and the one after that. Abby watched Scott carefully while he spoke, and admired the way he did his job. He focused right in on the questioner and never let his attention flag. He kept his answers short and to the point, and if his point wasn't exactly the one he'd been asked about he delivered it with such politeness and humor that no one got angry.

He would have been a good actor, she realized.

Then the gang questions stopped, and Abby raised her hand again. At last Scott's eyes found hers.

"Yes, Miss—"

"Abigail Keller, CNN. General, do you have anything further on the cause of the blackouts?"

Scott shook his head. "We do have ideas, Miss Keller, but nothing we're quite ready yet to share."

Even before the general had stopped speaking, Luka's

voice was in her ear. "Ask him about cutting off the grid in St. Louis—if he thinks that will have any effect."

Abby relayed his exact words.

"We'll have to see, Miss Keller," Scott said. He started to turn away from her.

"And the riots," Abby said. "Do you have any ideas what might be causing those?"

Scott's eyes fixed on hers.

"Let me say this," he said, and his eyes sparkled with a darkness Abby found no comfort in. "I think that very soon we're going to have everything under control."

LOS ANGELES AIR FORCE BASE

Eldon was on the cot next to his, sleeping in a little ball, his knees scrunched up against his chest. Every once in a while, Church looked over at him and thought, My son. Eldon's my son.

Church had been thinking about it a lot. It had made him both happy and sad. Mostly sad, he guessed, because it reminded him of just how stupid he was that he could have forgotten something so important for so long, and because of the way Eldon treated him sometimes, like when Eldon tried to get him to stand lookout while he and that other guy were robbing the clothing store.

Church held that memory up against another, which had just come back to him this very night, a memory from the time before those cops hurt him. He and Eldon were in a car together. He was driving, and Eldon was sitting on his lap, holding the steering wheel, and then he turned and looked up at Church and gave him a great big smile, the kind that only kids gave, the kind that held nothing back.

And now Eldon was embarrassed to have him as his father. He didn't want him hanging around at all. And who could blame him?

So Church was sad.

On the other hand . . .

At least he remembered Eldon was his son. That could change a lot of things. He could talk to the boy, at least. And who knew? Maybe there was a chance that he could get his son to like him.

As long as he was alive, there was a chance.

Church closed his eyes and decided to try and fall back asleep. Which was when he heard the voices.

"No difference in the pyramid: just who's at the top. And how much red tape has to get cut through, and frankly, there's no time for—"

"Excuse me, sir. Right through here."

Church opened his eyes and saw three figures enter the doorway of his big tent. He squinted: behind them, the sky was turning gray, so he guessed it was getting on toward morning.

The figures paused in the opening, which was near the first row of cots. Behind Church and down by the other end of the tent, one of the duty soldiers saw them and began waving his arm. Then he walked up the aisles until he got to Church's cot.

"He's right here, sir," the soldier said.

Church sat up and watched the three figures approach. As they got closer, he recognized one of them: Connors, the police officer who'd brought him and the kids to the Air Force base yesterday.

"Hey," Church called out.

The first one to reach him was a young black man in an army uniform. He stepped aside without a word and let Connors step up. "Hey, how are you, Church?"

"I'm good. Little hungry, but good."

Connors smiled.

"We're all hungry."

That was the third man speaking, a stocky guy in a uniform who put a hand on Connors's shoulder a nudged him to the side. "I'm Lieutenant Cook, Church. Greg Cook." He moved in closer and squatted down. "I wondered if I could talk to you for a minute."

"Talk to me?" Church looked from Connors to Cook and then back again. "What about?"

"The riots. You were there when they started down in Compton, Officer Connors tells me."

"I guess I was, but . . . I don't know what I can tell you."

Cook smiled. "That's what I want to find out. Just a few questions, all right?"

"Sure."

"Good man." He put a hand on Church's knee. "Let's talk outside, all right? So we don't disturb anyone else." He nodded behind him, in the direction of the tent opening.

Church frowned. "I don't know. I don't wanna leave my son here."

"I can watch him," Connors said.

Church thought about that. Eldon didn't usually like cops, but he and Connors had gotten along when they came into the camp yesterday.

"Okay," he said. He stood up carefully. Connors sat down in his place, and Church followed Cook outside.

Outside, they walked past the metal 5B sign in front of Church's tent. The tents had been set up on the parking lot, and a wide strip of blacktop left between the two rows served as a pathway. Tent 5A was right across from them, 4B right next to them, and so on. The toilets were all the way down by 1A and 1B. On the side closest to the main gate—up near 8A and 8B—the infirmary and the cafeteria tents were housed.

"So," Cook said. "Tell me about Compton. What happened there?"

"Well . . ." Church frowned. "Things just went kind of y, I guess. I don't know." He didn't really like thinking it; the look on that cop's face when the cop came after look on Carl's face when he'd gone after the cop. . . .

's the matter?" Cook asked.

"It was bad," Church said. "What can I say?"

"I understand, Church. It was bad everywhere. We're trying to figure out exactly what happened, and I think you might be able to help us."

"Oh." Church shrugged. "I guess I could try."

"I'd actually like you to talk to someone else, if you wouldn't mind."

"All right," Church said. "I could do that."

They passed 1A and 1B and came to the end of the path. There was a few more feet of what had been parking lot, and a soldier with a rifle held up his arm to stop them. A green truck full of soldiers zoomed past. Five more trucks passed before the guard waved them through.

Cook and Church followed a sidewalk up to a building with glass doors and went inside. Cook led him down the hall and into a small room. There was another man there, standing next to a table and two chairs. There was a briefcase on the table.

Church was suddenly a little uncomfortable, as it reminded him of being in a police station.

"Church, this is Dr. Wylie. Dr. Wylie, this is the man I told you about, Church Patterson."

The doctor was short and thin with glasses and slicked-back hair. He smiled and extended his hand. "Hello, Church. I'm glad to meet you."

They shook.

"Dr. Wylie," Cook said, "Church has agreed to talk to us about what went on the night the riots started."

"Good." Wylie smiled. "That's good, Church." He nodded toward one of the chairs. "Do you want to sit down?"

Church sat. Wylie sat across the table from him, and Cook leaned up against the door.

Church noticed that Cook had a little patch on the sl of his uniform. There was a drawing on it that reminde of a kid's Tinkertoy set.

Wylie set his hands down on the table. "Why

start by telling me everything you can remember about that night, all right, Church?"

"Sure." He went through it all again, starting with Carl waking him up, and going right on through to the part where he'd gotten into the fight with the policeman.

Then Wylie stopped him. "So right at that moment, Church," he said, "do you remember anything unusual happening?"

"What do you mean?"

"Did you feel dizzy, or smell something?"

Church shook his head. "No."

"Or feel something on your skin—like you were walking through fog, or a mist of some kind?"

"No."

"All right." Wylie nodded. "Let me put it another way. What do you remember about that moment? All the details you can think of."

"Well . . ." Church frowned. "I remember that policeman coming toward me, and then . . . I just got mad, so mad." He shook his head. "I felt like I wanted to kill him."

Wylie wrote something in his notebook.

"Go on," the doctor said.

"And I hit him," Church said, "and then—I don't know, it was like all of a sudden the moment passed."

"And that's all?"

Church nodded. "That's all I remember."

Cook stepped forward. "Church, as far as we can tell, all the rioting started down in Compton. And you're the first person we've found who was there, at the scene, when it started. So anything else you can think of . . ."

"I'll try," Church said.

He closed his eyes and concentrated.

He saw Eldon and the other guy running. He saw the cop ꞏg toward him, holding out his nightstick. And he saw behind him, framing the policeman in red and or-

. .

"The fire," Church said suddenly, opening his eyes. He looked up at Wylie. "The fire. That's what did it."

Wylie and Cook looked at each other.

"I don't understand," the doctor said.

"It was like—" Church started, and he knew this was going to sound crazy "—like there was a bad thing in that fire, and then all of a sudden that bad thing was in me."

"The fire . . ." Wylie looked over at Cook. He nodded. "That could be, yes."

"Does that help?" Church asked.

Wylie nodded and stood up. "It does. And there's something else you can help us with, Church."

"Sure, if I can."

Wylie opened the briefcase on the table and took out a needle. "If we can get a sample of your blood to analyze, to see if—"

"Oh, no." Church stood up and backed away. "Not a needle." He shook his head. "I don't like needles."

Cook put a hand on his shoulder.

"Church, I know you understand how important it is for us to stop more people from getting hurt. Isn't that so?"

"Y-yes."

"And you want to help us in whatever way you can."

"Well . . . yes, but not a needle. I don't like needles." In prison one time they'd stuck him with something that made him sick as a dog, and they said it was a mistake, but he swore that was never going to happen again, never ever again.

Cook looked over at Wylie. "Well, is there any other way to do this?"

The doctor shook his head.

"I'm sorry, Church," Wylie said.

Church started to sweat. Looking around, he charged the door, but two big soldiers were there to hold him b

"Come on, Church," Cook said. "This is importan

Church fought. He slammed one of the soldie

wall, then he picked up a chair and swung it over his head. A leg clipped Cook on the shoulder and he went down screaming.

More soldiers came rushing in.

Soon one was sitting on his back, twisting his left arm behind him while another held his right arm away from his body.

Wylie leaned over him. "You won't feel a thing, Church."

"Please!" Church screamed, twisting his body and crying. "No needles."

Someone rolled up his sleeve and he felt a pricking in his arm.

He looked up at Wylie then, and over at Cook, and just as everything started to go dark, Church realized that he was seeing the same thing in their eyes that he'd seen in the cop's, and in Carl's, the same thing he guessed was in his head a few minutes back when everything went crazy.

The bad thing from the fire . . . it was still in them.

Sunday 7:47 A.M., MST

NEAR ALBUQUERQUE, NEW MEXICO

Terry had been walking all night, waiting for the pills to wear   She didn't need pills anymore. What she needed was to   out her system, get some real food in her, and get a   ght's sleep. Then she needed a car. And a driver. The simplest thing to do might have been to stay with her father, let him take her, but that would have meant having him hanging over her, telling her what to do, what to wear, what to eat, when to go to sleep, when to wake up . . . and no way could she have handled that. Not now.

Now, everything was different.

She had to be careful, though. That was why she was staying off the roads, staying away from areas where trouble could occur; wherever people could congregate. She'd been careful crossing town, careful crossing the Rio Grande, and she was being careful now, even though most of the craziness seemed to be behind her.

She looked down at her shoes. The light dusting of snow on the ground was melting as the sun came up, and her feet were getting soaked. More than food and water, she wished she had a warm pair of shoes to walk in.

But there was another item even higher on her wish list: a weapon. A gun was the first thing that came to mind, but she had no idea how to use one. So a knife then, or—she thought from her dream—a switchblade.

Kerry smiled.

A switchblade. She would be good with that, but until she had something—anything—to protect herself with, she knew she needed to stay hidden.

From behind her to the left she heard the sound of a car engine and a scream—a girl's scream.

Hide, she thought.

Kerry was standing in the middle of an open field. There was a road, a fairly big road, somewhere off to her right, with a low wooden fence running along it. To her left the field rose slightly before stretching off to the horizon, with no cover in sight.

The field was scrub—dirt and hardy-looking tufts grass, pocked with puddles of icy water.

Kerry flattened herself on the ground just as a b

girl ran over the hill. She was sobbing heavily, and right after her, the car came—following—as whoops of laughter echoed from inside it.

It was like a game of cat and mouse, Kerry saw, as the girl dodged one way and the car followed. It looked to her like there were three or four people in the car, and they were all hanging out the windows and laughing and screaming, and though it was hard to tell from so far away, they all looked like girls.

Then the barefoot girl stumbled and the car sped up and slammed right into her.

The girl bounced off the front fender and rolled down the hill.

The car stopped abruptly and everyone piled out.

Kerry raised her head a little higher off the ground. It was definitely four and they were all girls, just as she'd thought. Probably around her age, though it was hard to tell from the distance.

They all gathered round the fallen girl and broke out into argument. Kerry couldn't hear any of it, but she was curious. She tried to get closer, scrabbling forward on her elbows and knees.

A dozen feet on she felt something hard and cold press into the back of her neck. She stopped.

"Well," a man's voice said. "What do we have here? Get up," he snapped, "and keep your hands raised. Turn around slowly."

Flushing hard, Kerry got to her feet. Turning around, she saw that he was in fact a boy, with longish brown hair and a half-smile on his face. And he held a rifle.

"Shit," he said, observing her. "You're just a kid."

He relaxed and let the rifle droop. Kerry thought she ~~ld probably get close enough to kick him in the nuts and ~~the gun. On the other hand, he didn't seem all that anx-
shoot her.

` out, she decided.

"Yeah, well . . . you don't exactly look like a senior citizen yourself," she said.

"Ha ha." He waved the rifle. "Come on. Let's get going."

"Where?" she asked.

"Thataway," he said, jerking his head in the direction of the car.

They started walking.

When they were halfway there, the others took notice of them. One girl walked out to meet them, hands on her hips.

"Who's this?"

"Beats me," the boy called back. "Found her lying on the ground back there, watching you guys."

"Did she see us?"

"Yeah, I think so."

"Shit." The girl who spoke—with long red hair and freckles—turned to Kerry. "Who the fuck are you?"

"My name's Kerry. Kerry Crescent. And if you think for a second I give a shit about *that*"—she pointed to the barefoot girl, who was lying still on the ground ten feet away from them—"you're wrong."

The redheaded girl eyed her suspiciously. "What are you doing out here?"

"I'm not doing anything," Kerry said. "I'm just walking along, minding my own business. Which I'd like to get back to doing, if that's all right with you."

The suspicion didn't leave the girl's eyes. "Yeah, well . . . we'll see."

Kerry was starting to wish she'd tried to make a break for it before.

"Roger." The redheaded girl crooked a finger at the boy and drew him aside. They began talking in hushed voices.

Shit, Kerry thought. Not good.

She had no idea who these kids were, why they were all together and why they'd been chasing the other girl, but it was clear they were worried about her.

She had to do something to let them know they could

trust her, that they didn't have to worry about her going to . . .

She had an idea.

"You guys want some pills?" she called out.

The redheaded girl stopped talking and turned toward her, surprised.

"What?"

"You want some pills?" Kerry reached into her pocket and pulled out a handful.

"What are those?"

"Amphetamines."

The red-haired girl stepped forward and held out a hand. "Let me see." Kerry dumped all eight or nine she had left into the girl's palm.

"You can have them," she said. "I don't need any more. I've been taking them all night."

One of the other girls, with long black hair and skin so pale Kerry thought she might be wearing some kind of makeup, stepped forward. "Hey, I could use one of those."

"Hold up," the red-haired girl said. She picked one of the pills out of her hand and held it out to Kerry. "You first."

Kerry shrugged. "Sure." She'd been hoping to clean out her system, of course, but one pill more or less wouldn't kill her.

She took the pill and swallowed it.

The black-haired girl stepped forward. "My turn."

The red-haired girl shook her head. Closing her palm on the remaining pills, she put them in her pocket. "Not yet. We've got to figure out how we're going to split 'em up. We'll do it back at the house."

The black-haired girl sighed. "Yeah, okay."

"And we've got to figure out what to do about you," the red-haired girl said, turning back to Kerry.

"Just let the kid go," the boy said.

"Shut up, Roger!" the red-haired girl snapped. She glared at him, then turned her glare on Kerry.

Kerry knew she had to think fast.

Food and water, a car and a driver: those were the things she needed. Here were two of the four, staring her in the face. She knew the others couldn't be that far away.

"Take me with you," she said.

The redheaded girl started in surprise. "I thought you wanted to get back to minding your own business."

"Plenty of time for that," Kerry said. "Right now, I need a place to crash."

"I thought you been taking your pills all night," the boy snorted.

"Yeah, well . . ." Her face flushed; shit, that was a fuck-up.

"You want food—is that it?" the red-haired girl asked.

Kerry nodded. "That's right. I'm starving."

The red-haired girl looked around at the others. "Well, I guess we got some of that. And a spare bed." She smiled, nodding in the direction of the dead girl.

Kerry smiled back.

Food and water, a car and a driver. And maybe, if they fit

The barefoot girl's shoes.

Kerry relaxed.

Maybe things weren't so bad after all

FREMONT STREET, LAS VEGAS

On the bright side, Danny thought, this was going to be the first time he'd ever left Vegas with more money than he'd brought with him.

He had to have ten thousand dollars in his pocket now, a wad of cash thick enough to choke a boa constrictor. All these old folks dead in the street still wearing their sweat-pants and carrying their vacation money. He just helped himself.

Of course, some of the bills were sticking together— blood did tend to make things a little gummy when it dried—but he wasn't letting that sort of thing bother him anymore. He'd stopped thinking about it a while ago. In fact, right after they'd walked through the wall in Indiana and stepped out onto Vegas Vic's head. That was pretty much when he decided he was in a padded cell somewhere, having had a complete mental breakdown. He'd even pinpointed the moment of that breakdown: when he'd been getting that last lap dance back in the strip club in New York. He must have had a stroke of some kind during that last lap dance, shot his wad and blown his mind at the same time, had a heart attack, whatever, and now he was lying in a hospital room with drool leaking out the side of his mouth.

Because everything happening to him was clearly a dream.

Walking through walls. Dead people waking up and screaming. Definitely a dream.

It was a colorful dream, though. A neon-lit, red and yellow and orange dream. Las Vegas was always colorful, of course, but now, with the fires and the blood—well, it was something special.

Too bad none of the casinos was open, Danny thought. Even if this was a dream, he'd like to lay a big chunk of cash down at the craps table and tell the pit boss to let it ride.

"Danny!" Claire snapped.

He looked up.

She was just ahead of him, on the street. She'd been stalking the boulevard ever since they'd gotten here, as if she was looking for something. Or someone.

He caught up to her, just as a cop turned the corner.

The cop was escorting a couple of thug-looking types down the sidewalk.

Claire walked right in front of them, blocking their path.

"Out of the way, sweetheart," the cop said. "These two guys are trouble."

"Trouble?" Claire looked over the two men, who were looking her over too. "Then shoot them."

The cop looked confused. Then he began to sweat.

"What are you doing?" he asked Claire.

She smiled.

It was like watching a tug of war, Danny thought. Two wills fighting for control of one body.

"Shoot them," Claire repeated.

The cop's hand reached for the revolver in his holster. The gun came out.

He looked at it as if it had a life of its own.

"Oh God," he said. "Don't—"

"Hey." One of the thugs stepped back. "What the hell is this?"

The gun went off.

Thug number one went down. Thug number two started to run.

The cop turned and shot him too.

Then he fell to his knees and started to cry.

Claire came and stood over him.

"I enjoyed that," she said. "Did you?"

He looked up at her.

Danny looked too.

Maybe it was his imagination, but he thought he saw a faint glow coming off her body, an aura, as if she was being lit from within. An aura of power, as if the killing, somehow, had made her stronger.

"No," she said. "I don't think you liked it at all, did you? Too bad."

The cop's hand reached down to his belt, and pulled out a fresh clip.

He started to cry all over again.

"Please," he said.

Claire shook her head. "I'm afraid you're just not my kind of man."

The cop put the clip in the gun. He put the gun in his mouth.

He pulled the trigger and blew out the back of his head.

"He wouldn't have worked out at all," Claire said, more to

herself than him. "So far it's just you and me, Danny. Though
I have a feeling," she said, putting her hands on her hips and
looking around, "that we'll find plenty of others around here
to help out in the cause. Don't you think?"

He nodded blankly.

She set off down the boulevard.

Suddenly he realized what was going on. The tag line
from that old army commercial came into his head: We're
looking for a few good men.

Claire turned around. He forgot. She could read his mind.

"Good doesn't enter into it," she said.

NEAR ALBUQUERQUE, NEW MEXICO

Introductions were made all around; the red-haired girl was
Jackie, the boy was Roger, the dark-haired girl was Simone.
The other two girls were Erica and Alex.

And the dead girl on the ground, Jackie told her, had been
Peggy.

They piled into the car. Jackie drove and Kerry was in
back, sandwiched between Simone and Alex.

"Where'd you get that bruise?" Simone asked.

Kerry's hand went to her face. The bruise from her
mother. It seemed like a lifetime ago.

"My mom," she said, figuring she had no reason to lie.

For some reason, that made Simone smile. "You're gonna
fit right in here then," she said.

Just over the hill there was a dirt road and a sign that said:

WILLIAMS HOUSE
GROUP HOMES FOR BOYS AND GIRLS

Group Homes. Kerry got it instantly. There was a group
home just outside Austin; a place for kids who didn't have
any other place to go. Kids who'd been in trouble with the

law for too much drinking, too many drugs; boys who'd done a little too much fighting, girls who'd gotten pregnant. Kids who came from broken homes, where the parents couldn't take care of them anymore. Kids who'd been abused by their parents, sexually or physically.

Jackie was eyeing her in the rearview mirror.

"You got a question?"

Kerry eyed her right back. "No questions."

The "Group Home" sign told her all she needed to know: why Simone thought she would fit in, why all these kids were together. It also told Kerry she'd better stay on her guard every second.

They were driving along a wooden fence and in a few minutes they came to a break in it. They turned down a long driveway. Above the road was another sign:

WELCOME TO
WILLIAMS HOUSE
ALL VISITORS MUST CHECK IN

Out the passenger-side window Kerry saw two long, low, one-story buildings that looked like old-fashioned log cabins. At the end of the drive, just ahead of them, was a white, two-story house with green shutters. A little bit of New England plopped down in the middle of New Mexico. A stone path led from that house to the two other buildings.

The car stopped in front of the white house and everyone piled out.

Jackie, Kerry noticed, kept the keys.

They walked up the steps of the house and through the front door. Kerry, bringing up the rear, heard shouts of greeting and name-calling.

She stepped across the threshold and found herself in a small vestibule; in front of her was a desk, with a logbook and a pen. Where visitors were supposed to check in, she supposed. To her left a set of double doors was open on a long, narrow room completely filled by a big wooden table covered with dirty dishes. The dining room, clearly. To her right was a much bigger room with a piano and a television set and a bunch of couches, on which were sprawled five or six other girls. All of them had stopped talking and were now looking up at her.

"Who the hell are you?"

Before Kerry could answer, Jackie stepped in front of her.

"She gave us these," the girl said, reaching in her pocket for the pills.

Most of the other girls got up and gathered around. A few seconds later they were all kneeling around a coffee table in the living room.

"Careful," Kerry heard Simone say. "Split it down the middle."

"I'm trying—shit!" Jackie screamed. "Fuckin' Peggy! I need a knife to do this right."

"Why is she mad at Peggy?" Kerry whispered to Erica.

"She hid the keys," Erica said, "to the medicine cabinet, to the kitchen knives . . . all the good stuff."

"She was in charge here?"

"No. She just was like—I don't know, the teacher's pet."

"That's why you were chasing her?" Kerry asked.

"Partly. Mostly because she was just a big fat pain in the ass."

Kerry nodded and watched the girls passing out the little pills. She suddenly wished she had pot instead of the amphetamines; pot or something else to make them all drowsy. That would give her a chance to get the car keys from Jackie, to go through the house and see what else she could find. Food for sure; she would need some for the drive. And a map wouldn't hurt either, though she could probably find an atlas once she got going.

She was still on the fence about needing a driver. The car in front of the house was an automatic, so she supposed she could handle that without too much trouble, except she knew nothing about cars, and if anything went wrong . . . a driver would be nice, someone who knew that kind of stuff. She could also use the protection a second person would afford. So she'd have to stick around for a while and see if there was anyone she could trust.

In the meantime, though . . .

She was hungry.

"Where's the kitchen?"

Erica jerked a thumb toward a door at the back of the living room. Kerry wandered in that direction and into the kitchen. It was huge, with a long wooden counter in the center, rows of white cabinets on either side, and a big walk-in refrigerator at the far end.

The countertops were all filthy, though, covered with dirty dishes and all sorts of open food containers. Kerry peered into each of them and found nothing that looked even remotely appetizing.

She started opening cabinets. In the first one she found a big box of pancake mix, and her stomach growled.

She walked back into the living room.

"Anybody want pancakes?" she yelled.

Heads turned.

"Yeah, all right."

"Make a lot."

Erica, who had sprawled out on one of the couches and was watching *Top Gun* on TV gave her a big thumbs-up.

Jackie, still kneeling next to the coffee table, smiled. A big phony-looking smile.

"Eggs and milk in the walk-in," she said. "Have fun."

A bunch of the other girls looked up then and smiled too.

Kerry nodded. Whatever.

She headed back in the kitchen and pulled the door to the walk-in open.

Something fell out, and Kerry jumped back.

It was a body.

A woman's body, a woman with a blue face and a stocking wrapped tight around her throat.

Laughter exploded behind her.

Kerry turned and saw half the girls from the living room crowded into the kitchen doorway, Jackie first and foremost among them.

"That's Miss Golding, our supervisor," she said. "Lying down on the job again."

More laughter, though not as loud as before, and a lot of the girls looked disappointed.

Kerry got it. She was supposed to be terrified. She should have screamed or something like that.

But she'd seen dead bodies before. Messier ones too.

At Mudge Pond.

Kerry knelt down next to Miss Golding and frowned. Then she looked back over to the doorway.

"You think she wants pancakes?" Kerry asked.

Now everybody laughed.

Everybody, that is, but Jackie, who glared, and stalked back into the living room.

Sore loser, Kerry noted, filing the fact away for future reference.

She got out eggs and milk, dragged the body back into the walk-in, shut it, and went to work.

She did a rough calculation of how many girls there were, and realized that she'd better make the whole box of mix. She ripped open the top and dumped the white powder in the biggest bowl. Then she added eggs and milk, took a long wooden spoon and started mixing the things together.

Right away she realized the bowl wasn't big enough; the mix was flying through the air and her arms were getting covered in white powder. So was her bracelet, so she took that off and placed it far from her on the counter.

She dumped some of the mix into another bowl, then went back to stirring the batter.

She hadn't done this since last summer, Kerry realized. Made breakfast for her parents on their anniversary. Brought it in to them while they were lying in bed . . .

Her dad, lying in bed.

Lying still on the motel bed, after she'd hit him with the lamp.

Kerry staggered on her feet.

She felt nauseous, like she was going to throw up any second. She braced herself against the counter and stood there a moment, her stomach rolling.

Oh God, she thought, gripping the counter so tight her fingers turned white. Oh God, what did I do?

The door to the kitchen opened and Roger stuck his head in. "Where're those pancakes at, kid?"

"Coming," Kerry said, turning away. "A couple more minutes."

"Make coffee too, will you?" he said. "It's in that cabinet up there."

She nodded without looking. "Sure. Uh-huh."

"Hey kid, up there."

She turned and saw Roger pointing to his right.

"Okay, got it," she said, her voice cracking.

Roger frowned. "Are you all right?"

She forced a smile. "Yeah. Guess that Mrs. Golding thing was a little creepy."

"Oh." He nodded. "Yeah. That." He shrugged. "Hurry up with them pancakes."

While they were all eating, Kerry forced herself to sit still and smile. Some of the girls asked questions about where she was from and where she was going, and she answered as best she could. The funny thing was, she knew she'd had a destination in mind that morning, but for the life of her she couldn't think of it now.

Finally, as the meal was winding down, she asked if there was someplace she could crash. Erica led her outside to one of the one-story buildings she'd seen on the drive in. It turned out to be where the girls who were in residence usually slept.

"Now we're all crashing at the main house," Erica said. "So this place is empty." She pushed the door to one of the rooms open and flipped on a light switch.

Kerry was looking at a little room, barely big enough for the single bed and chest of drawers. There was a poster of Ani DiFranco hanging over the bed.

"This was Peggy's room," Erica said. She looked at the poster and shook her head. "Weirdo."

Erica left.

Waiting until she thought it was safe, Kerry flopped down on the bed and wondered what the hell she was doing.

LAS VEGAS BOULEVARD SOUTH

Claire had been right. They found lots of people willing to help: a veritable army. Tuxedoed casino employees, showgirls, a fireman, a cocktail waitress—dozens of people following Claire and him down the street. Smashing. Burning. Killing. Danny didn't know how much longer he could keep it up.

He was tired. No, he was beyond tired, he was all used up. Exhausted. He wanted to find a dark, quiet room in one of the big hotels and sleep for a week.

They were in front of the Mirage casino. It was funny— the fake volcano next to the sidewalk was supposed to be spitting out flames, and it was one of the only things in the city that wasn't. The twin hotel towers behind the volcano sure were.

He spotted movement behind the trees. Another soldier for the cause.

He walked over to investigate. There was a foot sticking out through the undergrowth.

Gotcha, he thought, grabbing the foot, but something pulled back.

Danny looked up and saw a huge white tiger staring at him. It had one arm of the body Danny was pulling in its mouth. The tiger growled, and Danny dropped the foot and leaped backward.

"Holy shit!"

The tiger growled again and started gnawing on the arm.

Claire looked at it lovingly. "What a beautiful animal," she said.

"Yeah," Danny said.

Beautiful was not the first word that popped into his mind. It was more like "run." Though he barely had the strength to walk anymore.

"You're tired?"

Claire was looking at him with an amused expression on her face.

"Hell yes, I'm tired," he said. "I haven't slept since . . ." He struggled to remember. "Since . , "

"I have an idea," she said.

"You do?"

"A way to keep you from feeling tired for a long, long time. A way to make you feel stronger than you ever have in your life."

"Really?"

She nodded. "Yes. It'll hurt for a minute. But just a minute, I promise."

He sighed. He wasn't all that sure Claire's definition of "hurt" was something he wanted to experience. But she hadn't posed her idea as a question, so Danny doubted he really had much say in the matter. Besides, it would be good not to feel so tired anymore. "Okay," he said.

"Good." Claire took a step toward the tiger. It growled and rose to its feet.

She held up a hand and turned to Danny.

"Are you ready?" she called out.

Suddenly Danny had a very bad feeling about what was going to happen. He looked from Claire to the tiger, and shook his head.

"Uh—" he began.

Claire dropped her hand, and the tiger sprang forward.

WICHITA, KANSAS

At some point over the last half hour or so, the state highway Thomas was on had gone from a north-south road to an east-west one. Not good. Once he realized that, he took the next exit he could find, which dumped him onto a narrow county two-lane. At least it was going in the right direction— south—so he figured to stay on it awhile, maybe down to Oklahoma, and then pick up a bigger road so he could make better time into Texas.

The road led him into more rural country. It brought him past a string of berry farms, a riding stable and a nursery that advertised a special on Christmas trees.

Christmas trees.

He shook his head. God. When was the last time he'd had a proper Christmas, presents under the tree, turkey dinner, his family . . .

A lifetime ago, it seemed.

He looked down at the seat, where the crumpled-up article with Julie's picture lay faceup. He thought of her and the little girl back at the McDonald's. After he'd run out of there, leaving her father lying still on the table, he'd felt terrible guilt. He'd tried to pick up a local news channel, to see if they had any word of the man's condition, but there was nothing on the news but the waves.

Judging by what they were saying, he had until dinnertime before the car stopped working. And then . . .

Well, then he would see.

The narrow two-lane grew wider. He drove past a big supermarket with a parking lot so crowded that they had policemen directing traffic. He saw uniforms inside the store too, and at the doors. People were stocking up, he thought, the way they did in Massachusetts before a big winter storm.

He imagined them walking up and down the aisles, looking up at the shelves, looking down at their watches, judging how long they'd have to wait in line to pay for their purchases versus how much time they had left. Some of them were probably getting a little frantic, maybe fighting over the last carton of milk, the last box of Cheerios, things like that. That was probably why the cops were there.

Some of those people probably had other stops to make too. A Home Depot, or a place like it, a place to buy sheets of plywood, and nails to put those sheets up over their windows. More protection for their homes, their kids. Some of them were probably clearing out of their houses altogether, heading for the woods to take their chances out in nature. The camping supply stores, he thought, were probably very busy.

And the gun shops. Couldn't forget about them: they were probably the busiest of all. Which reminded him.

He pulled over and reloaded. Careless, that he hadn't done that earlier. Waves or no, he had to be prepared.

He took out his journal.

Look at that. He'd already started an entry for the day, and completely forgotten about it.

December 19

> *A lot of crazy people running around out there now. When I stopped for gas, there was an old woman handing out leaflets by the pumps.*
> REPENT, *the front cover said.* THE END IS NIGH.
> *She tried to give me one. I gave it back.*
> *"You don't have to tell me," I said to her.*

He finished off the entry quickly and got back on the road.

The county two-lane narrowed. It wound up a hill and then back down. At the bottom there was a car pulled over on the side. The hood was up and a woman stood out in the middle of the road, waving her arms in the air.

Thomas didn't want to, but he had to slow down: she was blocking his way. As he pulled closer he saw she had on jeans and a sweater. Her hair was shoulder length and brown. Her face was the shape of an oval, a perfect oval.

She reminded him of Julie. What his daughter might have looked like, had she lived. Had she grown up.

Thomas pulled over and got out, and the woman met him in the middle of the road.

"Hello," he said. "What's the problem?"

"It's my car," she said plaintively. "I think the engine broke down."

The car was an old blue Cadillac. Big old boat, a gas guzzler, the kind his grandparents used to drive. He walked over and peered under the hood. He saw the problem immediately: there was a big crack in the engine block. How the hell could she even drive with it?

"See here," he said, pointing, "you've got—"

The girl stepped back, and Thomas sensed movement on the other side of the car. Before he could make a move, though, he felt something sharp pressing into his back.

"Don't make a move, old man," a man's voice said. "That's a rifle pointing right in your guts, and it's loaded."

Thomas didn't turn around.

"Put your hands behind your head."

He obliged.

"Okay, now stand up and back away from the car. Slowly."

He did what the voice told him to do, and as he did, he turned and looked at the girl.

"Gotcha," she said, and now there was a nasty smirk on her face, and she didn't remind him of Julie at all.

"You shouldn't have done that," Thomas said.

Something in his voice made the smirk on her face disappear. "Sorry, mister," she said apologetically. "But we just got to get out of here, and we don't have a car."

"Never mind that," the man behind him said. He sounded young, as young as the girl. "Now listen, mister, you go on and get in this old car here, all right? We're gonna take your car. We're gonna be on our way and nobody needs to get hurt."

"I need my bag," Thomas said immediately. "There's a bag in the backseat, and I have to have it."

"Yeah? Why? Got your life savings in there?"

Thomas shook his head.

"Huh," the voice behind him said. "Now you done gone and made me curious. Jamie, go see what he's got in that bag."

"Stu," the girl said, "come on. Let's just take the car and go."

"Dammit!" Stu snapped, "I'll go see." Thomas felt the pressure on his back disappear. He turned around.

The boy, who was even younger than Thomas first thought, was backing away, holding the rifle waist high and keeping it pointed in his direction.

"Does this old guy look like he's got any money?" the girl said.

"No. But this old guy does look like Howard Hughes, and he sure had dough." The boy smiled broadly. "How 'bout it, mister? You got money like Howard Hughes? 'Cause you sure 'nuff got hair like him. Ain't you never heard of a barber?"

"I've got money," Thomas said. "I got twenty-four dollars. Right here in my pocket."

The boy grinned. "Yeah, right." He reached behind him and found the door handle to Thomas's car. "We'll see what else you got in here."

"Don't," Thomas said.

The boy reached into the backseat and came out with Thomas's suitcase.

"Come here, Jamie. Open this thing up."

The girl did as she was told. "It's just books," she said, flipping through everything. "Books, and some clothes, and—hey."

She pulled out the candlestick.

"What's this?"

"Looks like a statue," the boy said. "What is that, like a antique, mister? Is that valuable?"

Thomas's eyes flashed. "It is to me," he said. "Not to you."

"Like hell," Jamie said. She was holding up one of his business cards now. "Thomas Caruso—Antiques." She glared at him. "That thing's probably worth a lot of money. No wonder why he wanted the suitcase."

"I *told* you," Stu snapped. "Now what else does he got in there?"

"More clothes," the girl said. She threw them on the ground. "And what's this?"

She held up a flat piece of metal.

The boy's eyes finally left Thomas for a second.

"That's a magazine for a gun," he said. "This gun."

He reached behind him and pulled out the gun hidden in the small of his back.

"Drop the rifle, son," Thomas said. "Be smart. And we'll all just go on about our business."

The boy's eyes narrowed. "So you say."

"You have my word."

The boy's arm twitched.

Thomas fired.

The boy's chest exploded. He flew backward and into the road.

The girl screamed.

She ran to the boy and sank to her knees.

"Stu," she cried. "Oh, Stu." She looked up at Thomas and fear crossed her face. "Don't hurt me, mister, please."

He picked up the candlestick.

"I'm not going to hurt you," he said. But that wasn't what he was thinking.

That felt good, didn't it? a little voice whispered to him. *So come on, what do you say?*

Let's do it again.

He looked over at the girl.

"Go," Thomas said, in a thick, choked voice he barely recognized as his own.

She ran.

DENVER, COLORADO

Ten people died inside the cathedral, thirty-four in the city outside.

It was a miracle, everyone said. Hundreds in Phoenix, uncounted thousands in the other big cities, and less than fifty in Denver.

There was no way to explain it. So Bert didn't even try.

It was enough that for some reason—whether because they had more time to prepare, or what he'd done in the cathedral, or simply the luck of the draw—Denver had been spared the destruction wreaked on almost every other major city that had been affected. For the most part the police force had held together. So had the fire department. And while there had been riots reported in commercial districts, by and large the city had survived.

By dawn the power was back on and the worst was over.

The cardinal was fine. Father Larsen was fine. Connie and the girls were all fine. Bert was fine.

But Betty . . . Betty wasn't fine at all.

Bert was worried about her.

They drove her back to Connie's and put her in the spare bedroom upstairs.

Bert stayed with her. He pulled up a chair and watched her sleep. She tossed and turned. She moaned and cried out.

He wanted to help her, but he didn't know how.

Sunshine was peeking through the blinds. Bert got up and

closed them. He didn't want the light to wake Betty. Sitting back down, he stretched out his legs, folded his arms across his chest, and tried to get comfortable.

He was cold, so he got a blanket from the linen closet and sat back down.

Outside, he heard the occasional wailing siren. Betty shifted in her sleep. She had a lock of hair in her mouth and he leaned forward and brushed it away. Crazy or not, she was beautiful. He looked at her and felt the same sense of protectiveness he'd felt once upon a time with Sharon, and Rae before her. It was an urge to keep her safe from whatever harm might come her way.

One of Betty's hands lay open on top of the blanket. He closed his hand over hers and pulled it to his lap.

Closing his eyes, he was asleep and dreaming in moments.

In his dream, he was back in the cathedral. Betty sat next to him. They were holding hands. At the front of the church, the cardinal was speaking.

". . . the commandments that must be obeyed. For in return, we are promised eternal life." He looked down at the Bible and began to read. "Revelation, Chapter twenty-two, Verse fifteen. 'Blessed are they that do his commandments, that they may have the right to the tree of life, and may enter in through the gates into the city . . . ' "

While the cardinal read, Bert was struck by the oddest sensation. The man's voice, somehow, was starting to change.

Betty sat up next to him. "Oh my God," she said, staring at the cardinal. "It's him, Bert. It's him!"

Bert turned to her. "What?"

" ' . . . for without . . . ' " the cardinal continued.

Bert looked back at him and now he was positive. The man's voice was different—younger, stronger, more strident " ' . . . without are dogs,' " the cardinal went on, " 'and sorcerers, and whoremongers, and murderers and idolaters, and whosoever loveth and maketh a lie.' "

The cardinal stopped speaking and looked up.

It was Harold.

Bert had never seen the man before, but he knew him instantly. The thin face, the pale skin, the blazing eyes . . . the inch-wide gash across his neck that throbbed and oozed as he stepped away from the lectern.

"Any dogs or sorcerers out there?" Harold yelled. "Whoremongers? Murderers? Idolaters? Anyone?" He peered out into the crowd. Finding Betty, his voice lowered. "Anyone who loveth and maketh a lie?"

"He found me," Betty whispered.

Harold put a hand to his ear and smiled. "Ah. I think I hear someone now. A confessor in the audience. Come on, now, don't be shy. Stand right up! Let us know who you are."

Betty started crying.

"All right," Harold said, waving his arms. "I understand. It's hard in front of all these strangers, I know. I'll make it easy for you. Folks"—he raised his voice and threw his arms out wide—"let me introduce you to someone who not only loveth and maketh a lie, but is also an adulterer, a fornicator, a thief, and a murderer . . . yes, it's my own loving, ever lovely wife Betty! Betty stand up and take a bow."

Betty didn't move.

"Come on, honey," Harold said. "Don't be shy. Stand up."

Betty's eyes were wide and staring.

Harold slammed his fist down on the pulpit; the noise was so sudden that Bert jumped in his seat.

"Stand up!" Harold screamed, slamming his fist down again. "Stand up!" he demanded. "Stand up! Stand up!" and every time he said the phrase, he slammed down his fist.

The congregation did the same.

Bert turned to his left and saw Connie, slamming her fist down on the Bible and chanting along with Harold. Beyond her, Mary and Linda were chanting too, and the people on the other side of Betty were also doing it. The whole congregation was doing it, pounding their fists in time with Harold's, pounding on the pews, their Bibles, into their own outstretched palms, until the entire cathedral echoed with the noise—

"*Stand up!*

"*Stand up!*

"*Stand up!*"

Betty screamed and stood.

"There she goes, folks. The missus!"

Everyone began to clap.

Betty pushed past Bert and Connie and ran out into the aisle. Bert followed. She turned, sobbing, toward the cathedral doors.

"My hat's off to you, honey!" Harold cried after them. Bert turned and saw him take off the cardinal's red cap and fling it into the crowd. "I'm really proud of what you've done. In fact," he yelled, "my whole head's off to you!"

And then he grabbed his face with both hands and yanked up. Bert heard something snap—like a big rubber band—and then Harold's head was in his hands, a few inches above his neck, and the only thing still holding it to his body was a long, white, glistening sliver of bone.

The hands twisted again. There was a cracking sound, and then the head was completely off.

Harold's head smiled.

"Hold on!" Harold yelled. "Wait for me!"

His head plopped in his right hand, and the hand reared back and threw it.

The head landed in the middle of the aisle, bouncing once, twice, then rolling past them. It came to a stop in front of the cathedral doors.

Harold's eyes looked up at Betty and smiled.

"Till death do us part, honey. You know that. And it takes an awful lot to kill old Harold."

He looked at Bert with a curious gaze.

"Hey, honey—aren't you going to introduce me to your new boyfriend?"

Bert was walking back, away from the head, when he

tripped and fell. His head slammed onto the stone floor, and when he opened his eyes, Harold's dismembered head was smiling next to him.

"She's so bad about things like introductions," Harold said. "Not that you and I really need them, though. I know who you are. You know who I am." He winked. "Be seeing you around, buddy. Count on it. In the meantime, got a little something for you to remember me by."

Harold coughed and hacked up a big, bloody clot of phlegm, which he spat into Bert's eye.

"Here's blood in your eye, Bert!"

Harold started laughing.

Bert screamed

He woke to Connie shaking his shoulder

"Bert! Good God, Bert, you'll wake the dead. Are you all right?"

"Sorry, I—" He blinked and sat up in his chair. "I was having a nightmare."

He looked down to see he was still holding Betty's hand.

"It's almost noon," Connie said. "Don's not back yet, and the girls and I want to look for him. I didn't want you to wake up and find us gone without knowing."

"You're going out? But is that safe?"

She gave him a look.

"I wouldn't take the girls if it weren't. A few of Don's police buddies are downstairs—we're riding with them."

"Well . . . don't go taking any risks, Connie. Don wouldn't want that."

"I know. We'll be all right. Try to get some rest this time. We'll be back soon."

"Yeah," Bert said. "I'll try. Good luck."

Connie walked out and closed the door with a soft click.

Betty moaned and shifted in her sleep. Bert wondered if she was dreaming, and if she was, he hoped it wasn't anything like the dream he'd just woken up from.

He pulled the blankets around her and went downstairs.

In the kitchen, he put on water to boil for a cup of tea. It was a familiar routine. This was just as his life had been the last six months, coming downstairs when everyone was already gone for the day, puttering around the house for a while before he headed off to the cathedral. Of course, back then—at least for the first few weeks he'd been there—his biggest worry had been whether he could resist the liquor cabinet.

Times had certainly changed.

He took his tea into the front room and turned on the television—another habit he'd picked up. All the channels were dark, though.

He opened the stereo cabinet and put on the radio. He heard the emergency broadcasting system, a taped loop that said simply, "Please stand by for further instructions from the authorities." He frowned, wondering if everything was as under control as he'd been led to believe.

Then Betty screamed upstairs.

Dropping his cup, Bert ran up the stairs two at a time and rushed into the room.

Betty was sitting up in bed, her face ashen, looking as if she'd just woken and found the Devil himself lying next to her.

Bert took her in his arms. She was trembling all over.

"It's all right," he said. "I'm here now. It's okay. Shhhh." He stroked her hair.

She rested her head on his shoulder. "I'm falling apart, Bert."

"You need to rest."

She wiped away tears from her eyes. "This is getting to be a habit, isn't it? You coming in to comfort me after a bad dream?"

"I don't mind. You want to talk about it?"

She shook her head.

"It might help."

"I don't think so. I think what I want to do is shower and

get into some clean clothes. I keep falling asleep in the same old ones."

"There's your suitcase," he said, nodding over his shoulder. "And the bathroom is down the hall, second door on the right. Towels are in there too."

"Thanks."

He got to his feet. "I made some tea. You want some?"

"Sure. All right." She threw aside the sheets. "I'll be down in a minute."

He started toward the door.

"Bert?"

He stopped and turned around. Betty was sitting on the edge of the bed, hands clasped together, staring down at the floor.

"My dream," she said. "It was Harold again."

Bert nodded. "I thought so."

"It was different, though. He was here."

"Here?"

She looked up at him. "In Denver. At the cathedral."

Bert froze.

"It was terrible," Betty said. "Worse than the other dreams. Much worse."

Bert didn't want to hear any more.

"He was wearing the cardinal's clothes, and standing up there ranting and raving, and he was so angry, Bert. So angry."

Bert didn't say a word.

He couldn't even move.

"I'll get the tea," he said finally, and shuffled toward the door.

LOS ANGELES AIR FORCE BASE

Church opened his eyes.

He was in the big tent again, back on his cot. His right arm was throbbing from the shot. His left arm hurt too, from being twisted behind his back.

He sat up and looked for Eldon.

There was no sign of him, or the cop who said he'd watch him.

He got to his feet. "Eldon!"

There was an old man sitting on the cot across from him.

"Hey!" Church said. "Where's that little boy who was here before?"

The man frowned. "Heh?"

Church yelled again. "Eldon!" He turned all the way around. Everyone in the tent was looking at him. "Eldon!"

"Pipe down, man. We heard you the first time." A kid with a crewcut and a comic book across his lap glared up at Church.

"Yeah." A girl sitting next to him nodded. "Everybody heard you."

Church saw a soldier standing at the entrance to the tent. He ran up to him.

"There was a little boy—"

The soldier shook his head. "I heard you too, buddy. Sorry, I can't help you out. I just came on shift."

Church walked out of the tent.

It was still light out, but this time the smell of smoke hit him right away. To the rear of the base, floating high above the buildings, he saw a big black cloud that almost filled the sky.

The fire. It was close. Really close.

He walked into the next tent over and called Eldon's name. No answer. Same thing in the next tent, and the next, and the next. The same thing in all of them.

At the end of the line of tents, a soldier stepped in front of him.

"Sorry, sir. This is a restricted area."

"I'm looking for a little boy," Church said. "He—"

The soldier shook his head. "You'll have to step back, sir. This area is off limits."

Church turned around and walked to the medical tent. There was a long line of people waiting to get in to see the doctors. He walked down that line, but Eldon wasn't in it.

Oh no, Church thought, wondering if the doctors were doing to Eldon what they'd done to him.

He stepped up to the entrance of the medical tent; a soldier moved quickly in front of him to block his way.

"Sir." The soldier pointed. "There's a line."

"I'm just lookin' for a little boy," Church said. "His name is Eldon. I just want to see if he's in there."

The soldier shook his head. "You're going to have to wait."

Church wanted to argue, but he didn't know what to say, so he went to the end of the line and waited. When it was his turn, he peeked inside the tent, saw that Dr. Wylie wasn't there, and went in. The man he talked to told him they hadn't seen any boys matching Eldon's description that day.

Church left the medical tent. He felt lost and confused.

Eldon couldn't have just up and left, he thought. He had to be around somewhere.

Church walked past another line of people, waiting to use the latrines. He asked if they'd seen Eldon, but got a lot of no's and a lot more dirty looks.

When he got to the front of the line there was another soldier there, sending people off to use whichever latrine came free next. He gave Church a dirty look too, so Church turned and walked straight down the line of little white latrine sheds, wondering where Eldon could have gone.

At the end of the row there was a little patch of open cement, and then another latrine, turned sideways to the others. It had an official-looking OUT OF ORDER sign hanging from the knob.

As Church walked past he heard voices coming from inside. He also thought he smelled something burning.

He stopped and rapped on the door.

"Anybody in there?"

The voices got quiet.

"Hello?"

The door slammed open and a soldier burst out, glaring at him. He was about half Church's size and a little bit porky, but the look on his face was downright scary. He had a gun, and he looked angry enough to use it.

The name plate on his shirt said MAARTENS.

"Get the fuck out of here."

Church stuttered something and turned to go, and then he looked into the latrine behind the soldier.

Eldon was standing there, holding a little pipe in his hands.

Church felt relief, then smelled something burning. Angry, he charged past the soldier and grabbed Eldon by the arm.

"What are you doing?" he yelled.

"What does it look like I'm doing?" Eldon replied coldly.

Church grabbed the pipe and threw it on the floor of the latrine.

"What the fuck?" Eldon said.

"You can't be doin' that!" Church yelled. "You can't—"

Something whacked him hard in the back. He staggered.

Turning around, he saw the soldier holding his rifle like a club.

"You better get the fuck out of here," the soldier said. "Right now. And keep your mouth shut about this or you're toast. Got me?"

"That's my son," Church said, pointing at Eldon. "You can't tell me what to do. That's my son."

For a second both Eldon and the soldier looked surprised, then Eldon got mad.

"I ain't your damn son," he said. "Get lost."

The soldier started to laugh. "You heard what he said. Get lost."

Church looked from one to the other.

What could he do? He was about to say something else when he noticed a small tattoo on his son's upper right arm.

It looked like a big E.

Jimmy couldn't have hired anyone to script it better. He re turns to the base, Evans is on duty, and Evans swallows this cock-and-bull story about him losing it after Chou got shot and chasing that gang for ten blocks before realizing he was in a shitload of trouble, and how he was lucky to have made it through the night without getting croaked. Martinez was so busy he didn't even have time to give him more than a cold stare and put him to work. It was a big stroke of luck, especially because Jimmy could tell the sergeant didn't believe a word of his story.

Jimmy was assigned to patrol the base, which was fine with him because the place was like a foreign country now.

He needed time to get used to the changes. There were lots of soldiers he didn't know from Vandenberg and Camp Pendleton, and huge tents up in the middle of the parking lots, and all the scraggly, shell-shocked looking civilians. It was like walking into the middle of a third-world war zone, especially with the big cloud of black smoke hanging over the horizon. That fire down in South Central still looked like it was going strong, which surprised the hell out of Jimmy. He thought for sure they'd either have that sucker under control by now or that it would've burned itself out.

Well, no big deal to him, except for the stink of smoke. But it certainly wasn't going to interfere with his plans, because the armory, Jimmy had noticed, was in exactly the same place. He took a latrine break to figure out how to get at the guns and then what to do with them afterward. That's when he found a little kid doing crack cocaine in a latrine. He was about to drag his ass out of there and give it a sound thrashing when he saw that, lo and behold, he was looking at another Eighteenth Streeter.

Now he had a little partner in crime, but the little partner came with a big retarded guy who claimed to be his father and who Jimmy suspected was going to be a big pain in the ass.

But still, Jimmy thought, as he headed back to his shift, it couldn't have gone any better.

Which of course was right when his luck changed.

Throughout the camp, a big siren started wailing.

"Maartens!"

Jimmy turned and spotted Martinez heading right for him.

"I need you. Now!"

Jimmy followed the sergeant into the mess tent, where there were maybe 150 soldiers already gathered. Lieutenant Rogers was standing at the front, hands clasped behind his back, literally bouncing on the balls of his feet, waiting to speak.

Martinez walked past the waiting soldiers and right up to the front, next to Rogers. They spoke a moment, then Martinez turned to the group.

"All right, everyone, listen up!"

The words were barely out of his mouth before Rogers started talking.

"You all have eyes," Rogers said. "You all can see the monster out there. It's that fire. Its western edge is now less than a mile from this base, and though firefighting efforts continue, we are now convinced that those efforts will continue to prove unsuccessful. Fire Chief Delaney—anything you want to add to that?"

A man Jimmy hadn't noticed before, his face blackened by soot and looking more exhausted than Jimmy had ever seen any human look, rose from a chair next to Rogers and spoke. "No, sir. I'd say you summed it up fairly accurately. We can't stop the fire—we haven't even been able to slow it down. We've used foam, blew a trench, nothing's stopping it."

Delaney rubbed his eyes.

"We have two Search and Rescue units at Hawthorne Avenue right now, trying to pull out survivors. They'll also keep me apprised of exactly where the front line is. I'd have to say at this point, though, we're not fighting it, we're just watching it burn."

Rogers stepped up. "Thank you, Chief," he said, turning to the room. "There you have it, gentlemen. Clearly, we cannot stop this fire, and therefore we are initiating evacuation procedures immediately. We expect Los Angeles Air Force Base to be cleared by nightfall."

Whispers broke out around the room.

Jimmy was furious.

Goddamn it. Just when things were going his way. There it went, his golden opportunity right down the fucking drain. He knew the layout, he'd started on the plan already, and now—

"Attention!" Martinez called out.

Everyone fell silent.

"We're moving most of you to a refugee camp on Melrose Avenue," Rogers said. "This will be a fairly straightforward procedure, involving minimal risk. You will all report to your duty sergeants for assignment." He paused. "Sergeant Martinez?"

"Thank you, sir. At approximately 1100 hours this morning we established contact with the Army Reserve Center at Los Alamitos. Operating independently from the authorities here, they have managed to establish that base as a refugee center for several thousand people from the surrounding communities. They are completely out of food, medical supplies, and weapons. So they need our help." Martinez looked around. "I'll need two dozen soldiers for this mission. It's hazardous duty, people, so I'd like some volunteers first. Show of hands, please."

Jimmy looked around. A few arms shot up instantly.

Gung-ho types, Jimmy thought—anxious to go down in a blaze of glory. Los Alamitos was all the way on the other side of L.A.—on the other side of the fire. They would have to move through dodgy areas at the best of times, let alone through an inferno.

Wait a second, Jimmy thought, did he say weapons?

Suddenly everything seemed okay. It was the perfect solution to getting E Street their guns.

He raised his hand and stepped forward.

"Sir," he said, locking serious eyes with Martinez. "You can count me in."

NORTHEAST TEXAS

It took half an hour before someone finally let them merge onto the highway, and another half hour to travel to the next exit. Finally, they pulled off and stopped at a truck stop. Realizing that all the big roads were going to be jammed, Peter bought several maps to route an alternate course. They also tried to buy gas, but the pumps were empty.

A sign of things to come, he thought.

He still had half a tank left and they took off again. Finally, about an hour later, in a little town called Burke's Landing, they found a Mobil that had fuel.

They were also charging twenty-five dollars a gallon. Cash, up front.

"You'll burn in hell for this," Leo said to the attendant.

The man just smiled and collected his money.

He was still smiling as Leo took the wheel and peeled out of there. Peter had the map open on his lap, giving directions as needed and staring out his window the rest of the time.

Until then the view had been a familiar one. They took a long, sweeping arc across the northeast corner of the state, which led them into coastal Texas—which looked the same as coastal Florida, Mississippi, Louisiana, and all the wetlands and shopping malls they'd seen. But now the trees were gradually disappearing and the land leveling out. At last, Peter thought, they were into cowboy country. Texas Rangers, the Alamo, and John Wayne. The Wild, Wild West.

And it was going to get even wilder soon.

The waves were coming.

They were barely listening to the radio now, but even without the constant updates on which states, counties, and cities were going to lose power and when, you could tell by just looking out the window. There were almost no cars, every window was boarded up and every house had its curtains drawn. More than one roadblock forced them to take an alternate route. People, he realized, were battening down the hatches.

It was the calm before the storm.

It didn't take a rocket scientist to figure it out, of course, but Peter had always been able to smell trouble brewing—a skill that had come in handy back when he was a cop. He could be in the middle of almost any kind of bad situation—a drug bust, a barroom fight, a domestic quarrel—and tell whether or not things were likely to stay under control or flare up. He could even take one look around and tell who was probably going to cause it.

So why hadn't he seen trouble coming that one fateful night? And why couldn't he remember it?

Same old questions, wrapped up in a brand new package.

He remembered the man's eyes.

Like what you see?

Peter rubbed his face. The lack of sleep was catching up to him.

"I could use some coffee," he said.

"I could use a big fat steak," Leo replied. "But I don't think we're going to find either." He snorted. "Shit, and if we did, we'd probably have to pay through the ass for 'em."

"I don't care," Peter said, "I say we stop anyway."

He checked his wallet and realized he was down to his last twenty bucks. He looked at Leo. Now, more than ever, he would have to depend on his generosity.

"Hey, Leo," he said. "You know—I don't know if I've said thanks for a while."

Leo smiled. "You talking to me?"

"I am. And I want you to know I appreciate it—the car, you coming with me. Considering everything else that's going on. Considering you could be back in that nice big apartment of yours."

"Yeah. Guess I could. Broiling up some steaks. Watching the world fall apart on my big screen TV."

They both laughed.

Leo looked over at him. "How much further?"

"Another hour if we stay on this course."

"No reason why we shouldn't."

Then Peter did another calculation. He thought about the

waves. About three more hours till it hit. He went back to looking out the window. The sun was out, and mile after mile he saw wire fencing and green pastures.

He closed his eyes.

The next thing he knew the car was stopped and Leo was shaking his shoulder.

"We're here," Leo said. "And we've got a welcome mat."

Peter looked up. There was a sign on the side of the road.

WELCOME TO LITTLE CHAPARRAL

Next to it was a barrier blocking the way. An orange sign with black letters hung from it:

CLOSED TO THRU TRAFFIC

"What now?" Leo asked. "We didn't come all this way for nothing."

He got out of the car and moved the barrier. They drove on through.

Peter didn't know what the modern term was, but as they came to a stop in the heart of Little Chaparral, the only expression he could think of was one-horse town.

On their left was a gas station: a run-down shack with a single pump that Peter wouldn't have been surprised to learn dispensed only leaded gasoline. Beyond the gas station there was a one-story concrete house with a neon Coors sign in the window, and spray-painted letters along its side that said THE LAST ROUNDUP. Beyond that was what looked like an old-fashioned general store, called Fletcher's Five and Dime.

On their right there was only one building. Newer than the others, it had a faded red brick facade and an American flag hanging over the front entrance. Big black letters etched in the glass above the entrance proclaimed the building

Town Hall. Smaller letters underneath also identified it as the Sheriff's Office and Courthouse.

Just beyond those buildings, another road intersected the one they were on, and a construction barrier had been put up there as well. Parked on the road next to the barrier was a tan car with a siren on top, in front of which stood a cop wearing a cowboy hat. His back to them, he was scanning the horizon ahead, as if he expected to see the waves coming toward them.

Peter wondered if it was the same sheriff he'd spoken to on the phone.

The man turned and saw their car. He put his hands on his hips and stared a moment, and even from a distance Peter could tell he was angry.

"Oh boy," Leo said.

The cop got into his car, hit the siren, and headed straight toward them.

It was exactly the kind of entrance Peter hadn't wanted to make.

They were stopped between the five-and-dime on one side of the street and the town hall on the other. As the wailing siren got closer, the doors to both buildings swung open. A young girl in a gingham dress peered out of the store, a young boy's head popping under her arm a second later. On Peter's side of the car, a big, burly man stepped out of the town hall and put his hands on his hips.

Peter smiled. "Afternoon."

The man frowned and set his jaw.

The tan car came to a halt directly in front of them. Peter could see the words TITUS COUNTY SHERIFF'S OFFICE on it. The uniformed man stepped out of the car and walked toward them with an expression that was equal parts anger and confusion.

"What the hell do you think you're doing? You see that sign back there? Can you read English?"

He stood by the driver's side window.

Leo cleared his throat and spoke. "Yes, Officer"—Peter could see the deputy sheriff's badge pinned to the man's shirt—"we saw the sign, but my friend and I are working on a murder case in Florida—"

"What? Are you crazy?"

The deputy walked to the back of the car and looked at their license plate. "You drove here from Florida? Now?"

Peter leaned out his window. "I talked to the sheriff a couple days ago. My name is Peter Williams. Our case involves the killing of a Jacksonville police officer—"

The deputy drew his gun. "Out of the car," he said angrily, waving his weapon. "Come on, out."

He stood back as Leo and Peter unbuckled their seat belts and got out of the car. There was a full-fledged crowd watching them now; to Peter's surprise, at least two dozen people had come out of the five-and-dime and now stood on the edge of the road.

The deputy eyed them suspiciously. Then he looked over their shoulder and called out "Randy!"

"Yeah?"

Peter turned and saw the burly man.

"Come here a second." The burly man came over, and the deputy handed him his gun. "Keep an eye on these fellows. I'm gonna search their car."

"Now wait a second," Leo said angrily, "you can't do that. We haven't done anything wrong. We came here to see—"

Randy cocked the trigger. "Shut up, and don't take another step forward."

The deputy had their car door open and was looking in the glove compartment and under the seats.

Peter realized then that they were about to be in even bigger trouble than they already were.

"Well look at this."

He held up the handgun Leo had taped underneath the front seat.

"I got a permit for that," Leo said.

"Yeah. A Texas permit?"

Leo just stared at him.

"I thought so."

He slammed the front door shut and opened the back.

"There's another gun in there too," Peter said. "In that brown suitcase."

"*You* got a permit?"

Peter shook his head. "No. Listen, I told you we're here to see the sheriff. The guns don't matter, you can keep those till we leave, I just—"

"Oh, I'm keepin' these all right," he said. "Come on. Follow me."

He marched them into the town hall, with Randy following behind with the gun.

There was a woman in the vestibule talking on the phone. Seeing them, she spoke a few more hurried words and hung up.

"Ken? What the—"

"Where's Cade at, Lucy?"

"He's still out getting the supplies." She ran her eyes over Peter and Leo. "What's going on?"

"You know anything about two fellas from Florida he's supposed to see?"

"He didn't tell me anything."

"No," Peter said, stepping forward. "We didn't tell him we were coming, we—"

"All right," Ken said. "Let's go."

He pushed on a door labeled SHERIFF'S OFFICE, and they followed him through.

There was a large map of Texas on the wall, over a row of file cabinets. There was a big desk to their left, and a smaller one to their right. Behind the right desk was a jail cell.

"Oh no," Peter said. "Listen—"

Ken pulled the gate open. "Inside."

Peter and Leo hesitated a moment, but with nudging

from Randy, they stepped inside. Ken shut the door behind them.

"I'll let you out when the sheriff gets back. Shouldn't be long."

And then he and Randy left.

"Welcome to Little Chaparral," Leo mumbled.

The cell had been built to hold one man at a time. It was about eight feet square, and was furnished with a single cot, a small sink, and a steel bucket.

"Don't worry," Peter said. "The sheriff sounded like a reasonable man on the phone. I'm sure we'll get out of here when he gets back."

"Worried?" Leo said, sitting on the cot. "What do I have to worry about? A black man sitting in a Texas jail cell. I'll be fine." They both started laughing.

LOS ANGELES AIR FORCE BASE

It was just like Compton, Church thought. The smell of the smoke, the heat from the fire, everyone running around in a thousand different directions, each person in a bigger hurry than the next.

Only this time it was even worse, because number one, now he knew for sure no one could stop the fire, and number two, he couldn't find Eldon again.

Church was standing in a roped-off area at the base parking lot, crammed in with all the other people from 5B. Each tent number had its own roped-off areas for people to stand in, and soldiers were slowly loading them up into trucks.

Evacuation, they'd called it.

Church was hoping they wouldn't evacuate his group until he could find Eldon.

Church had been sitting on his cot, waiting for Eldon to come back, when the soldiers came to move them. He'd been waiting for Eldon awhile, thinking about what to say. He knew that the E on Eldon's arm meant that he was in a gang, and the crack pipe probably meant the gang sold the stuff. But he wasn't much of a role model himself, he thought, so how could he tell Eldon how to behave?

Church had thought long and hard, and finally decided the only thing he could say to his son was that he hadn't been a good father and he would try to do better. Then, if Eldon asked him for advice, he would tell him to never talk back to any cops, no matter what he did. But Church was starting to get the feeling he wasn't going to get the chance to talk to his son again.

He wondered where Eldon had gone. All the tents had been taken down now, the latrines were stacked up and being moved to a truck at the back of the parking lot. And the parking lot was slowly emptying.

Church scanned the lot again. Still no sign of Eldon. He started looking for that redheaded soldier, Maartens, when someone tapped him on the shoulder.

It was an angry-looking soldier pointing to his right. "I said let's go. On the truck."

Church followed his finger and saw everyone else from 5B walking toward trucks parked by the gate.

"I have to wait for my son," Church said. "He's from our tent too, but he's not here yet."

"I'm sure he's fine. He probably got on with another group. You'll all be together soon."

Church shook his head. "No. I been watching everyone get on the trucks. I think he must be back there somewhere." Church pointed toward the back of the big parking lot, where the latrines were being loaded, and where there were still lots of soldiers hurrying around.

"I guarantee you he's not back there, sir," the soldier said. "No civilians back there. Now come on"—the soldier took his arm—"let's go."

"Let me wait for the last truck," Church said. "Just to see if he shows up. Please."

"Sir, I need you to get on this truck. Now."

The soldier was starting to get angry. Church didn't want that, but he couldn't just leave Eldon.

More soldiers walked out of the building where Church had gone to see Dr. Wylie that morning. One of them was Maartens.

"Hey!" he said, pointing. "There's the guy my son was with. That soldier. Hey!"

Maartens turned and looked at him.

Of course, it was crazy—Church couldn't even see his eyes—but he had the feeling that Maartens had been expecting to see him, that he knew he was looking for Eldon, and that he knew where Eldon was.

"Sir."

Church turned around.

There were two soldiers facing him now, and both looked angry.

"On the truck."

Church sighed. Soldiers, cops, they were all the same. These two would hurt him if he didn't do what they said.

With a last look back at the redheaded soldier, Church got on line, and a second later he climbed into the back of a big green truck. It was already packed, so Church had to sit right where he'd climbed in, with his legs dangling over the edge, almost eyeball-to-eyeball with the soldier who'd made him get in.

"All right, everyone!" the soldier yelled. "Listen up!"

He waited for quiet, then spoke again.

"The trip to the Hollywood base should be about half an hour. Please don't make a lot of unnecessary noise; we don't want to do anything to call attention to this transport. All right?"

Church nodded, not really listening. He was watching the

red-haired soldier head toward the rear of the base. He squinted and saw six small trucks parked together there.

The engine to their truck started up and they began to move.

Church turned around and scanned the inside of the truck. He'd been hoping for a miracle, but there was no Eldon.

A second later he realized there were no soldiers either.

Jimmy had been walking away when the big guy yelled and pointed at him, and he thought, I knew he was gonna be a pain in the ass.

"Maartens!" someone called.

Jimmy looked up.

For once it wasn't Martinez yelling at him, but the sergeant who was in charge of his four-person detail. His name was Sergeant O'Neill, a marine up from Camp Pendleton who Jimmy had taken an instant dislike to.

The feeling was mutual.

"Are you coming?" O'Neill asked.

Jimmy realized now that he'd stopped walking when the big guy had pointed to him, while O'Neill and the two other soldiers on the detail—Haynes and Gathrid—continued to double-time it toward the waiting convoy at the rear of the base.

"Sorry, sir," Jimmy said, hurrying to catch up.

As Jimmy came up alongside him, O'Neill eyeballed him. "I'm not going to have to babysit your ass during this mission, am I?" he asked.

Jimmy shook his head. "No, sir, you're not going to have to worry about me at all."

Which was the honest truth. In fact, in about twenty minutes, Jimmy guessed, O'Neill wasn't going to have to worry about anything anymore.

Jimmy followed him and Haynes and Gathrid to the back

of the base, where the convoy bound for Los Alamitos was being loaded up. Half a dozen trucks filled with supplies—three with food, one with medical stores, two with weapons—and two jeeps to escort them. Jimmy was in one of the weapons trucks. He knew it was a lucky break that he'd been chosen for it, because otherwise he would have had to switch places with someone. Or just killed them.

Martinez was standing up in the rear of one of the jeeps, watching as the last of the food was loaded. When he saw the four of them approaching, he cleared his throat and spoke.

"All right. We're all here now, so let me go over the plan one more time."

Jimmy reached inside his coat pocket and as softly as possible flicked on the walkie-talkie he'd stolen out of supplies. He'd taped a transmit button in the bathroom fifteen minutes before.

"We're taking Rosecrans to Inglewood and heading south. We will skirt the edge of the fire as closely as we can, in order to minimize hostile contact. Once we're clear of the fire, we will roughly follow the 405 south and east toward Long Beach. From there we should be able to make contact with Los Alamitos and either pick up an escort or receive further directions. Any questions?"

No one raised a hand.

"Let's go, then." Martinez clapped his hands and everyone went to their vehicles.

Jimmy's detail had been assigned to handle the smaller of the two weapons trucks; bad break, he thought at first, then realized that the larger truck was mostly ammunition and small caliber weapons, and that in fact their vehicle had the good stuff. Grenade launchers and two cases of grenades. A half-dozen crates of M-1 ammunition, and twice that many of the guns.

Omar would be happy, he thought.

Jimmy volunteered to drive, but it turned out that Haynes

had driven tanks for the Marine Corps, so he was chosen. Jimmy volunteered to ride shotgun, but that was O'Neill's job, which left Jimmy riding in the back of the truck with the weapons and Gathrid.

"So how long you been in the service?" Gathrid asked as the truck began moving. The marine sat down on top of an M-1 crate and started polishing the end of his rifle.

"Too long," Jimmy said, moving around Gathrid.

Before Gathrid could say another word, Jimmy slit the man's throat. Gathrid slumped to the floor without making a sound.

Okay, Jimmy thought. No turning back now.

He took out his walkie-talkie. "Yo kid, you there?"

Eldon's voice came back fuzzy but clear. "Yo."

Jimmy smiled. He'd given Eldon the second walkie-talkie and snuck him outside of the base to wait for the convoy. But that was when Jimmy hoped to be driving. Eldon was going to run out in front of the truck, Jimmy was going to stop for him, and they would take it from there.

Now, though . . . they were going to have to improvise.

"Where are you?"

"Rosecrans and Inglewood," Eldon called back, sounding out of breath. Jimmy realized he'd probably run all the way there after listening in on the walkie-talkie.

"Okay," he said. "We're the fifth truck. Shoot the guy in the passenger seat."

"Huh?"

"Shoot the guy in the passenger seat," Jimmy repeated. "Out."

That was clear enough, wasn't it? He'd given Eldon a gun because he said he could use it. He hoped so. If not, Jimmy knew he would have to jump right back out of the truck and take his chances with Omar.

Jimmy flipped open the flap in the back of the truck to find out where they were, and his eyes went wide.

Martinez was riding behind them.

The sonuvabitch wasn't staying up front, he was moving back and forth along the convoy, keeping an eye out for trouble.

Shit.

Martinez saw Jimmy and gave him a curt nod.

Jimmy smiled and gave a big thumbs-up.

Fuck you, asshole, he thought, and stuck his head back inside.

There went that plan.

He reached for the walkie-talkie again. He'd have to tell Eldon to forget it. Maybe he'd have to forget the whole thing. Just wait until Martinez wasn't behind them and jump right out the—

He heard a gunshot, and a moment later the truck careened wildly to the left.

Sonuvabitch. Ten-to-one that Eldon, the stupid little fuck, had shot the driver.

The truck veered right; Jimmy ran back over to Gathrid, lifted him up by the hair and shot him in the throat. The head almost came off in his hand and blood exploded all over the back of the truck. Some of it got on Jimmy, but that was all right. The blast would hide the knife wound. At least for a while.

The truck veered left again. Jimmy ran to one of the grenade crates, pried open the lid and grabbed two. He stuck them on his belt and had turned toward the back flap when the truck crashed into something hard and he went flying forward. He slammed into a stack of crates. Slumping to the floor, he lay stunned for a moment.

"You all right in there?" someone shouted. One of the marines from Martinez's jeep stuck his head into the flap. His eyes went wide when he saw Gathrid.

Jimmy staggered to his feet, trying to sound as panicked as he could. "Those bastards! They got Gathrid!" He stumbled past the marine and out the back of the truck, onto the street.

The truck had run right into the side of a building. The entire convoy was stopped.

Martinez was helping another soldier pull O'Neill's body out of the cab. A dozen other soldiers stood facing outward from the wreck, forming a protective circle.

Jimmy heard the marine in the back of the truck.

"Shit! Look at all this blood."

I'm fucked, Jimmy realized. He had about five seconds before that marine looked a little closer at Gathrid's neck and saw his throat had been cut. Then they'd pull the knife out of the scabbard on his belt and—

Jimmy saw the other weapons truck stopped right behind him. There was only one soldier in the cab, and he was in the passenger seat.

What the hell, he thought.

He ran to the truck and climbed into the driver's seat.

The marine looked at him. "What's happening?"

"A lot of bad shit," Jimmy said, then shot him in the head. He took one of the grenades off his belt, pulled the pin, and threw it into the back flap of the truck he'd been riding in.

Martinez, kneeling on the ground over O'Neill, looked up then and saw him.

Jimmy gave him the finger and slammed the truck into reverse.

Martinez stood up and started waving his arms. "Get away," he shouted as he ran.

Too late, Jimmy thought.

The street exploded.

One minute he was looking at the soldiers, the next all he could see was a giant fireball that flew toward him. Jimmy screamed and raised his hands to protect his face. He felt something hot singe his hair and arms, and then the truck was slammed backward and sideways by the force of the blast. It was on the street, wheels barely touching the ground, spinning around like a top, and Jimmy shut his eyes and prayed that he'd die quickly.

The truck came to a screeching halt.

Jimmy lowered his hands.

They'd spun around 180 degrees and were facing the other way down the street.

Jimmy checked his mirrors.

Behind him the street was a wall of flame, and seeing that, he broke out laughing.

He'd killed the entire detail. And most especially— Martinez.

He reached down to shift the truck into gear.

"Hey!"

Jimmy turned and saw Eldon opening the passenger door.

"Stand clear," Jimmy said to the dead soldier, kicking him out of the van. Eldon climbed up next to him.

"You hit the driver," Jimmy chided him. "You weren't supposed to hit the driver."

"I only shot once, man. Musta hit 'em both." The kid looked up. "You're welcome, by the way."

"Yeah. Thanks," Jimmy said. Wise-ass.

He started the truck again. It made a hiccuping noise and Jimmy frowned. Something in the engine must've gotten screwed up when they did their little spin; he hoped it would hold out long enough for them to get where they were going.

Then he thought of something.

"The back of the truck." He reached for the door handle. "There could be more soldiers—"

"All clear," Eldon said. "I checked it." He put his feet up on the dashboard and leaned back in his seat, smiling. "You're welcome again."

Jimmy laughed. He shifted the truck into gear, and they started forward.

"So where we goin' now?" Eldon asked.

"We're gonna double back, past the base." He was going to copy Martinez's plan, only going in the other direction; stay close to the fire until he got clear of it. "Then on up into Bel Air. That's where we hook up with the gang."

"With Omar, right? You said Omar."

"Yeah."

"That's serious," Eldon said. "Omar is like . . ." He shook his head. "That's serious. And those are all guns back there?" He jerked his head toward the back of the truck.

"That's right."

Eldon slapped his leg and broke into a big smile. "That is serious! We are gonna be players, man. Big-time."

Jimmy smiled back, though what he was really thinking was, What's this *we* shit, keemosabe?

Then his smile disappeared.

Running down the street toward them, arms pumping like pistons, was Church.

"Not this clown again," Jimmy said.

"Slow down," Eldon said, pulling out the .45 Jimmy had given him. "Let me shoot him."

Jimmy shook his head. "What the hell does he want?"

"Me," the kid said.

"You?" Jimmy snorted. That was easy enough.

He slammed the point of his elbow into the kid's head.

Then he reached across, opened the passenger door, and kicked him out into the road. The kid hit so hard that he almost bounced back into the truck.

The big guy stopped running, and Jimmy only had to swerve a little to get past him in the street.

"There," he said, slamming the door, "take him."

Two pain-in-the-ass birds with one stone.

LITTLE CHAPARRAL, TEXAS

There was a window behind the big desk opposite them, and Peter had spent much of the last hour watching the sun head toward the horizon.

The window also gave him a good view of the front door of the five-and-dime across the street. Over the last few hours a lot of people had gone in through that door and hadn't come out. He'd heard a number of cars pulling up as well, but apparently the one they were waiting for—the sheriff's— hadn't arrived yet.

Either that or their good friends Ken and Randy had forgotten to tell the sheriff they were here. He supposed he could excuse them for that oversight, though.

The first wave had hit about forty-five minutes ago. But it didn't hit like a big deal. It hit like a breaker shutting off in a basement fuse box. The lightbulb in the middle of the room went out. Peter's watch stopped. He heard a few shouts from across the street.

And then things went on like before.

"Shit," Leo said. "I'm gonna end up having to use that bucket in the goddamn dark, aren't I?"

"We both are," Peter replied. "At least at this rate. Man, I really hope nothing happened to that sheriff. I do not want to be stuck in here when people start going—"

He stopped and looked down at Leo.

"Don't get me wrong," he said. "It's not you I'm worried about—"

Leo laughed. "I hear you."

But part of Peter was in fact looking at Leo and wondering if his companion might go crazy and attack him. Would the two of them end up knocking each other's brains out in an eight foot square Texas prison cell?

"I'm not worried about you either," Leo continued. "I think too many people are spending too much time worrying about what's happening, talking about the Bible and Judgment Day and hysteria and psychosis and stuff like that, when I think it's pretty clear what's going on. Don't you?"

Peter shook his head. "No."

"Come on, Pete." Leo pushed himself up off the bunk. "You should. You were a cop. You heard all this crap before. 'I was under a lot of stress that evening,' 'My client was emotionally incapable of distinguishing right from wrong,' all that bullshit. You know the truth—when you get right down to it, there's good people in this world and there's bad ones. Society sets up rules to keep the bad ones in check, and they behave. This wave thing, it seems, sets 'em free to do whatever the hell they want."

"Yeah, well." Peter shrugged. "Maybe. I don't know. Still, seems to me that there's gotta be more to it than that. Besides, you can't always tell who's who, right?"

"Oh, I can tell," Leo said. "I look 'em in the eyes and I know. That's how come I know about you."

"Well, good," Peter said. "Then I guess I know about you too."

The door burst open and a thin, wiry-looking man with a sheriff's badge pinned to his uniform hurried to their cell, fumbling a set of keys.

"I'm Sheriff Curtis and I'm awful sorry about this but goddamn you fellas picked a helluva time to come callin'." He slid the cell door open with a loud clang. "Don't you know what's goin' on?"

"We know," Peter said. "It's just that—"

The sheriff shook his head and turned around. "Well, listen, you'll understand I ain't got the time to talk to you now other than to say the same thing I told you on the phone. That fella Novarra is buried in a graveyard about ten miles west down the highway, and once the power comes back on, you can go and see it for yourself, all right?"

They followed Curtis outside to their car and Peter saw he'd been right: there were about twenty other vehicles parked in front of the five-and-dime store now.

"What's going on?"

"A bunch of us are fixin' to face this thing together," Curtis said. "Little Chap's a small town; we all know each other. Most of us lived here all our lives. We heard about what happened in Denver, and we figure we got a better shot at getting through it together than at home alone. The Reverend

Sanchez come down from Chap Junction, and he's here, and Randy's let us take over three of the big freezers in his basement to lay in supplies, in case some folks have to stay here for a while, and—" He shook his head. "Listen, I gotta get back. But the reason it took me so long to get you is that we've been talking over there, a few of us, and we decided that if you want to join us, you can."

Peter and Leo looked at each other.

"Well . . ."

"That's an awful generous offer, Sheriff," Peter said. "You want to give us a minute to think it over?"

"Sure. Fine. I'll be right inside," he said, and started toward the five-and-dime.

And stopped.

"Oh. One more thing. Your guns." He frowned, and shook his head. "I can't give 'em back to you just yet. Even if you decide to stay with us. I hope you understand. No one in the store's gonna have a weapon except me—and Ken. Once we make it through—"

"I understand," Peter said.

"All right, then," Curtis said. "Come tell me either way."

"We sure will," Peter said.

He turned to Leo when Curtis was gone. "So what do you think?"

"I think I want my damn gun back."

"Yeah. I hear that."

"And beyond that . . ." Leo shook his head. "I don't know. Sheriff seems like a good man. But I didn't really like that Ken guy—Deputy Ken, if that's what he was. And the people in there . . . I don't know about them either. Who knows? Could be a bunch of rednecks or two dozen more like Curtis. You take my point?"

"Yeah." Peter nodded. "But where else can we go?" He turned around in a big circle. There was nothing as far as the eye could see.

"Right. This sort of defines the middle of nowhere. What do you think we have, an hour?"

Peter looked up at the sun, which was hovering just above the horizon, and nodded. "About that."

"Well," Leo said, "I guess we don't have much of a choice, do we? Unless we want to just sit in the car. Or start walking in one direction and hope we can find our way back."

Peter's stomach growled. "I'm kind of hungry, to tell you the truth."

"And I gotta piss like a racehorse," Leo replied. "All right, then. So we're going in?"

"We're going in."

"You're gonna watch my back?"

"I'm gonna watch your back. And you'll watch mine?"

Leo nodded.

"Come on then," Leo said. "Let's go meet the good people of Little Chaparral."

Fletcher's Five and Dime was one of those places that was somehow bigger inside than it looked from without. The front of the store was a bewildering array of aisle after aisle of all sorts of foods and knickknacks and hardware supplies. Staircases led up the wall on either side of the first floor to a second level running halfway to the back of the building, which was filled with more of the same. And the back of the five-and-dime, where the building opened up, was a restaurant with a long counter that looked like something straight out of an old-fashioned soda shop.

The back of the store was also where the townspeople had gathered. Peter spotted Sheriff Curtis in the middle of a crowd and headed over to him. Heads turned as he and Leo passed, both of them nodding greetings and receiving similar greetings in return, as well as a few suspicious glances.

Peter wondered exactly how everyone had decided it would be all right for him and Leo to join them in Fletcher's.

"There you are," Sheriff Curtis said. He was talking to

Randy, the burly man who'd helped usher them into the jail cells earlier. "Have you decided what you're gonna do?"

"We're staying," Peter said. "If that's all right."

"You bet. Here, let me introduce you around a little. This is Randy Fletcher. He owns this place. Randy, this is Pete and Leo, and I'm sorry to say I don't know your last names."

"That's all right, Pete and Leo is fine." They all shook hands.

"Listen, I'm sorry about that before," Fletcher said. "Holdin' the gun on you. But you understand—everyone around here is a little on edge. More than a little on edge. No hard feelings?"

"Sure," Peter said. "No hard feelings."

But he noticed that Fletcher still seemed nervous.

"And this is Kate Harter and her husband Dave," Curtis said, drawing in a small, mousy-looking woman and a tall, lanky man with tattoos running down both arms. "This is Peter and Leo."

"Pleased to meet you," Dave said sullenly, sticking out his hand, though in fact Peter thought he looked anything but pleased, and kept a protective arm around his wife.

Then Curtis excused himself, and Fletcher took over the introducing duties, and Peter and Leo met Nora Santos and her twin daughters Isabel and Nina, and Hugh Flagg and his wife, Annie, who owned a ranch up toward Big Chap, which he learned was what they called the larger town of Chaparral farther to the north.

Everyone they said hello to was perfectly friendly, shook hands and smiled, but as they were introduced Peter kept thinking about what Leo had said before in the jail cell: "I look 'em in the eyes and I know."

He'd been looking the people he was meeting in the eye too, and while he wasn't so sure he could tell the difference between good and bad as easily as Leo said he could, there was one thing he could tell for sure and that was that none of them were all that thrilled they were there.

When the introductions were done and Fletcher left them alone, Peter turned to Leo.

"You get the feeling," he said quietly, "that maybe the decision to let us in here was not exactly a unanimous one?"

"Hell yeah," Leo said. "I felt more welcome at my ex's birthday party. You think we can change our minds?"

Peter looked up, and about ten heads swiveled in another direction. A lot of people doing their damnedest to pretend they weren't watching every move he and Leo made.

"Not without making a little bit of a fuss."

"Yeah, well, I don't mind making a fuss because I'm starting to get an awful bad feeling about being here when—"

Peter felt a hand on his shoulder.

"There you are," Curtis said. "I got someone else I want to introduce you to."

Peter turned around.

Curtis was standing next to a man in a priest's collar. But Peter didn't need any introduction.

The man was Diego Novarra.

INGLEWOOD, LOS ANGELES

The truck flew past him, engine hiccuping and the red-haired soldier at the wheel, but Church was barely aware of it. He had stopped and was staring at Eldon, lying flat and unmoving in the middle of the street.

"Oh no," Church whispered, walking toward his son. "Oh no."

He started running, and when he reached the boy's body, he bent down and looked him over. One of Eldon's legs was sticking out at a funny angle and there was a little pool of blood behind his head.

"Eldon?" Church whispered. "Eldon?"

His son's eyes were closed. Church lifted an eyelid, but he only got a blank stare.

Check the pulse. Church could almost hear Carl telling him, check the pulse.

He lifted the arm closest to him and felt Eldon's wrist. No pulse. He tried the other. Still nothing.

This couldn't be right, though. Eldon couldn't just die on the same day that he had found out who he was. That wasn't fair, Church thought, and God wouldn't let that happen.

Mouth-to-mouth, he thought.

He didn't really know how to do it, but he'd seen it on TV enough times to try.

He pried open Eldon's mouth as a little trickle of blood came out of the corner. Church wiped it away with his hand and took a deep breath. Then he bent over, putting his mouth over Eldon's and breathing out.

Church breathed out again, and again, a bunch of times, till he was short of breath. Then he lifted his head away.

Eldon still wasn't moving.

Church blew his nose on his sleeve and tried again.

No pulse.

He started to cry.

No, he thought. Don't go to pieces. Got to find a doctor. Go back to the base and get him a doctor.

Church bent low and picked up Eldon in his arms. Something fell out of Eldon's pocket and clattered to the ground; Church ignored it.

Eldon was so little, so light in his arms. How old is he? Church wondered. He couldn't even remember. He couldn't even remember Eldon's mother, or when he'd been born.

A doctor, Church remembered. Got to go back to the base.

And then he remembered the evacuation.

The base was empty. He'd seen it himself, just a few minutes ago, after he'd jumped out the back of the truck and run back there, running through the empty parking lot to the back of the base, toward the place where he'd seen the red-haired soldier, only he wasn't there, and then he had run out onto the street and kept going and had somehow found Eldon, only . . .

He was too late.

Church sank to his knees in the street and started to cry.

"Oh God, please no."

He let Eldon fall gently out of his arms.

He heard the sound of an engine then. A hiccuping engine. He looked up, but the street was empty. He looked down, and saw the thing that had fallen out of Eldon's pocket.

It was a little phone, and the sound was coming from it.

No. Not a phone. A walkie-talkie.

Wait a second, Church thought. Wait a second. The hiccuping engine . . . The truck with the redheaded soldier. What was his name again?

Maartens.

The hiccuping sound was getting all staticky. Church thought he knew what that meant. The truck was moving out of range.

Church stood up and looked around.

He needed a car.

LITTLE CHAPARRAL, TEXAS

"Reverend John Sanchez, this is Peter and Leo."

The man had his hands clasped behind his back, and there was a big smile on his face.

"Come all the way from Florida, I understand. This must be quite different for you." He looked deeply into Peter's eyes. "Like what you see?"

Peter thought he had to be wrong, that whatever he had expected to find in Little Chaparral, this couldn't be it.

But the second he said those words—

Like what you see?

Peter knew.

"It's you," he said. "Sonuvabitch, it's you."

Everyone around them froze. Peter's words carried to some of the other townspeople in the store, and he was vaguely aware of heads turning in their direction.

But mostly he was aware of Novarra.

The man's mustache was gone; the long hair was gone. But his face was the same; same hawklike nose, same thin mouth, same coal-black eyes.

Those eyes burned with amusement as he looked at Peter with a half smile on his face.

"What did you say?" Curtis asked angrily, and suddenly his down-home folksy manner was gone and his voice was like the crack of a whip, and Peter could tell there was a good reason this man had been elected sheriff.

"Pete?" Leo put a hand on his arm. "Are you all right?"

"It's him. Leo, this is him!" Peter said, aware that almost everyone in the room was watching him. "This is Diego Novarra. He's the guy that killed Kelly. Sheriff"—he turned to Curtis—"I know this sounds crazy but—"

Curtis stepped in between him and the reverend.

"You better put a sock in that, mister," he whispered. "Right now."

"But—"

Curtis grabbed his arm, and the same kind of iron that had been in his voice was in his grip. "I said, put a sock in it." He started to pull Peter back from the reverend.

The reverend held up his hands.

"It's all right, Sheriff," he said. "A case of mistaken identity, clearly."

Peter shucked off the sheriff's grip.

"I'm not confused. I know exactly who you are. You killed my partner."

"In Florida?" Novarra said, his eyebrow raised.

"You know goddamn well in Florida," Peter snapped.

"Mister, you're crazy," Randy Fletcher said.

"Pete," Leo whispered, "what's the matter with you?"

Then Kate Harter screamed, and a sudden light of understanding shone in her eyes. She took a step back from Peter. "I know what this is!" she yelled. "It's the waves! It's here!"

For a minute there was total confusion.

People who had been talking to one another suddenly stood apart. A woman grabbed a little boy and drew him into a protective embrace against her. Glass broke, and Peter saw a man—someone he hadn't been introduced to—walking toward him with a broken Coke bottle in his hand.

Curtis drew his gun.

"Everyone, stay right where you are," he said, and Peter froze, because he had absolutely no doubt that Curtis was going to shoot him if he moved another inch.

The man with the bottle froze too.

"All right, everyone." Novarra raised his hands over his head. "It's all right! It's not the waves. Believe me. We have time. It's not the waves."

He lowered his hands gently, and the temperature in the room lowered as well.

Peter caught a glimpse of his face then, and suddenly had the feeling that Novarra knew exactly what the waves were and knew exactly what was causing them.

In fact, he looked like he was waiting for them.

"Peter?"

Leo had his arm in a light grip and was leaning over him, whispering in his ear. "I don't know what the fuck you're doing and I don't know why, but if you don't shut up you're going to get us both killed."

"But—"

"Shut up," Leo said. He turned back to the sheriff.

"Listen. I'm sorry about my friend here, and I'm sorry for any confusion on his part, or any trouble we caused, and Sheriff, I think maybe it's best that Peter and I just go. All right?"

Curtis's face was like stone.

"Yeah. I think maybe that would be for the best."

Peter started to open his mouth, and Leo, who still had his arm in a tight grip, squeezed it so hard Peter winced.

They started backing away toward the front entrance.

Novarra took a step forward.

"Is this wise?" he asked, his eyes narrow and staring at Peter.

"Hell no, it ain't!" Fletcher yelled. "I was willing to let these two in here on your say-so, Reverend, but now that we know what kind of men they are, I don't think we can afford to let them go. We don't know what they might do out there when that wave hits. They might come back here and try to kill us all!"

Peter saw a lot of heads nodding in agreement, a lot of eyes blazing in assent.

"Run," Leo said.

Peter turned around with him, but Deputy Ken was at the door, holding a gun.

"I say we kill 'em now," said Dave Harter, stepping forward. "Before they kill us."

"No, no," Novarra said solemnly. "We're all civilized people here, we don't know for sure what these men are going to do."

He turned to Fletcher. "You have rope, though, don't you, Randy?"

Randy nodded. "Sure do."

"You've got to be kidding," Leo said. "You're going to tie us up?"

"That's exactly what we're going to do," Curtis said. "Because we're civilized folk here. Like Reverend Sanchez says. Otherwise, I might be more inclined to listen to Dave Harter there, and find another use for that rope."

Fletcher came back with the rope and Harter and another man brought over two wooden chairs.

Curtis waved his gun. "Go on, sit."

Leo shook his head. "Civilized, my ass," he said, and lowered himself into the chair.

"You're making a big mistake, Sheriff," Peter said. "That man is a stone cold killer. With my own eyes I saw him stab a woman and laugh about it."

Curtis shook his head in disgust.

"Gag him too," he said after they'd been tied, "so we don't have to listen to any of that crap."

"Oh, great," Leo said.

"Him too."

Leo's eyes went wide. "Me? Come on, Sheriff—"

But those were the last words Leo got out before Fletcher shoved a sock in his mouth and tied it tight with a bandana.

"Hope you can breathe in there," Fletcher snorted.

And then Fletcher stepped back, smiled, and joined the rest of the townsfolk of Little Chaparral at the back of the five-and-dime, where Sheriff Curtis was standing up on a makeshift stage, boards and milk crates, and raising his arms for quiet.

"I'm sure we all want to thank the Reverend Sanchez for suggesting this," Curtis said. "And again, with his help, I think we have gathered together a very special group here tonight. Now, despite that unfortunate interruption, I think this is going to be a wonderful, faith-affirming moment for all of us. And now I'm gonna let the reverend get on with it. Reverend Sanchez?"

Novarra stepped up next to Curtis and smiled as the room gave a polite burst of applause.

Peter's mind was racing. This was all Novarra's idea, he thought. I bet he helped pick—hell, he'd probably hand-picked—the people who were invited.

Peter had a sudden sick feeling that reached all the way down to the marrow of his bones. When the waves hit Fletcher's Five and Dime, it was going to be a massacre. And he and Leo were going to be the first to go.

DENVER, COLORADO

They were all eating dinner when Betty heard a car pulling up in front of the house. No, not a car, this sounded like a bigger vehicle of some kind. A truck.

A door slammed, and then she heard footsteps hurrying down the front walk.

Everyone else heard them too.

Mary bolted out of her chair and dashed out of the kitchen, Linda barely a step behind.

"It's Dad!" she yelled.

"Finally," Connie cried. She threw her napkin down on the table as a big grin spread across her face.

"Don?" she said, hurrying after the girls.

Bert smiled and got up too. "Sounds like somebody's home," he said, heading for the front door along with Betty.

Dinner up to that moment had been a grim affair, filled with uncomfortable small talk about General Dooley and the coup, about what was and wasn't safe for them to do on their own, about how long it would take things to get back to normal.

"Maybe they won't get back to normal," Bert had quietly suggested. "Maybe the cardinal was right."

No one had said anything for a moment. Connie and the rest of the family tended to look the other way when Bert started getting a little too "religious" on them, and that's just what they did then.

The only sounds at the table for a good ten seconds had been those of chewing and swallowing.

Finally, Connie spoke up.

"I'm sure there's a rational explanation for all of this," she'd said, and went on eating.

But Bert had noticed that no one at the table jumped up to offer any explanations, and not once during dinner did any of them address the most obvious topic of conversation: the empty chair at the head of the table. Don's chair. Connie and the girls had spent a fruitless afternoon searching for him, but had returned dispirited and disillusioned. Apparently, parts of the city were not as safe as they'd been led to believe.

Not that Bert pressed his sister too hard for details; he'd been fairly quiet all afternoon himself. But now that it sounded like Don was back, he hoped everyone would be in a better mood.

Only when the front door swung open, it wasn't Don.

It was the army.

Half a dozen soldiers, each of them younger, grimmer, and looking more menacing than the next, stood in the doorway. Each of them carried a rifle over his shoulder, and each wore a khaki-green uniform complete with combat helmet.

One stepped forward and spoke to Connie, who was now leaning on the door frame, her smile gone and her face a pasty white.

"Ma'am," he said, "I'm Corporal Caleb Josephs. Are you Mrs. Connie Mills?"

"I am. Is this about Don? Has something happened to him?"

"No, ma'am. I'm looking for a Bert Lyons."

Equal parts confusion and relief crossed Connie's face. "I—" She turned and looked at Bert, who looked as puzzled as she had.

"I'm Bert Lyons," he said, stepping forward.

"You were at the St. John's Cathedral yesterday evening, sir?"

"Early this morning, yesterday evening—yes. Me and a few thousand other people, I'd say."

The officer nodded. "Could you come with us please?"

"Why? What's this about?"

"I don't have that information, sir. I just need you to accompany us, please."

Bert frowned. "I'm not sure I want to do that," he said. "Unless you can give me a better reason."

"Sir." The soldier's voice, which up to that point had been crisply formal, took on an edge. "I don't need to give you a better reason. The state of Colorado is currently under martial law, and I am giving you an order to accompany us."

Bert locked eyes with the younger man. "And if I don't?"

"You will, sir. One way or another."

Connie stepped between the two men and stared at the soldiers.

"I want you all to get out of my house," she said.

Josephs ignored her.

"Mr. Lyons, I have my orders, and so do you. Please don't make this difficult, sir. Neither of us would enjoy it."

Watching him closely, Betty realized that wasn't quite true. There was something in his eyes that told her Josephs would enjoy making Bert's departure just as painfully difficult as it possibly could be.

Bert, she noticed, saw the same thing.

"All right," Bert said. "I'll come with you. How long will I be gone for?"

Josephs shook his head. "Again, sir, I'm afraid I don't have that information."

"Of course you don't."

Bert took a deep breath, and Betty could see how hard he was trying to keep himself under control. "Tell me this—do I need to pack a bag?"

"That won't be necessary."

The corporal stood aside then, and the soldiers parted so Bert could leave the house. Betty saw a green army truck parked at the curb, and another soldier standing in front of it, waiting.

Corporal Josephs cleared his throat. "Mr. Lyons?"

"Give me a minute." Bert turned to Betty. "I have no idea what this is about, but it can't be anything serious."

Betty looked at him with frightened eyes. "I hope so."

He hugged her. "I know so. I'll be back soon."

Then Bert let go of her, and turned to his sister.

"I'll be back," he said again, smiling at her and his nieces before walking out of the house.

Spinning on his heel, Corporal Josephs and the other soldiers followed.

INGLEWOOD AVENUE, LOS ANGELES

Nothing was ever easy.

The truck was only going thirty miles an hour, it was hiccuping worse than ever, and Jimmy had already taken one wrong turn and almost driven right into the fire. That had been a scary few minutes; there were too many abandoned cars in the street, not enough room to turn, and he kept thinking about what Lieutenant Rogers had said at the base.

"You can see that monster out there," Rogers had said about the fire, and Jimmy thought the lieutenant had nailed it. The thing was a monster, a hungry monster, and it was eating everything in sight.

When he finally got back on Inglewood, he made sure to say a couple of Hail Marys and to thank God for rescuing him. Going slow wasn't such a bad idea, he decided then. The last thing he wanted to do was somehow catch up with the convoy going north. Besides, the slower he went, the longer the engine would hold out.

He thought.

On the other hand . . .

Maybe he should just get as far away as he could from the fire, park the truck, and come back later for the guns. The flaw with that idea, though, was that he'd have to find someplace safe to park it, and as far as he could tell, there wasn't a safe place left on the planet. So it was Bel Air or bust.

The truck hiccuped and slowed again.

Jimmy checked the speedometer and groaned out loud.

Fifteen miles an hour? Christ, slow was one thing, but this was ridiculous. At this rate he might as well get out and push. But Bel Air was a long way off—and uphill to boot.

Something slammed into the back of the truck, smashing his head against the windshield and plowing the truck into a parked car.

"What the fuck . . ."

He looked into the driver's side mirror and saw a Toyota wedged up against the truck's rear fender.

That big guy—the same one from the base, the one who'd been chasing the kid—was climbing out of the driver's seat.

Jimmy slammed his hand on the steering wheel. "Goddamnit!" If that moron had fucked up the truck, he'd kill him.

What the hell, he'd kill him anyway.

Jimmy drew his pistol and opened the door.

The big guy was ten feet away and he looked mad.

Jimmy sighted down the barrel and pulled the trigger.

Click. Shit, he thought, no bullets.

He spun back into the seat, grabbed the wheel, and put the truck in reverse. It flew back and he kicked it into first and started moving forward. Reaching out to close the door, the big guy's hand closed over his.

"You killed my son," he said, looking up at Jimmy.

He grabbed Jimmy's shirt with his other hand and started dragging him out of the truck.

Jimmy shouted and tried to pull away, and the wheel spun in his hand. They were headed straight for a plate-glass window.

He spun the wheel again, and they turned onto a side street off Inglewood.

The fire was straight ahead of them, a block away.

"Sonuvabitch!" Jimmy shouted. "Let go! You're gonna get us both killed!"

"You killed my son," the big guy grunted, and began pulling himself into the truck.

Jimmy leaned back in the seat and kicked him in the knee.

Church grimaced, letting go of Jimmy's hand and grabbing him by the throat.

Jimmy gasped for breath and realized it wasn't just the pressure on his neck, but the fire. They were so close now that the cab of the truck was filling with smoke.

He reached down and pulled the grenade off his belt.

"This is a grenade," he said, choking out the words. "If I pull the pin—"

Church let go of his throat, ripped the grenade out of his hand and threw it out the window.

"Shit!" Jimmy jammed his foot up against the steering wheel and pushed back, flying into the passenger seat.

He looked down and blinked. The kid's gun was lying on the floor. He picked it up and fired. His aim was bad, though—the smoke, the heat—and the bullet caught the big guy in the shoulder. He howled in pain and grabbed the wound.

Jimmy reached behind him, opened the passenger door, and tumbled backward onto the hot cement just as the truck rolled forward into the blaze of fire and disappeared.

LITTLE CHAPARRAL, TEXAS

Sheriff Curtis talked about some of the neighborly things he'd seen people doing for each other over the last few years, and Kate Harter read a psalm. The sun went down, and Randy Fletcher and another man went around the room lighting candles.

Peter watched it all, feeling dread and horror growing in his gut like a cancer. He didn't know how Novarra had pulled off his masquerade, or how he had convinced the authorities that he'd died ten years ago, but he knew that if he and Leo didn't get out of there before the second wave hit, they'd be dead.

An hour or so had passed, all told, since they'd been tied up.

Any minute now, Peter thought.

And just as that thought occurred to him, Novarra rose to speak.

"I think the time has come for me to say a few words," he said. He smiled, and looked around the room.

"We've faced a lot together as a community over the past few years. We've experienced each other's triumphs"—he smiled at a boy sitting in the front row—"and shared each other's tragedies." He nodded toward Kate Harter, who bowed her head and began to cry softly.

"We've stuck by one another, and whenever I've had cause to be away from you, to be traveling"—and here he looked straight at Peter—"I've held you close, in my heart. I feel I've come to know all of you. The good and the bad."

There was a candle burning on the windowsill behind Novarra. Peter saw it flicker. And for a moment the dread and queasy anticipation that had taken up residence in his gut was replaced by something else.

Anger.

The crowd stirred, as if feeling it too.

Dave Harter snapped something at his wife.

Randy Fletcher turned to the man next to him and snarled.

Sheriff Curtis, who was standing to the rear of the crowd, directly between it and Peter and Leo, silently unholstered his weapon.

The second wave, Peter realized, had just passed through.

"Your cheap old man," Hugh Flagg said, getting to his feet. "Your cheap, penny-pinchin'—"

"Hush," Novarra said. "Hush."

He raised his arms over his head. "Be still."

And suddenly, everyone was: the inside of Fletcher's Five and Dime was silent as the grave. But the anger that had been so visible a minute ago was still there. Peter sensed it in the room, pulsing silently.

Novarra, he realized, was controlling it.

"As we have gathered here now, in the presence of a power greater than our own," Novarra said, and there was something different about his voice, something hypnotic, "I believe it only right that we stand up and acknowledge our own frailties. Who would like to go first? Anyone?" He looked around the room, and his gaze settled on a man Peter hadn't noticed before—a plump, freckled man in a crisp white shirt and a red bow tie.

"Frank?" Novarra prompted.

The man jerked to his feet like a puppet on a string.

"I have lusted after another woman. Other than my wife."

A leathery-skinned blond sitting next to Frank looked up at him with an expression of total surprise.

"That's not so bad, Frank," Novarra said. "That's only human. Only natural. I myself have felt lust, on certain occasions. As long as you haven't indulged that lust, why, everything's fine. No harm, no foul, as they say. Especially in the sight of the Lord."

Frank bowed his head and started to cry.

"You bastard," the woman said, jumping to her feet. "Who was it? Tell me it wasn't someone I know. Tell me—"

"Carla," Novarra said, "do you have something you'd like to add?"

The girl in a gingham dress stood up, and Frank's wife went wild.

"Your niece?" she yelled. She began hitting him.

Peter sensed the crowd eagerly, silently urging her on.

Hungry for the kill.

"Well," Novarra said. "At least we know now. We know. Some of us have fallen short of perfection. But that's all right, that's all right." He smiled. "Is there anyone else who has anything to share?"

"I got something," Deputy Ken said, and with that he turned around and shot Frank right in the face. Blood splattered everywhere as Frank fell. The girl in the gingham dress began crying.

"Hush, everyone," Novarra said softly, holding out his arms. "Hush."

Peter strained against his bonds and saw Leo doing the same.

"I can't abide this." Sheriff Curtis stepped forward. "Reverend, I'm sorry but I don't understand what you're doing here and I can't be a party to it."

"Rooting out those who don't belong," Novarra said. "That's what I'm doing."

Randy Fletcher stood up and pointed a finger at Peter and Leo.

"Them," he said. "They don't belong."

Almost as one, the crowd got to their feet.

"Now hold on," Curtis said. He raised his gun. "Let's not—"

Deputy Ken shot his weapon, and Curtis fell to the floor.

Hugh Flagg grabbed Ken around the neck and threw him to the ground. "What are you doing?" he yelled.

Novarra laughed out loud.

"Do as you will," he announced.

Leo stood up, the chair still tied to his back, and ran into one of the display cases in the middle of the aisle. It tumbled over with a huge crash, taking several others with it and knocking down displays all over the store.

Fletcher shouted and started toward them.

Peter got to his feet, intending to do what Leo had, but then stumbled and fell backward into the wall. Rolling over, he found himself face-to-face with Dave Harter.

Harter had a shit-eating grin on his face. "Where do you think you're goin', fella? Huh?"

Peter head-butted him, felt the satisfying thwack as his

forehead impacted Harter's nose. He did it again, before the man could stand up, and Harter fell back, stunned. His nose was gushing blood and his lower lip was split.

Harter shook his head, and rage filled his eyes. "You sonuvabitch, I'll kill you."

He got to his feet and kicked Peter in the head. Peter's vision blurred and blood trickled down his face.

Harter kicked him again, in the gut this time, and Peter felt the breath rush out of him and bile rise in his throat. He forced it back down, panicked. With the gag on, if he vomited, he would choke to death.

Harter reared his foot back for another kick, and then his face froze and he toppled to the ground.

There was a knife sticking out of his back.

Kate Harter stood over him, her eyes filled with tears and a madness that it hurt to look at.

"You bastard!" she screamed. "You were supposed to watch her! You were supposed to protect her! That was our daughter!"

She collapsed on the floor next to him, sobbing hysterically.

A shadow fell over Peter, and he braced himself for another assault. Instead he felt his bonds slip away.

He looked up and saw Leo standing over him, holding a sharp-looking hunting knife in his hands.

"Let's get the hell out of here," Leo said.

He turned toward the door.

Novarra was standing in front of him.

Before Leo could move a muscle, Novarra raised his hand. Metal flashed. Leo went down.

Novarra loomed over him. The spike was in his hand.

"Policeman," he said. "We have some unfinished business."

"Unfinished business," Peter said, "is right."

He swung his legs in an arc, sweeping Novarra's feet out from under him and sending him crashing. He was on top of him in a flash, pinning the man's hands over his head.

The spike dropped to the floor.

"What the hell did you do back there to all those people?" Peter yelled.

Novarra smiled. "The same thing I did to you."

"And what's that supposed to mean?"

"Don't tell me you've forgotten already," Novarra said, looking into his eyes. "Ah," he whispered. "You *have* forgotten. That's why it took you so long to come, isn't it?"

Peter was about to reply when he saw Novarra's gaze focus on something over his shoulder, but before he could turn around, something hard smashed into his head and he fell to the side.

Grabbing his head, he looked up and saw big Randy Fletcher standing over him, holding a shovel.

"He doesn't belong here, Randy," Novarra said, getting to his feet. "Does he!"

Fletcher raised the shovel again, this time like a spear, and brought it down hard. Peter rolled, and the point of the shovel buried itself in the floor three inches to the right of his head.

Fletcher grunted and started to pull it out. Peter grabbed the handle where metal met wood and yanked it away. Fletcher stumbled, and Peter jumped to his feet and buried the wooden end in his gut.

Fletcher went down, gasping for breath, and Peter took the shovel. Raising it over his head, he slammed Fletcher in the face. There was a sickening thwack and Fletcher lay still.

Peter turned and saw Novarra, still smiling. Deputy Ken was coming up from behind him. He held a gun.

Before Peter could move, he felt something sharp slam into his left leg. He howled with pain and dropped the shovel. Looking down, he saw a nail sticking out of his leg.

"Lost my revolver," Ken said, still coming, "but this oughta do the trick." He held up the nail gun again and shot.

Peter lurched ahead and fell to the ground just as another nail, and then another, slammed into the wall behind him.

He scrambled like a three-legged crab, darting away from Ken and down one of the aisles, toward the far side of the store.

"Stand still!" Ken yelled, charging after him.

Peter kept moving, eyes scanning the shelves for something he might use as a weapon. Cold cereal, hot cereal, laundry detergent, bleach—nothing.

He reached the end of the aisle and turned left into another. Toilet paper, napkins—nothing.

He turned down another aisle, heading back the way he'd come. Shampoo, hair spray—nothing.

He turned left again, and Novarra was right in front of him.

"How's the leg, policeman?"

Peter stumbled backward and knocked over a display behind him, and then he was falling too, landing on his back two aisles over—

Right in the middle of sporting goods. He saw a bat.

Deputy Ken turned the corner and smiled. He raised the nail gun.

Peter swung and caught him right between the eyes. Ken went down, dropping the gun as both hands went to his face.

Peter lunged forward and grabbed the gun. He held it on Navarro and got to his feet.

"Looks like it's you and me now," he said.

"That's right, policeman. You and me."

Novarra tossed the spike back and forth between his hands.

"Tell me," Peter said. "What happened that night?"

Novarra started laughing.

Peter took three quick steps forward and slammed the gun into his face—pushing him back against a wall. He hit it hard as Peter brought his knee up into his chest. Novarra grunted and dropped the spike. Peter slammed him back into the wall again, then grabbed Novarra's right arm, stretched it out along the wall, and drove a nail right through his palm, pinning it to the wall.

Novarra screamed.

Peter grabbed his left arm and did the same thing. Twice. Then he stepped back, and smiled.

"All right, you sonuvabitch. I want some answers."

Novarra was cringing in pain, his body twisting as he tried not to black out.

Then he shook his head—once, twice—and he seemed to come around. He looked to his left, then to his right. Then he looked straight at Peter, his eyes focused and clear.

"I don't like this position," he said, in the same matter-of-fact tone he might use to discuss the weather. "I don't like this position at all. It reminds me of something."

Peter was about to speak when Novarra strained and started to lean forward, trying to pull his hands free.

"I wouldn't do that if I were you," Peter said. "It's gonna hurt like a—"

"You're not me, policeman," Novarra replied, and, grunting, braced his feet against the wall and strained, ripping his right hand free.

Peter almost dropped the nail gun where he stood.

Novarra ripped his left hand free, and collapsed to the floor, a good half inch of skin and gore still stuck to the nails on the wall.

Peter couldn't imagine what sort of pain the man was feeling or how he'd found the strength to do that, or how he was even still conscious, still breathing, and . . .

Climbing to his feet.

"That hurt," Novarra said, and the look in his eyes was pure rage.

Before Peter could move, Novarra crossed the distance between them and backhanded him across the face.

Peter had never been hit so hard in his life. He went flying six feet in the air across the room and landed on his back.

When he opened his eyes, he saw stars everywhere, and Novarra leaning over him.

"You want to know what happened that night?" Novarra said. "Here."

Peter saw the spike, looming above him.

And then his world exploded.

Novarra stood caught in the glare of their headlights, the spike raised over his head.

A body lay at his feet.

"Police!" *Kelly shouted.* "Police officer! Step back from the girl!"

"You heard the man," *Peter shouted, drawing his gun.* "Step back!"

They ran down the alley towards Novarra, just the way it had happened that night. Peter saw himself wave Novarra away from the girl, saw Novarra drop the spike to the ground, saw himself look at the man and—

Freeze.

Like a statue.

"Like what you see?" *he heard Novarra ask.*

This was where, for the last six months, Peter's memory of what had happened that night ended.

Now at last, the scene played on.

Peter stood immobile over Novarra.

"Pete!" *Kelly shouted.* "Pete, what the hell are you doing? Drop that thing and cuff him. I got him covered. Cuff him."

But Peter didn't cuff him.

He kept staring at the spike.

And then . . .

"Look at me."

Peter turned his head away from the spike—reluctantly, it seemed—and towards Novarra. The two men locked eyes.

"That's it." *That was Kelly, stepping forward, holding his gun out in front of him, pointing it at Novarra. "I don't know what the hell's going on here, Mister, what you're doing to him, but I want you to lie flat on the ground, on your stomach, now. Do it." Kelly waved his gun. "Do it!"*

Novarra smiled and turned to Peter.

"Shoot him," he said.

Still holding the spike in his left hand, Peter raised his gun in his right and shot Kelly in the forehead.

Kelly's gun went off as he fell; Peter saw himself fall backward onto the ground.

Peter opened his eyes. He was flat on his back in Fletcher's.

Novarra stood ten feet away, holding the spike in one hand and flexing the fingers of the other.

He was staring at Peter.

"So now you know, policeman," he said, shifting the spike into his other hand and flexing the fingers of his free one. "Now you can die a happy man."

Peter felt numb. He felt sick. He had shot Kelly himself, after all, and it didn't even matter that somehow Novarra had made him do it.

A jumble of thoughts ran through his head. And then his brain registered what he was seeing before him.

It was Novarra's hands: There were no visible wounds on either one of them.

That's impossible, he thought, then realized he was looking at a man who was supposed to be dead but wasn't, a man who had made him shoot his own partner, a man who could convince a whole town to commit suicide. Maybe he wasn't looking at a man at all.

"What the hell are you?" Peter whispered.

Novarra shook his head. "No more questions."

Bending down, he picked Peter up by the collar and threw him halfway across the room.

Peter bounced off the top of a display rack and into another, knocking over both and landing on the floor in the middle of a sea of paintbrushes, rollers, and sandpaper. He stumbled to his feet in time to catch another backhanded slap from Novarra that sent him flying again, stumbling over the paint supplies and landing square on his ass amidst a sea of cereal boxes.

His hand found a pot, and he threw it at Novarra, who dodged and kept coming.

Peter got to his feet again, pushed over the display case in front of him and lunged into the next aisle, which contained shampoo and hair spray, among other things. The last aisle.

In front of him was the wall.

"End of the line, policeman," Novarra said.

Peter turned and saw the man coming.

Again he searched wildly for something to use as a weapon.

A lit candle, burned down almost to the wick, was on top of a display case a few feet away.

Peter broke into a big grin.

"I'm so glad to see you're enjoying this," Novarra said. "Perhaps we can draw it out a few minutes longer."

Peter grabbed the candle and held it out in front of him.

Novarra was ten feet away.

"Shouldn't that be a clove of garlic, or a cross, or something? Not that it would matter."

"This'll do," Peter said. He reached down and flicked off the top of a hair spray can with his free hand, brought it up before him and held up the candle.

Novarra frowned. "What are you—"

Peter depressed the aerosol button, and the spray blossomed into a jet of flame.

Novarra screamed. And burned.

He fell backward, and Peter stepped forward, still spraying, feeling the candle melt in his hand from the heat of the flame, wondering how long he had before it went out.

Novarra's clothes were on fire, his face was on fire, and he was twitching and screaming like a man with his finger caught in an electric socket.

He fell to the floor and tried to get up, and Peter kept spraying, until the smell of burning flesh was almost more than he could stand, until there was no more spray in the can.

The blackened husk that had been Novarra lay still on the floor before him, his skin still sizzling and crisping where the flames searched for something left to burn.

Peter looked up then, and realized that Novarra wasn't the only thing on fire.

The whole building was burning.

NORTHEAST TEXAS

Thomas wobbled and almost fell.

Then he caught himself and took another step forward.

One step at a time, that's how you ran a marathon, he'd always heard people say. That's how you climbed a mountain. That's how you got through life after your daughter was killed.

With the car dead, it was also how he had to reach his next destination. He couldn't wait the hours before the power came back; it might be too late then. He had to get there, and he had to get there now. Pain in his arm where the Johannsen woman had hit him, an empty hole in his stomach where hunger lived, a cramp in the calf of his right leg—but none of it mattered.

One step at a time. A step. A step. Another step.

The land was flat.

The road was empty.

After a while, in the pitch-blackness before him, he saw a glimmer of light. Enough that, when he came to the sign and stood next to it, he could read the letters.

WELCOME TO LITTLE CHAPARRAL

He smelled smoke then, and knew the light was coming from a fire. Praying he wasn't too late, he stumbled forward.

Peter found Leo lying on the floor. There was a pulse.

His friend was still alive.

"Thank God," he said, shaking him. "Leo! Leo! Come on!"

Out cold.

Peter reached under his arms and dragged him out of the five-and-dime and into the middle of the street. Then he went back into the burning building and searched for survivors.

He didn't find any, but he came upon Curtis's gun, still wrapped in the sheriff's hand.

Prying it loose, he started out of the building, and a few feet past the burned husk of Novarra's body he came upon the spike.

It lay on the ground, still glistening in the light from the fire. There was something almost hypnotic about the way the colors pulsed in time with the dancing flames—it beckoned to him.

Picking it up, he turned to go.

A man was standing in the smoky aisle before him.

Peter squinted. Was it a survivor? Someone he'd missed in the fire? No. It was an old man he hadn't seen before, a man who—

The man raised a shaky arm and pointed a gun at him.

Dropping the spike, Peter drew his weapon. "Don't—"

The man fired.

DENVER, COLORADO

After the soldiers left, everyone wore the same stunned expression Betty knew was pasted across her face. Connie went to the liquor cabinet, poured herself a drink and poured one for Betty too.

Betty swirled her drink and said, "They just want to talk to him," as if to reassure herself.

But Connie wondered why they needed to take him away under armed guard.

Her daughter Linda saw her worried expression. "It's the U.S. Army, Mom," she said. "We're all Americans. They're not going to hurt him or anything."

Betty wasn't so sure. She remembered the look in Corporal Josephs's eyes.

Connie, curious about what had actually happened in the cathedral, asked the others what they thought. Her other daughter, Mary, wondered what had blown out all the candles. It couldn't have been the wind because the door was closed.

Then Linda turned to Betty and said: "Who's Harold?"

Betty felt her face freeze.

"I mean, I heard you say that name in the church," Linda said.

Connie looked at both her daughters and said, "Girls, could you please excuse us?"

Linda gave her an apologetic look and left the room along with her sister.

"I'm sorry about that," Connie told her. "They don't know—about your husband." She looked at Betty sympathetically. "Bert told me."

Betty was surprised. "He told you? About Harold?" She couldn't believe it.

"Don't be upset," Connie said quickly. "After the cathedral, I practically forced Bert to talk about it—about why you were so upset. He didn't tell me much, though," she added. "I mean, no details or anything. Just that he'd been hitting you—abusing you—for a long time. And you left him."

Betty almost smiled. Then Bert didn't really tell you anything, did he? she thought.

Not that Bert knew all, or even a lot, of Harold's nasty little secrets. No, there were things about her late husband that Betty would never tell anyone, things she would take to the grave. And in a sick little way—a way that Harold himself would be proud of—that was only right, only fair. The sanctity of the marriage vow, she thought. Just like Harold always used to say.

Till death do us part.

"I'd really rather not talk about it," she said. Connie nodded. A few minutes later she excused herself and went up to bed.

Betty stayed where she was and looked at the door. Part of her was hoping that all the army wanted from Bert was a chance to talk to him about what had gone on in the cathedral. And if that was the case, he might just be back tonight.

She walked over to the bookshelf, looking for something to read, something to distract her and take her mind off things while she waited. But there were slim pickings in the Mills family library. Someone in the house was a big

Jonathan Kellerman fan, but that hardly seemed the kind of thing she was looking for. There were a lot of nonfiction books on parenting, as well as a handful of more recent bestsellers. Maybe one of those would do the trick. She picked up one and started reading, and put it down a few pages in. She flipped through a second, and that didn't interest her either.

But when she went into the kitchen to freshen up the ice in her drink, she saw a dog-eared copy of *Wuthering Heights* sitting on the counter. She'd loved the movie, and had always meant to read the book, but had never gotten around to it. She took it back into the living room and curled up in her chair.

She quickly realized, though, that the book was very different from the movie.

Thirty pages in, she got impatient. She started skimming, trying to find her favorite Cathy and Heathcliff moments from the movie—those big, mushy, romantic scenes, like the one where he cursed her and begged her to haunt him after she died—

Betty stopped. She dropped the book like it was on fire.

Begged her to haunt him after she died?

Harold's face came to her mind.

She realized then that she'd been kidding herself the last couple hours. She wasn't forcing herself to stay awake in the hope that Bert would come back. She didn't want to sleep because when she closed her eyes, she knew that Harold would come back.

He would be waiting for her, just like he always was.

Betty went into the kitchen, made herself a cup of coffee, and sat down at the kitchen table to wait for Bert. But at some point during the night her eyes must have closed, because the next thing she knew, she was dreaming again.

She was killing Nick.

She had a gun in her hand, and he was lying on the ground,

holding his hand to his stomach, and crying, and begging, asking her why she was doing this, and please, he had kids, please don't kill him. But to her horror, she wasn't listening at all. She was raising the gun and pressing it to his forehead and—

Bang.

She was looking at a copy of the *Asheville Herald*, at a small headline halfway down the front page which said SECURITY GUARD KILLED IN BOTCHED ROBBERY, and she folded up the paper and walked from the kitchen into the bedroom, where she saw herself lying in her bed, and she threw the paper down and said:

"Hey, your fat friend made the news."

And someone screamed and—

Bam, she was holding a bloody baseball bat and looking at Lou lying on the ground and dragging him into the trunk of the car and then stuffing a sock down his throat and tying and gagging him and down went the trunk and slam—

She was smacking her hand down on the desk and screaming, "Where is that goddamn magazine? What the hell did you do with it?" and striding right into the kitchen shouting things at the top of her lungs and she looked up and saw—

Herself, cowering, stumbling backward into the kitchen counter.

"You are going to have to be punished," she heard herself say, only it wasn't her voice, it was Harold's, and it was happening again. Somehow she was in his head, seeing what he did, feeling like he did, reliving first the killings and now this, the last few seconds of his life.

"The only question is how—" he said, charging forward, and Betty saw herself whip out the knife from behind her back, the big shiny bread knife and—

Cut.

Darkness.

It was over. All over.

But then . . .

Gray sky, coming in the living room window of their house in Asheville.

Opening his eyes.

Sitting up in the middle of the living room floor. Rubbing at his throat. Climbing to his feet, kicking over the coffee table. Where are you hiding, bitch? Slamming open the office door and the guest room. Don't think I won't find you! Throwing open the bedroom door, seeing the knife and spatters of red leading into the closet and clenching his fists and yanking that open, the suitcases were gone, and reaching into his pocket and —

Where is it?

Where is it?

Where is it?

And crash—

Hand right through the glass of the back door and climbing into the car and— —

Putting the pedal to the floor and—

Green and white highway signs whizzing by—

NASHVILLE

ST. LOUIS

KANSAS CITY

Nose to the ground, hot on the trail, a bloodhound who had the scent of his bitch locked down cold and was never letting go.

Till death do us part.

Betty jerked awake. Sweat covered her forehead, and her eyes darted around the room. She was still at the kitchen table. A butcher's block was in front of her and she grabbed a knife.

The front door quietly clicked open.

She stood up, knife in hand, shaking and fully expecting to see Harold come through the door.

I did it once, she told herself. I can do it again.

Bert walked into the kitchen.

Betty jerked in fear and dropped the knife. Her hands went to her face and she ran into his arms, crying.

"Hey," he said. "What's going on? Are you all right?"

"I am now," she whispered, wiping away tears and trying to get the dream out of her mind. "Just another bad dream."

She looked down and noticed he had a bandage on his right arm.

"What's this?" she said, breaking their embrace and pulling away.

"They took blood from me," he said, shrugging.

"Are you serious?" She looked in his eyes. "Why?"

"I don't know. They didn't say. They just—" He shook his head. "There's a military hospital at the edge of town. That's where they brought us. There were around two dozen people there. Everyone had been at the cathedral. They asked questions. They wanted to know what we'd gone through, how we'd felt. Then— Then they had a nurse come in and take some blood, and they brought us back. That was it."

"You're all right?" Betty asked.

"I'm fine. What about you?"

She bit her lip and looked away. "I'm okay now."

"Your dream . . . it was about Harold?"

She nodded. "It was the worst one yet."

"Do you want to talk about it?"

She shook her head firmly. She didn't want to talk about it, she didn't even want to think about it, because the idea that the morning after she'd cut Harold's throat he'd somehow gotten up and decided to come chasing after her was just too crazy to consider, too scary to contemplate, and way, way too much for her to handle. She needed to sleep, and now that Bert was back, she hoped she could. At least for a while. Without dreaming.

"Let's go upstairs," she said. "We can talk later."

She took his hand.

"Wait a second," he said. "There's something I want to talk about now. It was on my mind all day, and when I didn't know whether I was coming back or not, I was kicking myself for not saying anything before." He sat her down. "This morning—yesterday morning now," Bert said. "I had a dream . . ."

And when he was done talking about his dream, Betty shut her eyes, took a deep breath, and told him about hers.

LOS ANGELES AIR FORCE BASE

For the second time in the last few days, Jimmy was watching a Burger King burn. No more flame-broiled whoppers after this, he thought.

He was standing in front of the base's main building, staring down El Segundo toward the 405 overpass. The fire was just on the other side of it, and he could feel the heat coming off it. The smoke was gathering like dark clouds in the sky, and smoky fog covered the ground.

Jimmy judged it would be about ten minutes before the base was in flames.

He ran into the main building, darting from office to office and checking refrigerators and desk drawers for supplies that might have been left behind. He was leaving L.A., leaving behind his dreams of Lil' Kim and the gangsta life, maybe for now, maybe forever. Or at least until he could find a way to come back to the city without having to worry about what would happen if he crossed Omar's path.

Jimmy knew that Omar had let him live because he'd promised to get those guns. Without them, he'd be killed in no time.

In fact, he realized, picturing Omar's face and his nasty little smile, even if he had brought back the guns, he probably would have ended up dead anyway.

So maybe everything had worked out for the best, he thought. At least he'd gotten rid of that big guy. That pain in the ass was toast now—literally.

Jimmy leaped down the stairs to Command & Control and burst into the kitchen. In the refrigerator, he found a six-pack of Dr Pepper. In a cabinet, he found a box of Ritz crackers. He shoved both into his pack and dashed upstairs and out of the building.

An L.A. Metro bus with a big number 18 spray-painted on its side was parked right next to the gate.

"Oh, Christ," Jimmy said, taking a step back into the shadows. There went his wheels. He'd found a car with the keys still in it a few blocks from the base and parked it in the lot. But with the bus blocking the way, he'd have to go on foot for a while.

"Yo. Hands up," someone shouted from behind him.

Jimmy raised his hands. Shit, he thought. But when he turned around, he let out a huge sigh of relief.

It was Hector.

"Hey, soldier." Hector smiled. "Where is everybody?"

Jimmy shook his head. "They evacuated before I could get the guns."

Hector's face fell. "Oh, man," he said, shaking his head. "That's not good."

"I know," Jimmy said. He glanced over his shoulder.

People were getting out of the bus. One girl in jeans. Another in jean shorts. A big guy in a leather jacket.

Omar.

"Hector . . ." Jimmy started pleading. "You got to get me out of here, man."

"Shit." Hector stepped back. "I wish I could, man, but Omar, he wanted to come check up on you. I can't take a chance on him finding out I let you walk." Hector shrugged. "Nothing I can do. Sorry."

Jimmy felt his stomach flip over. This was not good.

Seeing them in the shadows, Omar swaggered up with a girl on each arm. Reaching them, he detached the girls gently, and turned to Jimmy.

"Soldier boy," he said, looking around. "I don't see any guns, man."

Jimmy offered a weak smile. "I know. Listen—"

"Ah." Omar held up a hand. "Just tell me. No guns?"

Jimmy nodded. "No guns, but—"

Omar drew a pistol and shot him without a thought.

LAS VEGAS, NEVADA

Claire's legs were wrapped tight around Danny's body. It was just what he'd dreamed of, ever since that lap dance back at the club.

Well, all right. Maybe it wasn't *exactly* what he'd dreamed of. Maybe things hadn't turned out quite the way he'd imagined them. But then, what did he expect?

After all, she wasn't Claire, really. She never had been.

And now, he wasn't Danny either.

Now he was the tiger.

How she had done it, he didn't know. All he knew was that one minute he was Danny, pissing his pants as he watched the tiger spring through the air toward him, feeling it slam into his chest, smelling its hot, foul breath, sensing his neck twist and something cut deep into his throat, and it was all happening too fast to do anything. And then he remembered seeing Claire leaning over him before everything went dark.

When he'd opened his eyes a moment later, his first thought was that something heavy had fallen on him. A rolled-up carpet. A chair. A fat man. But he looked up and saw Claire, kneeling next to him, holding her knife, with blood shining on its steel edge.

Danny had the sudden, awful feeling that he knew exactly whose blood it was. He tried to stand up. He only got as far as his hands and knees. Except he had no knees. He had no hands.

He had claws. Claws covered with blood and bits of flesh. Danny screamed.

What came out was a roar.

He tried again to get to his feet and stumbled. His nose rubbed against something warm and wet and rubbery, and he looked down and saw his own half-eaten face looking up at him.

And then he lost it. Completely and utterly. Images whipped through his mind—New York City, the trading floor, the strip club, his cousin Zeke, the motel, Vegas Vic, the tiger—and he felt an incredible sense of despair, worse than when he'd lost all his money. If he could have cried, he would have. Instead he just whimpered, and prayed there was a God who could somehow give him a do-over on the last few days.

Only he had no voice, so God couldn't hear his prayers.

When the world came back into focus, Claire was staring at him.

"Don't be scared, Danny," she said. "It's all going to feel a bit strange at first."

Strange wasn't the half of it, Danny thought. He took a step forward and realized the great weight he'd felt on him before was his own body. How heavy was he? He tried to remember how big tigers were—700, 800, 900 pounds? Seven, eight feet?

He had no idea. But however much he weighed, he didn't feel a bit of it when he moved. His every move was effortless. He even felt, for the first time in his life, graceful.

And thirsty. He bent down to the stream running next to the trees and drank. No, not drank. He lapped up the water with his tongue, which felt oddly natural to him.

Again, strange.

"Come here, Danny," Claire said.

In the back of his mind he remembered that he was angry at Claire, but he couldn't quite recall why. He padded over to her, feeling the strength coiled in his legs and realizing how powerful he was in this new body. Maybe this wasn't such a bad thing after all. Maybe—

Claire swung one leg over his back and mounted him. Her legs coiled tight around his body, and they strode onto the Strip, heading south.

It soon became obvious that unlike their previous wanderings, this time Claire had a definite destination in mind.

West.

Out of the city.

Which was not a moment too soon for him. The smells were unbearable to him now—the fire, the smoke, the foul air. He longed for the clean scents of the desert. Somehow the tiger's memory—what there was of it—was open to him. He knew that it had been a regular visitor to a specially constructed wilderness area outside Vegas, where it was able to run and hunt underneath the open sky. He pulled the memory of that place from within the dim recesses of the tiger's brain and savored it, allowing himself to get lost within it.

When he looked up, they were well outside the city and into the desert. The world was still. The only noises came from the shuffle of a multitude of shoes against the highway blacktop.

Claire's army.

The sky was pitch-dark, but to Danny the road and everything around it was as plain as daylight. He saw a jackrabbit crest a hill off to his right and stand a moment, nose twitching. As far off as it was, Danny had the crazy idea that he could smell it. Suddenly it froze, and a split second later shot out of sight.

Danny realized his crazy idea wasn't so crazy after all. He'd bet money that the rabbit had smelled him too.

A few hours on, he saw a light ahead of him on the highway. Arc lights, illuminating the road.

He growled in his throat.

"Don't worry," Claire said. She reached down to pat his neck. "I see them."

They drew closer, and what had been fuzzy a few moments earlier became distinct: two green canvas trucks, parked alongside the road. Green sawhorses were stretched out across the highway, the arc lights shining down on them. A half-dozen uniformed soldiers stood at those barricades, and several large tents were pitched in the desert off the right shoulder of the road.

The soldiers could see them too. Danny saw one of them holding a pair of binoculars to his eyes, lower them, and dart over to a tent. Not more than fifteen seconds later the first soldier and a second, older man popped out of the tent. The second took the binoculars and stared at them.

Danny could almost read his lips:

"What the hell?"

By the time they reached the line of soldiers, the small camp was wide awake.

Lettering on the side of the trucks read: NEVADA NATIONAL GUARD.

The older man stepped forward as they approached.

"All right, everyone, stop where you are." He tried to sound forceful, but to Danny's ears—his new, highly sensitive ears—he sounded strained and scared. And confused; no doubt about it.

It was the middle of the night, and they were a pack of Las Vegas refugees standing on the highway in front of him. Led by a woman riding a white tiger.

"Everyone halt. This border is closed by order of the Nevada governor."

"We're going to Los Angeles," Claire said.

Some of the soldiers shook their heads and whispered to each other. Was she serious? Going to Los Angeles? Nobody went to Los Angeles.

The commander raised a hand. "Quiet."

He turned to Claire.

"Listen, lady, I don't know what you think you're doing—" he paused and looked around at the legion of people standing behind her "—but you and all your people are going to have to turn around and go back where you came from."

A thin soldier smiled and poked out of his friends. "Gotta be Vegas, Sarge. Look at that tiger. Maybe they're part of the Siegfried & Roy Act."

A few troops broke out laughing.

"Enough, Carter," the sergeant said without turning.

Claire stared into the sergeant's eyes.

"We're going to Los Angeles," she said again. Giving Danny a squeeze with her legs, he started forward.

The sergeant held up his arms. "No, ma'am. I'm afraid you're not. You're going to have to turn around."

Danny and Claire kept moving forward.

"Carter!"

The sergeant snapped his fingers, and Carter stepped forward, his face serious now and his rifle raised.

The sergeant eyed Claire. "I won't ask again."

Claire didn't even stop.

Throwing a finger forward, she turned to the people behind her and said two simple words:

"Kill them."

Her army started to advance.

The sergeant's eyes widened.

Danny could almost read his thoughts: the people approaching him were unarmed. How could he fire on them? How could he order his soldiers to kill innocent people? It would be murder.

The soldiers were puzzled too. There were twenty-eight of them altogether; Danny had by now noted their number and position. They all had their rifles raised and he could smell each of them; their aftershaves, their sweat. They were confused. They didn't know what to do. They were looking to their sergeant.

The sergeant took a step backward.

Claire's cop with the ear collection on his belt was at the front of the line. The sergeant waited until he was almost on top of him, then fired. The bullet missed and struck the gondolier and he went down.

When he did, the trance was broken. Soldiers in the first line fired.

Claire's people screamed and charged, even as bullets riddled their bodies.

Danny roared.

With that roar, Claire jumped off and in two quick leaps Danny was among the soldiers. He decapitated one with a single swipe of his claw, and blood shot high in the air like a geyser.

Danny turned and roared again. Another soldier was right there, a boy who looked too young to be in the army. There was a shocked expression on his face and before he could raise his gun, Danny sprang forward and sent him sprawling to the ground.

Bones cracked as he landed on the soldier's chest. Jaws agape, Danny ripped the boy's face away and swallowed thick chunks of meat.

Mmmm. Tasty. He sat down on the road and began to chew. Around him, the screaming continued for a good long while.

NEAR ALBUQUERQUE, NEW MEXICO

Kerry heard a soft bang and opened her eyes.

The room was pitch-black and for a second she was completely disoriented.

Then she remembered she was in Williams House. Troubled kids. Peggy's room. She had gone to sleep at noon, and it seemed a lot later now.

Moving her head slowly, she adjusted her eyes to the darkness.

Someone else was in the room. Someone standing by the dresser, with its back to her, sliding the drawers open and going through them one by one.

Kerry couldn't tell who the intruder was from behind. One of the girls from the house, going through Peggy's things? A stranger, ransacking all the rooms? Should she scream? Pretend she was still asleep?

The person at the dresser turned, and Kerry saw it was a girl. She held something shiny in her hand, and it glinted in the darkness.

A knife.

The girl walked over to the bed, looking not at Kerry but at the wall.

Then she sat down on the bed and put the knife to Kerry's throat.

"Easy," she hissed. "Scream and you die."

Kerry swallowed hard. "I won't scream," she whispered. "Please, don't hurt me."

"You cry out, and I'll kill you. They might get me, but I'll kill you first."

The girl sounded as frightened as Kerry felt.

Kerry looked up, squinting into the darkness, and recognized the girl.

"You're Peggy."

Still alive, just like Roger had said, but looking much the worse for wear. Her face was covered with dirt and bruises, her glasses were bent, and her hair was a scraggly mess.

"Yeah," Peggy said, her voice trembling. "Who the hell are you? What are you doing in my room?"

The knife dug in farther.

"Talk."

Swallowing hard, Kerry told her how she'd run away from her dad, how she'd come to Williams House, and that she'd paid for it with the last of her amphetamines. Then she told her that Erica had brought her into the room to sleep.

"But I don't want to stay here," Kerry said, realizing as she said it that it was the truth. "I want to get out of here."

Peggy didn't move.

"I'm serious," Kerry said. "I have to find my dad. I won't scream."

Peggy shook her head. "I don't know," she said.

Voices and footsteps came from outside in the hall.

"Somebody's coming," Peggy said. She pressed the knife harder against Kerry's throat.

"Quiet. I mean it."

The doorknob turned.

The knife at her throat wavered.

"Hide," Kerry whispered. "Under the bed!"

Peggy dove for the floor.

The door opened and the light flicked on.

Roger and Jackie were standing in the doorway.

"Shit," Roger said. "She *is* here."

Kerry sat up and rubbed her eyes, pretending she'd just woken up. "Huh?"

"We're lookin' for a little privacy," Roger said.

He had one arm around Jackie's waist. She giggled.

"Never mind, we'll try the other house—"

He reached for the light switch.

"Wait," Jackie said.

She pointed to the dresser, where the drawers were still open. "What are you going through them drawers for?"

"Huh? Oh." Kerry yawned, trying to buy time. Her mind raced. "Just curious, you know?"

Jackie frowned. Roger nibbled on the back of her neck.

"Come on," he said. "Let's go."

Jackie pushed him away. "Hold off." She looked at Kerry. "You didn't find any keys, did you?"

Kerry shook her head.

"Well, if you do, I want 'em. Fatty had a set of keys to just about everything around here."

"Okay." Kerry nodded. "Sure. I'll look around."

Roger pulled Jackie again, and this time she went with him. He shut off the lights, then closed the door.

Kerry listened to the two of them laughing and giggling as they made their way to the other bunkhouse. A door slammed closed.

She waited a moment. "Okay," she whispered, getting to her feet. "I think it's safe."

Peggy slithered out from underneath the bed, a grimace on her face as she stood up.

"What's the matter?" Kerry asked.

"My back—where the car hit me. It hurts like hell."

"Let me see," Kerry said, reaching for the light.

"No!" Peggy said quickly. "No lights. It'll be all right, I just want to get out of here, find a doctor."

"Then why did you come back?"

"For the car. I can't walk that far."

"But . . ." Kerry shook her head. "Jackie has the keys."

"One set of keys. Not the only one."

Peggy walked over to the bed and jumped on it. She pulled out the bottom two thumbtacks holding up the Ani DeFranco poster and lifted it away from the wall.

"C'mere and hold this," she said to Kerry.

Kerry knelt next to her on the bed and held the poster. There was a hole in the wall behind it.

Peggy reached inside and grabbed hold of something—a string, Kerry saw, tied to a nail at the back of the hole. Peggy pulled on the string and something jangled. A second later she was holding a big set of keys. She untied the string and put the keys in her pocket.

Pinning the poster back to the wall, she looked at Kerry.

"Okay," she said. "Thanks, and thanks for not telling them I was here."

"No problem."

Peggy moved toward the door.

"Wait," Kerry said. "Take me with you."

They circled around the back of the main house, not wanting to chance running into anyone on the path. Ahead of them Kerry saw the car parked up on the lawn and started toward it.

"Shit."

Peggy put out a hand, stopping Kerry in her tracks. She pointed up toward the main house, where lights were still on in the front room.

"We better wait," Peggy said.

Kerry nodded, and the two of them crouched down in the darkness.

"So I don't get it," Peggy said after a while. "You run away from your dad, and now you want to go find him again?"

Kerry sighed and tried to explain: the last six months of her life, how crazy they'd been, the fights she and her mom had been having, the nightmares—

She stopped short.

"What's the matter?" Peggy asked.

Kerry didn't know quite how to answer, because she'd just realized that tonight, for the first time in a long, long while, she hadn't dreamed at all. No Mudge Pond. No John Topher. No bodies floating up in the middle of the lake.

"Nothing," she said. "Nothing's the matter."

Then Peggy told Kerry about Williams House. She'd been brought there as an orphan, had been there six years, and the other girls hated her because she was Mrs. Golding's favorite.

"I sure hope she's all right," Peggy said.

Kerry took a deep breath and wondered if she should tell her about the walk-in refrigerator, but just then the last of the house lights flickered out.

They stood up and walked quietly down the drive to where the car was parked.

Peggy went around the driver's side, Kerry to the passenger side.

Peggy opened the front door, and found Jackie sitting in the front seat.

Peggy jumped back.

"You stupid cow," Jackie sneered. "I can't believe you came back."

Kerry gasped, turned and ran.

Right into Roger, who came out from behind the bushes. He grabbed her by the arm. "Hey, look at this."

Jackie got out of the car, watching Kerry.

"I thought you might find those keys and get the idea to take off," she said. She turned to Peggy and smiled. "Looks like we get two birds with one stone."

Peggy pulled the knife out of her belt. "Get out of the way."

Jackie laughed. "Is that for real?"

"You're damn right it's real."

Kerry heard voices behind her and the porch lights clicked on.

"What's going on?" someone called out.

"Our favorite fatty is back," Jackie yelled. "Come and see!"

Peggy screamed and charged at Jackie. The two of them went down, disappearing from Kerry's view. She heard scuffling, and rolling around on the ground.

Then she heard someone grunt and cry out.

"Jack!" Roger yelled. "Jack, you okay?"

Jackie stood up. The knife in her hand glistened.

"I'm fine," she said. "Fatty, though . . ." She shook her head and turned to Kerry.

"Now, what do we do about you?"

LITTLE CHAPARRAL, TEXAS

Leo stripped down to his T-shirt to dig the grave.

He used the jack from the spare tire to break the hard ground, then scooped out the earth with his bare hands. He was sure there was a shovel somewhere in the burned ruins of Fletcher's, but he didn't think he could stomach what else he might find there.

He dug the grave long and deep, probably deeper than he needed to, but he didn't want some animal coming along and pulling Peter's body out.

And while he dug, he thought.

The last few days, ever since Peter had collapsed that morning at the Beaulieu mansion, had gone by like some sort of dream, driven by Peter's questions about what had happened the night Jack Kelly got killed. Leo didn't suppose Peter had ever gotten the answers he was looking for, and after last night at Fletcher's, Leo had even more questions of his own.

But he didn't feel the need to get all those things explained. The last few days had been too much, and the days that lay ahead promised more of the same. He couldn't go back to Florida because the waves were headed that way. All he knew was that he had to find food, he had to find gas, and he had to find out what Curtis had done with his gun.

But first things first.

He finished digging the grave, and hauled Peter's body from where he'd found it lying, sprawled out in front of Fletcher's with a bullet hole right in the middle of his forehead. Then he lowered him as gently as he could into the grave.

He supposed a few last words were in order.

He cleared his throat, trying to think of something appropriate to say. Maybe "the Lord is my shepherd" psalm? No, that wasn't what he felt.

He looked down at Peter and hoped his friend had found some peace, found a place where he could kick back with Jack Kelly and the two of them could sort out what had gone on together.

"Lord," Leo said simply, "take care of my friend."

Then he covered Peter's body with dirt, packed it in as tightly as he could, and went to see about the old man.

He'd dragged him into the shade of the town hall building before he dug Peter's grave, and although he still didn't know exactly what had happened out in front of Fletcher's, he had a gut feeling that the old man had shot Peter.

At first, when he woke up with his head aching and saw the bodies, saw what had happened, he'd thought about leaving the old guy out in the street to die. Why not? Leo didn't think the old man had long to live anyway. The wound in his shoulder was deep, and his clothes were already soaked through with blood.

He was also skin and bones, looking as if he hadn't eaten for months, and every time he breathed, a rattling sounded in his chest.

Leo knew he wouldn't last the day.

Leave him be, a voice had whispered in his head. *He killed your friend.*

And Leo almost did.

He knelt on the dusty road next to the burned-out shell

that had been Fletcher's and looked at Peter's body, then at the old man, and thought, You crazy old bastard, that's the last time you do anything other than die.

But then something told him there'd been enough death for the day. There was, in fact, plenty of death all across the country. So without knowing why, he picked the old man up and dragged him out of the sun, took off his knapsack so he could lie down, and left him in the cool shade to live or die as he would.

Then he turned his attention to the sack.

It was heavier than it looked, and made a rattling noise when he shook it that made him think the guy was carrying food cans.

But when he opened it, there was no food at all.

Inside was a cast-iron candlestick, heavy as a brick, and a pile of leather-bound journals, six, seven, eight of them. All had different dates on the cover, 1994–95; 1996–97, and so on.

He picked up the one on the top and opened it. A paragraph halfway down the page caught his eye.

> *I dreamt about Texas last night; a man there, wearing a priest's collar. Calling himself a man of God.*
> *Which God, he didn't say.*
> *His name is Novarra.*

A chill ran down Leo's spine.

He flipped through the diaries until he came to the one with the earliest date on the cover: 1990.

He opened it up and started to read.

June 12, 1990

> *My name is Thomas Kelleher and I'm writing this diary knowing the odds are that whoever finds this is going to think I'm crazy.*

In fact, I hope that's what happens. I hope that this ends up in a box in the corner of an attic someplace, and that twenty years from now my grandchildren find it, dig it out, and ask Mom and Dad who this crazy relative of theirs was.

But I don't think that's going to happen, for two reasons.

Number one, because I don't think I'm crazy.

Number two, because I'm never going to have any grandchildren.

My daughter is dead.

And I guess that's as good a place to start as any.

June 18, 1990

I made a vow to write in this every day, and of course I didn't. I had good intentions, though, and a few legitimate excuses. Some things happened that I wasn't counting on, but yesterday it hit me like a fist. I've been trying the wrong approach. I can't start by writing about Julie. That's too hard. I have to write about something where I can just lay out the facts.

So I decided I'm going to write about Coburn's ring.

It's right on the table next to me. It's a big plain piece of metal; it looks like a class ring, only without the writing, without any stones in the middle. At first you think it's just a plain old ring, but if you look closely you can see what looks to me like a snake etched into the metal, winding all the way around the band onto the surface. The serpent is an important mythological image. Set the destroyer, to the Egyptians. In Norse mythology, the world-snake, who plays a key role in Ragnarok, the twilight of the Gods. Satan, to the Christians. The evil one. The snake, in the garden.

More about that later.

I wear it on a chain around my neck. The ring is made of iron, by the way, which I understand is kind of unusual.

A few months back I flaked off a piece and sent it to a lab down in Princeton.

They wrote back a few months later.

Dear Mr. Kelleher:

We are unable to reliably date the sample you have provided us.

Sincerely,
Leslie Wickes

I called up Leslie and asked what she meant by "reliably."

"Our results were contradictory," she said.

"You tested it more than once and got different dates?" I asked.

"No." She hesitated. "We tested the piece three times, and got the same date—within an acceptable margin for error—all three times."

"So what's the problem?"

"The results are simply in error. According to the tests, the iron you provided us is somewhere between fifteen and twenty thousand years old."

"Wow," I said, "that's old."

"That's not old," she said. "That's impossible."

DENVER, COLORADO

They left right after breakfast.

Bert said they were leaving in order to get Betty away from civilization. Or what was left of it. She was falling apart, he confided, and he wanted a little time and space to put her back together. Take her into the mountains, find someplace safe to hide. Live off the land.

A lot of other people were doing the same thing, he heard. When she was better, they'd come back.

Connie said she understood their decision. She opened up Don's gun closet and let Bert take one of the big rifles as well as several boxes of ammo. She gave Betty a handgun and said she wanted them to take Don's truck as well.

"It's a gas guzzler, Bert, but if you really want to get off the road and into the mountains, it'll do you better than that jalopy of yours."

The way she said it, the look in her eyes when she handed him the keys, Bert had the feeling that she knew they weren't coming back.

They said goodbye just after nine A.M. Bert and Betty had agreed on a rough direction: southwest, heading for the wide open spaces of the desert. Beyond that they had no particular destination in mind. Someplace away from it all. Someplace hard to reach and harder still to find.

Half an hour later, having only gone a mile, they hit traffic. Major traffic. The army had set up checkpoints on all the roads leaving the city. They were searching every car because during the night a cache of guns and explosives had been stolen from the armory.

When it came their turn, Bert talked to the deputy. He told him they had guns but were getting out of the city and only wanted protection. Maybe it was because the deputy was young, or because Bert knew how to talk, or it was the look of pure fear and desperation on Bert's face, but the deputy let them go. And he let them keep their weapons.

The driver of the car next to them wasn't as lucky. As they drove off, Bert saw a soldier crack the butt of his rifle across the man's face, and when he went down, the soldier stood over him, breathing heavily, with a light dancing in his eyes.

Bert had the feeling that whatever miracle had spared the people of Denver, the madness sweeping across the rest of the country would not be avoided elsewhere.

They were getting away just in time, he decided.

"I dreamed he was alive," Betty had told him, leaning across the kitchen table and squeezing his hand tightly. "I dreamed Harold got up off the floor and went storming through the house, slamming doors and looking for me, and when he realized I was gone, he got into his car and—and—" She had stuttered in her rush to get it all out. "—somehow, I was inside his head while he was doing all this, feeling what he felt, like there was something connecting the two of us."

Bert had just stared at her.

"I know it was just a dream," she went on, "but there were parts in it that were real—parts where I was Harold and I was killing these people, my friends, Nick and Lou, just the way it really happened. Like I was right there. That's crazy, though—isn't it?"

"I had the same dream," Bert said, staring at her solemnly. "I think that's pretty crazy too. I think it's crazy that people are getting killed, and that the country's under martial law, and that no one has any answers about anything. I don't know what's happening. I don't know what's going on, but . . ."

He was about to tell her that he had to believe. He had to trust there was a reason, a higher power, that would steer them safely through whatever happened.

But he didn't.

Because, he realized, if you believed in a higher power, then . . .

Didn't you have to believe in one down below? So instead he turned to her and said, "I think we should leave here—right now, this morning. What do you think?"

Now, they circled Colorado Springs and Canon City, and when they were running low on gas, they siphoned it from cars that had been left on the highway.

Late in the afternoon the road split and there was a sign at the crossroads:

GRAND CANYON 183 MILES

An arrow pointed west.

Bert had wanted to keep going south, but Betty was staring at him with a big smile on her face.

"Want to take a detour?" he said.

"Yes." She clapped happily.

Bert laughed out loud. "Have you ever been there?"

Betty shook her head. "Jesus, no. Bert, I've never been *anywhere.*"

"Well, then," he said, "Grand Canyon, here we come."

PARAMOUNT STUDIOS, LOS ANGELES

Luka and Abby had breakfast with General Scott in the Paramount cafeteria, which had been transformed into a sort of officers' club. In contrast to yesterday's cornflakes and powdered milk, they had Danishes, bacon and eggs, orange juice, and coffee.

Abby's outfit was a contrast as well: instead of borrowed army fatigues, she'd raided the studio's dressing rooms and found something that looked like it was made for the TV show *Starsky and Hutch,* but it fit, and it was clean, and she wasn't going to complain, considering.

Luka told Scott that CNN in Atlanta wanted more stories out of Paramount.

"Human interest, that sort of thing. How people survived."

"That's fine," Scott said. "But not too graphic. We don't want to add to the panic."

"Agreed."

"At the same time," the general continued, "it would be

nice to try and let people know we've got things under control. That we know what's happening."

"And what is happening?" Abby asked.

Scott ignored her. "We could put on a psychiatrist. Someone who could talk about the importance of staying calm when the blackouts hit."

Luka nodded. "Maybe explain a little bit about why people react the way they do."

"Exactly." Scott smiled.

"Okay, so that's one angle. But I'd still like to know why you think the blackouts are spreading, and what the army's doing about it."

Scott shook his head. "Not yet, Andrew. I'm sorry. As soon as the general gives me the word, I promise you'll be the first to know. In the meantime, you'll just have to trust me. Everything is under control."

Abby almost spit up her coffee.

Everything was under control? Bullshit, she thought. Everything was falling apart. The camps were overflowing with people scared out of their minds—dozens of trucks had come in last night, bringing people from another abandoned base, and the scenes in the soundstages reminded her less of *Gone with the Wind* and more of *Calcutta*.

She'd gone back to the CNN trailer after the press conference yesterday and seen that the waves were continuing to spread everywhere: Texas, Oklahoma, Minnesota, Kansas, points north, south, east, west, a widening circle that was almost to the Mississippi River by now.

And the army had everything under control? She couldn't wait to hear that one.

About the only encouraging thing she'd seen all day was the news out of Denver, which had somehow managed to survive relatively unscathed. There were pictures of hundreds of people, pouring out of a cathedral and smiling, arms around each other, and even though she was an atheist, Abby thought they had the right idea.

Maybe prayer was the only way to deal with this.

"Excuse me? You there?"

She looked up, saw Scott frowning at her, and realized she'd been talking to herself.

"Sorry," she said. "Just thinking out loud."

"You all right, Abby?" Luka asked. "Sleep well?"

"Oh yeah. I slept fine."

And she had. She didn't need sleep. She just needed to get away from Scott's political bullshit. And rather than start the day off with a big fight, she decided she ought to get outside for a few minutes, get some fresh air.

Although the air outside didn't smell that fresh anymore. She'd noticed it on her walk over to the cafeteria this morning. The air smelled like fumes from the fire down in South Central L.A., which was still burning. Still spreading.

Just like the—

A thought hit her, and it was so ridiculous that she dismissed it. The fire had started the same night as the blackouts and the craziness. Could there be a connection?

No. Of course not.

Then she remembered standing at the guardrail on the 405, looking out at the fire and feeling—

Whoa, Abby told herself. Stop right there. Stop right there, and get out into that outdoor air, no matter how foul it smells, before you start taking out the Bible and shouting hallelujahs left and right.

"Excuse me," she said, interrupting Scott and Luka, who were still talking about the best way to manage their news. "I'm going to take a quick walk. I'll be right back."

She stood up, pushed her chair in, and noticed, at the table behind them, another officer looking at Scott with the same expression of disgust she knew she had just had.

If Scott was the prototypical war hero, this guy was the exact opposite. Dark where Scott was fair, stocky and solid where he was lean, brooding where Scott was all smiles and sunlight.

Their eyes met.

He picked up his mug and headed toward the coffee machine.

She followed, and stood next to him as he refilled his cup.

"I'm Abby Keller," she said.

"I know who you are."

"And you're . . ."

He turned the name tag so she could see it.

"Wieckowski," Abby read. She looked at the stripes on his sleeve. "Captain?"

"Lieutenant."

There was a patch on his shirt that Abby didn't recognize at all. Something that looked like a Tinkertoy symbol.

"You were listening to our conversation back there, Lieutenant. What do you think about what's happening here in Los Angeles? Think things are under control?"

He shrugged. "If that's what the general says, then I'm sure he's right."

"Correct me if I'm wrong, but from the look on your face, I got the distinct impression you didn't agree with him."

Wieckowski hesitated and Abby could feel he was struggling with himself, trying to decide what to say to her.

"Sorry," he said finally. "You're wrong."

Abby didn't think so.

"You've got the situation in hand?"

"I can't answer that."

She frowned. "How about this one: there's a rumor going around that the army is pulling out of Los Angeles. Any truth to that?"

"No." Wieckowski shook his head slowly. But again, his eyes told a different story. "Where'd you hear that? That's a dangerous rumor to be spreading."

Abby smiled. "I'll trade you—honest answer for honest answer."

Wieckowski's eyes went from her to Scott. He shook his head again. Then he put his cup in the dirty dish bin.

"Goodbye, Miss Keller. Nice meeting you."

He left the cafeteria.

Abby went back to her seat.

Scott and Luka were still planning her afternoon, but now Abby had an item she wanted to add: to make Lieutenant Wieckowski talk.

The lieutenant was on her mind during all her morning interviews. They started at Soundstage 12, which had been converted into the base's makeshift infirmary. The floor of the soundstage was covered by row after row of cots—there had to be hundreds of them, and virtually every one was occupied by a body. To attend to those hundreds, there were only a handful of people in white lab coats.

Abby talked to a half-dozen people there. Luka had given her a clipboard full of stock questions to ask—Where were you when the blackouts hit? Tell us how you got to the base? That sort of thing—and she wore an in-ear monitor so he could talk to her through the questioning. But she was getting comfortable enough to deviate from standard questions that called for a follow-up.

After the infirmary, it was on to the shrink—an army shrink, Dr. Francis Walters, who was in the corner office in the Roddenberry Building.

On their walk over there, an enlisted man waylaid Scott, who then disappeared in a hurry. He came back a few minutes later and waved Luka over for a conversation.

"The army wants us to go out live with this interview," Luka told her as they set up the shot. "Think you're ready?"

Abby tapped her earpiece. "I suppose you'll be in here, right? You'll coach me through it?"

"Actually, both of us will."

Abby saw Scott standing behind Luka, wearing a headset similar to his.

"Walters tends to be a little nervous," Scott explained. "I know the kind of questions that'll keep him at ease. So I'll feed those directly to you—all right?"

Abby looked at Luka, expecting him to object, only to see him turn and start talking to the cameraman about the setup.

She realized then that Luka didn't like Scott hovering around any more than she did. And that made her wonder who was really in charge of CNN's Los Angeles operation. Or their Atlanta one, for that matter.

Luka turned back in time to see the expression on her face.

"It'll be fine, Abby," he said. "Don't worry."

"Nothing to worry about at all," Scott chimed in. "Here's Dr. Walters now."

A middle-aged man with a beard and no mustache made his way to the chair opposite hers and sat down. He smiled at Abby.

She smiled back.

Luka cued her in. "Five—four—three—two—one—and we're live."

Abby turned to the camera.

"This is Abigail Keller for CNN, reporting live from Los Angeles. I'm joined by Dr. Francis Walters of the U.S. Army. Good morning, Doctor."

"Good morning."

Scott's voice sounded in her ear. "His specialty is mass psychology. Ask him to define it."

She nodded and spoke.

"Doctor, your specialty is what some of us might simply term 'mass psychology.' " She heard a snort of laughter in her headset—Luka, amused at her little joke? Or Scott, irritated by it?—and continued. "Could you explain what that is?"

Walters nodded. "Certainly. Mass psychology is simply the study of group behavior—the way people react as a group of individuals, which is, I must say, very different from the way that they as individuals might ordinarily react. For example, at a sporting event, you might see a man—maybe a father—caught up in the excitement of rooting for his team, and doing things he would never do outside of that particular context."

Walters leaned back in his chair and smiled, having delivered what was clearly a very well-rehearsed answer.

Abby had been on more than one talk show herself, and knew the same kind of thing always went on between guest and host. Questions—and answers—were often prepared beforehand. Still, in this context, the practice felt wrong.

"How does group behavior explain the violence?" Scott said in her ear.

She rephrased the question slightly for Walters. "Some people think this theory of group behavior may even help explain the violence we've seen across America."

Walters nodded. "You're talking about mass hysteria. A panicked reaction to the blackouts spreading across the country, a kind of paranoia made worse by the knowledge of what's happened in other cities. Some people—experts even, as you suggest—believe that is what's causing the wave of violence. I do not."

"And you, Doctor," Scott's voice prompted her, "what do you believe?"

Abby parroted the general's words.

"I believe," Walters replied, "that when one considers the totality of the circumstances— the blackouts that precede the violence, the spreading nature of the phenomenon—that the answer to what is occurring may in fact be very simple."

"Prompt him," Scott hissed. He sounded anxious, almost excited.

"Go on, Doctor," she said, realizing that "rehearsed" was the wrong word to characterize this interview. It was scripted.

"It may be that the hysteria we are seeing—the riots, the violence, all these things—have been artificially induced."

"By artificially induced," Scott said in her ear, "you mean—"

"Put that in plain English, Doctor," Abby said, cutting to the chase.

"I am talking," he said, "about biochemical warfare."

For a moment there was silence.

"All behavior has a biochemical component," Walters stated. "We know that if you change the levels of certain chemicals in the bloodstream—either increase them or decrease them—you effect a change in behavior. Testosterone. Caffeine. Even something as basic as sugar." He shrugged. "This is not new. What is new is how well we now understand the process and are capable of manipulating it. By we, of course, I mean scientists in general. Not just the United States."

Abby now saw where this was all going, and she didn't need a prompt for her next question.

"Are you suggesting," she said, "that America is under attack?"

Walters started a moment, probably thrown off his lines. Then he recovered.

"In my opinion, this is a strong possibility. If the behavioral changes we are seeing are the result of an artificially induced contaminant—"

God, this guy couldn't even talk in English.

"You mean a gas?"

He nodded. "A gas is a strong possibility. Or something in the water supply, perhaps. But I think a gas more likely: easier to disperse, particularly to more remote regions."

Abby's mind was racing. He could be right, she thought. Biochemical warfare, germ warfare, whatever you wanted to call it. It would certainly explain why, no matter how many times people were urged to remain calm, no matter how many police officers, county sheriffs, state troopers, and National Guardsmen they saw out on the streets to protect them, the violence went on just the same. It explained the violence in the rural areas too, as the doctor had said. A gas could travel everywhere. It could float across rivers, fly over deserts, climb mountains.

But then she thought about Denver and what she'd seen on television—the congregation walking out of the cathedral, arm in arm, smiling.

"Ask him what sort of gases would be likely to cause these effects," Scott said.

"Doctor," Abby began, "you know that in Denver, there was significantly less violence than in any other city. Can you think of a reason for that?"

"Denver?"

Walters started in his chair, clearly surprised by the question.

"I would suspect that the altitude there has something to do with it." He shrugged. "This is only a theory, of course."

She nodded. The altitude. That made sense.

If, she thought, other high altitude cities had been affected the same way. She'd check on that.

"Ask him about the gases," Scott repeated, a note of warning in his voice.

But Abby wasn't done yet. Something else had occurred to her.

"Have you seen the way the violence is spreading on a map, Doctor?"

Walters shook his head.

"It's spreading in almost a perfect circle, radiating out from Los Angeles. Would a gas be likely to spread that way?"

Walters frowned. "Anything is possible, though a perfect circle does seem highly unlikely."

His eyes brightened. "Perhaps what we're seeing is a series of attacks."

"And how would that work exactly," Abby countered, "given that the blackouts take place before the violence?"

"I don't understand."

"Nothing electrical works in the affected areas, Doctor. How would the gas be delivered?"

"Perhaps the weapons were placed earlier." Walters shrugged. "I am not an expert in this area."

"Commercial in five seconds," Luka said.

Abby put on a big smile. "We'll be right back with more

from Dr. Francis Walters of the United States Army. Stay tuned."

"And we're out," Luka said.

The spotlights above her and Walters dimmed.

Abby pulled off her earpiece and a second later Scott was in her face.

"What are you doing?"

"Following up a line of questioning," she said.

He shook his head. "No. Stick to the questions I give you. Unless you want me to find someone else to do this interview."

Abby looked up at him. "I didn't know that was up to you."

For a second Scott looked like he was going to hit her. And in that second, Abby thought she saw the same thing in his eyes that she'd seen in Carol's. The same thing she'd seen when she was looking into the fire.

She blinked, and it was gone.

"It's not up to Scott," Luka was saying, "it's up to me. And I'm telling you the same thing, Abby. Stick to the general's questions."

"Stick to the script, you mean?"

"That's why you're here," Scott said. "Because you can stick to the script. Not because you're a reporter."

The insult stung Abby like a whip.

"Do as you're told," Scott said. He turned and walked away.

Abby swallowed hard. "Wow. That was harsh."

Luka pulled off his headset and patted her shoulder. "Fuck him," he said, watching Scott go. "You did good, Abby."

"Thanks," she said.

Luka's words made her feel better, but Abby realized there was probably more than a grain of truth in what Scott was saying. The reason she was getting to play reporter at all was because of who she was—or rather, who she had been six months ago. A pretty face.

A pretty, well-liked face.

She was the spoonful of sugar they hoped would get their medicine down. She saw that now. And whatever that medicine was, they were using her to prepare the rest of the country to swallow it whole.

She finished the rest of the interview with Walters like a good little girl. She repeated Scott's questions word for word and by the end of the piece, she was sure that a large portion of the people watching believed the country was under attack. A two-pronged attack, the blackouts, and a biochemically induced mass hysteria. Say the word, name the enemy, and red-blooded Americans everywhere were ready to go charging over the hill.

But Abby didn't buy it for a second.

Her thoughts kept returning to the look she'd seen in Scott's eyes, and the smiling faces of the congregation coming out of Denver.

Later, back at the CNN trailer, she saw another piece, an interview with an army engineer and a civilian doctor, that discussed the spreading blackouts in terms of an attack as well. More than possible, the experts concluded.

Likely. Probable.

And still later in the day, there was an announcement from the Pentagon in Washington. A major address from General Dooley—and the deposed President—coming at nine that evening, EST.

That scared Abby. It sounded to her like the army was getting ready to fight back. Getting ready to show the world things were under control.

But things weren't under control.

And then she remembered someone else who felt the same way.

Lieutenant Wieckowski. She decided to go find him.

LITTLE CHAPARRAL, TEXAS

Smashing in the front window of the town hall building, Leo picked up the old man and carried him inside. It was getting hot, and he knew the man would need food and water if he eventually woke up.

After reading his journals, Leo wanted him awake.

He wanted answers.

He left the man in the hallway and checked the faucets. The sinks didn't work, but he found a cooler in the mayor's office with drinks inside. He also found a first aid kit and bandaged the man's wounded shoulder.

Maybe it was his imagination, but the bullet hole already looked better after only two hours.

There was a vending machine in the hall, and Leo kicked it over and broke in the glass. He didn't have any change, and he thought, Why not, the world is going crazy anyway.

He grabbed two bags of Cheez Doodles and two Milky Ways and, grabbing the journals, took one last look at the old man before sitting down in the mayor's empty chair. He broke open a Milky Way and got back to reading.

August 18, 1993

  Received a letter today from Professor Edgecombe.

Dear Mr. Kelleher:

  I have reflected on our conversation of last week, and feel I owe you an apology.

  I feel it is incumbent upon all professional scientists to welcome thoughtful, intelligent inquiries from an interested amateur in their field of expertise. And I feel that when the amateur tries to challenge accepted wisdom in that field—based on incomplete knowledge of the field as a whole—it becomes incumbent upon the professional to inform the amateur where their knowledge is lacking, in a forthright yet courteous manner.

All of which is to say that while I was certainly forthright in our conversation, it seems to me in retrospect that I was far from courteous, and wish to tender an apology herein.

Now. To the iron.

Your sources are correct; there is a myth, and it may be Canaanite, it may be Ugarit, we cannot be sure, as it comes down to us through the Greeks in a very imprecise fashion. The uncertainty surrounding the document's origin makes it very hard to be certain of the translation. In many primitive languages, the word for iron means sky-metal, and so, as to whether or not this is something that fell from the sky as, let us say, a meteorite, or a weapon actually bestowed by the gods . . .

Well, in any case, I am enclosing a copy of the only translation I have.

Please do accept my apology, and feel free to call on me again with any further questions. In the meantime, I do hope you will read up on some of the more orthodox sources within the field.

Sincerely,
Professor Harold Edgecombe

The Serpent-Queen of Gir-A-Desh

Long ago, in the days of the first sun, before the moon turned its face away from the stars, and the world ended and was reborn in the shape we now know, a mighty kingdom rose up in the oasis on the edge of the Western Desert. This kingdom was called Adesh, and at the height of its power and influence, a man could ride for a hundred days and nights without coming to the end of its borders.

At the heart of the city was a great castle, where the king dwelt and dispensed the law of the land. And of all the kings of fabled Adesh, the most revered was Enlil, a mighty warrior who was fierce in war, and generous in peace. Enlil's queen was Belissar. Together they ruled wisely over their subjects, and were much beloved by them.

Then one day, a terrible tragedy struck.

The queen gave birth to a child, a son named Enkinu. But the boy was stillborn, and this Belissar could not put behind her. She would not be comforted, by the king or the priests or her handmaidens. She would not let any of them touch her baby, nor take its body from her bed. She lay with it for a week, and spoke and thought as a madwoman.

At last, she agreed to see the priests. She begged them to make sacrifice to their god that Enkinu might live again. This, the priests would not do. And she wept, and howled, and begged a second time, and a third, but still they would not relent.

"It is against the laws of gods and men to seek a second life," they said.

At last she let Enkinu be taken from her, and given burial.

But she could not forget.

A dark cloud descended over the city of Adesh. The cries of the queen could be heard at night; the king's justice grew harsh, and harder to find.

One day a stranger came from the desert. He wore robes of black, and a hood covered his face.

In the castle gardens, he sought out the queen.

"It is said the gods have been cruel to you," he said to her.

She did not reply.

"You, who have raised temples to their glory, and showered riches on their priests, and justice on their subjects."

Still Belissar remained silent.

"These gods do not appreciate you, my queen," said the stranger. "And yet, there are others. Others who would restore what you have lost, and ask only a small token in return."

And now Belissar did look up, and speak to the stranger.

"I would do anything for the one who brought my son back to me," she said.

"Then listen now," he replied, and told her the things that would be required of her.

Thus it was that that night, for the first time since Enkinu's death, the queen returned to the marriage bed. She lay with the king, and when his passion was spent, and he slumbered, she stole from him the keys to the royal graveyard.

That very night, the queen dug up the body of her dead son and left Adesh for the western Desert.

She traveled for a week and at last, came to the ruins of a great city. And there before her stood the stranger in the black robe.

"This is Gehendron," he said to her, "where Yagunnata himself once ruled."

Belissar's heart trembled, and for a moment she knew fear. For she had thought the city and the Serpent God to be simply tales told in the night to terrify children. But if Yagunnata could restore her child . . .

"What must I do?" the queen asked.

The stranger bade her uncover the body of Enkinu, and lay it on the stone before them. Then he drew forth from his robes a great sword.

It was full the height of a man, and made of a terrible grey metal that seemed to pulse from within. Belissar knew this was a weapon forged by the gods, containing their own dreadful power, a thing mortals were not meant to trifle with.

Before she could speak a word, he raised the blade, and plunged it into the infant's chest. A terrible power seemed to flow from the sword to Enkinu's body, and a child's cry split the night.

When Belissar and her son returned to Adesh, at first, there was much rejoicing.

But as he grew, the boy Enkinu revealed himself an evil, willful child, and the king would have nothing to do with him. Indeed, the priests and the king's advisors feared mightily the day he would ascend the throne. At last, their words swayed the king, and he ordered Enkinu banished. That same day, he took a new wife.

That same night, Belissar poisoned the king.

Thus it was she ascended to the throne.

She tore down the statues of the old gods, and where their houses of worship had stood, raised up a great temple in honor of Yagunnata. In time, Enkinu rose to the throne to rule at her side. There were whispers that they lay together as man and woman as well. There were even those who swore that Enkinu was the Serpent-God himself, great Yagunnata reincarnated.

And according to these, it was only when the gods took pity on man and imprisoned Yagunnata beneath the Earth, shattering his sword, that the days of darkness and evil on the earth ended.

But this part of the story is hearsay, and not known to be true.

QUAKER HEIGHTS, ALBUQUERQUE

Steve had wondered if Alison would ever forgive him for taking Kerry.

Now, he guessed, he knew the answer to that.

He looked south, across the river, to where downtown Albuquerque—what was left of it, anyway—was burning, the flames rising up high enough to obscure his view of the Sandia Mountains beyond.

He could only hope that somewhere in that madness, Kerry was still alive.

"You hear that?"

Steve turned. The man who spoke, Lawson, was looking out the window of the jeep.

A second later he heard it too.

A supersonic whine, growing louder.

Lawson raised a hand to his forehead and scanned the horizon. "There he is."

Steve squinted. Then he saw it too: an Air Force jet hurtling through the sky, almost too fast to follow.

The mad bomber; what else could they call him?

The bomber and his plane were from Kirtland, the Air Force base just outside the city, and sometime yesterday morning he'd started taking target practice on Albuquerque.

Aside from a few hours last night—when Steve supposed he'd refueled and gotten more ammo—he hadn't stopped.

Now he was back.

As Steve watched, the jet went in low and released two missiles.

The whining noise became a screech as the missiles shot toward the city below, outracing the jet and trailing long thin plumes of smoke.

They hit the ground and exploded, twin columns of fire bursting into the air. From as far away as they were, Steve heard the muffled thump of the explosions. He even felt the ground shake.

Lawson shook his head. "He's got a thing for the Old Town today."

"As long as he sticks to that side of the river." That was Carew, who sat in the passenger seat.

Carew had that right, Steve thought. Albuquerque on the east bank of the river—downtown, the Old Town, the university—was mostly dead people at this point. He ought to know; he'd spent the better part of a day looking through the carnage for Kerry.

Lawson shifted the jeep out of park and drove on.

Steve had no idea where his daughter was now.

For all he knew, she'd died in the insanity of that first night and he would never see her again. Those first frantic hours after he'd woken up at the motel, he'd turned over every corpse he'd come upon, fearing the worst. And with every passing hour that he didn't find Kerry, a million gruesome scenarios as to what had happened to her, each worse than the next, ran through his head.

Late yesterday afternoon he'd decided that rather than fear the worst, he would assume the best: that Kerry had gotten out of the city and was somewhere safe, and that it was time for him to do the same thing while he still could, because the bomber wasn't the only mad thing running through the streets of Albuquerque.

So he'd crossed the river under cover of nightfall, and almost immediately ran into Lawson, Carew, and a half-dozen other men and their families who had banded together inside a high school gymnasium. The west side of the river, it turned out, was safer. Lawson and his people wanted to keep it that way.

Since the first night the waves hit, they'd been going methodically from neighborhood to neighborhood trying to organize the people who were still sane—and if need be, to shoot the ones who weren't. When Steve showed up yesterday, he'd volunteered to help them—not with the shooting, but at convincing people that there was safety in numbers; that rather than hide in their own houses and barricade the doors, they were better off bringing their families into the new high school out on Vizquel Boulevard and making it a safe spot.

The three of them had been at it since just after sunrise that morning. Now it was early afternoon and they'd gone to dozens of homes and sent maybe fifty or sixty people back to the high school. But at least twice that many preferred to stick it out in their own homes.

And then there were the dead, who outnumbered both groups put together.

"This is the end of the line, ain't it, Tim?" Lawson asked Carew. They'd come to the bottom of the mesa; to their right was a belt of green forest and a sign that said: RIO GRANDE STATE PARK.

Straight ahead was scrub, and the start of desert.

"Just about," Carew said. He wrinkled up his face and pointed left, almost due west, where there were still patches of farmland. "A few more houses out in that direction, I think."

"Let's try them," Lawson replied. "Then we'll head back to the school. You okay with that, Steve?"

"Sure." Steve nodded. He was along for the ride anyway. This was Lawson and Carew's ball game. Albuquerque was their town.

Both of them were longtime residents; grizzled, outdoorsy-looking types who could no doubt build a house from scratch. Men who, unlike him, could handle themselves in a fight. He hadn't been in a fight since his freshman year of high school, and only a couple of days ago had been knocked unconscious by his fourteen-year-old daughter.

He shook his head. No, he thought. That wasn't Kerry; that was the wave, or whatever the hell they were calling it now.

They turned left, and the road went from pavement to gravel to dirt. Up ahead on the right was a small adobe house. Pulling into the drive, they got out of the car.

Steve heard someone playing the piano. It was "Amazing Grace."

Lawson and Carew heard it too, and with a glance at each other, the three of them started down the front walk. The door to the house was wide open and a woman was sitting in one of the front rooms, hunched over a piano, facing them.

"Hello!" Steve called out from the doorway.

Sighing heavily, the woman stopped playing. Then, as if reaching an important decision, she slowly looked up at the three men. She was in her sixties, maybe even seventies, skin toughened to leather by the sun.

"The Lord took my boys," she said.

Lawson stepped into the house.

"I'm Judd Lawson. This is Tim Carew and Steve Crescent. We're from down by Quaker Heights."

"Elena Montero," the woman said, her hands drifting idly over the piano keys.

"Are you the only one here, ma'am?" Lawson asked.

The woman nodded. "I am."

Steve walked over to the piano. "Mrs. Montero, you said the Lord took your boys. What did you mean by that?"

"My husband. My son. They went out two days ago to get food. But they never came back." She looked up into Steve's eyes. "The Lord took them and lifted them up to heaven. Do you understand? They were judged, and embraced by the Lord."

Steve nodded. "I understand."

He understood because it wasn't the first time he'd heard someone refer to the waves as the Day of Judgment—as if it were God's way of deciding who was worthy and who wasn't.

Who knew, he thought, maybe they were right. When the wave had hit him—when he'd been holding Kerry and felt that power pass through him like he'd accidentally grabbed a high-voltage wire—he knew that something supernatural was happening. But if this was Judgment Day . . .

Then a lot of people were failing the test.

"Mrs. Montero," Lawson said, "we were wondering if you'd like to come back with us."

"Come back with you?" she said. "I don't understand."

Lawson explained, then, about the high school, about how dangerous it would be for her to stay out there all by herself. Carew chimed in as well.

But when they were done talking, the old woman just shook her head.

"No. No. I don't think so. I'll be safe here," she said. "My time will come. The Lord will give me a sign and take me up to be with my boys."

"Mrs. Montero," Steve said, "you can't—"

Lawson put a hand on his shoulder. "All right, Mrs. Montero. If you change your mind, remember McKinney High School. Vizquel Boulevard—take a right just before Central Avenue, all right?"

She smiled and nodded.

"All right, then. Goodbye, ma'am."

Steve wanted to say something else, but couldn't think of anything that would change her mind. "Good luck, ma'am."

The woman looked up and pointed to the ceiling.

"I don't need luck," she said. "The Lord will provide."

They left her playing another tune, and climbed back into the jeep.

They found two more farms along the same road, both deserted. Just past the second farm there was a sign:

WILLIAMS HOUSE
GROUP HOMES FOR BOYS AND GIRLS

"I know this place," Carew said. "One of my wife's friends works out here. Doris Golding."

"Let's check in on her," Lawson said. He turned at the sign and parked at the end of a long drive, in front of a large, Victorian-looking house.

Carew checked his gun before he got out of the car.

"Better keep an eye out, all right?" he said to Lawson. "Some of these kids are trouble."

Lawson pulled his gun out too. "I got it. Steve, why don't you just stay behind us?"

Steve nodded and followed them up the steps to the front door.

Carew banged on the door once. "Doris?" Then again, harder. "Doris, it's Tim Carew. Are you in there?"

There was no answer.

Carew turned the knob, and the door swung open with a loud creak.

His face blanched. "Holy . . ."

Steve peered over his shoulder.

There was a dead body lying in the entrance to the hall; a girl. Steve thought it was Kerry for a second and his heart leaped into his throat. Then he took in the long black hair and the tattooed arms and breathed a sigh of relief. It wasn't his daughter; it would have been crazy to think Kerry would be there anyway.

Carew unholstered his gun. Lawson did the same.

They stepped carefully inside.

There was a staircase in front of them, a living room to their right, and a dining room to their left.

There were more bodies in the living room.

"Jesus," Carew said, turning to Lawson, "what the—"

A gunshot rang out and pain ripped through Carew's right shoulder.

"Down!" Lawson screamed, pulling Carew to the ground.

Steve dove to his left, underneath the dining room table.

Another gunshot came, ripping up the wood in the entrance hall.

"Mrs. Golding's not home now!" a girl laughed from the top of the stairs.

Lawson raised his pistol and sighted carefully. He saw the side of a head and fired.

They heard a scream and the cracking of wood, and then a body literally flew through the air and landed on the ground in front of them. It was a redheaded girl.

Her body twitched once and then went still.

For a minute there was total silence in the house.

Lawson helped Carew sit up; the wounded man was pressing a hand to his shoulder, grimacing as he did.

"Damn," he said. "I didn't see it coming."

Steve walked over to the red-haired girl and stared down at her.

She was wearing Kerry's bracelet.

Monday 5:12 P.M., PST

PARAMOUNT STUDIOS, LOS ANGELES

Abby tried the straightforward approach. Her CNN badge allowed her free run of most of the camp, and she went to half a dozen places and asked twice that many soldiers about Lieutenant Wieckowski.

None of them had ever heard of him.

Then she tried the not-so-straightforward approach. She went to the quartermaster, whom she noticed, to her delight, had taken over an office in the old *Island Patrol* production department.

She lied and said she was supposed to meet a certain Lieutenant Wieckowski at a specified location, which she'd forgotten, but she had to get hold of him. She asked if he could help. To his credit, the quartermaster tried, but there was no record of a Lieutenant Wieckowski, Wikowski, Wiekoski, or anyone else with a similar name at the camp.

Discouraged but not defeated, Abby decided to wait it out and try to see him again at the cafeteria, but there was still more than an hour to go till dinner. To kill time, she decided to head over to the CNN trailer. Luka was there, talking on a satellite phone to Atlanta. She sat down and listened for a few moments, during which she noticed he was receiving what sounded like major abuse.

Luka slammed the phone down and turned to her.

"What?" he screamed.

"Whoa," she said. "Don't take it out on me."

He rubbed his eyes and took a deep breath. "Sorry," he said. "They're clearing out in Atlanta. The wave will hit there just before dawn tomorrow."

Abby couldn't believe it. She'd seen the map, but it hadn't sunk in until now. Atlanta tomorrow, and New York the next day. All the big East Coast cities—Boston, Baltimore, Philly, Washington—in the next thirty-six hours. Over half the country's population.

She remembered the throngs of people that had passed beneath her St. Mark's Place apartment every day and shuddered.

"Anyway," Luka said, putting his feet up on the long counter that ran the length of the trailer. "As long as you're here, we can talk about a few things for tomorrow. Atlanta wants interviews with some soldiers: happy rescue stories."

Happy stories, Abby thought. Sure. They'd just keep on dancing while Rome burned down around them.

"And I'm sure Scott will have some ideas of his own," Luka said miserably. "In fact, he usually hands me a long list of them by this time in the evening."

"He's probably getting ready for Dooley's speech," Abby suggested. Which was in less than an hour, she realized. "I'm sure you'll hear from him soon enough."

Luka nodded. "Yeah. He'll probably do a little Q and A afterward too. You should plan on being there."

Abby frowned. That would mean missing out on a chance to intercept Wieckowski at the cafeteria.

Her disappointment must have been obvious.

"What's the matter?" Luka said. "You got something else going on? A hot date?"

She laughed and shook her head. "No. I'm trying to find somebody."

"Somebody. Who?"

"A soldier."

"Any soldier?"

"Just someone I want to talk to."

"Why?"

"I have a few questions."

Luka stared at her. "That's all you're going to tell me?"

She nodded. "That's all I've got right now."

He looked at her a moment longer and smiled. "Well, I think someone's turning into a bonafide reporter."

She smiled back. "Is that a bad thing?"

Luka picked up the satellite phone again. "I don't know. Let's find out. I'll cover Dooley's speech, and Scott. You go find your soldier."

Five minutes after the cafeteria opened, Abby was standing by the doors. And it was a good thing. Otherwise she would have missed Wieckowski.

He strolled out of the cafeteria with his hands in his pockets and his head bowed, and he was ten feet past Abby before she realized it was him.

"Lieutenant Wieckowski!"

He turned around. He looked even less happy than he had that morning.

"Miss Keller," he said, nodding hello. Then he turned around and continued walking.

"Wait!" she yelled, and ran to catch up with him.

"I can't wait," he said. "I have someplace I need to be."

"I just wanted to ask you a couple quick questions."

"I don't have time," he said.

"But—"

He stopped and turned to face her directly. "Miss Keller, I don't have time to talk to you right now."

She smelled alcohol and realized he'd been drinking.

"Are you all right, Lieutenant?"

"Fine," he said in a clipped way that let her know that he wasn't fine, not at all. "Thanks for asking. Now I really have to go."

"Wait," she said again, putting a hand on his arm. "I wanted to ask you something. Please. One quick question."

He hesitated. "Why are you so insistent on talking to me? Isn't Scott supposed to be the one you deal with?"

"Scott issues press releases. Scott thinks things are under control," she said. "I don't think he's telling me the truth."

He shook his head. "I'm not sure I can do that either."

She raised an eyebrow. "What's that supposed to mean?"

He looked her dead in the eyes. "Ask me your question."

Abby thought a moment. Of course, she didn't have just one question for Wieckowski, she had about two dozen: Why don't you think things are under control? Why don't you like Scott? What do you think about the coup and General Dooley? Is there anything the army can really do to stop what's going on?

She could have sat the Lieutenant down and done a longer interview with him than she had with Walters. But there was no time for that. He had someplace to be. And she had time for only one question.

She hoped it was the right one.

"I'm waiting," Wieckowski said.

Abby nodded. "Okay. How come I had such a hard time finding you?"

"That's your question?" He smiled. "That's easy. I guess you haven't been looking in the right places."

"No, that's not what I mean. I mean nobody seems to have heard of you here. I walked all over the base this afternoon, asking just about everyone in a uniform where I might find you, and no one knew your name. I went to the quartermaster's office and they swore up and down you weren't assigned to this base."

"Somebody screwed up somewhere, obviously, because I'm here, aren't I?" But he wasn't smiling anymore.

"Lieutenant, if I asked CNN back in Atlanta to use sources to run a check on your service record, what would I find?"

He didn't answer.

"What part of the army do you work for, anyway?" She pointed to the Tinkertoy patch on his shirtfront. "What does that stand for?"

He sighed. "You *are* persistent, aren't you?"

"Comes with the job," Abby said.

"You're good at it."

"Thanks. I'd like to be better. Maybe when I grow up."

For some reason, his face changed, and he looked almost upset.

"Lieutenant? You still haven't answered my question."

"Yeah." He nodded.

He looked at her seriously for a moment, sizing her up. He looked at his watch. "What the hell," he said. "Walk with me, I'll answer your questions."

Lieutenant Lee Wieckowski led Abby down an alley between two soundstages. It dead-ended into a T and they turned left, coming up on a guard post. Abby showed her CNN badge, and Wieckowski nodded at the guard. The sentry waved them past.

Then Abby recognized they were going to the Paramount back lot, where the studio kept all its standing sets, the ones used, as needed, in its various television and film productions. Normally, the sets included a replica of a New York City street, a medieval marketplace, and a beach boardwalk, which had been used regularly on *Island Patrol*. Abby had spent a lot of time on the lot, and she was looking forward to a stroll down memory lane, but when they turned the corner, she saw that everything was gone.

It was completely empty.

The entire back lot, which was the size of a football field, was now bare cement. In the middle of it were two huge tractor-trailers, both with satellite antennas bolted onto the top. Fist-thick black cables ran back and forth from one trailer to the other, and more cables led from the trailers, across the cement, to the main part of the lot.

There were barbed wire circles around the trailers, and at one break in the fence stood two ramrod-straight soldiers.

They walked across the lot, Abby looking around in wonder.

"What is this?" she asked.

Wieckowski didn't answer.

They walked up to the guards and Abby held out her CNN badge.

The guards raised their guns and moved forward to block her.

"Easy," Wieckowski said. "She's with me."

They looked at him and lowered their guns.

"Sir?"

"It's all right, Corporal. She's with me."

One of the soldiers shook his head. "Unauthorized personnel are not permitted, sir. You know the rules."

"Check with General Scott, Corporal. He'll clear her."

"I'll do that."

"In the meantime," Wieckowski said, "I'm taking her in."

"Sir—"

"I'm taking her in."

And Wieckowski did just that, moving with her past the startled soldiers and into the perimeter of the fence.

"What are you doing?" Abby asked. "Scott won't vouch for me. He'll tell them—"

"Scott can't tell them anything," Wieckowski said. "He's on a plane to Washington."

Abby's heart skipped a beat. "What? Why is Scott—"

They reached the trailer. "Inside," Wieckowski said, and when she complied, he shut the door and locked it.

"Welcome to my little home away from home."

Abby looked around. The interior of the trailer was packed, floor to ceiling and both walls, with electronic equipment. Monitors, scopes, digital displays—there was barely enough room between the opposing walls of equipment for the two chairs. Wieckowski threw his coat over one and sat down in it, and pushed the other chair in her direction.

"Have a seat. I need to do a few things."

"Why is Scott on his way to Washington?" she said. "What's going on?"

"Give me a minute," he said. "I'll answer all your questions."

Abby reluctantly sat down and watched him make adjustments to some of the equipment. She swiveled in her chair, taking in the trailer.

There was a steel attaché case on the floor, and spray-painted on its side was the same Tinkertoy emblem that was on the front of Wieckowski's uniform. Underneath the emblem were the words:

UNITED STATES ARMY
CHEMICAL WARFARE DIVISION

"There," Wieckowski said. "All set." He turned in his chair to face her. "Now, ask your questions."

Abby reached down and picked up the attaché case. "Chemical Warfare Division?"

"That's right. Which is why you couldn't find me through anyone here at the base. I'm not officially here."

"Do you know Dr. Walters?"

Wieckowski nodded. "Sure. Dr. Walters, Dr. Wylie, Secretary Kennedy—we're all one big happy family."

"And where do you fit in?"

"Me, I'm just a small cog. A small but important cog." Something beeped behind him, and he held up a finger. "Excuse me a second. I need to make a little adjustment."

He pushed backward to a computer keyboard and typed something in. "There," he said, and rolled back to her. "Now where were we?"

Abby shook her head. "I don't understand what's going on. Where's Scott?"

"On a plane to Washington, like I said. Well, actually, he'll get as far as he can by plane. Then he'll walk." He snorted. "Or make someone carry him."

"Why?"

Wieckowski's eyes sparkled. "Haven't you guessed?"

Reaching into his pocket, he pulled out a silver flask and took a long slow swig, then offered it to Abby. "Want some?"

"No. I want to know what's happening."

"You were pretty close this morning," he said, "with your little interview piece with Walters."

Abby stared at him. "America is going to war?"

Wieckowski burst out laughing and held up the flask. "Hell, yes!"

It all fell into place for her.

"That's what General Dooley is going to speak about tonight." She looked up at the clock. "In about fifteen minutes."

Wieckowski leaned back and read something off one of the digital readouts behind him. "In exactly fifteen minutes and twelve seconds, to be precise. You want a little preview of his speech?"

"You know what he's going to say?"

"Not word for word, but the substance—yeah, I know that."

"I'm all ears."

Wieckowski smiled. "I'll even deliver it to you in the general's own inimitable style. Everybody says I do a pretty good Dooley, anyway."

"Sure," Abby said, thinking, Why the hell not? How much more surreal could things get?

Wieckowski stood up.

"My fellow Americans," he began, and damned if he wasn't right, it was a pretty good Dooley, "we have determined that the cause of the violence sweeping across the country is the result of an attack by a foreign power—"

Wieckowski abruptly stopped and switched back to his own voice for a moment. "He's going to point the finger at China, I think, that was the last I heard. Though it still might be Iraq or Libya, I don't know."

He cleared his throat and started up as Dooley again.

"—a foreign power that has detonated a biochemical weapon on our shores. The devastating effects of this weapon have been felt from the West Coast to the shores of Lake Superior, and are now on the verge of striking at the heavily populated Northeast corridors of our country, placing literally millions of lives in peril. While we prepare a suitable response to this vicious, unprovoked attack, we must first confront the immediate danger to our own citizens."

Wieckowski coughed and took another swig from the flask. "You sure you don't want some of this?"

She shook her head. "I don't drink."

"You might want to take it up, while you can. All right. Let me finish here."

Abby was getting impatient. "Can't you just cut to the chase?"

"Hey," he said, feigning upset. "This is my big moment. My biggest moment since Wilmington Junior High . . . did *A Connecticut Yankee in King Arthur's Court*, and I was Merlin. Big bad Merlin. Long white beard, black robe, and a magic wand. Shit, I could use that magic wand now."

He took another swig, and Abby realized that the dour Lieutenant Wieckowski was getting drunk.

"How about the rest of Dooley's speech?" she pushed.

"Glad you asked."

He changed voices and continued.

"If we lose the Northeast, my fellow Americans, for all intents and purposes our country will cease to exist. We cannot permit this to occur, at any cost."

Something beeped behind him. Wieckowski held up a finger, went to the keyboard and typed in a few keystrokes.

"Okay," he said, turning back. "Where was I?"

She sighed. It was eight minutes till Dooley's speech. At this rate she might as well hear it from the general.

"Ah. I remember," he said. "Right at the kicker. You ready?"

"Lieutenant," she said, "just tell me what they're doing."

He looked at her with glassy eyes. "They made something. No, they didn't make something. They took something that already existed, I think. It's code-named Hemlock. I don't know, it's probably an acronym of some kind."

"Hemlock," Abby repeated. "That's a poison."

"This isn't a poison, actually. It's a microorganism. They're going to use it to stop the gas."

"How?"

Suddenly, Wieckowski sounded stone-cold sober. "They think the gas spreads by bonding with oxygen molecules. That's how it travels so fast, so regularly. Hemlock interrupts that bonding process by disrupting the O^2 molecule."

Abby looked confused.

"Hemlock prevents the gas from spreading," Wieckowski went on, "and it will disrupt the contaminated O^2 molecules as well, effectively neutralizing the effects of the gas in places that are already contaminated."

"Wait a second, wait a second." Abby's head was spinning. "Go back. Hemlock disrupts the O^2 molecule?"

"That's right."

"O^2, meaning oxygen?"

He nodded.

"Isn't that what people need to breathe?"

"Bingo!" Wieckowski shouted. He got to his feet. "Give the little lady a gold star!"

"Jesus Christ."

Abby's blood ran cold. They're going to wipe us out, she thought. They're going to kill us all. We're like sacrifices.

"You're kidding," she whispered. "Tell me you're kidding about all this."

"Kidding? Oh, no." Wieckowski tilted his flask back. "I'm drinking."

"Lieutenant, please—"

"I'm not kidding you, Miss Keller. A warhead containing the Hemlock microorganism was loaded onto an ICBM earlier today in Griffith Forge, Virginia. I've got the video here, if you'd like to see it."

"This is crazy. Do they even have proof this gas exists?"

He shrugged. "Oh, you know the government. They can make the facts say pretty much whatever they want them to. I know they've been running some experiments. Taking samples from people all around the country. Got video of those too." He shuddered and gave her a conspiratorial glance. "But those aren't for the squeamish."

"Where are they planning on detonating this warhead?" Abby asked.

Wieckowski set down his flask and took her hand.

"Come here."

He pulled Abby to her feet, then led her halfway down the aisle that ran between the opposing walls of equipment and pointed up at the ceiling.

"You see that?"

Cables ran through the roof of the trailer and outside, to a satellite dish on the trailer next to them.

"Yeah."

Wieckowski slapped the roof. "You are now standing about two hundred feet below ground zero."

Abby stared at him. "They're setting it off here?"

The beeping noise sounded again.

"Excuse me." Wieckowski pushed past her and went back to his work station.

"But this is crazy," Abby said. "Why are they dropping it here?"

"This is where it all started," he said. "Hemlock's going to spread just like the gas did, following in its wake. Only much, much faster—catch up with it and kill it in about six hours. Before it gets to the rest of the country."

"And then it's going to stop?"

"That's the theory. If they've loaded up the right amount. If Hemlock works the way they expect it to. If if if if if . . ."

Abby sat down and held her head in her hands.

"This is insane," she said. "Absolutely, positively, fucking insane."

"I tend to agree with you," Wieckowski said. "But who knows? Maybe the general and his little weapons are right. Maybe this will stop the gas. That is, if there really is a gas. Which I don't think there is, but hey—" He shrugged. "Like I said, I'm a little cog."

Abby shook her head. The general and his little weapons.

She recalled the look she'd seen in Scott's eyes, when Walters was talking about biochemical warfare and how the United States was under attack, and Abby wondered exactly whose little weapon the general was.

"We have to stop them," she said. "Lieutenant, you can't let them launch this thing."

"It's too late for that. It's too late for anything, really."

Wieckowski walked over to the clock he'd been looking at and turned it around so she could see it.

The display read 00:08:08.

"Hemlock launched this morning. We now have eight minutes until impact." He sat back down in his chair. "By the time Dooley gives his little speech, you and I will have already made our noble sacrifice for America."

"But—" Abby shook her head. "That can't be it. There's gotta be something we can do. There has to be!"

Wieckowski raised his flask and smiled.

"I'm doing it."

January 5, 1994

Have not been keeping up entries; for one thing, forgot to note that Margaret phoned the other day. She's moving again, so the pictures of Julie she has are all boxed up. She promised to send me some when she settles into her new home, though she conveniently forgot to say exactly where it is in Chicago she's moving to.

Where was I?

Yes. Professor Edgecombe.

I was in New York today, and went to see him, to thank him for his letter over the summer. I showed him the Durer woodcut—St. John's vision of Christ and the seven candlesticks.

"Suppose," I said. "Suppose there really had been a sword? And it was shattered, just like in the myth?"

He frowned. "Mr. Kelleher. Have you been drinking?"

I took out the ring and laid it down on the table.

"No. Not at all."

January 5, 1994 Later

Edgecombe wouldn't touch the ring.

He hemmed, and hawed, and finally threw me out of his office. I think he was scared. Who could blame him?

What if, indeed?

What if the sword of Yagunnata was real?

What if the ring I have is one piece of it?

And what would happen if you put all the pieces back together?

I'm beginning to think I know the answer.

PARAMOUNT STUDIOS, LOS ANGELES

The clock read 00:05:42.

Five minutes, and everyone within a fifteen hundred mile radius was as good as dead. And Abby knew there was nothing she could do except sit back and watch it happen. Nothing, that is, except take Wieckowski up on his offer and grab the flask.

That same little beeping noise went off again.

Wieckowski rolled his chair back and typed at the computer.

"Why does it keep making that noise?" she asked.

"To let me know I need to make a course correction."

"For . . . ?"

"For Hemlock."

Abby's pulse quickened. "Wait a minute. You can change that thing's course?"

He snorted. "Don't get your hopes up. I'm just verifying the onboard computer's accuracy. I can't actually change where it's going."

"I don't understand."

"It had to pass through the blackouts to get here, so the guidance system was out for nine hours."

Right. Of course.

"It didn't crash because they shoot it up like a rocket. Way, way up, so it would do an unpowered orbit. Then when the guidance system switched back on, I started guiding it down."

"How?"

"The missile's computer sends the coordinates it thinks it's aiming at. I send back the ones that it's actually targeted."

"So you can change the coordinates?"

"Sure, I can change the impact point by a few miles, but not enough to matter."

A few miles.

"Wait a second," Abby said. "How about twenty miles?"

Wieckowski was looking at another display. "Sorry?"

"Can you change where it hits by twenty miles?"

He shrugged. "Maybe. But that would be about the limit."

"Twenty miles west . . ."

He stopped what he was doing and looked her in the eye.

"The ocean," she said. "You can send it into the ocean."

He shook his head. "No, I can't do that."

"Why not?"

"Listen, I'm no scientist, but to send something that's going to destroy oxygen molecules into the ocean . . . we could destroy all the sea life."

"Better them than us!"

"Yeah, except Hemlock was designed to work in the atmosphere. We don't know what effect it will have in the ocean. It might do even more damage."

"And it might not do anything at all."

"And it might work just the way Dooley thinks it will. It might give the rest of the country a chance."

"Come on, Lieutenant," Abby pleaded. "What are the chances of that happening?"

He shook his head. "About the same as me sending it into the ocean. Sorry, Miss Keller."

Abby took a deep breath and ran her fingers back through her hair. She looked at the clock: 00:04:36.

That was it, then. The Abby Keller story, finis. All she wrote. From actress to reporter to witness to history. It had been a hell of a ride. She might as well have a drink to celebrate.

She was about to ask Wieckowski for a hit off his flask, when she thought of something she'd rather have.

Abby stood up and unbuttoned the top of her dress.

Wieckowski had his back to her and had switched on the television monitor.

"Maybe we'll be around for the first minute or so of Dooley's speech," he said. "Might as well see how close I came to getting it right."

"Lieutenant," she said.

"What?"

"Turn around."

He did.

She smiled at him and undid another button.

He laughed—quietly at first, and then burst into full-out gales. "Come on," he said after he'd caught his breath. "You can't be serious. You're trying to seduce me?"

"Would you like that?"

She walked over to him, moving with the curves of her body.

Wieckowski's smile faded. "Yeah. I would." He stood up. "But I don't think there's time."

"You're sure?" She smiled and walked closer. "I'm quick."

Reaching around his waist, she grabbed his gun and ripped it out of its holster.

"See?"

He fell back into his chair and started laughing again. "What are you going to do, shoot me?"

"Do it," Abby said. She waved the gun at him. "Change those goddamn coordinates."

"Come on. You don't even know how to use that thing," he said.

She clicked the safety off. "Want to bet?"

"Look at this," Wieckowski said. "I answer all your lousy questions, and more, and this is the thanks I get?"

Abby pointed the gun at his head. "Change those goddamn coordinates!"

"No."

"I'll shoot you."

Wieckowski shook his head. "I don't think you will."

They locked eyes.

"Fuck!" Abby shouted, turning away.

Wieckowski started laughing again.

"Get out of the way, then, goddamnit. Get out of the way and let me do it."

"Really?"

"Really."

He was still smiling. "Sure. Be my guest." He sat back in his chair and rolled it all the way to the other end of the trailer.

Abby leaned over the monitor.

There were two rows of identical numbers on the screen:

34 16 118 52
34 16 118 52

The bottom row was blinking.

All right, Abby thought. Simple enough. The blinking ones had to be the numbers Wieckowski was changing.

She hit the 5 key to test her theory.

The computer beeped, and a message flashed across the screen

REQUESTED VALUE IS OUTSIDE ALLOWABLE PARAMETERS

"Sorry," Wieckowski said. "Wrong answer."

"Shit!" Abby hit the countertop, and the display changed back to the two rows of numbers.

All right, she told herself. Stay calm. The first key she was hitting, that was probably changing the first number. The 3, in the 34, 5 was too much, 4 was probably too much. What would happen if she hit the 3?

She tried it.

The 3 in the bottom 34 stopped blinking.

Abby smiled.

"Figure out something, did you?" the lieutenant called out.

She didn't answer.

Now came the tough part. What the hell did those numbers mean?

They were coordinates, Wieckowski had said. Right. But what did they stand for?

Longitude and latitude? Maybe, but why were there four of them? She wracked her brain trying to remember geography; longitude and latitude were in degrees and minutes, that's why there were four numbers.

She looked at the display again.

34 16 118 52
34 16 118 52

So that was 34 degrees, 16 minutes, and 118 degrees, 52 minutes. Fine.

But which was longitude and which was latitude?

She looked at the clock: 00:03:06.

"Fuck!" Abby shouted. "Fuck fuck fuck!"

Wieckowski was still laughing.

"Goddamn you!"

Abby's eyes filled with tears. She couldn't think of a single longitude or latitude reference point to compare those numbers to.

Wait a second.

Zero degrees latitude was the equator.

The computer beeped again.

"All right," Wieckowski said, getting to his feet. "Playtime's over. Let me make sure this comes down right, at least give everybody else in the country a fighting chance."

Abby shook her head. "No. Stay back. I'm doing this."

"Get serious. Let me back in there."

He moved toward her.

"Damn it." She turned away from the display and saw the clock at 00:02:47 and Wieckowski getting closer. She pointed the gun at him.

"I'm not fucking around!" she screamed. "Sit back down!"

"Come on," Wieckowski said, "give me the gun."

He was five feet away.

Abby shot him.

Wieckowski slumped to the floor, a red patch slowly spreading across the front of his shirt.

"I can't believe you fucking did that," he said. "Shit."

"I can't believe it either."

Abby put the gun down and turned away, staring at the numbers once again.

34 16 118 52
34 16 118 52

Zero degrees latitude was the equator. Globally, Los Angeles was not that far from the equator. So the thirty-four degrees sixteen minutes measure was probably the latitude. Latitude was north/south. Longitude was east/west. So the 118 degrees fifty-two minutes was what she wanted to change. She wanted to send it west, as far as she could.

But which direction was west?

Damn damn damn!

Abby's mind raced. All right. The equator was zero degrees latitude. What was zero degrees longitude?

She had absolutely no fucking idea.

"Shit!" Abby yelled. "Shit! Shit! Shit!"

She looked at the clock: 00:02:29.

She pounded the desk.

"Don't break anything."

She turned and saw Wieckowski sitting on the floor, still with a half smile on his face, blood bubbling between his lips.

"Zero degrees longitude? What is it?" she yelled. "What is it?"

He shook his head.

"Yahhh!" she screamed in frustration, and pulled at her hair.

The computer beeped.

Abby picked up the gun and almost shot the display. Instead, she took a deep breath and started calculating again.

All right. They start counting latitude at the equator. Where do they start counting longitude? Come on, Abby. Think. Think.

Nothing.

Come on. Where do they start counting longitude?

"I don't know!" she shouted. "Wherever the fuck they want to!"

They. Who was they?

The fucking British, right? Weren't they the ones who came up with longitude and latitude? Or was she confusing that with time zones, A.M. and P.M.? She had no idea.

She had two minutes.

Okay, she thought. So let's pretend longitude starts in England. If England is zero, and Los Angeles is 118, then the higher the numbers go, the farther west you are. So she needed to make the numbers higher.

34 16 118 52
34 16 118 52

She punched in the 4, and that stopped blinking, and then the 1, and the 6. That took care of the latitude.

Now for the longitude.

Two minutes left to impact, she didn't think it was worth trying to convince Hemlock it was hundreds of degrees off course. She punched in the first two digits—1 and then another 1—and then, after quick consideration tried a 9.

REQUESTED VALUE IS OUTSIDE ALLOWABLE PARAMETERS

She waited a second, and the screen cleared, and she hit the 8.

Now there were only two numbers blinking, the 5 and the

2, the fifty-two minutes in the longitude. Fifty-two minutes out of sixty, she supposed; there were sixty minutes in an hour, so probably sixty minutes in a degree too, but she tried a 9 anyway.

She got the "requested value" error message again. She tried the 8, then the 7, and finally the 6, and the same thing happened all three times, so she ended up punching in the five.

One number left.

The two.

She punched the 9 key, and the computer beeped.

The second row of numbers disappeared, and now the monitor read simply:

34 16 118 59

Abby let out a long, slow breath and leaned on the counter.

"I did it," she said.

She glanced over at Wieckowski, who was still smiling.

And then she had a horrible thought.

"The missile's computer sends the coordinates it thinks it's aiming at," Wieckowski had said. "I send back the ones that it's actually targeted."

She told the missile it was aiming further west than it should be, so didn't that mean it was going to adjust its actual trajectory eastward?

"Fuck!" Abby screamed; 00:01:48.

"Wieckowski!" She bent over him and shouted in his ear. "Are you alive? Goddamnit, answer me! I fucked up, I fucked up!"

He opened an eye and stared at her.

"Listen to me, I screwed up big-time, I thought I was sending it west but I sent it east instead—how can I fix it?"

He shook his head and mumbled something. She couldn't hear. She leaned over him and put her ear next to his lips.

"Bad girl," he said, and then breathed out once, sharply, and closed his eyes.

"Wieckowski!" She shook his shoulder. "Wieckowski!"

He didn't move.

"Shit!"

Abby got back to her feet and went to the monitor.

There was still only one row of numbers on the display. She had to get that second row back. She had to convince the missile it was off course again.

How the hell was she going to do that?

She didn't have a clue: 00:01:23.

"God!" she yelled, leaning her head back and turning her face up to the roof of the trailer. "I need a miracle, please! Okay? This is Abby Keller, begging you for a miracle! Please, please, please do whatever it takes to make that computer start beeping again, so I can have another chance to send this fucking Hemlock monster off course!"

She squeezed her eyes shut, squeezed her hands into clenched fists, and waited, praying for the little beep of the computer.

Nothing.

That was it.

Finito. Kaput. End of story. Abby fucks up and blows chance to save world, but at least no one will be around to report it, she thought, because we'll all be dead, dead, dead, dead, dead.

She opened her eyes and saw the cable leading out to the satellite dish on the roof of the trailer.

Ground zero.

She jumped on the counter and started slamming the roof of the trailer as hard as she could. It was a silly idea, but it was all she had now, and there was no sense in not giving it her all. She reached over and yanked on the cable too, for good measure.

The computer started beeping madly.

Abby jumped down from the counter and looked at the screen.

SYSTEM ERROR
PLEASE WAIT

"Oh, great," Abby thought, looking at the clock: 00:00:54. Was there even time to change the course now?

The computer was still beeping.

SYSTEM ERROR
PLEASE WAIT

"Come on, you bastard!" Abby slammed her hand down on the counter.

The display cleared.

34 16 118 59
34 16 118 59

The second row of numbers was blinking.

Abby entered in 34 16 118 54. The letters flashed solid and disappeared. The time read: 00:00:31

She collapsed into her chair.

She'd done what she could. All she could hope for was that it was enough.

The television monitor at the very end of the trailer went from blue to black. Solid white letters appeared on the screen.

PLEASE STAND BY FOR THE COMMANDER-IN-CHIEF OF THE UNITED STATES.

Abby waited, watching anxiously. The clock on the wall went to zero. The monitor stayed dark.

A muffled ringing filled the trailer. Abby looked around. She couldn't tell where the sound was coming from.

She looked down. Wieckowski.

There was a cell phone in his inside jacket pocket.

She pulled it out and pressed the talk button.

"Hello?"

"Wieckowski! Is that you? What the hell happened?"

Abby smiled.

"Hello?" the voice on the phone demanded. "Hello? Is anybody there?"

"Yes," she said, realizing suddenly her eyes were moist. "Yes. We're all here, you bastard. Every last one of us."

The voice on the other end sputtered.

Abby hung up, and went to find Luka.

WILLIAMS HOUSE, NEAR ALBUQUERQUE

Steve finished searching the last of the second-floor bedrooms and started back down the stairs, anxious and angry and frustrated. He'd already done the attic, and he and Lawson had started with the two rooms downstairs, so that meant Kerry was nowhere in the house.

So where was his daughter?

"Nothing?"

Lawson was sitting at the dining room table, reapplying bandages to Carew's shoulder with a first-aid kit he'd found and waiting for Steve to hurry so they could get Carew back to the school—and a doctor.

"No sign of her." Steve shook his head. "Damn it. She's got to be around here—or somewhere near."

Lawson nodded. "Yeah."

But he didn't sound convinced, and for some reason that made Steve angry.

"Well, what else could it be? Why else would the bracelet be here?"

"The girl could have met your daughter anywhere," Lawson said. "She could have traded the bracelet."

"Yeah." Steve nodded. "Maybe."

"Or it might not be the same bracelet."

"No." Steve shook his head. He was sure of that; he'd been with Kerry when she bought it. He pulled the bracelet out of his pocket and held it up. It was heavier than it looked; solid. He wondered what it was made of. Iron?

"Let me take one more look around," he said.

"Steve—"

"One more look around, damn it. Five fucking minutes, what's the big deal?" He glared at Lawson, whose eyes were wide with surprise.

Lawson nodded. "Five minutes. But then I'm going. With or without you."

"Yeah." Steve shrugged. "I got that."

All right. He'd been through the living room, but the kitchen . . .

That was the first room they'd checked, but he hadn't been thorough. He walked in and noticed the big walk-in refrigerator. He went up to it and pulled it open.

There was a girl lying on the floor.

He turned her over.

It was Kerry.

They gunned the jeep all the way back to the high school. Kerry lay down across the backseat, her head in Steve's lap, shivering, floating in and out of consciousness.

He put his coat over her and rubbed her hands. Her eyes fluttered open.

"Dad," she whispered, hugging him. "I'm sorry," she said, shaking her head. "It wasn't me, I swear. That wasn't me who did that."

"Shhh." He pushed her hair back from her forehead and smiled, glad to have her back in his arms. "It's all right."

When they got back to the school, Steve carried her into the gym and they were surrounded as soon as they entered. One woman led Steve over to a cot in the corner of the gym, where he lay Kerry down.

"It's all right," he said. "You'll be safe here."

"Mr. Crescent?"

Steve looked up and saw a woman staring down at him.

"I'm Dr. Riser," she said. "Mr. Carew, who has major gun-shot trauma, seems to think your daughter needs to see me more than he does. Insists on it, in fact."

Steve turned and saw Carew watching them. The man gave him a thumbs-up, and Steve returned a grateful smile.

"This is Kerry," Steve said, standing up. "My daughter. She—"

"Mr. Carew told me," Dr. Riser said. She put a hand to Kerry's forehead, then felt her hands and legs. She put a stethoscope to her chest and listened.

"Hypothermia," she said. "How long were you in that freezer?"

Kerry shook her head. "I don't know. Half a day, I guess."

"Shouldn't be any permanent damage. Hot liquids, plenty of rest," the doctor lifted up her chin, "and stay warm."

Kerry smiled wearily, and the doctor smiled back. Then she left.

"I don't understand," Kerry said after Steve came back with a cup of tea for her. "How did you ever find me?"

"It's a miracle," he said, shaking his head. "All I can say is it's a damn miracle. That, and—" he'd almost forgotten, "your bracelet."

Kerry's brow furrowed. "What?"

"That bracelet you bought last summer," Steve said. "I found it on one of the girls back at that place." He reached into his pocket for it. "See?"

The moment Kerry saw it, a strange, angry expression came across her face.

"Are you all right?" Steve asked.

"I'm fine. Can I have that back?"

"Sure." But when he went to hand it to her, he realized she had turned cold on him, and after he'd saved her and brought her back, her attitude made him so mad—

She took the bracelet and, abruptly, he wasn't angry anymore. Just like that.

"Wait a second," Steve said. "Wait a second."

He took the bracelet back from Kerry.

"Hey," she said, "what—"

"Shhh," Steve said, and concentrated.

He was quiet a long, long time.

Finally, he opened his eyes. "You were right," he said. "It wasn't you at all."

He held up the bracelet.

"It was this."

GRAND CANYON NATIONAL PARK

They stuck to the back roads, through the northwest corner of New Mexico, through the Navajo Reservation and into Arizona. Bert had been to the canyon before, driven through the country around it more than once, and it looked exactly the same—untouched by the waves that had ripped through a couple days ago.

The familiar surroundings, the open spaces, the small scale of the places they passed through, all combined to make him feel safer than he had in days.

But as they got closer to the canyon, the landscape changed. The rock formations became forests, the back roads began flowing together, and at the edge of the national park they found themselves, for the first time since leaving Denver that morning, driving down a road that had a route number attached to it—Highway 64, heading west into the village of Grand Canyon.

Bert sat a little straighter in his seat and adjusted his rearview mirror. He began checking it, and the road ahead, very carefully.

"What is it?" Betty asked. "There isn't anyone following us, is there?"

He shook his head. "No. But even though it's winter, I'd

bet there are still a lot of people around here. I'd like to get off the highway, find a trail, and get out of sight. We don't know what sort of reception we're likely to get."

Five minutes farther on they found out.

A big banner hung across the road, stretched between two telephone poles: U.S. ARMY NO! The words spray-painted in huge red letters.

The bodies of a half-dozen dead soldiers swung from the phone lines next to it.

Bert had been driving with his rifle on the seat next to him. Now he stopped the truck and got out Betty's handgun as well.

"We're not going on, are we?"

Bert thought about that. It was at least ten minutes back to where they'd merged onto 64. "We'll give it five minutes in this direction," he said. "If we don't find a place to turn off by then, we'll swing around."

"You know, I've never used one of these," she said, fingering the gun nervously.

"Hopefully, you won't have to. Just keep an eye out. Yell if you see anything. Don't shoot unless I tell you to."

He started the truck up again.

Not more than two minutes down the highway he found what he was looking for: a park service road partially obscured by thick undergrowth, and chained off from the highway. The chain was fastened to two stout, short logs buried in cement. Using the axe they'd brought, Bert chopped off one of the logs and the chain swung free.

They pulled into the forest.

The woods closed instantly around them; the majestic evergreens, the scraggly junipers. The bare branches of towering pines, dusted with snow, hung over them like the gnarled fingers of ancient, cranky sentries, set to guard the forest from human intruders.

Like the apple-throwing trees in *The Wizard of Oz*; like the Ents in *The Lord of the Rings*, Bert recalled from books he'd read in high school. Then his attention was drawn back to the road by a fallen trunk blocking their path.

He had to get out and move it, and then he had little time to do anything other than watch the road, which had abruptly turned into little more than an unpaved, winding trail. He lost it more than once, at one point taking a wrong turn that almost ended up stranding them in a creek bed. The deeper into the woods they got, the more grateful he was to Connie for giving them the truck, because there was simply no way in hell they would have made it through with his car.

They went on that way for what had to be half an hour, and just when Bert had begun to think that the road wasn't leading them anywhere in particular, they burst through the trees onto a rocky mesa. Not a quarter mile ahead of them lay the rim of the Grand Canyon, the rocks burnished a thousand shades of red and gold and orange by the setting sun.

"Perfect," he said, stopping the truck and thanking God. "Perfect timing. Let's go take a look."

He opened his door.

"My God," Betty said. "That's beautiful."

He smiled. "Wait'll you see it in morning. That's when it's really something."

"Can we camp out there? By the rim?"

Bert hesitated. He didn't like the idea of being out in the open like that, but something about the idea intrigued him too. To wake up and see the sun . . .

"We'll see," was all he said. Then he took her hand and they walked out to see the canyon.

They ate dinner right at the rim: peanut butter and jelly sandwiches, cheese and crackers, and lemonade to wash it all down, almost all the perishables they'd packed. Tomorrow they'd have to break out the canned goods or go hunting. Bert had told her there were deer around that were so tame and so used to the tourists, they'd walk up and take the food right out of your hands.

Betty was in heaven. She stuffed a cracker into her mouth and lay back on the blanket Bert had spread out. It wasn't quite picnic weather, more like campfire weather, but Bert had refused to light a fire out in the open, and it was still warm enough that they could sit out in the night air with their coats on and be comfortable.

Bert put the leftovers back into the big duffel bag.

"You don't happen to have a bottle of wine in there, do you?" Betty asked. "I could really use—" Then she remembered and flushed. "Oh, I'm sorry."

"It's all right." Bert smiled. "Tell you the truth, I could use a glass of wine too. My problem is, I'm not sure I could stop with one."

Betty nodded. Bert looked into her eyes. He leaned over and kissed her. Then he kissed her again, and Betty smiled as he did.

And suddenly the last lingering clouds of Harold and the nightmares and the army and the waves and all the madness of the last few days just blew away, and it was just her and Bert, and the cathedral of stars above them, man and woman. And she was feeling something inside her that she hadn't felt in a long, long time, something she hadn't been sure she would ever be able to feel again.

"Where are we going to sleep?" she asked.

Bert smiled. "You want to go to sleep?"

"You know what I mean."

Instead of answering, he unzipped the duffel bag, reached inside and pulled out a sleeping bag.

Betty started laughing. "Right here? Under the stars?"

"Why not?" he said.

She had a big smile on her face.

After they'd kissed and hugged and made love, Betty lay next to Bert in the sleeping bag, looking up at the stars, and every few minutes breaking into a smile. It felt good to smile. It had been a long time since she'd done much of it. That, and making love.

She was looking forward to more of both.

Suddenly, she was ravenous. Easing back into her jeans, which were crumpled into a ball at the bottom of the sleeping bag, she slipped on her sweater and got up. She ate the last peanut butter sandwich and realized it was now very cold indeed.

Warm as it was inside the sleeping bag, she knew she should wake Bert. He'd want them to spend the night in the forest, nearer to the truck, in case they needed to make a quick getaway. She knew she shouldn't let herself fall asleep out here. But it had been a magical night and she didn't want it to end.

She climbed back into the bag, still fully dressed, and snuggled in next to him.

Then she closed her eyes.

She and Bert were standing together, arm in arm, looking out over the edge of the canyon. She turned to face him, and suddenly he was Heathcliff and she was Cathy, and he picked her up in his arms and she said, "The heather, Heathcliff. I want to smell it one more time before I die."

And he laughed, because they were only playing, and then he set her down on her feet again and they were back to being just plain old Bert, plain old Betty, and her dream was just a replay of those moments when they'd first come out of the forest and seen the canyon, walked out across the mesa to the very edge and looked down into the vast, empty darkness below, while the moon shone full and bright above them.

Except it had still been daylight when they first got to the rim.

Betty opened her eyes and blinked.

Bert stood at the edge of the canyon, silhouetted against the darkness.

She opened her mouth to call him back, to come lie down in the sleeping bag with her again.

Then the last vestiges of sleepiness dissolved and she realized that Bert's warm body was still pressed right up against hers. The man at the edge of the canyon turned, and the moonlight fell on his face, and Betty screamed and started to cry at the same time.

"Well, missy," Harold said, taking a step forward. "You've got some explaining to do."

Bert was on his feet in a flash, but for a second thought he was still asleep. He had to be asleep, he had to be dreaming, because Harold—Harold from the cathedral nightmare, Harold from the stories Betty told him, Harold who was supposed to be dead but looked very much alive at this second— was standing not ten feet away.

"You're Bert." Harold smiled. "And you're naked."

Bert was, but he didn't feel it. He was consumed with the man standing before him. The moonlight could only hint at the jagged, oozing wound across his neck, right where Betty said it was, but it certainly looked like it should have been fatal; but of course it hadn't been because here he was, large as life.

Betty scrambled out of the sleeping bag and stood next to Bert, shaking as hard as he was.

"Now, Bert," Harold said, "to tell you the goddamn truth, I'm a little upset. That's my wife you're sleeping with, mister— and I'll grant you that she's still wearing her clothes, so I don't have any actual proof of anything, but I wasn't born yesterday—well, actually, in a manner of speaking you could say I was, but that's neither here nor there at the moment— and I think that whatever it is you're doing needs some explaining. Or didn't she bother to tell you she was a married woman?"

Bert reached down into the duffel bag and pulled out the handgun.

"Go away," he said, and he was ashamed at the tremor he heard in his voice.

"Excuse me?" Harold said, taking another step forward. "You're telling me to go away? Listen, buddy, in case you hadn't heard, the marriage vow is a sacred contract. Sacred in the eyes of God." He wagged an admonishing finger at Bert. "Believe it or not, I take those kinds of things very seriously."

Bert shot him in the chest.

Harold fell back and landed spread-eagle on the ground, face looking up to the stars.

He coughed once, twice, and climbed back to his feet.

"I had hoped we were going to be able to have a civilized conversation about this, but I can see—"

Bert dropped the gun. He pissed all over the ground.

"I can see," Harold continued, "that you have a very strange idea of civilized behavior. Damn." Harold shook his head. "What kind of man have you taken up with here, Betty?"

Bert didn't bother trying to make sense of what was happening; he didn't try to pick up the gun and shoot Harold again. He grabbed Betty's hand and ran for the truck.

His mind was racing too; the rifle was in the cab underneath a blanket. It was loaded and ready to fire, and it was a big gun; one round from that thing, right in the face, would blow Harold's head right off his shoulders.

Or maybe they should just get in the truck and drive. Maybe—

Bert stopped running, and Betty, whom he'd been tugging with him, stopped too.

The truck was locked. The keys were in his clothes, back in the sleeping bag.

"What's the matter?" Harold called out. "You have a change of heart? You want to talk things over, mano a mano?"

"The keys," Bert said to Betty, and now he felt the cold. His fingers and toes were already like ice cubes, and he didn't know if he'd be able to hold the keys to start the car or fire the rifle or—

He couldn't think about that now.

"They're in my pants."

Betty gasped and began to cry again.

"I'm going to try and draw him away from there. You get them. You go. Even if I can't get back to you, you go, understand?"

She stifled her crying and nodded mutely, tears still streaming down her face.

Bert turned back toward the canyon and started walking. He circled one way, Betty the other. He stubbed his toe on a rock and could barely feel it. His teeth started chattering.

"You know something?" Harold called out when Bert was about fifty feet away. "I think you two are trying to gang up on me. Now that doesn't seem fair, does it?"

Bert didn't bother answering. He bent down and picked up a good-size rock and kept coming.

"I guess we're not going to be able to talk this out after all," Harold said.

Bert saw Betty moving behind Harold, heading toward the sleeping bag.

"I think you're right," he replied, trying to keep Harold focused on him.

"Good." Harold smiled. "I'm glad you see things my way." He had the handgun now, raised it and fired.

A scream rang out. The bullet had slammed into Bert's gut, and the next thing he knew, he was sitting on the ground, holding his stomach in his hands.

"Oh no," he said.

He looked up, and the stars were going out. Everything was going black.

Harold leaned over him and put the gun against his forehead. "Goodbye, Bert," he said, and pulled the trigger again.

Another scream came from behind him, and Harold turned around to face Betty.

"Now," he said, "I believe you have something that belongs to me."

Betty dropped the sleeping bag and scrambled backward.

"Wait," Harold said. "Don't—"

Taking a few more steps back, her eyes went wide as she dropped off the edge of the canyon and screamed.

Harold got to the rim just in time to hear her scream abruptly cut off.

"Oh, for crying out loud," he said, squinting down into the darkness. "Why can't anything be easy?"

It took him two hours to find her body, and he was lucky at that—she hadn't fallen all the way to the canyon floor, but had landed only partway down, bent over like an upside-down U on a long pointy piece of rock that hung a few feet above the path.

Harold took hold of her arm and yanked.

Betty flopped down onto the path before him.

Her pretty face was all smashed up, and her beautiful body wasn't so beautiful anymore. But he wasn't interested in those things anyway.

He had no time.

Kneeling down next to her, he pulled out the wad of bills she'd stolen from him. It didn't feel appreciably smaller, and he was grateful, because over the years, they'd had more than one argument about money. She always seemed to think it grew on trees.

Ah well. No more of that.

He pulled the bills free from the money clip and tossed them into the darkness below.

Then he held the clip up to the moonlight and frowned.

The gold plating had been almost completely scraped off, and a second later he realized why—the bitch had been keeping it in the same pocket as her house keys. That made him mad for a second, until he realized she was dead, and that the gold plating wasn't important anyway. It never really had been, of course.

What mattered was the iron underneath.

Harold turned around and was about to start hiking back up when he realized he still had one more thing to do.

He had to say goodbye.

He dragged Betty back to her feet and held her up so they were face-to-face.

"Well, babe, here we are. The end of a long, winding road. I'm sorry things didn't work out, but I know I did my bit. I said the words, and I meant them, I really did. Till death do us part."

He shrugged.

"So . . ."

He heaved her body over the side of the ledge and watched it bounce all the way into the canyon below.

Then he hiked back up to his car and started the long drive west.

LITTLE CHAPARRAL, TEXAS

Leo put down the last journal and rubbed his eyes.

It was late, and he was tired, and he had no idea what to make of what he'd just been reading.

The old man—Thomas—had been running all over the country for years, collecting these pieces of iron. A ring. The candlestick. The spike. Trying to put his sword back together. There were other pieces out there too that he was still looking for. Leo didn't understand everything he'd read; half the time, the guy wrote like he was on drugs. Especially in the later entries, where he sounded totally paranoid. Trying to connect the sword to the waves. Rattling on about some woman.

Leo heard footsteps. He looked up.

The old man was standing in the doorway.

"I want the candlestick," he said. "Give me the candlestick, and I'll let you go."

Leo rose from the desk. This was his first good look at the old man. He had long, white hair, past his shoulders, pale skin, and blazing blue eyes. He had on a long, green trenchcoat, stained with Leo-didn't-want-to-know-what.

He looked like a crazy man.

He took a step forward toward Leo.

"Please. Give it to me, and I'll let you go."

"You'll let me?" Leo laughed. He had fifty pounds, six inches, and at least two dozen years on the guy. "After what you did . . . I oughta kick your ass."

"What I did?" The old man—Thomas—nodded toward the desk, at the journals strewn across it. "You know what's happening. You know why—"

"You crazy sonuvabitch!" Leo shouted. "You killed the wrong guy!"

The old man blinked. "What?"

"You killed the wrong guy," Leo repeated.

He told Thomas about Peter's search for Novarra and the spike. Even before he finished, Thomas had gone chalk-white.

"Oh God." He turned away, shaking his head "I'm sorry. God, I'm sorry. God damn it!"

He slammed his fist into the wall. It went right through the sheetrock and Leo heard the crack of wood splintering as well. A support beam?

The old guy was a lot stronger than he looked, Leo realized.

And he'd just punched with the arm he'd been shot in.

"Careful," Leo said. "Your shoulder . . ."

Thomas pulled back his shirt.

The wound was completely healed.

"How . . ."

"The iron," Thomas said. "It has powers."

"I remember," Leo said. He reached for the candlestick.

"DON'T TOUCH THAT!" Thomas shouted.

Leo's hand froze, an inch away from the metal. Thomas strode quickly across the room, and picked up the candlestick. His face twisted a moment. Then he put it, and the journals, back into the knapsack.

"Is that your car out front?"

"Yes," Leo said. "Why?"

Thomas held out his hand. "Give me the keys."

Leo looked at him. He had no doubt the old guy would take them if he didn't turn them over. He also had no doubt he could do it easily.

"Wait a second," Leo said.

The old man shook his head. "Now. There's no time."

"I said wait!" Leo shouted. He was surprised at the anger in his voice.

So was Thomas. The old man frowned.

"Explain all this to me," Leo went on, more softly. "Tell me what's happening."

Thomas sighed. "It's not that easy. I . . ."

His voice trailed off. His eyes went to the bookshelf behind the Sheriff's desk. He reached up and pulled down a book.

The Bible.

"You know the Bible?" Thomas asked.

"No. Not really." Leo hadn't been to Church in years for anything other than a wedding. Sundays, as far as he was concerned, were for barbeques, and football.

"Revelations," Thomas said, opening to the back of the book. " 'And I saw an angel come down from heaven, having the key of the bottomless pit, and a great chain in his hand. He laid hold on the dragon, that old Serpent, which is the Devil and bound him a thousand years.' "

"So?"

Thomas looked up. "And after that, he must be loosed." He flipped the book shut. "The sword is the key. Once all the pieces are put together, then—"

"The devil is set loose?" Leo interrupted. Saying it like that, he wanted to laugh. The expression on Thomas's face stopped him. "What about these waves? Seems to me it's loose already."

"Oh no," Thomas said. "It's just waking up. Once she puts all seven pieces together—"

"Whoa, hold up," Leo said. He looked at Thomas. "She?"

LOS ANGELES AIR FORCE BASE

He was dead.

Or well on the way, Jimmy thought. He had to be. Omar had shot him right in the forehead from a foot away, no way to dodge that bullet. And he could remember a split second of unbearable pain before everything went dark and he went numb all over and was dead.

Except . . .

Here he was. But where was here? Limbo? He'd seen a Jerry Springer show once where they put on people who'd had near-death experiences. They all talked about being someplace between life and death before they returned to their bodies through some miracle or another, about seeing a white light at the end of a long tunnel, hearing the voices of their loved ones, the heavenly choir.

Which was definitely not what he was getting.

What he was getting was more like that scene from *The Wizard of Oz*, where Dorothy's house went for a ride on the twister and all those people drifted past her bedroom window. But instead of Auntie Em and the wicked witch, he was getting Omar. That big guy and his kid. Hector. Tina. And Martinez, fucking Martinez.

And here came someone he didn't know at all, a woman, a beautiful woman with long dark hair, and right behind her—

A white tiger?

Metal flashed. Something struck him full in the face.

Jimmy screamed and opened his eyes.

The woman with long dark hair was leaning over him.

The tiger was next to her.

Whoa. Definitely not in Kansas anymore.

He groaned and sat up, his hands covered in something black and sticky.

Tar, he realized. Melted tar.

What the hell . . .

He looked around. It was dark; the sky was lit by a hazy reddish-orange glow.

He was inside the fire.

"How do you feel?" the woman asked.

"Not good. Weird." Very weird, he thought. He couldn't smell a thing. Couldn't taste a thing either. He tried to stand up. His legs wobbled. They felt weak, as if he hadn't used them in a long time.

"What's the matter with me?" Jimmy asked.

The woman smiled.

"Not a thing. Not anymore."

Tuesday 8:50 A.M., CST

I-40, SOMEWHERE WEST OF AMARILLO

The old man drove, and Leo read. Leo never read; he watched sports. He went to movies. He watched TV. He hadn't read so many words since college.

He fell asleep reading, with the old man hunched over the wheel beside him, his eyes seemingly glued open.

When he woke, he started reading again. He went through the journals a second time; there were parts he didn't understand, parts he'd skipped.

The old man drove, and Leo read.

January 3, 1991

In 1977, I was a reporter for the Bergen County Examiner. *I'd just gotten promoted from the city desk to*

street crime, and I guess I was a little eager. Malachi
Coburn was the biggest story I'd ever had. Maybe you remember his name. Maybe not. It was a long time ago.
The headlines might ring a bell, though. My favorite was
SECAUCUS SLAUGHTERHOUSE. I wrote that one, and the article that went with it. Could probably still cite every
word. But I'll spare you the details, and go straight to the
highlights.

Coburn was a serial killer. A particularly nasty one.
Tortured his victims in ways I could never have imagined
possible. Until I began to dream about them.

The dreams started the first day I brought the ring
home. But I'm getting ahead of myself.

Leo looked up.

"I remember Coburn," he said. "Sick sonuvabitch. It's his
ring you have."

Thomas nodded. "That's right."

Leo held up the journal he was reading. "There's nothing
in here about how you got it."

"No big mystery," Thomas said. "After the cops shot him,
I found it in his things."

"Aren't they supposed to give those to the next-of-kin?"

"He didn't have any kin. They couldn't even find a birth
certificate for him. For all they ever knew, Coburn wasn't
even his real name."

"So they gave you the ring."

Thomas shook his head. "No. I took it. I was alone in the
room with the body and his things, and I saw the ring
and . . . I had to have it. Had to." He fell silent a moment, lost
in thought.

"What is it?" Leo asked.

"If only I hadn't taken it," he said quietly. "My daughter
would still be alive."

"How do you figure that one?" None of this was in the
journals.

"I had the ring. Coburn came to get it. Julie got in the way. So it's my fault, really."

There was a world of pain in the way he said those simple words.

"Wait a minute." Leo frowned. "I thought you said the cops shot him."

"They did."

"You made it sound like he was dead."

"He was."

"But—"

"Haven't you been paying attention?" Thomas asked. "Dead doesn't matter. Not when you have the iron."

Leo remembered the old man's wound, how it had miraculously healed.

"All right," he said. "But Coburn didn't have the iron. You did."

"He had it when he was shot," Thomas said. "That was enough. My fault," he repeated.

And no matter how Leo argued, he couldn't convince Thomas otherwise.

BOOK III

REVELATION

BEL AIR, LOS ANGELES

Jimmy pushed open the front door of the mansion and walked inside.

There was a party going on.

For a second he was pissed. While he was out getting his ass kicked, stabbed, and shot at, these bastards were relaxing by the pool. Mixing up drinks. Scoring with chicks.

On his right was a big living room, with a white carpet and brown leather furniture. There was a man sprawled out on a La-Z-Boy, toking on a big fat joint. He did a double take when he saw Jimmy.

"What?" Jimmy said. "What the fuck you starin' at?"

The guy got up off the couch, shaking his head. "You dead, man. I saw him shoot you."

"You were there?" Jimmy walked up to the guy, getting angry all over again.

The guy shook his head. "Look at you, man."

Jimmy poked him in the chest with a finger. "Hey. You were there?"

The man slapped Jimmy's hand away. "Yeah, motherfucker. I was there."

"Thanks for the help," Jimmy said. He punched the man in the face.

Bones cracked. The guy's, and his. The guy fell to the ground, slobbering. Jimmy held up his hand and studied it. The knuckles were all crooked.

Weird, he thought. He couldn't feel a thing. What the hell had that woman done to him anyway?

He headed back out into the hall.

It opened up into a huge atrium, with a pool in the middle. Music was blaring. Tables full of food and liquor ringed the pool.

Someone tapped him on the shoulder.

Jimmy turned around and saw one of the girls who had been with Omar at the base when he got shot. She was wearing tight hip-huggers and a tighter halter top.

"Hey," Jimmy said. "What's goin' on?"

"What's goin' on?" The woman shook her head. "I tell you what's gonna be goin' on in about five seconds. You gonna get fucked up somethin' fierce. When my man comes—"

"Omar?" Jimmy interrupted. "You're talking about Omar, right?" He scanned the crowd. "Where is he?"

"I wouldn't be in a big hurry to find him if I were you." The girl put her hands on her hips and curled her face up in distaste. "What the hell happened to you?"

Jimmy frowned. The guy he'd punched out had also said something about how bad he looked.

"Is there a bathroom around here?" he asked.

"What?"

"A bathroom," he said, getting up in her face. "What's the matter, don't you speak English?"

For a second she looked ready to come back with another smart remark. Then she saw the look in his eyes and backed off.

"Right there." She pointed.

"Thanks," he said. At the door, he turned around. The girl was still staring at him. Damn. She was fine. "What's your name?"

"Rose."

"Thanks, Rose. Excuse me a minute."

He locked the door and looked in the mirror.

What he saw made him queasy. He was a walking horror show. There was blood all crusted up in one eyebrow, his skin was all black and blue, and there was an honest-to-God hole in his forehead where Omar had shot him. A freakin' hole. He poked a finger in and wiggled it around. He didn't feel anything weird.

He tossed his shirtsleeve in the wastebasket, checked the bandana one more time, and opened the bathroom door.

Omar was standing there, arms folded, staring at him.

"You gotta be fuckin' me," he said. "You gotta be fuckin' me." He took a step forward, his voice rising. "You come here and you—"

Jimmy's hands shot out and grabbed Omar's head, one on each side. He started to twist.

Omar screamed.

Jimmy applied more pressure.

"Just shut up," he said, still twisting. "I risk my goddamn life to do you a favor, and you shoot me in the fucking head? What kind of bullshit is that, huh?"

He twisted Omar's head down so the two of them were face-to-face, less than an inch apart.

Omar was crying. "Oh God, *madre*, please," he whimpered.

"Not so tough now, are you?" Jimmy said. He looked up at the crowd of people that had gathered around, all of whom had been smiling a few seconds ago and whose faces were now screwed up in expressions of shock. "Not such a tough guy now, is he?"

No one said a word.

Jimmy caught Rose's eye and smiled.

"This your man?" Jimmy shook his head. "This mama's boy?"

She opened her mouth but no words came out.

"He ain't shit," Jimmy said, and twisted even harder.

Something snapped.

Omar's eyes went blank and he toppled to the ground. A stream of piss puddled out from underneath his body. "Gross," Jimmy muttered, stepping back.

"Hey. Asshole."

Jimmy looked up. Another tough-looking dude, one of those who'd been in on his initiation, stepped forward, holding a gun.

He shot Jimmy square in the chest.

The blow hit him like a sledgehammer. He stumbled backward.

"Huh," he said, looking down. There was no blood.

He stepped forward and grabbed the gun from the man, who had shot him.

Jimmy shot him back.

"Anybody else?" He put his hands on his hips and looked around the room defiantly. "Anyone else got something to say to me? To the new boss?"

He waited a moment. No one moved.

"Good." Jimmy nodded. "Then I'll say a few things. First of all, I want you all to know that I don't hold any grudges. What's done is done, okay?" He looked around the room. "Some of you might remember that I was trying to get all of us guns from the Air Force base. That didn't work out, but—"

At the back of the crowd he saw a familiar face.

"Hector!"

"Hey, Jimmy." The man smiled nervously.

"Hector." Jimmy waved him over. "C'mere."

The crowd parted, and Hector stepped hesitantly forward until he stood facing Jimmy.

"It's all right, dude," Jimmy said. "It's all right."

He put an arm around Hector's shoulder and turned back to the crowd.

"As I was starting to say, the guns didn't work out, but I have focus now. A new mandate." Actually, it wasn't his mission, it was the woman's; but did they need to know that? No.

There was a table right behind him with a turkey carcass on it. Lying next to the carcass was a carving knife.

Jimmy picked up the knife and held it high in the air for everyone to see.

He held Hector close and slashed his throat.

Blood gushed out, coating his arms and the front of his shirt. He couldn't feel that either.

The corpse fell to the floor.

People gasped; people moaned and looked sick. Jimmy watched until they were all quiet again. "As I was saying, our new mandate is pretty straightforward." He smiled. "We kill whoever we can get our hands on."

Wednesday 3:40 P.M., PST

MALIBU, CALIFORNIA

They were doing a long, slow coast down the canyon road, and Abby's legs appreciated the rest, after a morning and afternoon of laborious uphill pedaling. She didn't appreciate the chill air whipping into her face, though; today was as cold a day as she'd ever experienced in Los Angeles, cold and wet and gray, and along with the wind, her face was getting pelted by thousands of needle-sharp droplets of mist.

And then there was the smell.

It had been getting worse ever since they crested the mountains, heading toward the coast below, and Abby had a feeling in her gut—a sick, nauseous feeling—that she knew what that smell was.

By the grim expression on his face, Luka—who was coasting along beside her on a messenger bicycle borrowed, like hers, from the Paramount lot—knew what it was too.

For two days, since the night of Dooley's speech, she'd been begging for someone, anyone, to take her to the ocean so she could see the damage Hemlock had done. She'd stopped the bomb from going off over Paramount, or anywhere in the atmosphere—at least, she assumed that's what had happened—but no one could, or would, tell her where, or even if, it had gone off.

Dooley's speech had been delayed half an hour, and when he came on he made no mention of Hemlock. He did speak about China, as Wieckowski had guessed, promising "swift and forceful retaliation for the cowardly attack on our country." But they'd never heard from the general again: Atlanta was gone the next day, no more CNN, and Washington shortly after that, so no more Dooley. They had no way of knowing if he'd made good on his threat.

There were rumors, of course: we nuked China, they responded in kind, Russia dropped a few bombs too—and so on. Abby and Luka tried to confirm some of those rumors with the base's new commander, a Lieutenant Rogers, but Rogers had little interest in talking about them or—as he put it—Abby's "conspiracy theory."

Especially since she didn't have a shred of evidence to back up her assertions. Wieckowski's trailer was gone, so was his body, and no soldier on the base would admit to seeing him, or anyone with a little Tinkertoy symbol on his chest, for that matter.

But Abby knew what she'd seen.

Now she needed to know what she'd done.

She'd badgered Luka all day yesterday, and this morning he'd finally gotten the two of them bicycles—gas was in short supply, and the army was controlling it tightly—an armed escort from Paramount out to Topanga State Park, and a promised pickup at nightfall.

That was hours ago. And now they were racing down the narrow canyon road through the last of the forest. For a second she felt like a little kid again, leaning forward over the front wheels, trying to get every last bit of speed out of their bikes. She took a quick look back at Luka, half a bike length behind her, and grinned. He gave her a thumbs-up.

She turned around just as the canyon road took a sharp bend, and there, ahead of them, was the Pacific Coast Highway, and beyond it the ocean.

Abby braked and came to a stop.

The smile that had been tugging at the corners of her mouth disappeared, her stomach flipped, and something caught in her throat.

The water was the wrong color.

Not blue, not blue-green, but black. A thick, brackish, unhealthy-looking black, the color of rot and disease, the texture of used motor oil, a dark oozing black with flecks of white floating on top.

As Abby watched, a wave formed out in the water; the flecks of white floated to the top of the crest, the larger ones took on a shape, and Abby realized what all the flecks were.

Fish. Dead fish.

She swayed on her bike and almost fell over.

Luka had come to a stop beside her. He looked at the water and didn't say anything for a moment.

"Oh dear God." His voice came out a whisper.

Abby let out a choked gasp and pedaled forward.

"Abby!" Luka called. "Wait—"

But Abby wasn't listening. She was halfway across the highway. On the other side of the road was a rusted steel railing, and beyond that a parking lot. She pedaled into the lot and dropped her bike at the far side, next to a white sign that said:

LAS TUNAS COUNTY BEACH
LIFEGUARDS ON DUTY 8 A.M.–5 P.M.
SWIM AT YOUR OWN RISK

Beyond the lot was a long flight of concrete steps leading down to the beach. Abby took them two at a time, the smell rising up to meet her, overwhelming, unbearable, like being trapped inside the hold of a fishing trawler with a week-old catch.

She stumbled down the last few steps, and fell face first into the sand. Even before she looked up, she knew what she was going to see.

Dead things.

Dead, rotting things covering the beach in front of her. Thousands of them, a decomposing carpet of fish and all sorts of sea creatures—a seal, a dolphin, a shark, crabs— anything that lived in the sea, though now nothing lived in the sea, thanks to her. There were plenty of living things mixed in with the dead before her, though; sea gulls and other birds were hopping all around the beach, pecking away at whatever pile of rotting flesh took their fancy.

Not five feet away from her, a particularly large gull, its beak smeared with reddish gore, stopped its pecking long enough to look up at her quizzically.

It uttered a single, emphatic squawk, and turned back to its food.

Abby laughed hysterically.

"Was that a thank-you?" she asked the bird. "Was that a thank-you?"

The bird looked up and squawked again.

"You're welcome!" Abby screamed. She stumbled to her feet and ran at the bird, which took two quick hops backward and then, squawking madly, took off into the air.

"Hey!" Abby shouted. "You're very fucking welcome!"

She looked around, aware that the beach, which had been quiet a moment ago, was now a cacophony of squawking flapping birds, backing away in confusion from this madwoman who had suddenly appeared to interrupt their feast.

Abby threw her arms open wide. "You're all very fucking welcome!" she yelled, and she spun around, taking in the entire scene, the birds, the fish, the ocean, the highway above them—

"Oh," she said, and started laughing again. Because it was right here, or right around here, anyway, they'd shot the big climactic scene of the second season finale for *Island Patrol*, the end of the two-parter with George Hamilton—or was that David Hasselhoff? she couldn't remember—as the greedy oil tycoon whom she fell in love with and was all set to marry until one of his tankers ran aground off the coast and killed a whole school of dolphins.

They'd filmed the final moment at sunset, a classic California sunset, he holding her in his arms while she told him she loved him, she loved him, she really did, but she couldn't marry him, not now, not ever.

"You killed them," she'd said, big tears welling up in her eyes, "all those innocent, defenseless creatures. Even if you didn't mean to do it, you killed them."

And then she'd pushed away from his embrace and walked off into the sunset without another word, wearing a string bikini, of course, and everyone on the set had given her a big round of applause, and that was her big moment, really the highlight of her career.

Until now.

She started to laugh again.

"Abby."

She looked up and saw Luka standing a few feet away.

"You can't do this, Abby," he said. "You can't blame yourself."

"Gee, I'm sorry. Who should I blame?"

"You know. It was Dooley. And Scott. And Walters an

Wieckowski. All of them. The ones who made the gas; the ones who launched it. You—" He shook his head. "—you saved people, Abby. Millions of people."

"Yeah." Sure. He was right; she had saved people.

But you killed them. She remembered saying the lines, batting her baby blues at Hamilton, yes, it was definitely Hamilton, not Hasselhoff. *You killed them, all those innocent, defenseless creatures.*

She looked out on the black ocean.

The Pacific was huge, far bigger than the area of land Hemlock was intended to affect. If what Wieckowski had been telling her was right, a huge chunk of ocean remained untouched, pristine water. Everything there was still alive.

If, she thought.

If, if, if.

Luka put a hand on her shoulder. "We should go."

"Yeah." She sighed. He was right. They should be getting back. It was going to be a long trip. Their bikes were made for shuttling around between offices on the Paramount lot, not going up a mountain. They were clunkers, old machines with no gears and heavy iron frames. She and Luka had to walk them up several particularly steep sections of road on the way here; she had no doubt they'd be doing the same on the way back. And the sun was already going down, settling into a band of dark clouds at the horizon.

God, she realized, that's a big storm. A hell of a big storm. They'd been having shitty weather for the last two days, and this looked like more of the same, or even worse. They were going to get drenched. Abby felt like she deserved it. She turned and followed Luka back up the steps to their bikes.

QUAKER HEIGHTS, ALBUQUERQUE

There was a legend Steve was trying to remember; something about iron.

He had the bracelet on the table, directly in front of him, stacks of books spread out on either side, and a yellow pad on his lap full of hastily scribbled notes.

He knew he wasn't going to find the legend in any of these books. The Quaker Heights School Library had only general reference volumes—the *Encyclopaedia Britannica*, D'Aulaire's *Book of Greek Mythology*, a young adult picture book of myths from around the world. The books were just to jog his memory. The legend lurked somewhere to the back of his mind, a reference he'd glimpsed once while researching a book.

A reference to the forging of iron, in a time long before the knowledge of how to draw that metal from the earth existed.

"Dad."

Steve looked up.

Kerry stood there, holding another stack of books. "I found a few more."

"Thanks, honey." He shoved aside the stack on his right, and she set the new pile down. Her eyes went to the bracelet; he could tell that part of her still wanted it. Wanted to pick it up and put it back on.

No way in hell was that going to happen, though. He had his daughter back, and he wasn't going to lose her again.

"Did you find it?" she asked. "The thing about the iron?"

"Not yet." He smiled, and tapped the new pile of books. "Maybe these'll help."

She nodded over her shoulder. "I'm going to keep looking, okay?"

"Sure."

After she was out of sight, Steve leaned back in his chair and rubbed his eyes.

He needed a real library, damn it. A research library. He needed Hesiod, Homer, and Herodotus; he needed Frazer, and Guthrie, and Flamieux. If he could go online, he could probably find what he was looking for in a minute, but of course he couldn't go online anymore.

He sighed and opened the first book on the new pile Kerry had given him. It was titled, simply enough, *Iron*.

On the title page there was an epigraph, a quote from Pliny the Elder: "I look upon iron as the most deadly fruit of human ingenuity."

A little tingle of recognition buzzed up his spine.

There was something there. Iron as a weapon? That meant second century B.C., Asia Minor. The Hittites. Not his specialty, though; doubtful that would have been the reference he'd seen, so . . .

Pliny had written that a long time ago. Back when iron weapons really had been the deadliest things around. Now, of course, human ingenuity had come up with much deadlier fruits.

Like the bomb.

According to the rumors that had been spreading through the school yesterday, America had dropped it. Not once, not twice, but several times. On Iraq, according to some. On China, said others. And only after we'd been hit several times.

Steve hoped not. That would be like the end of the world. That would be like—

A memory stirred in the back of his head.

Ragnarok.

The Twilight of the Gods. There was a book around here, he remembered, thumbing through the piles Kerry had left him. *European Folklore*. He cracked it open and checked the table of contents. Sure enough, there it was: Ragnarok.

He turned to the chapter, and skimmed down the page. A line near the bottom caught his eye:

> *Jormundgant, the world-Serpent, shall break the chains that bind him. He is the first herald—*

Steve sat bolt upright in his chair.

The Serpent-God, breaking free.

Yagumata's sword.

The door to the library swung open.

Lawson stood there with two men Steve didn't recognize. Newcomers to the school, one black, one white, much older, the latter staring at him with an intensity that was almost frightening.

"Two guys here," Lawson said, "They want to see you."

The older man pushed past Lawson then and into the library.

"The bracelet," he said. "Where is it?"

THE WASTELAND, LOS ANGELES

Claire was having one of her moments.

It was just like before, back in the motel in Indiana, after she'd killed Zeke. Now, since finding that soldier and sending him off with a few well-chosen words, Claire had been sitting on the ground, staring off into space. Almost like she was dreaming with her eyes open, Danny thought.

After a few hours of watching her, he'd left her to go exploring. But after going only a few blocks, he'd come back. The sidewalks and streets were literally knee-deep in ash; he didn't like the feel of it on his paws, he didn't like the smell of it in his nose, and he didn't like the way it tasted when an errant piece flew into his mouth.

He didn't like this place at all; he wished they were back in the clean, dry desert, or even better, in the indoor habitat in Las Vegas. Now that was the life: three squares a day—actually, it was one square, but one big, big square—an indoor pool, and trips out of the city every few weeks to romp underneath the open skies. Those were the tiger's memories, of course, not his, but he could still enjoy them.

Better those memories than these gray skies, these bad smells, and the ash. He was getting hungry too, which didn't help his mood any. He sniffed the air regularly, hoping to pick up the scent of something that might be food, but he' found nothing yet. As far as he could tell, in fact, he and Claire were the only living things in this place. And he wasn't so sure about her, actually.

Burned-out buildings gave way to heaps of rubble, which gave way to a flat, desolate landscape—add a few craters, and they could have been walking on the surface of the moon. Claire was heading for the center of the fire, he realized, the place where it had all started. Because the more they walked, the more complete the devastation got.

They turned a corner, and before them was a burning building. A church, he realized, seeing the cross on top. Or to be more precise, on top of the building the fire had taken the shape of a cross.

Claire walked up a short flight of steps toward the entrance. Danny stopped in his tracks and growled.

"Easy, Danny." Claire turned. "It's all right."

No, he thought, it wasn't all right, not at all. It was wrong.

The church was burning, but he couldn't smell fire. The church was burning, but it was still standing. Through the door, which Claire held open, he could see that the aisles and the pews inside were all made of fire as well. Everything was just off a little, like he was looking at a distorted, fun-house mirror reflection of the world.

Claire strode down the burning aisle toward the front of the church and stopped at the front pew.

There was a corpse there. A burned, unrecognizable husk of a human, with something shiny and gleaming in its hand.

Claire bent down and took it.

"There you are."

Danny's head swiveled. A man stepped forward from the shadows.

Food, Danny thought. Then he caught a whiff of the newcomer and slumped back in disappointment.

Damn. This guy was dead too. The man stepped into the light. He had a great, gaping wound at the base of his neck; he skin flapped when he talked.

"You wouldn't believe the time I had," the man said.

"I know," she said.

He took something out of his pocket and handed it to Claire. Another piece of metal. She held it up and smiled.

"You've done well."

"What can I say? I love my job." He frowned suddenly. "Where are the others?"

"There's a problem," Claire said, and as she explained, Danny understood at last what this was all about. The iron, that's what she wanted.

So what are we waiting for, he roared. Let me go get the old man. Let me get the rest of the pieces for you.

Claire shook her head.

"No, Danny. It can't be you. We need someone a little more . . . subtle."

The man with the neck wound grinned. "Subtle? That's my middle name."

Thursday 3:40 A.M., MST

QUAKER HEIGHTS, ALBUQUERQUE

Leo was having a hard time sleeping. For one thing, the cot they'd put him on was too small. His feet hung over the edge, and the mattress was so thin that his weight pressed it right into the hard gym floor. His knees dug into the wood when he slept on his stomach; if he tried sleeping on his side, his elbows rubbed against the floor, and if he lay on his back, his butt got it. He flipped from position to position, hoping to fall asleep before he got too uncomfortable in any one.

For another thing, he was woken up by explosions every hour or so; this mad bomber they kept talking about was having a time of it, and with every pass, he seemed to be zeroing in on their location. Leo knew it was probably his imagination, but it made him nervous to think that on any one of his runs, the high school might be next.

Making all of it worse was the caffeine buzzing through his system from the six-pack of Coke he'd bolted down during the last part of their drive. They'd come across a stalled tractor-trailer on one of the mountain roads into Albuquerque, and pulled out a case of the stuff. Leo was so happy to see caffeine that he went overboard, which he was now greatly regretting.

He finally decided to get up and go for a walk, see if that would calm his nerves.

He all but tiptoed out of the big gymnasium. Down the hall there was a light on; he went to the door marked LIBRARY and peered in.

The guy who'd had the bracelet—Steve—was sitting at a big table, surrounded by Thomas's journals.

Leo pushed the door open. Steve started, and Leo realized the man had been sleeping.

"Wha—Oh." Steve blinked and rubbed his eyes. "Hey. What's up?"

"Sorry," Leo said quickly. "I didn't mean to wake you."

"No, that's all right. I want to finish these."

Leo stepped inside. "Your kid's sleeping like a rock, by the way," he said. He'd seen the girl lying on the floor in the gym, dead to the world.

Thomas was just a few cots down from her; when he'd heard that Kerry had been wearing the bracelet for the last six months, he became very concerned, and asked her—and her father—a lot of questions. He'd stood over her for a while after she fell asleep, then gone to the nearest cot to rest himself.

Leo hadn't been able to tell if he was sleeping or not. The old guy was weird that way: during the drive from Texas, he'd barely shut his eyes at all. Sometimes he would just stare off into space for hours, dreaming with his eyes open.

At times, Leo would look over at him and decide that this whole thing was a crock—the iron, the sword, all of it. He'd just about managed to convince himself of that when they'd hit Albuquerque and the old man had guided them straight to this spot, and the bracelet.

That's when the last of Leo's doubts vanished.

Now he sat down across the table from the girl's father and sighed.

"You look pretty comfortable here."

"I'm used to libraries. They're a big part of the job description," Steve said. And he told Leo about his work back at the University.

"So you've heard of this sword before?"

"Once. A long time ago." He stood up and stretched. "When I was a grad student, I helped a professor do research for a paper on the Signs of the Apocalypse. Apocalypses, actually."

"There's more than one?"

"Sure. Depends on which religion you're talking about. Different religions, different signs. Heralds, if you want to call them that. The Messiah, for Christians. Sishyot, for the Persians. Vishnu—"

"For the Hindus."

Leo looked up. Thomas was standing in the doorway.

"Don't let me stop you," he said to Steve, and sat.

"I got a question," Leo said. "So this woman is like a herald, too?"

"She's out of my area of expertise," Steve said.

They both turned to Thomas.

"I suppose so," he said after a moment. "That's a good way to think of her, and what's happening. She's the herald, and this—"

"Is the apocalypse?" Leo shook his head. "Nothing good about that."

"Well," Steve said. "Some religions have it that creation goes in cycles. That every age has a natural lifespan, so when this world dies, another begins. If it's any consolation."

"It's not," Thomas said. He turned to Leo. "Let's go."

"Go?"

"We need to leave," he said. "Right now."

"What's the rush?" Steve asked. "Wait until morning. I think I can get you some weapons, and—"

"No," Thomas said. "We can't wait."

"Why?"

"The herald."

"What about her?" Leo asked. "She needs all seven pieces of iron, doesn't she? Without all seven, no sword. Without a sword, no Apocalypse. So she can't do anything without the three things we have."

"You're wrong," Thomas said. "She can kill. She's doing it now."

"How can you possibly know that?" Steve asked.

Thomas got up. "Keep reading," he said. He turned to Leo. "I'll be out in the car."

"Wait," Steve said. "Please, let us help you. Just give me until morning."

"It's only a few hours until dawn," Leo added.

Thomas hesitated.

"All right," he said finally. "Until morning, and no later."

He turned and left the library.

Steve convinced Lawson to give him fifteen minutes to speak after the regular morning meeting. That didn't give him time to put together much of a presentation; he was going to have to wing it.

As he sat in a chair in the front of the gym, he spotted Irene Garza, an elderly woman who wore her hair in a tight bun, washed her hands obsessively, and always carried a Bible. In fact, she'd started a prayer session every morning with those so inclined among the hundred or so people in the high school. Out of everyone gathered here, he felt, she would understand what he was going to say.

They were all gathered around tables in the gym, running through the agenda for that day. Steve hoped to change that agenda. Lawson had promised him five minutes during the meeting to speak. Thomas and Leo had agreed to hang around until then.

"So more ammunition is available," Lawson was saying. "It's just a question if we can get there and back on the gas we have. That's what we'll try and figure out this morning." He turned and gestured Steve forward. "And now, I promised a friend of ours a few minutes to talk. Steve . . ."

Steve pushed back his chair and stood.

He felt as if he were about to give a lecture.

Okay, class. Today's topic: the Apocalypse, and how to stop it.

He took a deep breath.

"A lot of what I'm about to say may not make much sense, but that's only right, I think, because it seems to me that about a week ago the world stopped making sense. Except—" he looked at Irene Garza "—except that if you stop trying to look for rational, scientific explanations for what's been happening, and start taking things on faith—"

"Oh, brother." Toby Carwell, a big bear of a man who'd been one of the first to come into the high school, stood up. "I don't think I need to hear any more Bible-thumping today, Steve. Excuse me."

He turned to go.

"Wait, Toby. I'm not going to talk about the Bible," Steve said. "Not exactly."

"What do you mean by that?"

He took a deep breath. And then he told them about the iron, and the sword and the herald.

When he finished, Steve looked around the room. There were a few nods and whispers of agreement—along with snorts of laughter and some amused smiles.

Tim Carew stood up. "So this herald, where exactly is he?"

"She," Steve corrected. "Los Angeles."

Carew frowned. "You want us to go to Los Angeles with you? Now?"

"I've heard enough of this." Carwell stood up. "I've got work to do. I think we all do."

"Hold on," said Steve. "I wanted to—"

Lawson rose from his chair. "I think that we got enough on our hands here, Steve, without worrying about stopping your, ah—" He looked around and smiled. "—herald."

"Can I say something?"

Heads turned.

Thomas, who was standing toward the back of the gym, stepped forward.

"You're all going to die."

The room erupted in shouts of anger.

"Mister," Lawson said, "you got a helluva nerve—"

"You're going to run out of food," Thomas said. "You're going to run out of water. Gas is going to get harder and harder to find; so is ammunition for your weapons. You'll start killing each other to survive."

The gym was dead quiet.

"I can promise you, you're all going to die unless we stop the herald."

Steve looked around the room. "What we're doing here is fighting a holding action. The real war—the real enemy—is out there. In Los Angeles. That's where we have to go if we want to live." He nodded to Lawson. "And now I guess I'm done."

As he left the room, very few people met his eyes.

Steve went back to the library to collect some books, and his notes. He was just about finished packing up when he felt, all of a sudden, like someone was watching him.

He looked up and saw a man standing at the back of the room. Which was strange, because the entrance was at the front. He must not have heard him come in.

"Hi," the man said, stepping forward.

He was a stranger. Steve looked at the man. He'd never seen him before.

"Who are you?" Steve asked.

"Harold Garson." He stepped forward, and held out his hand to shake. Steve took it.

It was cold and clammy to the touch.

"Heard you were going West," Harold said. "I wanted to join up."

Harold didn't look healthy. His skin was pale, and waxy, and he had a scarf wrapped tightly around his neck.

"Are you sick?" Steve asked.

"This?" Harold held up the scarf. "No. I just get cold easy."

Steve frowned. "I appreciate the offer, Harold, but this is going to be dangerous work."

"I know. I understand that." He smiled again. "Let me come with you. I know lots of people in Los Angeles."

PARAMOUNT STUDIOS, LOS ANGELES

The rain had started falling during the night.

It was a dirty rain; the feel of it on her skin left Abby wanting to shower. But there was no water for showers anymore; they were rationing that too, a cup a day for everyone to drink, or to brush their teeth with, for those who had toothbrushes. Abby didn't; but then, they were down to one meal a day too, so her teeth weren't getting all that dirty either.

At least she had a poncho, borrowed from one of the soldiers; at least she could go out in the rain without getting soaked, without ruining her clothes. Not like the rest of however many of thousands of people trapped in the soundstages, where there was barely enough room to sit down now, much less sleep. She tried not to feel guilty about that.

She was trying not to feel guilty about a lot of things.

She looked up and realized she'd walked all the way across the Paramount lot. In front of her was the barricade, and the gate to the street. To her right was the big parking lot, where the CNN trailer had been. Luka had gone out with a few soldiers that morning, after they'd gotten back from the ocean, to try broadcasting from somewhere up in the mountains. He had the idea that in the higher elevations he might be able to pick up something from elsewhere in the world.

"Hey."

Abby turned. A soldier was walking toward her.

"Excuse me, ma'am. You're not supposed to be here. This area is—"

Abby flashed her badge. "I'm with CNN. Check with Lieutenant Rogers. He'll vouch for me."

Rogers was the new commander. He'd come in a couple days ago with a large contingent of soldiers from another base; he'd taken charge after Scott disappeared.

The soldier stepped forward and took hold of her badge, held it up so it caught the light from the spots by the gate. He looked it over carefully.

Abby did the same to him.

He was about her height, but stocky. The weight looked to be muscle, not fat; the veins in his arms stood out like a roadmap. The left side of his face was very badly burned; the burn stretched down his neck and disappeared underneath his uniform shirt. The skin was still peeling away at the edges of it; he had to be in a lot of pain.

He dropped the badge and stepped back.

"All right," he said. "Sorry to bother you."

"No problem." She offered up a smile.

He returned it. "You're the one who stopped HEMLOCK, aren't you?"

"That's right."

He looked her in the eye. "That was a goddamn brave thing to do. Thank you."

Abby nodded, and felt something catch in her throat.

"What's the matter?" he asked.

"Nothing." She smiled. "It's just the first time anyone's thanked me for doing that."

"Well. A lot of people are thinking it, I can tell you. You'll have to excuse their lack of manners." He slung the rifle over his shoulder, and held out his hand. "I'm Martinez, by the way. Sergeant John Martinez."

They shook.

"Abby Keller."

"Yeah. I know that. I should have recognized you before. From your show." He frowned. "So when did you become a reporter?"

Abby laughed. "About three days ago."

"You must be a quick study." He nodded towards the empty space where the CNN trailer had been. "Looking for your friends?"

"Yeah."

"No word from them in a while. But they have a transmitter. If you let me know where you're sleeping, I'll send someone the moment we hear anything."

"Thanks. But I'm not calling it a night yet." A sudden gust of wind whipped across the lot; Abby shivered and wrapped her arms around herself. Damn, it was cold. Even for Los Angeles in winter.

"I hate this weather," she announced. "You wouldn't happen to know whether or not the sun was coming out anytime soon, would you?"

"Afraid not. But I wouldn't count on these clouds breaking up for awhile."

"How do you know that?"

"Trust me. I do."

"Really?" She laughed. "What do you have, a Farmer's Almanac or something? Al Roker locked up in that guardhouse over there?"

He shook his head. "No."

"So how do you know what the weather's going to be?"

"Believe me, I know. I know it's going to be winter for a long, long time."

He pronounced the forecast like a curse. Abby smiled, and shook her head.

"All right, I believe you," she said. "I don't love the cold, but you don't have to make it sound like the end of the world."

He looked her dead in the eye. "I'm trying not to," he said.

"What?" Abby said. She was confused.

Then a little bell rang in her head.

The dark clouds she'd seen from the beach yesterday. The rumors about China, and bombs dropping. The wind. The rain. The cold.

Nuclear Winter.

Her hand went to her mouth.

"Oh my God," she said. "Oh my God."

She wobbled on her feet; Martinez reached out a hand to steady her.

"They did it, didn't they?" Abby said. "Those idiots. They dropped—"

"I can't talk to you about that," he interrupted sharply. "Orders. I'm sorry."

She nodded distractedly; he was telling her something she wasn't supposed to know. They couldn't discuss it openly.

Nuclear Winter. She remembered the vague outlines of the theory. When a nuclear bomb went off, it sent up vast quantities of dust into the atmosphere. Set off enough bombs, the resulting cloud would be big enough to block out the sun for years. The temperature would drop. The planet—and everything on it—would freeze.

"Jesus Christ," Abby said. "We're all dead."

"Not me." Martinez shook his head. "Not me. I don't plan on dying for a long, long time."

"Nobody plans on it," Abby said.

Gunfire erupted behind them.

Abby turned just in time to see a man fall to the ground, and two army trucks slam through the wooden barrier at the main gate.

Martinez unslung his rifle.

"Stay!" he yelled at Abby, and took off towards the gate. He was one of many; soldiers were swarming in that direction from all over the base.

The first one there stared down the street and shouted after the trucks.

"You goddamn cowards!" He raised his gun, and sighted down the barrel.

Martinez ran up beside him and knocked the gun up in the air. "No sense in it, Collins. Let 'em go."

"Sarge!" Another man was kneeling next to the soldier on the ground, motioning Martinez over. Martinez ran to his side and knelt down.

Abby joined him.

The man on the ground was Lieutenant Rogers, the base commander.

He wasn't moving at all.

"Shit." Martinez pulled the lieutenant's poncho up over his face.

"What happened?" she asked. "What's going on?"

"Deserters. I told him to let them go. I told him . . ." He sighed heavily. "Damn."

He looked up, realized he was the center of attention, and frowned. "All right, everyone. Back to your posts."

The soldiers scattered. Abby watched them go.

"Have there been a lot of deserters?" she asked.

"Since everybody figured out what was happening with the weather," he said, "yes."

"I thought you couldn't talk about that," Abby reminded him. "The bombs."

"I can do whatever I want now," Martinez said, getting to his feet. "You're looking at the base's new commander."

He hadn't come back yet.

Friday 10:40 A.M., MST

FLAGSTAFF, ARIZONA

The weather was getting colder. Much colder.

In the end, they'd convinced two dozen people to come with them. The little convoy—half a dozen cars and one big truck—had stopped in front of a Wal-Mart just off the highway. A half-dozen men stayed outside, keeping watch, while everyone else went into the store to look for warmer clothes.

The place had been pretty well ransacked; there wasn't much left. Kerry found a University of Arizona varsity jacket underneath an overturned rack of children's clothing. She picked it up and dusted it off; farther down the aisle, she found a Tweety Bird sweatshirt to go with it.

Women's Clothing ended right where Home Entertainment began; that area of the store was a disaster, display cases shattered, videocassettes and CDs scattered all over the floor. Music, Kerry thought; it might be nice to get something new to listen to for the rest of the drive. The car she and her dad were riding in was old, though; it only took cassettes. Kerry sorted through the debris before her and came up with a few tapes, including the latest Prophecy and the new Jody K. Two of her favorite groups, and she hadn't realized either one of them had a new record.

Boy, she really had been out of it these last six months.

She turned the corner at the end of the aisle and almost walked right into the old man.

He was holding up a videocassette of *Peter Pan*, a wistful smile on his face.

"Sorry," Kerry said, and turned to go.

"No, it's all right." He put the video back on the shelf. "You found a few things, I see."

"Yeah." She held up the Tweety Bird shirt. "Not exactly high fashion, but—"

"Better than freezing."

"That's right."

She hesitated a moment.

She'd been peppering her dad with questions about the old man—Mr. Kelleher—and the iron, for almost the entire drive. But there were still a few things she wanted to know.

"Can I ask you something?"

"Of course."

"The guy who had the bracelet before me, the one in my dreams—the one from the lake?"

"John Topher," the old man nodded. "I remember."

"Whatever happened to him?"

"He's dead. When they caught him, when they took away the bracelet—he killed himself."

Kerry was about to ask why, then realized she knew the answer.

"He couldn't live without the iron?"

"I think so," Thomas said. "I think, if you have it long enough, it somehow becomes part of you. And you become

part of it, I suppose. That's why you were reliving what Topher did."

Three sharp blasts of a horn sounded—the signal that it
was time to go.

"I'd better try and find something warm myself," the old
man said. "Excuse me."

She watched him go, and then remembered something
else, something her dad had told her.

Coburn, the guy who had the ring before Thomas, had
killed the old man's daughter. Which meant that Thomas
had to relive that in his dreams.

Kerry shuddered. And she thought she had it bad.

BEL AIR ESTATES, LOS ANGELES

Jimmy lay in bed with his arms folded behind his head and
sighed.

"It ain't happenin' , babe," he said to Rose. "Not your fault;
it just ain't happenin' . "

Her face fell for a second; she climbed off him and sat
down on the edge of the bed.

"Come on," she said, trying to smile. "Just tell me what to
do to make the Little General happy. I'll do it. You know I
will."

He didn't doubt that; since yesterday afternoon, when
he'd first dragged her into the bedroom, she'd been only too
anxious to obey his orders. That was when she'd started with
this "Little General" business; Jimmy thought it was kind of
funny at first, but now he was getting tired of it.

He was getting tired of all this; it was time to face the cold
hard facts. Ever since he woke up back at the Air Force base,
he wasn't the same old Jimmy.

His mind was still as sharp as ever, but his body . . . the
body was definitely going. His skin was getting all squishy; he
was starting to smell. People wrinkled up their noses when he

walked by; they stood well away from him whenever he stopped to talk.

He'd put on deodorant head-to-toe this morning, and that seemed to help for a while, but now whatever funk he carried around with him was back. He could tell by the glimpses he caught of Rose when she thought he wasn't watching her. Worst of all, the Little General seemed to be unable to perform any of his customary duties.

At first Jimmy had felt sorry for himself, that the pleasures of the flesh were slipping away from him. He tried to look on the bright side: Maybe he was evolving beyond his body, becoming a creature of pure intellect. Just like those aliens on the original *Star Trek*. The Asshead people, who could make everyone see what they wanted and do what they wanted. They moved past the hungers of the flesh. Maybe he could, too.

Rose got up from the bed and put on a CD.

It was Lil' Kim; Jimmy recognized it right away. "Let Me." Great song. Great beat.

"How about if I dance for the Little General?" she asked, standing at the foot of the bed and starting to sway back and forth.

Jimmy shrugged. "Sure." Why not?

She licked her lips and started to move.

Jimmy took hold of the Little General.

He tried to remember what it felt like to get excited down there. What used to work for him? Lil' Kim was the right music, and Rose was providing the right visuals . . .

He closed his eyes and tried to think back.

For some reason, the image of Tina Chou popped into his head.

There. That was a little tingle.

Jimmy grabbed harder, but the tingle quickly vanished. Damn. Maybe he should try and find that woman who had woken him up at the base; maybe she could help him. Though he had the feeling that helping Jimmy get his rocks off was not high on her priority list. In fact, now that he thought about it, she probably wouldn't appreciate his problem at all. She'd given Jimmy a to-do list with only one item on it, and she wouldn't want to hear he was making time for anything else. No, he'd do better to—

Whoops.

Jimmy looked down. He'd been yanking away while he was thinking, and it seemed he'd yanked a little too hard.

He was holding the Little General in his hand.

"Look at that," he said, more surprised than anything.

Rose stopped dancing, and looked. Then she screamed, and ran out of the room.

Jimmy sighed and got to his feet. Someone would bring her back; someone had brought her back yesterday, the first time she'd run away after finding out what he wanted her to do. He would have a talk with her. Not a big deal.

There was a knock on the door.

"Come," Jimmy called out. He put the Little General into the pocket of his robe so as not to freak Rose out again.

The door opened.

But it wasn't Rose. It was Oscar.

Oscar was Jimmy's new number one man. He was a fat, creepy-looking dude with a skinny mustache and a wall eye—one of those that stayed fixed in one position, no matter where he looked.

Jimmy had put him in charge of executing the mandate the woman had given him. Oscar had gone off happily this morning with half a dozen buses full of guns and gangbangers. He didn't look so happy now.

"What's the matter?" Jimmy asked.

"Did what you asked, man, but . . ." He shrugged. "Not a lot of people around."

"What are you talking about, not a lot of people around? That's crazy. This is Los Angeles. There's millions of people here."

"Not anymore. We went downtown, Venice, Santa Monica—it's like empty."

The hall behind Oscar was full of other gang members. They were all nodding furiously.

"For real, man," another chimed in. He looked scared. They all looked scared.

"For Christ's sake," Jimmy said. This would not do. Lots of people, the woman had said.

A little light bulb went on in his head.

"When we were evacuating the Air Force Base," Jimmy said, "they were bringing a whole lot of people up to Hollywood. Someplace safe."

"Yeah, Paramount," Oscar said. "They turned it into an army base."

"Paramount? The movie studio?"

"Uh-huh."

Jimmy started laughing. "Only in California."

The sea of gang members facing him suddenly parted, and Rose was dragged forward.

"All right," he said. "So tomorrow we hit that studio."

"That's the army you talkin' about, man." Oscar looked nervous. "That ain't goin' to be easy."

"Nothing worth doing ever is," Jimmy said. He smiled, and held his hand out to Rose.

"Ain't that right, honey?"

Her eyes rolled back in her head. She hit the floor.

Saturday 1:40 P.M., PST

NORWALK, LOS ANGELES

All the way through Arizona they'd been making plans.

Steve and Kerry had switched cars so they could ride with Leo and Thomas; they'd talked about the herald, about the iron, about what some of the research the old man had done might mean.

But all those plans went up in smoke when they hit the outskirts of Los Angeles and saw the river burning.

Impossible, Steve thought.

It was an oil spill burning off. Or one of the trash barges from the big sanitation facility at the water's edge, flaming up. Or an optical illusion from a burning building on the other side of the riverbank.

But when they got as close as they could to the fire—fifty feet or so before the heat forced them back—he realized it really was the river, truly and impossibly, ablaze.

What made it an even more astounding sight was that the blaze ended on their side of the riverbank; in the hour or so they'd sat parked before it, with the giant metal machinery of the county sanitation facility looming behind them, the fire hadn't moved another inch, as if it had run out of gas and was saying, "This far and no farther."

If any of the people who'd come with them harbored

doubts about what they were up against, seeing the burning water completely erased them.

Irene Garza had started right in with talk of the lake of fire from the Book of Revelation, saying that they now stood before that holy flame in which all evil souls would supposedly be destroyed, according to the Bible.

It hadn't helped when Thomas announced that the herald was inside that fire—and that was where they had to go.

No one had a clue how they were going to do that; it may not have been ordinary fire in one sense, but it still burned, and they could barely get within fifty feet of it before the heat drove them back.

Steve had asked Thomas for his journals again; the old man had taken a lot of notes while doing all his research on the iron. Steve was hoping there might be a reference to this fire, but beyond the mention in both the Ragnarok and Revelation myths, he hadn't found anything.

He had the journals spread out on top of a trunk full of weapons in the back of one of the vans they'd brought. Next to them were the other three pieces of iron—the spike, the candlestick, and the bracelet. Steve didn't like having them so close; he remembered how even just holding the bracelet for those few moments had affected him.

He heard the crunch of footsteps on gravel and looked up.

"Harold," Steve said. "What do you want?"

For the first time in what seemed like years, Kerry was warm.

For that reason alone she didn't mind waiting around in front of the fire while Thomas and her dad tried to decide what to do next.

It warmed her right down to the bone, banishing the chill she'd been feeling ever since getting locked in the walk-in, back at Williams House.

No one else was within a hundred yards of her; they were

all gathered together in various groups back by the cars, waiting, she supposed, for her dad to come up with some sort of miraculous idea.

She wondered how he was doing; she supposed she ought to go see.

Turning, she saw one of the men who'd come with them from Albuquerque—walking straight toward her.

He was holding the bag with the iron in it. Thomas's bag.

"Hey," Kerry said, reaching out to grab him. "What—"

The man shoved her aside and continued straight on toward the fire.

Kerry hesitated only a second, then stood up and sprinted after him. She caught up twenty feet away from the edge of the river and tried to pull the bag away from him.

"Uh-uh," the man said. "Finders keepers."

He grabbed Kerry's wrist and smiled.

"And look what I just found." He started dragging her toward the fire; the heat was incredible.

Until her hand closed on the man's wrist.

Then a chill penetrated Kerry right down to the bone.

The man's skin was ice cold; cold as the grave.

He turned and fixed Kerry with a glare. "So willing to sacrifice yourself, child?" he asked. "Very well, then."

His free hand fastened on Kerry's throat, and it was like being caught in a vise. Kerry couldn't get any air; the world around her started to go dark.

The man dragged her into the fire.

I'm going to burn up, was Kerry's last thought. I'm going to burn up and die.

But she didn't.

She touched the flames and felt nothing but cold.

Ice, ice cold.

BEL AIR ESTATES, LOS ANGELES

Whoever used to live in the mansion had a massive collection of porn movies; Jimmy took a big stack of tapes into the bedroom and started watching them with Rose. But he lost interest an hour or two into the pornathon, and left Rose snoring on the bed in front of something called Thunderballs.

There was a little party going on downstairs; maybe a dozen people drinking what was left of the liquor in the house and dancing. Everyone stopped what they were doing and smiled up at him nervously when he passed through.

"Carry on," Jimmy told them, and walked outside.

It was still raining, fat drops that had made a big mud puddle out of the front yard. Jimmy didn't care; he splashed through the squishy mess and out into the street.

The sky was gray. It was morning already. No sun. He didn't care about that either. He was losing interest in a lot of things he used to care about. Food. Water. Sleep. Sex.

About the only thing that gave him pleasure these days was seeing people jump to it when he barked out an order. Being in charge was something he was getting used to.

He went back into the mansion and woke up Oscar.

"Let's go," he said. "We got work to do."

An hour later, half a dozen of them were in one of the buses, cruising slowly down Melrose towards the studio.

"I don't know, man," Oscar said, turning around in his seat to face Jimmy. "I don't think this is a good idea. They gonna shoot us up like fish in a barrel."

Jimmy shook his head. "I don't think so," he said. "I don't think they'll shoot unless we do. They have to be conserving ammunition, because they know they're not getting resupplied anytime soon."

"That's it right there," the driver announced. "Paramount."

Jimmy squinted out the window. It was all fogged up. He couldn't see a damn thing.

"Hold up," he said, getting to his feet.

The driver turned around, eyes raised. "Say what?"

"I said hold up. Stop the bus."

The driver looked unhappy, but he did as he was told.

The bus had an emergency exit built into the roof; Jimmy released the latch, opening it to the chill outside air, and boosted himself up and on through.

He stood on the roof a moment, in the wind and rain, and surveyed the base in front of him.

He didn't like what he saw. They'd built a raised catwalk just beyond the studio walls; it was packed full of soldiers and civilians alike, a lot of whom had their rifles trained right on him. Beyond the catwalk, the mist swallowed everything up; still, he thought he could make out the outlines of some bigger vehicles, one of which he thought was an armored personnel carrier of some type, and one that had to be a tank.

He stood up on the roof and shouted, "Hey! Hey, in there! Paramount!"

He saw movement by the gate, and a second later a megaphoned voice came back: "State your business."

"State my business." Jimmy started laughing. "Sure. I'll state my business. *I'm gonna kill every last one of you!*"

Another flurry of movement by the gate, and then a different, megaphoned voice.

"Jimmy Maartens, you little shit. This is Sergeant Martinez."

Jimmy's eyes went wide in surprise. Martinez? Oh, this was too good.

"I've got ten guys here who survived your little stunt with the weapons convoy, Jimmy. Ten guys who are itching to put a bullet in your head, and a hundred more who are itching to do just the same to your little gang-banging buddies. I don't want to waste the ammunition on you, though, so I'll give you ten seconds to turn your little bus around there and get out of my sight."

"Tell you what I think, *sir*," Jimmy said, stressing the last word sarcastically. "I think the truth is you don't got enough ammunition to take on me and all my little 'gang-bangers,' like you put it. I think—"

A gunshot rang out, and a second later Jimmy felt something slam into the side of his head.

His right ear fell on the roof of the bus next to him.

He glared at the studio gate and imagined he could see Martinez glaring back at him.

"All right!" he yelled. "So you want to play rough, huh?"

He jumped back into the bus.

"They got tanks in there, man," said Oscar. "I saw one."

"They ain't got shit," Jimmy said. "We're gonna wipe that place off the face of this planet."

THE WASTELAND, LOS ANGELES

Kerry had been scared before. Terrified, even. The first time she'd become John Topher in her dreams and relived those killings without knowing what was happening and why, she'd woken up and turned on all the lights in her room. Then she'd gone into the closet and come out with her favorite stuffed animal, a bear named Tubby that she'd gotten when she was three years old. She sat up with Tubby until dawn, clutching that bear like a life preserver until the sky was light.

But it was nothing compared to how she felt now.

"Almost there, sweetheart," the man said. "I'd tell you to relax, but there's really no point to it. Besides, I think the woman I work for really appreciates a good loud scream. So do I, to tell you the truth."

Kerry didn't say anything.

She was trying to think of a way out.

But all she could see around her was a deserted, devastated landscape.

Then a figure rose up in front of her. A burned, hulking giant of a man.

"Whoa," Harold said. "Who the hell are you?"

"My name is Billy Ray," the man said, stepping forward. "What are you doing with that girl?"

PARAMOUNT STUDIOS, LOS ANGELES

Supplies in the camp were running low. They were down to two meals a day. Late breakfast, early supper. The morning meal had been oatmeal and a pack of crackers. Supper, which Abby had just finished, was chicken soup and a pack of crackers.

Earlier in the day, she had snuck a peek inside the supply building. It looked to her like crackers for a few more days. And after that . . .

The soldier next to her got to his feet and saluted. She looked up and saw Martinez entering the room.

"At ease, at ease," Martinez said, walking up to the podium at the front of the stage. "We don't have time to stand on ceremony."

They were in Soundstage 14, the same place Scott had given his first briefing. The atmosphere, though, was decidedly different. That day, there had been a palpable sense of urgency, of can-do-it-ness floating around the room.

Now Abby saw a lot of long faces.

"Let's make this short and sweet," Martinez said. "I want a summary of our current assets from each of the company commanders. Then we'll talk strategy." He pointed toward a soldier in the front row. "Sergeant McCauley."

The man stood. "Twenty-eight men, sir. As many rifles. Concussion grenades. Two launchers. A handheld—"

"Just a personnel count now," Martinez said. "I'll take the weapons separately." His eyes found Abby's. "You're getting this?"

She nodded. "I'm getting it."

Abby had a laptop open in front of her. She entered the information from McCauley. Martinez pointed to another soldier.

"Corporal Wyatt."

"Sixty-eight men, sir."

Martinez signaled to another man. The count went on for a few more minutes.

"Two hundred ten soldiers, sir," Abby announced at the end of it. That number was down from the one he'd given her yesterday. Considerably.

More men had deserted during the night.

They did weapons next.

When Abby finished cataloging, she announced those numbers as well. She didn't know what the numbers meant. But from the grim expressions around the room, it wasn't anything good.

"We have to resupply." That was Potter, one of the company commanders. He was older than Martinez, with a gruff voice and a three-day stubble on his chin. "Weapons and—while we're at it—food."

"Last truck that went out never came back. Ten soldiers," Martinez said, shaking his head. "We can't afford to lose that many men again."

"I don't see as we have a choice. We couldn't hold off a Girl Scout troop with the weapons we have now."

"Where would we go to get more?" Martinez asked. "And could we be sure about doing it before this gang attacked? That's a rhetorical question, people, no need to answer. We make do with what we have. Now. Strategy." He looked around the room.

"J. B. What do you know about these guys?"

An older man in uniform stood up. "Eighteenth Street Gang. Biggest in the city. Biggest in the country, as far as I know. They seem to be pretty well organized. Plus they got access to the police department armory. I'd say there's more of them, and they're better armed."

"We're better trained."

"You don't need much training to fire a gun," Martinez said. "What do we think they want?"

"They?" another soldier said. "Aren't we talking about Jimmy Maartens here?"

"Yeah. Though how he ended up in charge of a street gang . . ." Martinez shook his head. "The question is, do we believe what he said he'd do?"

For the first time, civilians chimed in with their thoughts. The consensus was Maartens had meant what he said.

The consensus was evacuation.

The officers took over the discussion. They talked strategy for another ten minutes or so, till Martinez called a halt to the talking.

"So we're agreed?" he said. "Skeleton crew on the walls, and three rapid-response teams. We can deploy them wherever they're needed. Potter and McCauley to handle evacuation procedures with civilian consultation. That's it, unless there are any other ideas?" He looked around the room. "Anyone?"

Abby looked at him and shook her head.

And at that moment, her eyes fell on a partially disassembled set at the back of the podium. It looked like something from one of the *Star Trek* shows.

Phasers, she thought wryly. We could sure use some of those. Hell, we could use the whole starship *Enterprise*.

Abby cleared her throat. "I might have something," she said.

Later that day, Abby and Martinez were up on the catwalk ringing the studio walls, looking out to the city beyond.

"That was a damn good idea," Martinez said. "We just might be able to pull that off."

"I hope so."

He leaned out over the wall, pulling the hood of the poncho back from his face. It was even colder, and grayer than yesterday. The sun hadn't peeked through the clouds once all day.

"Damn, it's cold," he said.

Abby nodded, shivering inside her poncho. She thought, suddenly, of the big, handknit wool sweater Carol had sent her from Ireland last year; it was sitting in a box on the top shelf of her closet. If there was one thing she wished she could get from her apartment right now, that was it. How good would that feel to have on right now, to protect her from this wind, and the rain that never seemed to—

Abby frowned.

She looked up at the sky, and realized it wasn't rain anymore.

It was snow.

"Look," she said to Martinez. She held out her palm, and showed him a handful of flakes.

"You know what this means?" she said. "You know what day it is?"

He frowned for a second. Then he got it.

"Oh," he said. She saw a smile tugging at the corners of his mouth. Then he actually started to laugh.

Abby laughed too.

"White Christmas," he said. "I've lived in Los Angeles my whole life. I never thought I'd see one."

"Me neither. I wonder if anyone else realizes . . ."

Her voice trailed off.

"What's the matter?" Martinez asked.

She pointed behind him, up towards the Hollywood Hills.

An endless stream of headlights, stretching back west as far as the eye could see, were heading in their direction.

"Shit," Martinez said. "Here they come."

THE WASTELAND, LOS ANGELES

Church—no, Billy Ray, he was Billy Ray now—didn't know how he'd come to this place. He remembered Eldon dying, and then finding the police car. He remembered chasing Maartens, and driving into the wall of fire. When he woke up, he was in this weird, deserted landscape, and his memory had come back to him, and he didn't know how those things had happened either.

One thing he did know: he didn't like the looks of this guy in front of him. This pale-skinned man with the scarf, who had a grip so tight on the arm of the girl with him that red marks had already risen on her arm.

"You let that girl go," he said.

The man grinned. "You make me."

Billy Ray shook his head. He remembered how to fight now; he remembered what it felt like to hit people, how to use his strength.

"I don't want to hurt you," he said, stepping forward.

The man started to laugh. "Oh, I wouldn't worry about that."

He twisted, and the girl screamed again.

He had the girl's wrist in his right hand; his left was free. Billy Ray bulled forward, ripping the girl's arm free from the man's grasp with one hand and straight-arming him backward with the other.

At least, that's what he meant to do. His body was slower than he remembered it being; weaker too. All those years of drinking and eating junk food, not doing anything other than sitting on his butt, had definitely taken their toll.

He couldn't break the man's grip on the girl. Which was strange: the guy was half his size. He ought to be able to—

The man grabbed the fingers of Billy Ray's left hand with his free one and squeezed.

Billy Ray screamed in pain. He tried to pull his hand away but couldn't.

He heard bone snap.

The man squeezed again, and Billy Ray screamed.

Tears filled his eyes.

The man forced him down to his knees, squeezing harder, and he still couldn't understand what was happening. Going through the fire must have weakened him more than he realized; that had to be it, because there was no way this guy could be so strong, it wasn't right, it wasn't—

Natural.

Billy Ray balled his free hand into a fist, drew back and struck the man square in the gut. He laughed. He did it again, and again, and then he stopped and grabbed at the hand that was breaking his and tried to pull it away and he couldn't do that either.

Oh Lord, he thought, and grabbed a handful of ash and threw it in the man's face. That didn't do anything except make him cough.

His hand flailed again, and closed around the edge of the man's scarf. Church yanked involuntarily.

The man made a gurgling noise.

Church yanked again.

The scarf got tighter. Suddenly the man's head was flopping on his shoulders.

"Hey," the man said. He let go of Church's other hand. "That's not—"

Church gathered all his strength, and gave one last yank.

The man's head came off.

Church gave it a great big kick, and it rolled down the street.

The girl collapsed, sobbing.

"Oh thank you, thank you," she said.

All of a sudden, Church heard a roar behind him. He turned.

A woman stood there. Next to her was a white tiger.

The woman looked at Billy Ray. She looked at her tiger. "Get him," she said.

The animal gathered itself, and sprang.

NORWALK, LOS ANGELES

"This is a bad idea," Thomas said. He walked down the line of cars that stood at the entrance ramp to the bridge, revving their engines, and shook his head.

"You're going to burn up!" he shouted.

Lawson, who was driving the lead car, stuck his head out the window.

"You're wrong, mister. We'll be going way too fast to get anything but a sunburn."

Thomas looked across the bridge. Lawson and the others had found two sanitation trucks and used them to clear one of the lanes right up to the wall of fire. Then they'd put the trucks front to back and used a tractor trailer as a wedge to push them right through the fire. And beyond, hopefully, clearing space on the other side for their cars once they burst through the fiery barrier.

Thomas didn't think they were going to make it, though.

Even before the other trucks had disappeared beyond the curtain of flame, Thomas swore he'd seen them start to burn. Not the seats, not the interior, the metal frames of the trucks themselves.

"This isn't an ordinary fire," Thomas said. "You can't just get a running start and drive through."

"We can't just let that little girl die," Lawson said, and ducked his head back inside the car.

Thomas could barely stand to watch.

There were five cars, spaced evenly apart from each other along the road. Lawson gunned his engine again, louder this time. And then he was off.

They'd spaced the cars well, Thomas saw. Given plenty of

room for the drivers to build up speed, to be at, by, and through the wall of fire before anything could burn them.

Lawson's car was moving. He didn't even slow down as he neared the halfway point, where the flames waited, like a mythical boundary line.

Then he was through. Gone. Vanished from sight. For a moment there was silence.

And then cheering.

"He's through!" one woman shouted. "He's —"

There was an explosion. A shower of different-colored flames added to the inferno.

The other cars quieted.

Thomas shook his head.

Now they would try it his way.

Thomas's way was him and Leo. Alone and on foot.

"I think that's how Harold got through," Thomas said. "Holding the iron. So that's how we'll get through—holding my ring."

"Isn't it a little small?" Leo asked.

"Take my hand," he suggested.

Leo did.

Thomas stared up at the wall of fire before him. It was fully two stories high.

"No man born of woman has done what you have asked," he said.

Leo turned and stared at him. "Huh?"

" 'No mortal man has gone into the mountain; the length of it is twelve leagues of darkness; in it there is no light, but the heart is oppressed with darkness. From the rising of the sun to the setting of the sun there is no light,' " Thomas whispered.

Leo frowned. "What is that? Some kind of curse?"

"It's from Gilgamesh."

"It's damn depressing," Leo said. "I don't like it." He shook his head. "And I don't like this. For all we know, she's already got the girl. And those three pieces. And the girl's probably—"

"Don't." Thomas shook his head. "Don't even say it."

"All right." Leo threw up his hands. "Even if she's not dead, is you going in such a good idea? Bringing her the last piece she needs?"

Thomas stared at the wall of fire a moment.

He suddenly felt an overwhelming urge to enter; a primal, primordial desire.

"It's stupid to talk about this anymore," he said. "We're going in there, we're going to find the herald, and we're going to kill her. All right?"

"Sure," Leo said. "I hope."

The two of them joined hands and stepped forward.

MELROSE AVENUE, LOS ANGELES

Jimmy had been content to let Oscar coordinate the whole attack—he just wanted to be one of the first ones in, so he could rip Martinez's head off his shoulders—but when Oscar started talking about taking their time, about being cautious, Jimmy felt he had to step in.

"Cautious is not in the mandate, remember?" he said, taking the walkie-talkie from Oscar.

He ordered the attack to start, and he could tell Oscar was pissed, because attacking without a plan firmly in place meant a lot more of their people would die. But he didn't care about that, or if Oscar got mad.

Besides, if Oscar knew what else he was thinking, what else had occurred to him about the mandate the woman had given him, he would be even more upset.

She just said kill.

She didn't say who, exactly.

THE WASTELAND, LOS ANGELES

Danny stood over the big man's corpse and thought:

Dinnertime. At last.

He was about to tear into his fresh, hot meal when Harold came walking up.

"I'm all right, I'm all right," Harold said, heading back towards them. He had both hands pressed to the side of his head, and was leaning his neck from one side to another. Trying to stretch, Danny thought at first.

Then Harold frowned, and crooked his head down till it was almost touching his shoulder. That's when Danny noticed that the head and the body weren't attached to each other anymore.

"I'm going to need some help here," Harold said to Claire.

She nodded. "Soon. Soon we'll have all the time in the world."

The girl started to cry again. Danny could tell Claire was getting mad, that she didn't want to listen to the younger girl whine anymore. Maybe, he hoped, she would give the girl to him.

He'd rather have her any day than the big man lying on the ground. He sniffed, trying to catch her scent—an intoxicating mixture of youth and fear. But there was something else in the air; he growled, a low rumble.

Claire turned to him.

"You're right," she said. "Someone's coming."

Thomas seemed to know exactly where he was going.

Which was a good thing, Leo thought, because he had absolutely no idea where they were. The street signs were covered with a thin coat of ash, which made half of them impossible to see. The ash was everywhere, in fact, a gray powder that made it seem like they were the last people on earth, walking through the ruins of a nuclear explosion.

"This place gives me the creeps," Leo said. "I wish—"

Suddenly he was flying through the air: he landed on the ground with a hump and for a second was completely, totally disoriented. He'd never felt so strange in all his life. He looked around.

A huge white tiger stood over him, snarling.

On the ground next to the tiger was a body.

Leo realized that it was his body.

Leo frowned. Body there, head here. Then how—

Oh.

He closed his eyes and died.

Danny stood back from the man's decapitated body and drooled.

Damn, that looks good, he thought. I'm starving.

He heard a gun go off and felt fire spread across his insides.

He turned and saw the old man holding a pistol.

The man fired again, almost at the same time Danny jumped. The bullet hit him in the shoulder and he roared in pain and lashed out with his paws, taking a big chunk out of the man's chest.

All these bullets were starting to hurt; luckily, Claire would fix him up. Claire would put him back together again, all shiny and new.

As soon as he brought her what she wanted.

"The old man has the last piece of iron," she had told him. "A ring. Bring it to me."

The man raised his gun again.

Danny sprang through the air and bit clean through, severing the hand at the wrist.

He spit the gun out and swallowed the fingers.

Whoops.

The ring.

PARAMOUNT STUDIOS, LOS ANGELES

The soldiers on post near the gate were firing their weapons frantically down into the street. Their fire was being returned fivefold; as Abby watched, two of the soldiers went down.

Other soldiers were running from elsewhere along the catwalk to try and help.

"Stay on your posts!" Martinez screamed, waving them back. "Stay on your posts!"

He'd been on the Bronson Gate, covering a hole that had popped up in their perimeter there. Now he leapt up the ladder leading to the catwalk, taking two rungs at a time. As he reached the top, another soldier fell.

A hand appeared at the lip of the concrete wall. And then another.

Martinez slammed the butt of his rifle down hard, and the hands disappeared. He reached down to his belt, and snapped off a grenade.

He threw it over the wall. A big explosion sounded.

There was a lull in the firing.

It was the first one since the attack had started, over an hour ago.

Abby climbed the catwalk and stood beside him. She looked out onto the street in front of them.

It was a slaughterhouse.

"Don't they care how many people they lose?" she asked.

"Apparently not." Martinez pointed west, down Melrose, where dozens of buses were idling, white exhaust steam rising up in the air and mixing with the seemingly never-ending fall of snow. "As long as it gets them closer to us."

Abby nodded. Judging by the ferocity of the gang's attack, their leader—Jimmy—hadn't been making idle threats. Killing was their first priority.

Also their second, third, and fourth.

"Sir!"

A soldier who didn't look old enough to drink was standing below them.

"Sergeant Wyatt says we're ready."

Abby smiled. She and Martinez exchanged a glance.

It was time to put her plan into action.

Her thinking had gone something like this.

"If we want to evacuate, we'll need a distraction," she'd said in the meeting. "A spectacle. And isn't that what the movies are all about?"

And what made movie explosions so spectacular, she'd told them, was flash powder.

And Paramount's in-house prop department had barrels full of it.

Jimmy was surprised Martinez hadn't tried to make a break for it yet. If he was in the sergeant's position, he would have done it hours ago. Last night, even, under cover of darkness. But now it was too late.

Now Jimmy was getting in on the fun himself.

He'd been content to sit on the sidelines for the first attack, but now that the blood was flowing, he wanted to be in the thick of things.

He was in the first bus coming back down Melrose when the street exploded in front of him. It was the goddamn biggest explosion he'd seen yet.

Maybe this was it, he thought. Martinez's big breakout.

They were going to try and walk right out the front door.

Jimmy pulled out his walkie-talkie.

"Oscar!"

"Yo."

"They're going out the main gate. Pull everyone you can, and get 'em there. I don't want a single soul to escape."

"But shouldn't we—"

"No buts," Jimmy said. "Do it."

It took longer than he wanted, but at last the soldiers on the catwalk out front stopped firing, and the buses rammed through the front gates and onto the Paramount lot.

Except for the scattered sounds of gunfire in the distance, the studio was completely deserted.

"Hey!" Jimmy screamed. "Where is everybody?"

THE WASTELAND, LOS ANGELES

Danny trotted into the church.

Claire had bound the girl; she knelt on the ground next to the altar, tear tracks running down her face.

Claire frowned as he drew closer.

"The ring, Danny, where is it?"

He growled, remembering the taste of metal as it slid down his throat. That had hurt.

He knew it would hurt even more, coming out the other end.

"Oh, Danny." Claire shook her head. "I can't wait, I'm sorry. I just can't wait."

He growled questioningly. What do you mean, can't wait?

She bent down next to him and stroked his fur.

She looked into his eyes.

She rammed her hand down his throat and started feeling around in his stomach.

Danny writhed in agony; he twisted and tried to bite her arm. It was like his jaws closed on nothing but air.

He whimpered once more, and died.

Claire pulled her arm out of the tiger's throat. It was drenched with blood and gore.

She held the partially digested finger up in the air and pulled the ring off it. Then she frowned.

"Wait a second," she said. "Something's not right."

"Looking for this?"

She turned.

Thomas stood at the entrance to the church.

In his hand—his one remaining hand—he held up the chain with the ring on it.

HOLLYWOOD, CALIFORNIA

The huge flashpowder explosions—enhanced by a few strategically timed shells from their rapidly dwindling arsenal—had convinced the gang to concentrate their forces by the main gate, while at the rear of the studio, under cover of the smoke and snow and gray skies, a meticulously organized evacuation took place.

First they blew a hole in the back wall, between Paramount and Hollywood Memorial Park, the cemetery that bordered it. Then they ferried out the civilian population through the cemetery, and into the streets beyond. Every group of civilians had a military escort; every one of them had the same destination in mind. The Santa Monica Mountains National Park. How they got there was their own business.

The entire operation had taken a little under half an hour, and they'd gotten almost all the way through it before the flash powder ran out, and the gang stormed the front gate.

Now Abby and Martinez were providing cover for the last civilians out.

A man came running at them from the front of the studio; somehow, every single bullet fired at him seemed to miss.

"Jimmy," Martinez said, raising his own rifle and smiling. "Say bye-bye."

He fired.

The slug hit Jimmy in the arm. He kept coming.

Martinez fired again. Jimmy staggered, hit once more.

And still, he kept coming.

"Martinez!" he shouted. He looked ready to kill. "Martinez! You sneaky, lying, no-good sonuva—"

"I can't take all the credit," Martinez said. He nodded toward Abby. "It was her idea."

"I'll deal with her later," Jimmy said. He stopped running. "How do you want to do this?"

The sergeant stepped forward. "You and me. *Mano a mano.*"

"Can't do, Sarge," Jimmy said. "I'm no longer a mano, sorry to say."

He picked Martinez up off the ground and snapped him in half.

Then he turned to Abby.

"Next."

Abby was sitting in the jeep she and Martinez were supposed to escape in. She floored it out the hole in the wall by the cemetery.

The jeep slammed into a tombstone and knocked it over; she kept going.

Jimmy was right behind her, on a motorcycle.

She had no idea where she was going; she just wanted to get away from him.

She kept climbing, going farther up into the Hollywood Hills. She passed a sign:

PRIVATE ROAD RESTRICTED ACCESS

There was a cul-de-sac at the end of the road.

No place left to hide.

She got out of the jeep and started to run.

She looked behind her; through the mist, and the falling snow, she could see Jimmy coming after her. Gaining on her, in fact.

She burst through the trees, and skidded to a halt.

She looked up.

Fifty-foot-tall letters looked down at her.

She was right underneath the Hollywood sign.

Jimmy had always wondered how you got to the sign. Now he knew.

It was the Hollywoo sign at this point. The last "D" had toppled over—or been pushed—and lay on its face on the steep hillside, one end on the ground, the other sticking up in the air—a good couple hundred feet down the slope from where it had originally stood.

The girl was circling the "D" now. She seemed to be slowing down. Jimmy saw that, and smiled. Only a matter of time, he thought. Only a matter of time.

He grinned, and started after her.

The hill was steep, and slippery. Probably tough to climb at the best of times, he thought, and these weren't the best of times. The ground was slick with snow; he slid backwards every few feet, scrambling for purchase. There were no trees to grab onto, just scraggly little bushes on their last legs, about to succumb to their harsh new climate. Tough luck, Jimmy thought.

To make way for the new, the old had to die.

Up ahead, the girl had reached the base of the first "O." Almost at the exact second she touched it, a recorded voice filled the air.

"Warning. You are in a restricted area. Warning. You are in a restricted area . . ."

The voice continued, ad nauseum, getting louder as Jimmy drew closer to the "D." Which was even bigger up

close than he'd expected. It took him what seemed like forever to get all the way around it.

When he reached the far side, the girl was nowhere in
sight.

"Shit!" Jimmy shouted. Where the hell had she gone?

He started running up the hill, legs pumping, slipping
and sliding all the way, looking repeatedly back and forth
from left to right.

Fifty feet away from the first "O," Jimmy ran past a metal
pole with a speaker on it.

"Warning. You are in a restricted area. Warning. You are
in a—"

"Shut up, already," Jimmy said, and punched the speaker
as he went past. It made a fizzling, crackling noise, and then
fell silent.

He reached the "O." Still no sign of the girl.

More snow, though; it was coming down hard enough
that he had trouble seeing more than a couple dozen feet in
front of his face. He squinted into the gray sky and frowned.
Where had she gone?

A creaking noise came from somewhere above him.

Jimmy squinted up, into the falling snow, and saw a dark
speck moving above him.

She was climbing the sign. The second "L," to be precise.

"Damn it!" Jimmy shouted. "Don't make me come up
there after you!"

The girl didn't answer. She just kept climbing.

He frowned, and looked up. The "L," just like all the other
letters, stood on a base about ten feet off the ground. There
was a metal ladder leading from that base to the back of the
letter.

Jimmy reached up with his good arm, and pulled himself
onto the ladder. First one rung, then the other.

He felt his hands sticking to the cold metal surface of
the ladder; it was a good thing he couldn't feel cold any-

more, or this would have been an even more uncomfortable climb.

The ladder ended, and Jimmy stood at the bottom of the
letter itself. The back of each letter looked like an erector set,
crisscrossed with metal scaffolding.

The girl was at the top of the "L" now. She had no place
else to go.

Jimmy smiled.

"Ready or not," he shouted, "here I come!"

And he started to climb.

What a stupid idea this had turned out to be.

Not only because she was now trapped up here, with no
way out and Jimmy coming straight for her, but because the
higher she got, the more the letter swayed.

And now she couldn't get any higher. Abby was standing
on the top crossbeam. The top of the "L" came up to her
neck.

She shielded her eyes from the snow and looked down the
hill at the fallen "D."

Oh God. Please don't let this big hunk of sheet metal fall
down too. Please.

As if in response, the wind gusted again. The letter swayed.

The crossbeams were about six inches wide, and slippery.
Abby's left foot skidded. She just managed to right herself.

She looked down.

Jimmy was twenty feet below her and climbing.

God, she thought. She'd even picked the wrong letter to
climb. There was no place to go on an "L" but up or down. If
only she'd picked an "O." Or the "W." Jimmy would have had
a harder time cornering her then.

He was ten feet below her.

"Been saying your prayers?" he asked.

She looked to her right. The other "L" was barely visible.

But on the other side of the tree, to her left, the top of the "Y's" outstretched arm was only a fifteen-foot jump away.

Right, Abby thought. Only fifteen feet. From one narrow six-inch ledge to another. In the middle of a winter storm.

Piece of cake.

Jimmy's hand cleared the edge of the support beam.

Abby took a deep breath, and a running start.

And then she was flying.

The snow swirled around her; she was weightless. She saw the top of the "Y," she threw out her arms and strained forward and—

Her hands grabbed metal. Sharp, slippery metal.

She felt it cut into her skin. She grabbed on for dear life.

It was a fifteen-foot jump. She'd done it. Exactly.

But the support beam was another half foot away from her dangling feet.

She could swing herself like a pendulum and try and get those last few inches.

But doing that might make her fall.

On the other hand, if she didn't do something . . .

She hung there, swinging in the wind, struggling to maintain her hold on the letter's slick metal surface.

Slowly, her fingers began to slip.

THE WASTELAND, LOS ANGELES

Thomas took a step forward, into the flaming church.

It had the feel of some ancient, primordial site. Stonehenge. A place where gods gathered to decide the fate of the world.

There was an altar ahead of him. Before it stood the woman. The herald.

The altar was splattered with blood. To the right of it lay the body of a tiger, the white tiger, its face frozen in a particularly human expression of pain.

To the left knelt Kerry, her wrists fastened behind her back.

"I've been expecting you," the woman said.

Thomas pulled the gun out from the small of his back and shot her. Once, twice, three times.

The bullets passed right through her, with no effect.

"You didn't really think that was going to work, did you?" she asked.

"Worth a try," he said. He tossed the gun aside.

Kerry raised her head. Her face was bruised all over. "Mr. Kelleher," she said. "Help me. Please."

Thomas nodded. He would; he would save her, the way he hadn't been able to save Julie.

He owed Steve that much, at least.

"Don't worry," he said. "I'm—"

Pain exploded in his chest.

Thomas looked down and saw a jagged piece of metal sticking straight out of his body.

He heard Kerry scream; he gasped, and stumbled, the pole sliding out of him as he fell face first toward the ground. He put his hands out to break his fall, but of course he didn't have hands any more, he had only the one hand and a stump, and so he fell awkwardly, jamming the fingers of his one remaining hand and falling hard on that same shoulder.

He looked up and saw a man standing over him, holding a long, jagged piece of metal in one hand. In the other was his head. The head smiled.

"Gotcha," it said. The man bent down and ripped the chain—and the ring—from Thomas's grasp.

The world around him began to fade away.

"No," he said. "No."

He could feel his heart pumping, the warm blood spilling out through his wound. It seemed to be slowing down.

Get up, damn it, he told himself. He groaned out loud

and got his one good hand under his body. *Get up. This is everything.*

He managed to rise up off the ground for a second, and then flopped over helplessly onto his back.

All out of miracles, he thought, and closed his eyes.

When he looked up again, the woman was standing over him, holding out the ring for him to see.

He tried to speak but no words came out.

She moved away, out of his field of vision.

Clouds took her place; dark, swirling storm clouds that moved far too quickly, like film projected at the wrong speed up in the sky.

The stars, he saw, were gone.

End of the world, he thought, end of the world.

He took a breath and cried out in pain and frustration.

Somehow, he managed to prop himself up onto one elbow.

The woman was standing at the altar.

As he watched, she took the ring from her hand and laid it down on the dark stone platform. Then, one by one, from within her robes, she withdrew the other pieces of iron, those he had seen only in his dreams, those he had held only hours ago.

The bookmark, the money clip, the candlestick, the spike, the bracelet.

His ring.

Close. He'd been so close.

"Now," she said. "We need a sacrifice."

She lifted her head and looked across the altar to Kerry.

"One human sacrifice coming right up," the man said.

"No!" Thomas's voice came out as a weak, feeble croak. He tasted blood in his mouth.

The man walked over to Kerry. She threw herself backward, trying to get away from him.

"Leave me alone!" she shrieked. "Leave me alone!"

The man set his head down on the floor of the church. "Why," it said, "does everything have to be so difficult?"

He grabbed Kerry's ponytail and dragged her, kicking and screaming, back to the altar. He threw her down at the woman's feet. She lay there a moment, still screaming.

The woman had begun chanting.

She spoke words that were not English, not anywhere close even, and yet somehow they struck a spark of recognition in Thomas. He mouthed them along with her silently for a moment before he realized what he was doing.

Then, not taking her attention at all from the iron on the altar before her, the woman grabbed Kerry by the hair and pulled her up onto her feet, as if she were simply grabbing another ingredient. Kerry was still shouting.

The woman slammed Kerry's head into the side of the altar, and the girl fell silent.

She pulled something else out from her robe. The hilt of a sword.

She raised it high above her head.

"No!" Thomas lunged forward. High above Kerry's body, the jagged blade came down.

He flopped onto his stomach, and didn't even have the strength to turn away. All he could do was close his eyes so he didn't have to watch.

But he could still hear.

Kerry's scream lasted forever.

When he opened his eyes, her body was slumped on the ground.

The blade's edge glistened with blood. And at the back of the altar, behind the woman, something was happening.

A wall of fire; a gathering of energies.

A door, waiting to be opened. And on the other side . . .

Apocalypse.

The woman held the hilt of the sword above the altar; her eyes blazed. A cloud of white-hot energy swirled around the scattered pieces of iron; it began to flow up, toward the blade in the woman's hand. That too was enveloped in a white-hot light, blindingly bright; Thomas had to squint to keep watching.

The light grew brighter. Thomas finally had to close his eyes. He sensed, rather than saw, the final burst of energy. When he looked again, smoke was rising from the altar. The iron was gone.

And in her hands the woman held a long, gleaming sword. The edges crackled with power.

The ground shivered. And shook again. Thomas could sense something beneath, straining to be free. The sword was the key. All the woman had to do was use it.

The door behind the altar blazed.

He howled in frustration. "Don't open it! God damn it. Stop!"

The woman lowered the sword. "Don't open it?" She studied him a moment.

Her gaze bore into him.

He felt something reach into his mind then, rip it apart like a kid looking for a Cracker Jack prize. Everything that he ever knew, thought, dreamed, came pouring out of him.

He screamed.

And when he was done screaming, Thomas looked up and saw the woman standing over him.

She was laughing.

"I'm not the herald, you fool." She shook her head. "You are."

Thomas struggled for words, and came up empty.

"What?" he said finally.

"I'm not the herald, or whatever you want to call it," she repeated. "That's your job. One, I might add, that you've failed miserably."

He still didn't understand. His job?

"That's right," she said, walking around him. He realized she had been—and still was—reading his mind. "Your job, to use the sword and open the door. Complete the cycle. Release the evil. However you want to put it. Not mine."

"But—"

"Not mine," she repeated. "I like things just the way they are now. I plan on keeping them like this for a long, long time."

A glimmer of understanding dawned. Steve's words came back to him.

Every world has a natural life span. When this one dies, another begins.

That's what was supposed to happen now; what had to happen now, he realized, thinking of all the death and destruction in the world outside.

Apocalypse and rebirth; it was all up to him.

He was the herald.

Thomas forced himself to his feet.

"Give that to me," he said, stumbling forward. "Give me the sword."

"Sorry, friend."

Thomas turned.

The man with the head under his arm stepped forward.

"That's as far as you—"

Thomas lunged forward and punched the head.

It popped out from under the arm it was stashed under, and rolled back down the aisle.

"Hey!" he heard the head say. "Where'd everybody go?"

The woman stepped down from the altar to the floor of the church and started walking toward him.

"You want this?" she asked, holding out the sword. "You really want this?"

She ran him through with the sword. He felt something inside him shatter, explode.

The woman smiled and started to pull the blade free of his body.

"So much for the herald," she said.

He put his one remaining hand on the hilt of the blade, next to her two, and stopped her from pulling it out.

"That's right." He looked up at her and spoke through clenched teeth. "I'm the herald."

For the first time, fear crossed her face.

"No," she said, trying to wrench the blade free. "Let go—"

He did.

Only long enough to wrap his arms around her and pull her close in an embrace that drove the blade of the sword all the way into his body again.

Blood bubbled out from between his lips, and it felt like holy fire upon his skin, washing him clean.

He stepped up onto the first stair of the altar.

Now it was her turn to scream.

"No! Let go of me! Let go!"

He took another step up.

She beat on his back with her fists; she clawed at his face with her hands.

He smiled and embraced her even tighter.

The fire burned inside him; growing like a seed, he thought, like a flower waiting to explode.

A new world, waiting to be born.

They were at the altar now; he glanced down quickly at Kerry, and allowed the shadow of a smile to cross his face.

The door loomed behind him. And he was the key.

He looked up into the woman's anguished face.

"Apocalypse," he said, and stepped forward, into the fire.

Sunday A.M.

THE CITY OF THE ANGELS

One minute Abby was clinging for her life to the Hollywood sign.

The next, she was dead.

She saw the tunnel, and the white light at the end of it; she heard the voices and the music all around her. It was just like everyone who'd been there and come back said it would be; just like they'd written it in the fourth season finale of *Island Patrol*, when her character almost drowned while saving two little boys who'd paddled out too far into the ocean in their kayak. She was in the middle of a spiritual crisis on that show, prompted by the reappearance of her terminally ill father—played, she remembered now, by George Hamilton—whom she hadn't seen in twenty years. He died during the show, and after she'd rescued the boys in an almost suicidal act of heroism, she met him again in the tunnel—in the waiting room, as it were, for the Great Beyond.

"It's not your time yet, Cristina," he'd told her. "You have to go back. You have so much more to do with your life."

He'd embraced her then, and the soundtrack changed from a heavenly choir to Kenny G and the sound of waves slapping against the shore, and she'd opened her eyes to find Milch and Casey standing over her, tears of relief on their faces.

Cut then to Abby, praying in church, crying her own tears of relief, prompted—according to the script, at least—by the knowledge that her father was in a better place.

So, Abby wondered, where exactly was she?

She heard waves slapping on the shore and the cry of a gull. A salty breeze blew across her face, and she felt the warmth of the sun shining down on her.

She sat up and opened her eyes.

She was lying on the beach. The ocean was blue. A bright, shining blue.

The sun was bright in the sky above her; the clouds at the horizon were white and fluffy. Everything looked clean, untouched. Brand-new.

She heard someone calling her name.

She turned and saw Martinez walking toward her, a whole gang of people following in his wake. She thought she recognized some of them. Wasn't that Carol? And Luka?

She got to her feet and went to go see.

Author's Note

Although the name on the cover of this novel is mine, the original vision for what became *Black Dawn* came from a series of editorial meetings at the offices of Avon Books in early 1999. While much about the book has changed since then, I hope the editors at that meeting will find that I have done justice to their original idea.

I must also thank the following: Lou Aronica; Lisa Bankoff; Avideh Bashirrad; Jon Beauregard and Betsy Isrodit for information on the Hollywood sign; Matt Cassel; Lana Dubin, girl genius; Tom Dupree; Lloyd Fukuda of the Los Angeles Fire Department; Shawn Gonzalez of the MTA; Max Greenhut for Malibu; Dave Grossman, Sergeant Mike Ford, and everyone at Los Angeles Air Force Base for showing me around; Janet Holliday, a.k.a. "Doc"; Kathy Jones for the ride along the beach; Matt Lait of the *Los Angeles Times*; Shelly De Los Reyes of the LADOT; Lauren "Pancho" McKenna; Erin Macphee for the Aggie Lou; Sean O'Sullivan and Alison Fast for breakfast at Denny's; Patrick Price; L.P.S. and, of course, B.C.S.; and Roger Tierney for valuable background info.

Any errors of fact (beyond those of fictional license) are entirely my own.

Finally, there are two people whose constant encouragement made this book a reality under some very trying circumstances.

First Josh Behar, at HarperCollins, an invaluable sounding board and a valuable editor.

Second, my wife Jill, whose support is priceless.